TOXIN

TOXIN

ISBN-13: 978-0-9859223-3-7

Published by

Wittmann*Blair*

St. Louis, Missouri
wittmannblair@charter.net

TOXIN

Paul Martin Midden

Never was anything great achieved without danger.
—Niccolò Machiavelli

Chapter 1

Even though I was walking, I could feel my eyelids beginning to droop as the speaker droned on in a practiced midwestern accent. He was a lobbyist—something to do with guns, I think. The kind that button-holes you on the Capitol steps and doesn't let go until you either get into a car or get rude. Beyond his right ear, just to the left of his moving mouth, the instrument of this momentary torture, I caught a glimpse of my driver pulling up to the curb. I forced my eyes open to full alert and made my own mouth move. "Gotta go," I said, interrupting him. "My ride's here."

I slipped into the car wondering if every congressman and senator was as annoyed by these guys as I was. I have been in the Senate for almost two years now, and my disdain—no, my contempt—for these bastards has not diminished a bit, not a single iota. It's all about money, money, and more money. It's a child's pretend game. They pretend they are providing a service, and we pretend that what goes on is not a half-step away from bribery, if not closer. Once I was safely ensconced in my limo and moving away from the noxious presence, I could shake my head and put the annoying mini-drama out of my mind, like changing the channel from an especially soporific soap. Unfortunately, I knew in the back of my mind that I probably wasn't finished with these guys for today.

I forced myself to focus on what lay ahead of me. I was on my way to meet with a woman I had never met. She was not, thankfully, a lobbyist, or at least I didn't think so. And the voice on the telephone was redolent with such sincerity, such strength of purpose, and such clarity that my interest was piqued. Or at least piqued enough to agree to meet with a woman I did not know for a reason I only dimly understood. I have always been a sucker for women with sexy voices, and hers was one of the sexiest I had ever heard.

When I called for my ride, I gave George the address that the woman, Isadore, had given me. My thoughts turned to Isadore, the name attached to the sexy phone voice. There was something about her: a potency, a determination, something that enabled her to get through to my private phone without getting derailed by the various ploys routinely used by members of Congress to dodge real-time phone encounters. No one in this town wants to talk to anyone unprepared, and I am no exception to that rule. It keeps my life uncluttered, or at least less cluttered.

But Isadore vaporized those defenses like a twelve year old vanquishing mousy little figures in a computer game. When I picked up the phone, I glanced at Sarah, my secretary, the overseer of my entire office fortification. I looked at her with a question in my eyes as I picked up the phone, and she just shrugged. *Fifty years old with thirty years experience at fielding calls, and she just shrugged. This caller must be something*, I thought.

Isadore did not waste time once she had my attention.

"Senator Telemark," she began in a silky alto. "My name is Isadore Hathaway, Frank Hathaway's daughter. I need to see you."

The natural response to a statement such as this would be "Why?" For reasons I am still digesting, that little three-letter word did not cross my mind. It was her tone, I think, her certainty. It didn't hurt that she was related to the fabled Frank Hathaway, recently deceased senatorial powerhouse of the era just before I joined the Club. Frank had been revered by friend and foe alike,

2

mostly because he was tirelessly committed to working the system. Legend has it that Hathaway did not talk to anyone on whom he did not have the goods. A walking, talking, late-twentieth-century inquisitor. He scared people on both sides of the aisle and even in other branches of government.

"When?" I asked Dora. Even now, as I am being driven to a small restaurant across the Potomac, I am not sure why she got to me so effortlessly. *Hypnotic suggestion? Some mysterious powder she had planted on my phone? Don't be silly*, I thought. *She's just a woman. A compelling woman but a mere mortal.*

"As soon as possible," she had said, without skipping a beat. "At the Emporia restaurant in Alexandria. Can you come this afternoon?"

I momentarily regained my senses. "May I ask what this is about?" I countered weakly.

"I will tell you more when I see you, but for now, please understand that I have something to share with you that matters to our country and in which you have a personal stake. You will understand as soon as I am able to explain it to you in detail. I am sorry I can't say more on the phone."

Silence. I was pinned to the mat. All she had to do was wait until I recognized it.

"OK," I said for lack of any real alternative. "I'll meet you in an hour."

When I put the receiver back, I realized I was sweating. Not out of anxiety, but out of, well, I am forty-eight years old, but I felt like a high school nerd who got asked out by the prom queen. All fluster and flush. It did not help that I was single and not involved with anyone at the moment. My last train wreck of a relationship had ended three months ago, and I guess I am still pretty vulnerable. But the wreck in question had only lasted about two months, so I can't really claim any profound emotional loss. I am just ready.

I guess I wanted to be intrigued. I wanted to have some sexy female voice on the other end of the line entice me to lunch at a restaurant in the middle of my work day with vague promises and even vaguer intentions. Besides, DC is beautiful in the spring, and the three thousand Japanese cherry blossom trees don't hurt. I'm a romantic at heart; I just play a senator on TV.

George pulled up to the Emporia, got out, and opened the door. This little door-opening ritual continues to embarrass me. Even though I am a life-long republican, the scion of a family of multigenerational republicans, we did not have money. Or servants, or drivers, or any of the other perks that come along with the kind of money that most of my colleagues in the esteemed chamber of the Senate have had from their earliest days. Both my parents were teachers. Smart; loved their work; loved me. But money was scarce. I did have an uncle once who people said was loaded, but he could have been the mayor of some town in Kazakhstan for all I saw of him, or his cash. In our family, life was simple and honest.

I looked at the restaurant and realized that I had no clue who I was looking for. The woman with the sexy voice. Maybe I could ask the dozen or so women within my field of vision to say my name. On the other hand, I would prefer to leave lunch without getting arrested.

It didn't matter. A woman who could only have been named Isadore Hathaway was walking straight toward me without a hint of hesitation in her stride. I blushed; it wasn't just her voice. Tall, thin, elegant—very attractive. Dressed in a simple black dress with a single strand of pearls with matching earrings. The kind of body men long for, the kind that is splashed across more than one weekly style magazine to entice male and female readers alike.

"Mr. Telemark?" She asked, extending her hand, which I was relieved to take. "I am Isadore Hathaway." Her voice was the same strong alto I had heard on the phone. Her handshake was firm and her gaze unwavering.

I tried to respond with similar strength. I looked her straight in the eye and said, "Call me Jake."

"Call me Dora," she said, softening just a tiny bit. I did not think it was an invitation to familiarity so much as a more efficient way of relating, of doing business. "Please come with me," she said, and turned on her heel and headed into the main dining room of the restaurant.

I followed and had to pick up my pace to stay with her. She seemed headed toward a table at the back of the room, and the fifteen seconds it took to get there gave me some time to organize my first impressions. She was a very attractive, pedigreed woman who obviously had an agenda. I wondered why I had never heard anything about her before. If she was this potent a presence, was associated with DC, and was the daughter of Frank Hathaway, it didn't seem likely that she could fly under the radar. Not with her lineage.

To my surprise, she walked straight into the kitchen through a door at the back of the dining room. She did not even turn to make sure I was following. I guess she just assumed I would. *Pretty sure of herself*, I thought. The nagging sense that something was amiss wasn't improving. *Why had I not heard about this woman before?*

Dora walked straight out the kitchen entrance of the restaurant and nodded to a car waiting in the alley. She did not need to say the words. Our eyes met momentarily as I opened my car door and she opened hers. She knew she was in complete control as she had been since the unexpected phone call an hour or so ago.

The car was manned by a huge African-American who drove slowly down the alley. I could see his eyes in the rear view mirror flit back and forth across his field of vision as he edged the limousine slowly into the street. As soon as he entered traffic, he picked up speed. Just beyond the speed limit. He was headed south.

"Mr. Telemark. . . I mean, Jake," Dora began. "Thank you for meeting with me. I asked to see you because I have recently become aware of something I hope you can help me with."

She paused and glanced at her hands, as if organizing her

thoughts for the presentation. "There are some men of my acquaintance who are planning to overthrow our government. I need your help to stop them."

As soon as she said this, it clicked. The reason I had never heard of this delicious and enticing woman before: she's a nut case. Crazy as a loon. Paranoid. A conspiracy theorist. I was instantly embarrassed that I had allowed myself to be so taken in so easily. Her name probably wasn't Hathaway, or if it was she was probably from some branch of the Hathaway family that broke off generations ago to think up kooky thoughts in the hinterland somewhere. The hills of Tennessee, maybe, or the badlands of Montana. I took a deep breath but made no move to speak. I immediately began to think of how I could get away from this crazy woman who was wrapped in such an agreeable package. But it was her car and her three-hundred-pound driver in the front seat; so nothing seemed plausible at the moment. I tried to look calm on the surface.

"What I am about to share with you is something I trust you will hold in the highest confidence." She pulled out a small, high-end laptop and opened the screen.

What appeared to be a home page was emblazoned with a large cross, the kind that you see a hundred times a day in various settings across our country. It was rough-hewn, a symbol of ignominy or splendor, depending upon one's point of view.

The image faded into a collage of twelve faces, each one smiling sanctimoniously. I recognized three or four of them, men I had met during my time in DC. Men I did not particularly like. One was a senator, another a representative, and another an appellate judge. Another may have been a military man of some sort, a colonel perhaps or maybe a general, but not a high ranking one. I wasn't certain. The collage was distasteful to me; an unsavory collection of militant evangelicals, the kind that have haunted the District since the original swamp was drained to build there. Men most people just tolerated.

Dora looked at me. "You recognize at least some of these men," she began. "You probably don't like them."

As crazy as I was sure she was, she had my biases nailed. "That's correct," I replied, still pondering escape scenarios in my mind.

"These men want to replace our current form of government with a managerial council of twelve. As you can see, they have very clear ideas of who those twelve people—all men—will be."

I looked back down at the computer screen. It was indeed a website of evangelical government officials, the type that has grown increasingly common these days. It was fashionable in this segment of time in the US for educated officials in the government to flaunt their religious preferences. They were always praying in public and advising others to do the same. Websites like this were popping up all over the Net. I thought it was revolting.

Dora was watching me watch the screen. I thought maybe she could sense the disgust that must have been written somewhere on my face. When my eyes rose to meet hers, the businesslike air was gone, replaced by a look of warmth and conspiratorial empathy. "These are dangerous men," she said softly.

I am such a sucker for smart, pretty women. Every cell of my higher brain pointed to the fact that this was a deranged, sick woman lost in a conspiracy theory she may have constructed all on her own out of bits and pieces of news strung together in her mind to support it. My limbic system, however, was more equivocal; more disposed; more attracted. These animal/rational collisions were not uncommon in my life. I was always disgusted that, for the most part, the animal won. I began to have that sinking feeling that always accompanied the abandonment of my good sense.

"Dora," I said. "What in the world are you talking about?"

Dora leaned back a few inches against the soft leather interior of the limo as if she had won. I was still sure she was nuts, but I was not in control of the vehicle, so I leaned back too, wondering what her next move would be. I did not have to wait long. Dora launched into a detailed story that didn't sound so whacked out as it might have twenty years ago. She spoke calmly, even thoughtfully, as she detailed just how twelve fanatical government officials planned to turn the US into a theocratic oligarchy.

I had to admit, if there was a plot, it was a pretty good one as sinister plots go. The gist of it was straightforward: these twelve driven men were going to provoke a crisis, call for a constitutional convention, and propose that democracy as it has been practiced in the United States for the past two hundred years had had a good run, but that it was inefficient, dangerous to the safety and to the morals of the country, and could advantageously be replaced by an executive council of twelve chosen from all parts of the United States land mass who would serve twelve-year terms to safeguard the economic, social, and moral well-being of the citizenry. The long terms of office would give them a chance to keep the longer-term interests of the populace in mind, and the attentions of the country would not be so distracted by frequent elections the way it has been these two centuries. Given the mess that the country is forever in, they were banking on the educated populace doing what an educated populace had done on more than one occasion within the last hundred years, that is, surrender their rights for greater efficiency, greater security, and more relief from fear. You did not have to look back to the Third Reich to see that this strategy could work; you just had to review some of the legislation that followed the horror of 9/11.

In addition to the crisis, there were two other elements of the strategy that were high on the agenda of these men. One was to neutralize the independent judiciary so that no threat could come from the courts to claim that what they were doing was unconstitutional, even though it violated every authentic American impulse. The second was to stage a catastrophe in an effort to entice the citizens of the US to surrender their rights voluntarily in an effort to be safe, the kind of thing that started with the Patriot Act after 9/11. Open records; surveil anyone; dismantle the Bill of

Rights. *In process*, I thought.

There were obstacles of course. They needed a credible crisis, not just another three-hour headline on CNN. And it couldn't be something that struck the US from afar. That would just coalesce the status quo and rally patriotic fervor around the existing system. No, what was needed was a home-grown act of terror, something that reflected the extreme moral decay of the prevailing political and cultural mores. What they needed was a renegade liberal, a deranged hippie, an amoral lunatic who was both widely known and who could credibly be accused of trying to destroy the country. What they needed was Willy Maelstrom.

Chapter 2

Willy Maelstrom was the *nom du plume* of William Mechalowski, a street-smart Chicago kid with a big mouth, liberal views, and enough charm and verbal facility to talk his way from the gritty South Side to a spot first on talk radio and then to his own TV show, which aired on cable and satellite channels. The Willy Maelstrom Show was vibrant, controversial, leftist, and intelligent. Despite the goofy stage name, Willy hosted some of the most thoughtful men and women in the country, who joined in his ongoing conversation about the strengths and weaknesses of American democracy. Unsparing, irreverent, unable and unwilling to suffer fools gladly, Willy did not so much preach his brand of liberal politics as he deduced it, arriving at conclusions that typically seemed self-evident and incontrovertible. He was thorough, thoughtful, and deeply desirous of making the US not just a cart that carried big companies but the kind of society that would serve as a beacon to the world. The kind that took care of its citizens and held them accountable. The kind where no one could go broke because he got sick and no one could claim that he did not have the opportunity to become educated. The kind of place where streets were safe and the police even safer, where industry held the common good in mind in all its decisions, and where the thought of cutting pensioners off because of financial constraints would be unthinkable. Like Europe but permeated with the American spirit. Willy believed in this America, and he worked hard to bring it about.

Of course, many different kinds of people hated him. After exposing just how frequently large corporations were able to renege on their contracts with former workers after a court decision allowed businesses to abandon their promise of health-care for retirees, Willy blasted the corporate culture of the United States in a rant that was mostly unable to be broadcast on network television. Immediately, the political right wing accused him of betraying the country, the religious right questioned his morals, and a presidential spokesman called him obstructionist. But his ratings soared. After years of right-wing control over all branches of government, the people of America were finally catching on that they had been sold a bill of goods. That behind all the pious and patriotic talk, the safeguards they did have were being whittled away. That the tax cuts granted to the wealthiest among us undermined the fiscal stability of the country. And there was a growing recognition that the premise of democracy was that the people ruled. Willie knew this, and he thought his time, and the time of his ideas, was on the horizon. To bolster this view, he was riding a growing tide of popularity. His simple, no-nonsense approach to problems was beginning to appeal to more and more people. In other words, he was dangerous to the status quo.

Dora looked at me thoughtfully. "I think they're going to set him up for something big," she said.

"Why Maelstrom?" I asked. "Wouldn't he be too obvious a target? Why don't they find some no-name liberal goof-ball from Omaha?"

"I think they're shooting for the moon, Jake," Dora said. "Willy has been getting more and more attention in the neocon press. *American Spectator* ran articles on him three months in a row. The conservative talk show circuit mentions him routinely. He's riled up everybody at Fox News for months now."

I sank more deeply into the soft leather of the long vehicle. I could smell the new-car scent and looked around to admire the upholstery. My cerebral cortex was reasserting its authority as the puppy dog limbic system slinked back into its ramshackle cage. *Okay, she may not be a nut, and maybe she is who she says she is, but how close do I want to get to anything associated with Dora Hathaway or with some lunatic government officials? Or with Willy Maelstrom, for that matter? I have always seen my job as doing the best I could with what was in front of me and avoiding fiery polemics and grandiose strutting around. After all, I started out as a teacher. I ran for my first office on a drunken bet. It wasn't my fault I won.* I sat there surveying the whole improbable series of events that led up to my sitting in a chauffeured limousine being driven around the hallowed environs of Washington DC, being targeting by a beautiful but possibly deranged woman of some prominence who wants to drag me into something in which I was about as interested as knitting doilies for elderly unmarried virgins.

"Dora," I finally said. "I can understand why this would be upsetting to you. Or to anyone with your background. From what I hear of your father, he was the last great lion of the left in the Senate." I paused and weighed the next part as carefully as I could. "But I am not the crusader type. I'm more like the dutiful, service-oriented type. The kind that wants to make things work smoothly." I looked at her doubtfully. "You know, demure, hardworking, live-and-let-live. Republican."

Dora's gaze, though softer than before, continued unwavering. She did not speak. I hate that about her, and I've only known her for seventy-five minutes.

"Would you say something," I finally said.

"I was thinking, Jake," she said with a new level of softness. She turned her face to look out the window at the refulgent Virginian sunshine. Of course, it made her look radiant. I figured she was doing this for my benefit. I liked it.

"What do you want me to do, Dora?" I said, surrendering.

Her head turned slowly back toward mine. "I want you to kill these twelve people," she said softly.

Chapter 3

Dora's words hung in the air. So did my insides. I was experiencing what psychologists call depersonalization, a momentary loss of the stuff of my normal personality. I felt the moment stand still; I could hear my heart beating. My eyes could move a little but not my body. I sat frozen. I couldn't believe Dora had said what I knew she had said, but there was no trace of humor, irony, or ambivalence in her voice or in her demeanor. I knew my face had no color; I had felt it drain away in an instant.

In this moment, I saw my life in one grand sweep. Well, maybe not grand, but of a piece. My whimsical decision to run for alderman; my lucky run for the House of Representatives; my improbable appointment to the Senate. I'm a teacher—that's how I started—that's all I ever wanted to be. Never in my time in Washington had any hint of criminal activity crossed my path. I never saw or heard of anyone taking a bribe; I never saw anyone robbed. I have heard of someone padding his expense account a little, but that seemed like a victimless crime. But murder? Except for crime bill discussions, I don't think I ever spoke the word out loud. I may not be religious, but my family was strict Episcopalian, and the thought that some member of our family would even be riding in a car with someone who broached the possibility of killing another human being filled me with an ancient fear of my father's vengeance.

There was, however, another side to these reactions, which reflect the way I think about myself now, the way I present myself to the world. This other, deeper part has to do with a secret and restricted part of my past, a part to which no one is privy. A part that is protected both by law and by the demands of my sanity, and that I could certainly not voice to Dora or to anyone else. I had to stay away from this. I couldn't even risk asking her why she picked me.

My body was beginning to stir. I inhaled for the first time in what must have been minutes. I slowly drew my head back and looked at Dora, not quite so entranced by the high cheek bones or the well-coifed hair or the elegant dress. I drew another breath to speak. "What?" I said.

Dora looked at me calmly. "These men are dangerous, Jake," she said soothingly. "And they are well-shielded. Two of them are highly placed in the FBI; two others are federal judges. A fifth is an Assistant Attorney General. Others are similarly in positions where they can operate with impunity. They are out to wreck our system of government; they are fanatics. And they must be stopped."

I could see fire in Dora's eyes, but her voice was steady. I just wanted the car to stop so I could get out and be free of this hellish experience. But the car kept moving. And Dora kept looking at me. "You're out of your mind," I said at length.

A grim smile crossed Dora's lips. "I wish I were," she said. Her eyes flickered just a bit. "But there is another, even more compelling reason for you to do what I suggest." Another long pause. "If you don't kill them, they will kill you."

I was close enough to normal to have a reasonable thought. "That's preposterous!" I said. "Nobody wants to kill me."

Dora looked back out the window, as if she were putting up with a recalcitrant child. Her head swung quickly around, and her eyes blazed. "Oh, yes, they will, Jake, whether you think they will or not." The belief in her voice was unmistakable.

"What possible reason on earth would these people, fanatical as they might be, want to harm a junior senator from a fly-over state?" Dora wasn't the only one who was angry now. "Why, Dora?" I shouted. The driver's eyes glanced at the rear view mirror.

"Because you stand between them and their objective," she retorted. "Because the success or failure of their plan depends on the amount of opposition they get, and you, as a reasonable member of the Senate, have been tagged as a potential obstacle. You and a half-dozen other senators and a couple dozen representatives." Another pause. "Along with a number of strategically placed judges, cabinet officers, and assorted bureaucrats."

The color had returned to my face. I could feel the hot blood rising up my cheeks. I was furious. None if this sounded in the least bit plausible, except for my emotional reaction. I wanted out.

"Stop the car!" I demanded.

The car did not stop.

Dora was breathing more heavily now. I could sense that she was trying to re-establish control, although it was difficult for me to assess if she ever lost it. She obviously did not want me to end this conversation.

"Stop the car!" I demanded a second time. Another glance into the mirror by the driver.

Just for a moment, Dora looked torn. Her eyes darted quickly to the driver and then back to me.

"No!" she said.

The locks on the doors all went down with an audible thud. My chest tightened.

Dora continued, "Listen to me, Jake. I am not telling you this because I am some misbegotten paranoid who's trying to get a rise out of important people. I am telling you because . . . because it's just not right what these people are planning. You are in danger. You have been targeted. You and several of your closest allies in the Senate. These people are deadly serious about their agenda.

They will not let you or any other reasonable person stand in their way." She paused and looked away momentarily. "And they know how to use violence to maximum effect."

For the next few minutes, neither of us spoke. We drove on in the Virginian sunshine, which contrasted sharply with the thunderclouds filling my mind. I still could not grasp the notion that someone, anyone, would want to harm me. It's never happened. Even having this conversation without reporting it to the proper authorities may set me up for a conspiracy charge.

I had to get out of this car and away from this woman. I glanced at the beefy driver whose biceps stretched the circumference of his already large coat sleeves. *I guess he's here in case I get rowdy*, I thought.

I looked back at Dora. "How do you know these things?" I asked, trying to buy some time to think.

"About two years ago, I dated one of these men. He was a friend of a friend. He worked in the AG's office, and I didn't think twice about danger. He was just another guy. I've been around DC for a while—grew up here, practically—and I've always been drawn to men in government. Must be in my genes. Anyway, to make a long story short, I discovered that he was an evangelical. I didn't care; a guy's religion makes no difference to me. One day, I made a crack about it, and he went ballistic. Prior to that moment, which happened about two months after our first date, I had no inkling that there was anything wrong."

"What did you say?" I asked.

Dora looked away for a moment and blushed ever so slightly. "I told him it didn't seem to interfere with his appetites," she said. "It was an innocent comment. I didn't mean anything by it. We had been having sex for weeks."

"What was his reaction?" I pressed.

"Well, a lot changed in that moment. Prior to that, I would not have believed in split personalities, but Roger—his name is Roger Bandera—started shouting and calling me names—whore, slut, temptress. He was waving his arms and poking his finger at me. I thought he was totally bonkers. I was also a little scared."

"Dora," I said not without sympathy, "What did you do?"

"I walked out," she said. "Both my parents had always been very clear about one thing: if a guy goes off on you, dump him. So I walked out. We were at his apartment, and I left a few clothes and things, but no one, I mean no one, talks to me that way. It had never happened before."

This made me wonder how old she was, but it did not seem like an opportune moment to inquire about that sensitive topic.

"After I calmed down," Dora continued. "And that took me a while, but after a few days I began thinking back to the time we spent together. Something didn't add up. Successful government guys are control freaks. Also, they think they're important and they often allow their social lives to be interrupted by business. One phone call and the evening is shot. There is no such thing as a brief interruption. I think the guy thinks it makes him look important and a lot of the women in this town seem to agree, so everyone puts up with it. But with Roger, it was different. Roger and I would go to dinner and he would get a call on his cell and excuse himself and be gone for all of three, four, maybe five minutes. Then he would return and act as if nothing happened. It was kind of nice at first; I mean, we didn't ever have to trash the entire evening. But it happened all the time. His calls came like clockwork. I tried to think back if there was a time when one of our times together was not interrupted, and I don't think there was a single one. Not just dates in public, but when he would stay over at my place or if we were at his apartment. There was always a brief interruption. Or two." Dora looked at her hand and shook her head. "I didn't think anything about it except that it was curious. Until the blow-up."

Dora paused and looked at me. God, she was beautiful. I wished at that moment we had met under different circumstances. Like not when she was telling me I would be killed.

She continued, "After I left, I started to ask around about Roger: who he hung out with, who he knew, who he was close to. I googled his name. Turns out that he was one of the cameos on that website I showed you. So I started digging deeper. Really, at first I was just angry that he had mistreated me, and I think I just wanted to get back at him. But the more I learned, the more intrigued I became. This guy was very well-connected to a group of highly placed officials who meet every week for a prayer breakfast at the Press Club." Dora paused to take a breath. I could sense the wear and tear of this business on her young and lovely face.

"Then I met a woman who had dated another one of those website guys, and we started comparing notes. She had almost the exact same experience I did, both with the interruptions and with the blow-up. Only she did not walk out. She and Walt Zimmerman had been dating for over six months—practically a marriage in this town—when he blew up at her for some off-hand remark. Not only did she not walk out, she sat and listened and tried to make sense out of what was happening. After Walt dumped all his sanctimonious crap on Madison, my friend, he broke down and wept in her arms like a little boy." Dora looked away. "Cried for hours. Told her some of the things that I've been telling you. How the country was off track with how the wicked were spreading their irreligious ways; how democracy was an antiquated system of government; how management by a council of twelve would be more efficient, more long-term, and more far-sighted. He told her that there needed to be a change and that there would be one. A big one. He said that the wicked would have to mend their ways or pay big time."

There was silence for some minutes. I was almost completely absorbed now, but I was still uncertain of what I would or could do about this whole situation. I waited because I didn't know what else to do and because I could tell that Dora wasn't finished.

"Madison and Walt had a series of conversations over a couple weeks. It was during this time that I met her. I am not one to get close to someone right away, but I liked her; strong, smart, powerful woman—older than I am, but very engaging. She seemed more than a little preoccupied. She and her family had been big fans of my father, so she felt a bond to me immediately. On our third lunch, she asked if she could share some private things with me. That's when she told me about her experience with Walt."

"Was she still seeing him at that point?" I asked.

"No. She had just decided that Walt was too unbalanced for her, and she ended the affair. After that first night, Walt tried to put a different spin on things, diluting what he said at first and never explaining why he had gotten so emotional. She knew he was lying, or at least covering something up. She was scared and didn't want to have anything to do with him or his right-wing conspiracy."

My stomach began to sink at this point. I was having inklings of how this story would go. I hoped I was wrong but was getting more certain by the moment that I wasn't.

"Dora," I said, "What happened?"

Dora looked at me with the saddest eyes I had ever seen, which confirmed my worse fears. "She was killed in a hit-and-run accident about two weeks later," she said. Tears began flowing down her lovely face.

I could feel the warmth of my own tears welling up in the corners of my eyes. Tears of sadness for what this woman in front of me had gone through. And tears of anxiety at what she was sharing with me. I took her hand. "I am so sorry," I said.

Dora looked up at me. "That's when I started looking even more deeply into this," she said, ignoring my hand but not pulling her own away.

"I knew some women—they were acquaintances, really—they dated men for a fee, as a service. A dating/escort service. Young women just out of college, mostly, working in the District and trying to jump start their careers. They needed cash. And a lot of men in this city need escorts. I had hit a dead end with my contacts and with public information, so I suggested to my acquaintances that, if they got organized, they could make some good money targeting some of the members of this group. I gave them strict instructions on how to behave: what to say, what not to say. They were just looking to make a splash, have a good time. . ."

"They're not. . .?" I interrupted.

"No, Jake; they are all alive as we speak." Dora almost smiled. "But don't think I haven't worried about them every day for the past two years. I am still worried about them."

"Anyway, I called Roger after a while and told him I knew our relationship ended abruptly and I didn't want to be enemies and I am sure our last time together included a lot of misunderstanding. I gave him a clear signal that I wanted a truce but that I did not want to get back together. This is a common thing in this town, as you must surely know. No one wants to make permanent enemies. Roger was civil and understanding about it, almost but not quite apologetic. In this conversation, I mentioned that I had some friends who were putting a little business together and wondered if he knew any other guys who needed dates from time to time for official functions. He said that occasionally he did have some use for these services, strictly on a platonic basis, and he took the names of the girls—all aliases, of course—and their telephone numbers. It turns out there wasn't a single date that was arranged that wasn't with one of these twelve guys. Many of whom are married."

I was listening so intently that I didn't realize we had stopped. I turned and looked out the window and saw the front entrance of the Emporia restaurant, where this outrageous rendezvous started. I looked at Dora with a quizzical expression, and she said, "I'm hungry."

This woman knows how to throw me off, I thought. But then I realized that I too was hungry and that I was more than happy to join her for lunch.

Chapter 4

Lunch seemed like a return to what I thought of as normal day-to-day life. That is, up until a few hours ago. We sat at a small table near the window of the upscale eatery, sipping white wine and talking. It was after four, so it was hard to call it lunch, but we were both famished. I guess hearing about threats on your life does that.

But all that weird stuff was not on the table. Rather, Dora talked about herself and her famous—and, some would say, infamous—father, the man who prided himself on getting things done, who worked for the people. In truth, I had a lot of respect for Frank Hathaway. His methods were probably not always kosher, but he could get things done, and in general he did keep the welfare of ordinary Americans in mind. He was a good man, a good citizen, and a good senator, even if he sat on the other side of the aisle. It was clear that Dora adored her dad; when she spoke of him, her face glowed. At one point, I could see the moisture of an incipient tear glaze her eyes. It was less than three years ago since he died, and the pain had not completely receded.

Two glasses of wine on an empty stomach began to cloud my thinking, and my thoughts were not completely cleared by simply eating. Mental images and possibilities began to crowd my mind, and I knew I needed some time to sort out what I had heard and what my own reactions were. After we finished eating and after a momentary pause in the conversation, I called for the check and then looked directly into Dora's eyes.

"How long do I have?" I asked.

Dora paused. "I am not sure. My best guess is that this drama will play out over the next six to twelve months, although that is just a guess based on scraps of information I have been able to collect through the friends I mentioned earlier." She looked down at her empty plate and then back up at me. "Some of this depends on how threatened these guys feel. They may have a 'prep list' and strike out preemptively. But they might just wait until specific threats appear. It's hard to predict paranoid behavior, but the numbers are fluid."

The check came and Dora took it. "Jake, I will give you a few days to think about this, and then I will be in touch again," she said. She signed the bill, took her copy, left the merchant copy on the table, and stood up. I followed.

I nodded and thanked her for lunch. We shook hands and lunch ended just the way it does in the thousands of business lunches that occur across the US everyday. Formal but friendly. I walked out into the early evening light and spotted George standing idly by my limo, reading a magazine.

It was too late to return to the office, so I directed George to drop me off at my apartment in Georgetown. My head was swimming, and I had no idea what to do or even what to think. The alcohol had taken the edge off my anxiety a bit, except when I pictured Dora's lovely face telling me that I had been targeted for assassination. Then my stomach roiled and my breathing got shallow. I tried to inhale deeply, but it was only a palliative. The cure completely eluded me.

I thanked George and walked slowly up the steps of my apartment building. I have always felt lucky to live in Georgetown, one of the most charming neighborhoods in the country. I always felt happy to be home in this enclave of professional and government workers. The Georgetown neighborhood felt more like home than the Wisconsin town where I grew up. I hated small town life.

But this evening the usual glow of satisfaction and homecoming was gone. I lumbered into my apartment, threw my keys on the kitchen counter, and plopped down onto the leather couch that faced both a small fireplace and a television. I did not turn on either. I just sat there in disbelief, staring into space for probably a half hour before I decided to make some coffee and get my mind in gear.

I turned on the TV while the coffee was brewing. Nothing special on the local news. I flipped to CNN. Same there. These simple, homespun tasks felt different today. I felt disconnected. What I was doing seemed like a parody of a life as opposed to my life. I guess I was scared. No, I knew I was scared; I just wasn't sure what to do about it.

I poured myself a cup of coffee and stood looking out the window at the night descending on the old buildings of Georgetown. It was then that another layer to my reaction started making itself felt, something I did not want to face. It has been so long since I thought of my other life; most often I pretended that it never happened. I was a teacher, an alderman, a representative, and then a senator. I was a do-gooder who was able to maintain idealism as fifty approached. I was unfailingly polite, well-mannered, and cautious. But distant. The distance made personal relationships hard, especially with women who wanted more of me, as most women do after a few months. I don't blame them, but nor have I wanted more closeness. Emotional distance keeps me safe. From my past; from myself. It allows me to pretend that there was not a time in my life when I was a killer.

The unconscious thought that had been knocking around in the back of my mind slowly dawned into the forefront. Isadore Hathaway knew about my past. That was how her father operated. Frank Hathaway was legendary for finding out the whole truth about people, including the sordid parts of their lives that no one wanted revealed or exposed, especially in public. No one knew exactly how he did it. He had contacts, as did most congressmen who spent more than one term in office. But he never revealed the extent of his network, not to the press or to his colleagues. He did not have a *protégé*, the way a lot of self-important people in this town do.

The insight widened in clarity. Dora must have some access to whatever network her father had. She did not flinch when she told me she wanted me to kill these men. She must have known that it wasn't so far-fetched a request as most people would imagine. She must have known about my past. But how? And the way she put our conversation away when we entered the restaurant. She had no way of knowing if I knew that she knew, but she demonstrated that she could change personalities as smoothly as I have learned to do. She showed me how I do it. I blushed a little at the thought that I could be so transparent.

I felt the blood chill in my veins as I commanded myself to look at the past that I had forced out of my conscious awareness years ago. I closed my eyes and tried to picture the four years I spent in the Army. Just out of college and full of energy, I joined the Army because I wanted the experience and the GI Bill that went with it. Even though that Bill did not provide the generous benefits it did after World War II, it was still a great way to fund advanced education—in fact, it did pay for my night-school law degree.

I looked down into my nearly empty coffee cup in an effort to ward off the shame that was percolating into my consciousness. I was so young, so eager. I volunteered for everything and anything. It turned out that I was better at some things than at others. And one of those things was shooting at far-away objects. I was a good sniper. I was a great sniper.

So I spent two years shooting people. At first it seemed like a game. I could hit a target a thousand yards away without being seen, using the finest and quietest equipment in the world. I was the good guy; the person in my scope was the bad guy. It worked okay in combat situations or in war situations, but when I was transferred to the Special Ops Unit, the good vs. bad thing wasn't so clear to me. After the transfer, the targets in my scope were most often not wearing uniforms. Often they were wearing business suits. Some of them wore dresses. I was always assured that these people had done terrible things, criminal things. They were people who, if they were not killed, would do more terrible things. They were dangerous. The macho culture of the Army, and especially of my unit, did not encourage questioning of orders. We were in the service of the United States government. That's all we needed to know.

I wanted to vomit. Dora was no nut case; she knew exactly what she was doing. I don't know whether to believe her about my being a target. That would enhance my motivation, and it is possible that it's true, but I am doubtful. What I do know is that she wants those twelve guys dead.

My thoughts returned to the end of my sniper duty. To the day I just couldn't do it anymore. I had the target in my sights. I had checked my equipment and the ambient conditions. I was well hidden and could walk away easily after the job. I was psyched mentally. I had put my ambivalence, my qualms aside. I was all robotic intellect and physical power. But the image in my scope unknowingly looked straight back at me. He was about my age, mid-twenties. His face was full of life and optimism. He probably had done some bad things, but my job was killing people, and whatever he did probably paled in comparison to what I did. At that moment, my mental clarity collapsed, and dammed-up guilt and shame flooded my head. I rolled over and looked up at the twilit sky. What I was doing was wrong. More than wrong. It was a crime against nature, against life itself. Maybe in some grand scheme it was justified, but to me I was killing people I did not know because someone else I didn't know told me to. It sickened me now just to think of it, and I put my coffee cup on the window sill so I didn't drop it.

I hung my head and looked unseeing at the floor. I had always thought of the rest of my professional life as serendipity. Wild chances and lucky breaks. I loved teaching, but I went to law school because I could. I ran for alderman on a drunken bet. Same for my first run for a House seat. The appointment to fill a vacant senatorial term was also sheer happenstance. None of this seemed to get near the seriousness of my life as a sniper. And with good reason.

They said I cracked up. Lost it; lost my nerve; lost my "objectivity". No kidding. That kind of objectivity may be useful for psychopaths, but it was not how I saw Jacob Tobias Telemark filling up his four-score years on the planet.

When I was in the Army I couldn't tell anyone what I did. Some of the guys around me knew I was a sniper, but almost no one talked about it. Most snipes are introverted guys who don't fraternize much. But I love to be around people, and I drank quite a bit, so I often hung around with other members of my unit. But even so, talk of death and dying was not done in the Army. It was understood that killing was the reason we were in the organization, but it was considered low-life and cowardly to talk about it. An almost superstitious air surrounded the topic if it ever came up. Sudden silence, eyes cast down, total discomfort.

So I never talked about it with my buddies. Nor could I tell my parents or my family. My mom and dad were okay with my being in the Army, if not wild about it, but they were mostly glad because they thought it would allow me to continue my education. I scraped through college, much to their dismay. They saw me as a bright kid who was in imminent danger of throwing away the opportunity to make more of himself. Though republican, they were the more traditional variety and were generally opposed to interventionist wars. They supported the big ones: World Wars I and II; Korea. But from Vietnam onwards, they were more skeptical than not. They disapproved of the current president's Middle-Eastern policies, seeing them as unnecessarily burdening the American taxpayer with the costs of building someone else's country. But they respected the modernized military and the discipline that came along with it. They hoped it would make a difference in my life.

They never knew about the crack-up. I told them I had been redeployed when my commanding officer sent me to the psych ward. There may have been some unpronounceable word to describe the condition I had, but I thought of it as breathing fresh air, of health. To me, it's healthy to want to stop killing anonymous people for whatever reason. And it's healthy to talk about what you do. I appreciated the time on the locked unit. I had people to talk to, and I talked and talked. I not only talked, but I cried the tears that I had not allowed myself for the two and a half years before I walked into that sacred space. I was there for a month.

At the end of my stay, the handwriting was on the wall. I could be honorably discharged and leave quietly—and sign a million forms swearing me to secrecy—or I could risk court-martial for failure to perform my duties and a dishonorable departure from the Army. The decision in my mind was made the minute I rolled over on my back in that shit-hole in Africa and let my mark live. No more killing. That was that.

And from that time to this, I never looked back. I did everything I could to imagine my life without two years of murder on my tab. I knew the body count—36—and couldn't erase it from my mind if I wanted to. But I worked hard to make sure that my public self-presentation, which meant my new self, was seamless, always acting as if my conscience did not torture me relentlessly for the first few years as I took up my teaching duties and pursued an evening course in law. I needed to fill up my time. Time alone was dangerous.

I knew what I had; it wasn't really so unpronounceable. PTSD: Post-Traumatic Stress Disorder. They taught me all about it in the hospital and they told me the kinds of things I could expect. Even the depersonalization I experienced in the car earlier today with

Dora was part of the package. It's unpleasant as hell to go through, but it's not so scary when you know what it is. Especially when you've gone through it before.

For the first few years out, I had panic attacks and episodes such as the one this afternoon on a more or less routine basis. Each time, I had a therapist I could talk to. I could hold on and get through it. After a while, the frequency diminished, as did the intensity. Occasional nightmares occurred for about ten years, but it has been a long time since I've had one of those. The truth was that I began to see my symptoms as fair punishment for my sins, if not for my crimes. So while I never welcomed them and was always glad when they receded, I met them with resignation and acceptance. Screwed up, maybe, but that's how I always felt about these experiences.

But Dora did an end run around my defenses. I sat down on the chair and kept looking out into the night that had fallen. I felt strangely free. Dora had reached into my past and forced it into the present and maybe even into the future. I felt defeated but whole. All my efforts to put the sniper story away lay in ruins. This was me. As much as I believed I had succeeded in pushing my past away, it left me at odds with myself, disowning one of the most formative periods of my life. There were other snipers in the world, but to the thirty-six dead people on my dance card, I was the only one that mattered. I did it. I did it again and again. Thirty-six times. Son of a bitch.

Chapter 5

I don't remember falling asleep last night. I remember switching from coffee to scotch, and I can see the half-empty Dewar's bottle on the coffee table in front of the couch where I spent the night in my clothes. I remember the dreams. The nightmares, of course. Any undergraduate psych student would have predicted that my dreams would be wracked with frightening images of the past. But there was another piece: I dreamed of a hunchback who stood up straight. The details are fuzzy, and the dream segment was surrounded by explosive and terrifying images of dead people. I don't know how the humpster went from being bent over with a grotesque hump to standing erect, but I sensed enormous relief that this unidentified presence was free of his deformity.

I looked at my watch. 6:30. I am surprised it is so early. I stumbled into the bathroom and looked at the person in the mirror. Not a happy sight. I tore off my clothes and fell into my bed hoping that sleep might return.

It did. I had two hours of dreamless—that is to say, uninterrupted—sleep. I awoke to the ringing telephone. It was Jamie Steward, my Chief of Staff. The scheduler of my life.

"Jake," she said too loudly. "Where are you?"

I thought this an ill-considered question, given that she dialed my home number. "At home," I replied.

"You have a meeting with the Select Committee in ten minutes," Jamie said.

I looked over and found the clock. So I do. "Listen, Jamie, I am under the weather. Please make my apologies to the Committee and clear my schedule for the day."

Jamie's tone changed instantly. "Are you OK?" she asked.

I considered this question. *No was the real answer, but I didn't want to explain the entire situation to Jamie. On the other hand, it wasn't like me to take a day off for any reason.* So I replied with the truth, "No, I am not, Jamie," I said.

"Jake," she said with growing concern. "Is there anything I can do?"

"Yes, Jamie, you can cover for me and clear my schedule."

"Consider it done. Please call me if you need anything."

"I promise."

I held the phone in my hand for some minutes before I returned it to its cradle. I lay in bed pondering my next move, especially now that I had the day free. I got up to do my morning ritual. These homey tasks helped me feel grounded and helped clear my head after the psychic storm that was yesterday and last night. I showered, shaved, dressed in chinos and a polo shirt, and went to the kitchen to make breakfast. I collected the newspaper from the front stoop and sat sipping coffee and going over it at the kitchen table. Just another day.

Beneath the look of the normal day, however, my insides were in open revolt. I couldn't really concentrate on the paper. Nor could I put my finger on what was happening to me emotionally and psychologically. I had not forced myself to look at my life, my whole life, so clearly in almost two decades. I never wanted to remember; I wanted to forget. But I had to admit that, though this internal experience was discomfiting, I was beginning to feel whole again. Real again. It was like the first time I told my story to my therapist aloud and said the words I dreaded:

"I killed people. I stalked them, lay in wait for them, and blew their brains out."

Therapeutic silence.

"Usually I came in the day before the job and scoped out the place. I had everything I needed. Afterwards, I packed up my stuff and disposed of it according to plan. Then I usually stayed around for a day or so to blend in, to catch the sights. It was like... it was like getting out of town for the weekend with a simple job to do. Shooting people isn't hard, especially when you've been trained as well as I had been."

"You stayed around?" asked the middle-aged white guy who was so good at silence.

"Yeah, I stayed around. I did it out of, I don't know, respect maybe. A death is something important; a person shouldn't run away. You should be respectful."

Even now, thinking about this first session, the tears burned as they ran down my cheeks. I was glad I stayed. It was the right thing to do. Maybe there was some other weird psychological reason for it. Maybe I wanted to get caught or some other nonsense. But the truth was I just wanted to pay my respects to the place my victims last walked the earth.

I flipped through the newspaper trying to distract myself from the memories of my life, but more than once I put the paper down and re-entered the vivid and detailed history book that was my imagination and my memory. I felt such relief at being able to think about my whole life. There were even moments when the shame was not so damned debilitating. I remember the first time I felt that, in the hospital. Holding the truth of my life in my mind without being dragged down into the craggy abyss of self-loathing. It was the truth; I killed people. I did it as respectfully as I could, but I killed them.

I picked up the paper from the table in the breakfast nook of my tiny kitchen and tried to concentrate. I felt another thing I hadn't felt in years: excitement. The thought that someone was out to harm me was troubling, but it stimulated me. Maybe it seemed like justice. Hell, it would be justice. But I don't want to die; I just want to play a more serious game. I want my life to matter more than being some middle-of-the-road congressman who gets invited to everyone's parties. I want to live with more intensity than I had been. *Wouldn't take much*, I thought.

It was then that I noticed the small headline on the bottom of page four. *College student found dead in alley on K Street.* The picture showed a pretty early-twenties woman with a bright smile. Obviously a school picture. I immediately concluded the worst, that this was one of Dora's girls. A flash of fear swept through my body. And then the phone rang.

It could only have been Dora, and it was. "Meet me in ten minutes," she said. "Outside."

She hung up.

God, this woman is a control freak, I thought. But I took her call as confirmation of my worst fears. I was also glad in an eerie kind of way to be in the loop, to be part of the action. Unfortunately, I did not know what part. I grabbed a sweater and left my apartment.

Dora did not need ten minutes. She pulled her 3-series BMW alongside a parked car within minutes and motioned with her head for me to get in the passenger side.

"One of my girls was killed last night," she said with no introduction as she moved the car forward.

"My girls?" Odd way to phrase that, I thought. "Same girl in the paper?" I asked.

Dora nodded. A single tear rolled down her cheek. I said nothing.

"I am concerned that the timetable I outlined for you yesterday may have been too optimistic," she continued. "I now think things are going to move much more quickly." She paused. "They may already be in play."

Yesterday I had the luxury of savoring the attentions of this hot, smart, urbane female. Today there was no place for that. I had to make some determinations, and I had to make them quickly.

I turned to Dora. "Look," I said, "You need to level with me. What is your involvement with these girls? How do you get your information? What are you up to?"

Dora did not take her eyes off the road. She didn't say anything. I kept my gaze locked on the right side of her face. A face that was hardening into one of grim determination.

Suddenly, Dora's hand grabbed the parking break of the 340i and the nimble machine did a fast and screechy U-turn in the middle of the street. After a block, she made a sharp right, then a left, then a right again. She came to a sudden stop in front of a nameless apartment building and killed the engine.

She didn't take her eyes off the rear view mirror. "I think we were being followed," she said softly. "Don't move."

I didn't. As sudden as these movements were, the events of last night must have recalibrated my body to be ready for anything. I wasn't anxious; nor was I alarmed. I was calm, focused. As focused as training my silenced Remington sight on an unsuspecting mark. I looked across Dora's lap to her side-view mirror, which gave me the best view of the rear field of vision without turning around.

"Clear," I whispered after a couple minutes. "Let's get out of here."

Dora fired up the car and edged it slowly into the side street. She went the opposite direction than we had come. I had not seen what had alarmed her, so I didn't bother to look for a specific car. "What was it?" I asked.

"Black Lincoln with government plates," Dora replied. "Four guys, dark suits, sunglasses, trailed us from two cars behind. Standard FBI procedure. Stopped suddenly when I made my move. Three of the guys looked our way; one was focused on driving. Turned his blinker on; made the turn." She was speaking rapidly with shallow breath. "I was able to turn twice before they caught up."

We both sucked in deep breaths at the same time. "Let me repeat my question," I said. "What are you up to?"

Dora glanced in my direction with a resigned expression on her face.. "Let's go somewhere," she said.

The somewhere was in Maryland, just north of Ocean City. Coastal property: isolated, windswept, and beautiful in a rugged way. She drove up to a small cabin and pulled into a single car garage. "We'll be safe here," she said.

I wasn't so sure. I didn't know if whoever was following her was following her or following me or following us both. "What is this place?" I asked, not confident about getting a straight answer.

"It's a family place, but it's off the grid," Dora replied. "My dad kept it as a retreat for himself and his very closest friends. It's mine now."

"How can you be so sure it's off the grid? That's pretty hard to pull off these days." I was more than a little skeptical.

Dora looked at me with an especially patronizing expression. "You didn't know my father," she said as she unlocked the front door of the modest cabin.

The cabin was small but well-appointed. It had comfortable furniture and seemed to be well-stocked. It did not have the look of neglect. In fact, Dora acted like she lived there, throwing her keys on the small kitchen counter and going right to the coffee maker.

"Coffee?" she asked.

"Sure," I said.

Dora motioned to the couch with her head and went about making coffee. She seemed lost in thought, and I was getting irritated at having to wait during her long process times. I knew a lot had happened to her, but a lot had also happened to me in the past twenty-four hours. I needed some answers.

"I am going to restate my question for a third time," I began.

"I heard it the first time," she replied. But I lost her to her own thoughts one more time.

"Jesus, Dora!" I blurted. "Don't you understand that until yesterday I was leading a peaceful life as a senator from Wisconsin and that today I'm running away from people who might well be government agents or police with someone I barely know? Can you allow that this is a little disconcerting for me and that I might want some answers?"

The silence was broken by the gurgling of the coffee maker. Dora turned to get two cups, poured them both, and brought them over the where I was sitting on the couch.

She looked straight at me. "Yes, I do, Jake," she said soothingly. "And I am sorrier than I can say that I dragged you into it." She took a sip from the hot liquid. "But I decided that letting you in on this was better than letting you die."

I decided to go with the obvious. "Why would you care about the death of someone you don't know?" There was more sarcasm in my voice than I intended.

Dora looked across her coffee cup and blew gently. She took a small sip. "There are some things I can tell you and some I can't, Jake," she said. "What I can tell you is that I think Deborah was killed last night because she had a similar experience to mine and Madison's. That somehow, despite the fact that I warned all the girls very specifically not to comment on any matters religious or political, she had crossed the line and made herself a target."

Deborah, I thought. *She was close to this woman.*

"But there is another explanation," Dora continued. "They may have discovered she was working for me. They may have tortured her for information before they killed her."

I looked at Dora as I considered the implications of what she was saying. The girls work for her. They sleep with government officials and spy on them and collect information those officials are very interested in. This situation is getting more serious by the moment.

"What about the guys who were chasing us?" I asked.

"Following, not chasing," Dora replied. "I have been under surveillance off and on for the past few months. Those guys were just the latest batch."

"Four guys?" I asked.

"It's always four guys," Dora replied. "I'm not sure why. Strength in numbers maybe." She raised her arms slightly as if to underscore how not dangerous she was and took another sip of her coffee.

"Why are they following you?"

Dora did not respond at first. She looked around the room as if seeing it for the first time. Then her gaze descended upon me. "These guys on the website I showed you yesterday; they might have figured out that I know something they don't want me to know."

"And what is that?" I demanded.

Dora put her coffee cup on the rustic coffee table and took a breath. "For the past two years, I have been assembling information about the conspiracy I told you about yesterday. It has come in bits and pieces, mostly through the girls I told you about." She paused and looked down. "Deborah and the others. The picture that is emerging is, well, it's frightening in its scope. These people are fanatics, Jake. They dress like you and me and talk like you and me, but they are not normal people. They have a radical agenda that makes present Washington DC feel a lot like Germany in the thirties."

Then her eyes looked directly into mine. "I heard you speak at a foreign policy conference this past fall. I went to check out if you might be one of them. You are republican, but you were talking about pulling back from our international involvements. That's part of their agenda. *Questionable Practices* was the title of your speech. It sounded moralistic and high-handed to me, so I thought you were involved." Dora picked up her coffee cup and took and sip. I thought I was going to lose her to thought again, but she put her cup back down and looked back to me.

"Your name had come up at some parties that the gang of twelve had hosted. It was unclear if they saw you as a potential proponent or a potential problem. That's why I went to check you out. That's also why I did a little background check on you." She picked up her cup but did not drink. "Interesting stuff," she said.

I looked at Dora with a mixture of apprehension, anger, and mistrust that was complicated by her forthrightness and by a fact that was beginning to seep into my consciousness that, when tragedy struck, she came straight for me. I had to allow for the possibility that she wanted me on her side and that she was protecting me. I let that one ride and didn't respond to her last provocative remark. I wasn't going to spill the beans on my past. If she found out about it, OK; but she would have to show her hand first.

"I know about your history, Jake," Dora said softly. "It took some doing, but I had to know if you were one of them or not." She looked at me almost apologetically.

"What do you know?" I asked, looking straight back into her eyes.

"I know that you were a sniper with Alpha Unit in the Army about twenty-five years ago. I know you cracked up, or so people said, and that you spent a month in a top-secret psych hospital where guys on secret missions go when they crack up. I know you saw a shrink for a long time afterwards to put that behind you." She looked into my eyes with a firmness that matched my own. "And I know you kept every promise you made to the military to keep your activities quiet. And that you live as if those dreadful years did not exist."

My lips wanted to spread into a smile, so good was it to hear someone talk about my past with a candor I have never been allowed. But I commanded my face not to move, and I held Dora's gaze. After a moment, I stood up and walked to the window.

This chick is tough, I thought as I turned my attention to the emerging spring outside the window. *And thorough*. I put my hands on the window sill and kept peering outside. I did not know exactly what to say. I began to think about last night and how all those memories came flooding back. I thought about the nightmares and the lie I live. I considered that Dora was not threatening me; in fact, she might be saving my life. I wasn't sure about that, but it was a possibility.

I did not move when Dora's hand touched my shoulder, but my insides shuddered. I had been so lost in my own thoughts that I didn't hear her move. My muffled startle reaction got her attention, and we both chuckled. Then we hugged. The hug lingered. And then, dammit, a big fat juicy tear rolled down my cheek. I didn't mean to or want to. I didn't even think about that happening—I hadn't cried in years. But it's been over fifteen years since my last therapist and from then till now I have not spoken of my past with a single human being. I never thought about it. I was sure it was behind me.

Now, in Dora's arms, the tears came and my body shuddered. Dora did not pull away. She held me until the storm passed. I put my hands on her shoulder and straightened my arms. I forced myself to look directly into her eyes. "I'm sorry," I said. "I didn't expect this."

Dora shrugged slightly and said, "It's OK, Jake."

But it wasn't OK, not for me. Number one, it wasn't OK for someone, anyone to know about my past, except those persons sanctioned by the military. Number two, I had just humiliated myself in front of someone I barely knew and who may or may not be on my side. I pulled back.

"Please forgive me, Dora; that will never happen again," I said with a cold-heartedness I did not feel. I walked back to the coffee table and picked up my cup.

Dora stayed by the window and leaned against the sill. "I decided several months ago that you were not one of the conspirators but I began to check on why your name kept coming up. Evidently, the twelve has targeted middle-of-the-road congressman from both parties who they see as people who are willing to speak out against their fanatical plans. You are on that list."

"Targeted me for what?" I asked, trying to re-organize my thoughts.

Dora looked at me as if I just wasn't getting the reality of what she was saying. "For assassination, Jake. They plan to kill you." She looked at me doubtfully. "I told you this yesterday."

So she had. I wasn't thinking very clearly. I looked at Dora with what must have been a quizzical expression on my face, because she nodded and motioned for me to sit down.

"Look, Jake," she began. "I understand that a lot is happening right now and it's a lot to digest. I can only imagine how this information about your past is hitting you. So relax, clear your mind as best you can, and we'll talk some more later." She patted my legs as if to direct them to move up onto the couch. "Why don't you take a little nap. We're safe here."

I fell into a deep sleep.

Chapter 6

The same humpback guy who visited me last night reappeared in my dream. He wasn't quite so erect now, but he wasn't stooped over either. He was walking.

He was sandwiched between explosive scenes of war and mayhem. I didn't know what that was about in my dream. It seemed like generic war-movie stuff, the kind of stuff that most people never actually experience in their real lives. Only in the movies. Only in their nightmares.

I awoke and it was still daylight. In fact, it seemed only to be about mid-afternoon, a fact confirmed by a glance at the watch on my wrist: 3:22. I knew where I was, but Dora was not in the room. I sat up and listened. Nothing.

Dora had removed my shoes and covered me with a macramé shawl of some sort. I lay back down and luxuriated on the comfortable couch. It was something I learned in the Army: indulge comfort when you can.

After a minute or two, I got up and put my shoes on. I walked into the little kitchen area and poured myself a cup of coffee. It had gone cold, so I popped it into the microwave for a minute or so. While I was waiting, I looked around. Old photographs lined almost every wall of this cozy little redoubt, and I casually perused them. I recognized many of the faces. Dora's dad was in many of them, usually mugging with other senators or politicians of renown. I saw him with Reagan and Carter; there was even one with Gerald Ford. I figured he had probably been in physical proximity to every president since Nixon. Maybe even Johnson.

I removed the cup from the microwave and saw the steam rising. I blew across the top of the cup and took a tiny sip. It wasn't great, but the warmth of the liquid felt good in my mouth.

I heard a noise behind me and turned to see Dora walking in through the front door.

"You're up," she said.

"Yup," I said noncommittally.

"How do you feel?" she asked.

I looked at her for a moment before responding. *On what level are you asking?* I thought. *Physically? Mentally? Spiritually?* At the moment, it was go on all three, although I wasn't sure how long that would last.

"OK," I said. "How 'bout you?"

Dora looked at me with that schoolmarmish expression I had seen more than once. "Fine," she said.

"Well, then," I said. "Let's get on with it. You were telling me these guys were planning to kill me." I looked at Dora with the most disinterested expression I could muster.

She did not skip a beat. "Yes," she said. "If they believe you will oppose their plan, they are not above murder."

"Dora," I said. "Do you really expect me to believe that these men are out to do harm to me or to the country?" I was feeling a very strong urge to be done with all this conspiracy stuff and re-connect to the life I had. The safe, predictable life.

"Yesterday, you said that you wanted me to kill these men. I guess you thought me capable of that because of my background." I paused and stared across the room for a moment. "I don't know how you found out about my past. I do know that it is highly classified information, and the fact that you found it probably means you violated a good half-dozen laws."

Dora did not respond.

"You misjudged me," I said. "I'm not the killer you think I am." Silence. I took a breath. "I think we are done here."

Dora shrugged and said nothing.

It was quiet on the ride back. I had a lot of thoughts; some were jumbled, but some were crystal clear. I did not want to be involved with this woman. I did not want to be seen with her, identified with her, or connected to her in any way. I wasn't too familiar with rural Maryland, and I had only the vaguest idea of where I had spent the better part of the day. I didn't care. I just wanted to go home.

When Dora pulled up to my apartment building, she reached into a pocket and pulled out a printed card with her name and phone numbers on it. "Call me if you change your mind," she said. I nodded and got out of the car. I didn't say anything.

I entered my apartment with great relief. It was just about 6:30 p.m., and I was hungry. I foraged through the fridge to see if there was anything edible. Beyond an especially bland variety of low-fat yogurt, I was disappointed.

I sat down on the couch in my small living room and flipped on the television. I felt as if I had visited some eccentric parallel universe today, losing a day of real-time work and production. I was angry with myself and tried to put what Dora had said out of my mind. It was outlandish. Every part of it was improbable. I felt played. *There was no doubt she knew things about my background that were far from public knowledge, but her family probably had connections to account for that. But murder? I don't think there is anything short of an immediate threat to my own life that would inspire me to even consider it, and Dora would need a lot more evidence than some coincidental tragedies in the DC area.* The more I thought about it, the angrier I got.

I had to admit, however, that revisiting my hidden past had a stimulating effect on my mood and on my outlook. Maybe that made the whole bizarre experience worthwhile. I doubted that, but I was still savoring the opportunity of thinking about something I had shoved way down into the bottom of my psychic closet. It felt tantalizing, like getting away with something. And it was mine; it didn't belong to anyone else. Or at least to anyone I cared about.

I decided to go out to eat something real. Except for that yogurt, I hadn't eaten all day. So I walked down to a local eatery and got a table for one. I grabbed the *Washington Post* and read the mindless articles about this or that failure in the city and in the nation. Liberty is hard on the status quo.

After dinner, I stopped at a pub on the corner nearest my apartment and sat at the bar. The place was eighty percent full of college students—older ones, probably graduate students—from Georgetown University. They were a smart and verbal lot, and the intense conversations going on around me were stimulating. I just listened, lost in my own enigmatic re-connection with a past I had long pushed away. I walked home an hour later.

I guess it was predictable that Dora showed up in my dreams that night. She didn't do much; mostly she just hovered in the background, watching things. Watching the humpback, watching the carnage. Watching me. Just like how she was: thoughtful and beautiful.

Other than the far-fetched prospect of getting offed by middle-aged evangelical fanatics, the biggest thing I missed about Dora was looking at her. It was time for me to find someone to date, and she would have been near the top of my desirable list. Except that she was spying on government officials, probably providing them with the services of prostitutes, and surely nosing around in classified files. And she wanted me to kill people. I lay in bed and looked out at the early morning sky glad that she would no longer complicate my life.

Chapter 7

For the next few days, I had the advantage of feeling more whole than I had in years, and I went about my life with a new sense of purpose. A bounce in my step. Jamie was mightily relieved to see me show up on time in a more or less healthy state, and she told me—commanded me, really—how I would catch up the lost day and a half I had spent messing around with Dora. Neither she nor Sarah asked about lunch the day before yesterday.

Also, there were no more killings. At least none involving pretty young college women who dated government officials. At least none that I knew about.

I almost succeeded in putting this madness out of my mind. After all, I was practiced at doing that. I dove into my work like a first-year grad student and spent most evenings working late in the office. Work was the method I used to pull my life back into the range of sanity. Or of something that looked like sanity.

I didn't have any more nightmares. One night the humpback returned, but it was a vague and barely recoverable dream fragment. Dora showed up there too, but again in an unmemorable way.

During the next two weeks, two things happened that caught my attention. One was learning that Dirk Gruber, one of the senators from Maine, was floating the prospect of a congressional investigation into one William Mechalowski for subversive activities. He brought it up at a luncheon of northeastern senators. I was there because Max Johansen of New Hampshire, a friend of mine who was invariably on the same side of every issue as I was, had invited me to tag along.

"We could start a congressional investigation," he said unceremoniously to a table of eight senators.

"For what?" Max asked. "Having opinions we don't like?"

Gruber reddened slightly. "No," he said, "For obstructing the law, especially the Patriot Act."

Max frowned. He was a personable man, but he was from the Live Free or Die State and proud of it. "Dirk," he said. "It's almost impossible not to obstruct the Patriot Act. Unless you relinquish your library card."

The chuckles around the table were a signal for Gruber to back off. He was just floating the idea, and he got the information he wanted. No way he could start any kind of investigation on Willy Maelstrom today. I didn't say anything.

The second thing that got my attention was the thing I was dreading. I was working late in the office, and Jamie and Sarah and the rest had already left. The phone rang—one of the back lines where the number is not listed. I watched it ring for a few minutes, and then I picked it up.

"Hello," I said.

"Hi, Jake, it's Dora," said the velvety alto.

I didn't say anything.

Neither did Dora. I sat there thinking that the silence routine worked less well for her on the phone, especially because I was still mad at her for trying to drag me into something that had no upside.

For the past two weeks, I began to believe less and less in her story. Not that there weren't some right-wing sickos out there dreaming up alternative forms of government—I'd guess that's been going on since the Republic was founded—but the interest of those people in a guy like me: it just didn't add up. As for the prostitution ring she implied she was running and the deaths: well, DC is a rough town, and hookers probably get killed with some regularity.

So when I heard her voice, I wasn't keen to get caught up in the whirlwind.

"What do you want?" I said.

"I was wondering if you had thought about what we had talked about." She paused but without relinquishing her momentum. "And if you'd like to have dinner with me to talk about it." Now she was done.

Dinner with a lovely young woman sounded good; the topic did not. So I said, "Dinner sounds OK, if you promise not to bring that stuff up again."

Long pause.

Finally: "You don't believe me, do you?"

No response from me.

"OK," she said. "Dinner about 8:00?"

"Where?" I asked.

"How about Galileo's on 21st Street?"

Good taste, I thought. "See you there," I said and hung up the phone.

Why in the world I said yes to this invitation is beyond me. My brain was clear that this woman, drawn to her as I was, was trouble. She is pushy, domineering, smart, tactical, and conniving. She knows too much about me and apparently too much about a lot of people. She is clearly up to something that at minimum involves prostitution and some level of espionage. She is being tracked by the FBI, which means that I may already be tracked as well. Just being around her is probably dangerous to my career if not to my physical safety and well-being. I couldn't wait to see her.

Chapter 8

Galileo's is not a casual restaurant. It beckons the wealthy and elite members of the District to dine in its tasteful and antiseptic rooms and curries favor by offering fabulous food and impeccable service. Attentive but not smothering, the wait staff keeps a respectful distance but when needed, a server is there within seconds of being summoned by the slightest gesture of the eye, head, or hand. I like it, but I don't go there very often because of the sheer investment involved. I decided to take a taxi, and I was just trying to work out how to handle seeing some of my colleagues there when it pulled up to the restaurant. *I guess I'll just be polite*, I thought while tipping the driver.

I walked into the room and scanned the patrons trying to find Dora. I didn't see her. Before I could find the *maitre d'* to ask about a table, he found me.

"Mr. Telemark?" he asked.

"Yes," I replied, certain that I had never laid eyes on this man before. "This way to your table, sir." he said and turned on his heel.

This treatment did not surprise me completely. This place was known for the skill with which it catered to its august clientele, and I was, after all, a United States senator. The seamlessness of it, however, suggested Dora's skilled hand. I felt certain that she had arranged this entrance down to the last detail.

After seating me, a server appeared and asked if I would like something to drink. "Vodka," I said. "On the rocks." He waited for just the moment it took me to specify a brand and when I did, he promptly disappeared.

I took a deep breath and looked around the well-appointed room. I never resented the fact that my parents did not care much about money. They were correct in believing that it too quickly becomes an end in itself. On the other hand, I loved what money could bring: the food, the service, the style; being treated as someone special. Nonsense, I knew, but charming nonsense.

Dora appeared within ten minutes. *An acceptable interlude*, I thought. I was getting ready to order a second drink when I saw her walking gracefully toward me. I stood up.

"Hello, Jake," she said, taking my hand and turning her cheek in my direction so I could kiss it. I planted a greeting kiss as gently as I could.

"Hello, Dora," I replied.

She sat down and we sat looking at each other across the white tablecloth. The waiter came and brought Dora a clear, fizzy drink in a tall glass. Gin and tonic, maybe. We continued to look at each other.

Simultaneously, we said each others' name, chuckled, and then Dora began, "I was the one who invited you, Jake," she said. "The conversation is my responsibility." She looked straight into my eyes.

I was completely charmed. The warmth of the vodka helped, but seeing Dora stimulated me more than any substance could. "How have you been?" I asked, attempting a casual approach. I realized, as I said this insipid thing, that Dora was the one who lost someone close to her when we were last together, yet she was the one who had attempted to console me. It seemed longer than two weeks ago, but it felt like a loose end. I began to think of ways to apologize.

"It's been a rough two weeks." Dora replied, setting the stage for less insipid communicating. "After Deborah died, all the girls were shaken up, and I've been spending a lot of time holding hands." She paused and looked down into her glass. "Some of the girls have left town. I understand that, but…" Her voice choked ever so slightly. "But these girls had dreams, Jake; they wanted to make a difference in the life of the country. Now there's such disappointment, even bitterness. It makes me sad. I understand it, but it makes me very sad." Her eyes returned to mine.

I looked at Dora for a few moments. She was being disarmingly transparent, and transparency is not a common trait in DC. It felt like an invitation, and I wanted to match the evident sincerity Dora was showing me.

"Dora," I began. "The last time we were together, you had the good grace to be nice to me when I broke down. I completely ignored the fact that Deborah was your friend and that your feelings were probably quite raw. I am sorry."

Dora did not say anything. Instead, she reached across the small table and put her hand on mine. "I didn't think you broke down, Jake. I just thought you were having some pretty strong and understandable emotional reactions. I was glad to be there for you." She pulled her hand away.

I love it when a woman touches me, but I especially love it when an attractive woman touches me. I took a sip of my drink and tried to act as if I wasn't getting turned on. I am sure I failed.

"Why don't we order?" I said, hoping to return to the safety of innocuous conversation.

"Sure," said Dora.

We spent the rest of dinner talking about ourselves the way people do when they are getting to know each other. It was a bit of a replay of the late lunch we had two weeks earlier when we first met, but there was a palpably deeper bond between us. Even though I was on guard against the prospect that at any moment Dora could cross the line and try to entice me to assassinate someone or some group of people, I enjoyed her company. She was obviously bright, but she was down-to-earth in a way I don't often find in this city. Smart with no need to prove it.

When dinner ended, I leaned back in my chair and looked at Dora. The obvious and last question of the evening hung between us. I looked at Dora. "Why did you call me?" I asked.

Dora did not hesitate to respond, "My offer is still on the table, Jake. I want to know if you will do what I requested." Silence.

What offer? I thought. *An offer to assassinate a dozen men? In return for what? My life? So she was still very much on-message. This was another opportunity to entice me to get involved in something that seemed to have no upside.* I was dismayed for thinking there was even a possibility that this relationship could be about more than what she wanted me to do. *How stupid. What did I think? That she called me because she liked me? Junior high déjà vu.*

I took a breath. *Now, I suppose, was the time to make a decision. I either throw my lot in with this complex, attractive, and possibly deranged woman or go back to living my shallow but at least safer-on-the-surface life.* The moment was potent; I could feel a bead of sweat forming across my hairline. Dora knew her talent and was skilled at using it. I saw that. I also saw that my reputation and possibly my career in the Senate were in the balance.

In the middle of these ponderous thoughts, Dora picked up her purse and said, "Let's go."

I looked at her quizzically, but she was already on her feet, so I reflexively stood up. "Where to?" I asked lamely.

"Follow me," she said and turned around and headed for the door. I paused for the briefest moment before I galloped to catch her.

At the door, she turned and noticed me, as if for the first time. "The check?" I asked. "Taken care of," she replied.

Now, I appreciate planning. In my sniper days, the Army drilled the importance of preparation into your head. Be Prepared: Boy Scouts on steroids. I was always, and I mean always, prepared. It was part of the my-life-or-the-target's-life kind of thinking that enabled me to live for two years shooting people. So I respected

Dora's planning, but I felt too much like a target.

Dora's BMW was idling in front of the restaurant. We got in the back and drove off.

"Did you see the paper this morning?" Dora asked.

"Yes… No… I saw it and perused it, but I didn't read it closely," I stammered.

"Page six, bottom story. Chemical spill in West Virginia lake kills two kids swimming in it."

"Yeah? So?"

Dora looked at me like I was being obstinate. "It was a trial run."

"A trial run for what?" I asked.

"For the above-referenced catastrophe on which the heinous scheme of twelve malevolent men is based," she said in a gently sarcastic voice.

I was pissed. Why was she talking to me this way? My feelings were jumbled. I guess I have that single guy thing about thinking women are interested in me when they act interested. I wanted a date. Obviously, Dora still wanted an assassin. I am slow this way.

Dora pulled out the morning edition of the *Washington Post* and showed me the article.

"What makes you think this was deliberate?" I asked.

Dora took a breath before she responded. "I have received a lot of information in recent months about a trial run, a small-scale experiment to see if the scheme could work."

"From your hooker friends," I said, trying to match her earlier sarcasm.

"Yes," she said, glaring at me with a hard look I had not seen before, "from my hooker friends."

It was then that I noticed that the driver had the same twenty-inch biceps that were so familiar from my last chauffeured ride with Dora. *This woman doesn't quit*, I thought.

"Look, Dora," I began. "I don't think…"

"What you think is not really relevant here, Jake. What is relevant is that, whether you believe me or not, this situation that I have been describing is not a paranoid fantasy. It is as real as the seat on which you are sitting."

I shifted in my seat. "OK," I said. "Tell me more."

Dora's look softened but not much. She looked out the window before she turned her head to me and began to speak.

"My girls have independently been hearing indications of some kind of experiment. We couldn't find out what it was specifically, but we learned that it involved some kind of industrial or chemical accident that would have a huge impact. There were to be several trial runs before the final scenario."

I listened as intently as I could from the vantage point of a humiliated man. I hate myself in relationships with women, mostly because I often feel less mature and less in control that they are. I am usually both. When a woman lectures me the way Dora was doing, humiliation is my main reaction. I compensate by looking serious and acting as if I'm listening. Years of therapy have been very helpful in this regard.

I thought this time I would try to rise to the occasion. "OK, Dora," I said. "If you can prove to me that this isn't some kind of tragic coincidence; if you can link this in a convincing way to a plot or even a deliberate act on the part of any of the men you showed me on that website, I will believe you." I sat back and folded my arms.

It was then that she got me. She pulled out a PDA and turned it on. On the small color screen was a grainy video of a man and woman in bed talking. I strained to look at the picture closely and listened intently. It was one of the cameo heads from the website. This was obviously a pillow-talk conversation between him and a woman I could only presume was one of Dora's "girls". He was half-lecturing the young woman on the need for change and the changes that would be occurring in the coming months. "They'll start small," he said in a distinct and unrehearsed southern drawl. "But within the year, you'll see big changes. Big changes." And then he turned over and went to sleep, snoring loudly.

The camera must have been in the woman's handbag or on a dresser, because she got out of bed and completely filled the screen before it went black.

I looked at my lap, momentarily lost in thought. Dora looked at me intently. "I have more of these if you would like to see them, Jake," she said softly.

I looked at her with none of the timidity I felt earlier. "I would like to see them, Dora," I replied.

She showed me three instances where a similar conversation took place and another two where even more specific references to an "experimental run" were made. I began to think that she had something.

Oddly, the fact that Dora had collected this information by means of prostitution did not seem to faze me. I had been a killer; I knew how to walk the line in the regular world and work in the nefarious one. It was like putting on an old coat.

"I'm still open," I said.

Chapter 9

The next few days resembled Carroll's rabbit hole more than anything. That evening, Dora's Sasquatch driver delivered us to her DC apartment, a small but nicely appointed unit in the Watergate. Once there, she opened a long drawer full of documentation: written notes, videos, audio recordings which were all obtained through her "network" and all neatly arranged by date and cross-referenced by target and government agency. We spent the rest of the already-late night going through the stuff. By 3:30 a.m., I was bleary-eyed and overloaded with information.

"I'm shot, Dora. I can't do this anymore."

She showed no sign of fatigue, but she nodded as if to forgive my lesser-mortal self for hitting the wall. "OK," she said with feigned cheerfulness. "Let's put the rest of this stuff off until tomorrow." She stood up. "I'll have Jefferson take you home."

Jefferson, I presumed, was her pet gorilla and part-time driver. I couldn't imagine that he was still awake, but the truth was I didn't know where he was and didn't care. I just wanted to go to bed.

Dora walked me to the door and put her hand on my hip. "Thanks, Jake," she said with what seemed like real affection. "I know this has been hard for you." She brushed my cheek with her lips.

If I had been less tired, I would have kissed her. Throughout the cramming session, I had not lost sight of the fact that she remained the object of my desire, if not my affection. At the moment, however, I couldn't rouse enough energy to do much more than say good-night.

Jefferson appeared at the door and escorted me to the garage where the BMW was parked. He opened the door for me; I got in. Wordlessly, he drove off.

The District at night looks like a fabulous stage set: grand buildings with long shadows and watchmen visible outside. It's as lovely as it is during the day, but with an eerie feel, as if it were thinking about the next day.

We got to Georgetown in record time—no traffic—and Jefferson stopped in front of my door. "Good night, Jeff," I said and got out. He drove off without a single word.

Inside my apartment, I spent a few moments reviewing the events of the long evening. I knew that, once again, I would have to clear my schedule for the next day, and I called Jamie and left her a voice mail to that effect. Then I plopped into bed.

Unfortunately, sleep did not come immediately. I stared at the ceiling; I knew that I was moving toward doing something that I vowed I would never do again. Neither Dora nor I mentioned that part of our deal during the entire evening, but it was pinned to the back of my mind throughout. I figured I had time. No one was going to start shooting until shooting needed to be done. Somehow, that vague bit of pap was enough for me to fall into a deep sleep.

I awoke at 7:00 a.m. without my alarm. Despite the small number of hours of sleep, I felt refreshed and relaxed. I went into the bathroom and did my morning thing, and then I called Dora, who was also awake.

"Now what?" I asked.

"Jefferson is on his way," came the unhesitating reply. I wondered if she slept, or if she spent the whole night waiting for me to awaken.

I figured Jeff would be at my door by the time I got there, and I was right. I saw the silver BMW idling at the curb as I closed the door behind me.

"Morning, Jeff," I said.

He nodded, and off we went. *I guess only Dora gets to hear him talk.*

Dora offered me coffee right after I entered her apartment, and I did not decline. We sat on the couch for a few moments, and she began reviewing what we had gone over the night before. The content of that material touched upon two things: the upcoming catastrophe, and, as he was commonly referred to, "that liberal son of a bitch Maelstrom." No mention of the independent judiciary or of assassinating politicians. I was actually a little relieved by this last point, given what Dora had said about my name being on the to-be-cancelled list.

"I think that's a minor part of the plan," she said matter-of-factly.

"Minor part of the plan!?" I looked at her askance. "Doesn't seem so minor to me."

Dora looked at me for a moment before she began speaking. "As events unfold, I believe these people have prepared a list of potential obstacles, people who could get in their way. They are not eager to kill them outright, but are prepared to do so if the opposition to their plan gets too vocal." She paused and looked at me intently. "That's what I meant by minor," she said.

"Oh," I replied. *What was I worried about?* I thought.

Dora continued, "I don't know exactly how they're going to go after Maelstrom, but I don't think that will be too difficult. They have been compiling data on him for years. The tough part is going to be neutralizing the independent judiciary. Some of these men are, after all, judges, who know how deeply rooted the tradition of the independent judiciary is."

"How do you know that neutralizing the judiciary is part of the plan?" I asked. "Wouldn't a constitutional convention override the judiciary?"

"Possibly," Dora replied. "But the judicial system in this country has been at the vanguard of protecting American democracy, as the founding fathers envisioned. I can't imagine they wouldn't want to limit its power at the outset. Also," Dora paused in a lovely and thoughtful pose for a moment, "there has been a movement spearheaded by the right to neutralize the judiciary for years. Roger brought it up when I was with him, and several of the other clients also mentioned how troublesome 'activist' judges are."

I was still skeptical. After all, if the goal was to declare a state of emergency, civil rights would automatically be suspended for the duration. Then it dawned on me; these guys were after the independent judiciary, but they wanted judges to actually have power. Their judges. Their power. "Neutralize" was beginning to sound more like "eliminate".

I looked at Dora. "They want to get rid of them, don't they? They want to get rid of all the judges who would stand in their way?"

Dora nodded slowly. "I think so, Jake, although I have no direct information about that. But remember, these men are fanatics."

I let go a long, low stream of air. *More like lunatics*, I thought.

There was a knock on the door. It was Jeff. He entered and walked over to Dora and handed her a note. He left. Dora fell silent and kept sorting through the materials on her lap.

At the risk of sounding impolite, I ventured the obvious question after the door was again closed, "What was that about?"

"Willy Maelstrom has been arrested," she said evenly.

"For what?" I asked.

Dora looked at me with a face two shades paler than a minute ago. "Treason."

Treason? I tried to think back to the last person prosecuted in the Untied States for the crime of treason, and I couldn't even think who that might be. *There were some spies convicted of espionage and some Americans convicted of war crimes, but treason?*

"Why?" I asked Dora.

"I don't know, Jake, but I will find out. Please excuse me." She turned her head away.

I took that to mean that I should leave, but I wasn't sure where to go. I looked at Dora quizzically, but I could see that her wheels were turning in many directions to which I was not privy. So I left; I walked out the door. I stood in the hall for a moment, half-expecting Jefferson to appear, but he didn't. So I took the elevator down to the ground floor and found a coffee shop a half block away.

There was a TV on the wall at the end of the counter showing a special news report on Willy Maelstrom. Details were sketchy, but he was evidently arrested at his home in the early hours of the morning. The images on the TV screen showed SWAT teams with guns at the ready surrounding a suburban Arlington home. News trucks were also there, suggesting that it was the intention of whoever engineered this to have it hit the news big time. Willy was shown being led out of his house in handcuffs. The commentator was saying that a charge of treason had not been lodged against an American citizen since 1946 when Ezra Pound returned to the US to face such charges, only to be deemed insane and admitted to a psychiatric hospital, where he spent the next twelve years. The look on the commentator's face suggested that this situation was equally preposterous.

The few patrons in the diner were either bored with the news or perplexed by it. Almost everyone knew Willy Maelstrom and everyone knew that he was controversial. But this is America, and controversy is part of our national character. *But treason? Nonsense.*

My gaze was fixed on the television, as was the gaze of a few other patrons. But news stories like this tend to be repetitive and ramble on in an effort to cover up the fact that not much was happening. Ezra Pound must have been a lucky find, probably due to some bright bookworm intern at the network.

Beyond the bland stare directed at the TV, however, my mind was rumbling. I know anxiety when I feel it, and I could feel it percolating inside me; not a torrent or even a stream yet, but a vague but unmistakable rumble that starts simultaneously from the pit of my stomach and the tips of my fingers and toes. Eventually, I knew it would collide in my chest, making it hard for me to breathe deeply. I kept looking at the TV, hoping that no visible sign of my internal state showed itself.

Mentally, I knew where this was going. Throughout my life, one of the few things that helped me calm down, that made me feel OK when chaos swirled around me or fear welled up inside me, the one solid thing I could hold on to, could count on to make me feel more secure was the feel of a gun. Everything about it helped me focus and calm down. To feel its heft and weight; to hold the stock tightly and insert my finger into the trigger guard; to load it shell by shell; to sight down the top of it at a faraway object; to hold it in my arms as if hunting or to aim it deliberately at someone or something. The gun itself, the rituals around it, the care and feeding of it, and even the use of it brought me focus, peace, and a sense of security. Always.

In the last months of my service as a sniper, I knew I was getting more and more roiled up about my job. But every time the roiling threatened to bubble up over the surface, I took my gun and cleaned it, polished it, and practiced shooting it. I held onto it the way I guess most men hold onto their women. When I was in lockup and the gates of hell had already been passed, grief for the loss of my gun was just part of the torrential emotional storms that wracked my mind. I felt naked and unprotected without it. But I didn't talk about that; I talked about every other aspect of my experience, every other feeling and event. But I never talked about my relationship with my gun. Some things are too private, even for therapy.

After I got out of the hospital, I knew I was leaving the army, and I didn't want to walk away with the Remington I had used most often, although that would have felt good. Uncle Sam had learned to be more careful with his dangerous toys over the years, and every gun part and piece of ammunition had to be accounted for. Besides, I didn't want trouble. The Army could make my life very, very difficult. I had some money, and I figured I would be able to find a gun to my liking when I got out. I knew then and know now that this was a stupid plan; that there was no reason on earth for me to be in possession of a sniper rifle. But I also knew how safe and secure it made me feel. So a few weeks after I got set up in my apartment, I started looking. This was when I realized that you can buy anything online. It was a snap.

I never used it. It's in pieces in my apartment, and the pieces are spread throughout different rooms. Every once in a while I'll collect the pieces and assemble the rifle. Sometimes I would load it just to feel the power in my hands. But I never pulled the trigger. That was my deal with myself. I would keep this little secret, this little indulgence, from everyone on earth, and in return I would never fire it. I was tempted a few times, but I never fired it.

As the anxiety was coursing through my body on its way to the appointment in my chest, I felt two things that turned my stomach. One was that I would be playing with my rifle soon enough; the other was that, if Dora is right and this conspiracy is going the way she says it is, I would break my promise to myself. I wrapped my arms together across my chest. I felt cold.

Chapter 10

I didn't see Dora any more that day. Or the next day. Willy Maelstrom was still in jail, his bail denied. The Civil Liberties Union was up in arms, but it was a shrill and solitary voice in a curious void. Except for the occasional line in the occasional speech, the mood in the country was oddly quiet about this absurd situation. Some small protests, but nothing big. Mostly like, "The government must know something we don't." Another legacy of 9/11.

After the coffee shop, I decided to go to the office anyway in the hope of getting lost in the humdrum life of a US senator. Neither Jamie nor Sarah nor anyone else there seemed surprised when I showed up. There was always a lot to do in a senatorial office: phone calls, requests from constituents, mail, mail, and more mail; snail mail, e-mail, voice-mail— congressional offices are inundated with mail that they encourage in order to discern the mind of the electorate.

It wasn't working. Jamie and Sarah both barraged me with questions that seemed urgent to them but pointless to me. Until Jamie looked at me point blank and asked, "Are you going to make a statement about Maelstrom?"

I did not respond right away. I looked down at my desk as if I were thinking about it. "I'm not sure," I finally said.

Jamie looked at me with wide eyes as if to say, "And why the hell not?" Instead, she said, "May I ask why not, sir?"

I hated it when she called me sir or some other formal name. When things were okay between us, it was always Jake. Just Jake. Not sir or Senator or Mr. Telemark.

I look at her through slotted eyes, calling her on her sudden coldness. "Why not, Jake," she said after a minute. "You are one of the few moderate voices in the Senate who is known for speaking his mind. It will be noticed if you don't say something."

She was right. Even after just a couple years here, it was clear that my turf was part of what the old Democratic Establishment used to do—speak up for the little guy, for those people wronged by our system. Follow the sensible middle way.

On the other hand, I was thinking about putting my neck on the line. I wasn't sure I wanted to draw attention to myself just yet, making myself an easy target in a minor aspect of this explosive cultural war. "I'm thinking about it," I told Jamie. "Give me a little time, OK?"

Jamie shrugged. My call, I knew. I also knew I didn't have much time. I was seized with a sudden desire to speak to Dora. "Excuse me, Jamie," I said. She knew that was her cue to leave my office and close the door. After she left, I swiveled in my chair and put my hand on the receiver. I hesitated, uncertain if I should take this step closer to a woman who was so sure of herself about this. I thought for a moment that Willy's arrest and her friend's death and her being followed might have a more benign, more normal explanation. Shaking my head, I dialed her number.

"Yes," came the very businesslike voice on the other end.

"Dora, it's Jake."

I paused, but she did not say anything.

"I am in the middle of preparing a statement regarding Maelstrom's arrest," I said. "Any input on this?" I waited.

I could hear Dora let out a breath on the other end of the

phone. She was at least thinking about it. Maybe she was relieved. I was a little tired of guessing what she was thinking and planning.

"What kind of statement are you thinking of making?" Dora asked.

"Something vague about protecting freedom of expression and the First Amendment. You know, the predictable stuff," I responded with more than a little sarcasm in my voice.

The line was quiet. I wasn't sure she had taken offense or whether she believed me.

"The truth is, I'm not really sure what I should say at this point," I continued in a more sober vein. "I don't think this is something that should be allowed to pass with no comment from the centrist part of the party. I'm just not sure how far to go." I paused and leaned into the receiver. "I'm also aware of what you told me about that, um, minor part of the scenario."

"Jake," she said. "I think it's a good idea for you to make a statement. Somebody has to." Another pause. "I also think you should proceed to do what you believe is the right thing."

This last statement had a very slight touch of recrimination to it, as if she were confronting my cowardice. *Ouch. Take the direct approach*, I told myself.

"You don't think this makes me any more or less of a target?" I asked.

Dora thought for a moment. "I don't think so. Not yet anyway. I don't think they will start gunning for opponents until things get a lot heavier."

I reeled inside at her choice of words and tone of voice. She was so damnably matter-of-fact when it came to the little detail of my life. My feelings, however, were not germane to the conversation.

"OK," I said after a while. "I'll put out a statement that's as strong as I can make it. I'll probably be able to find some other senators to co-author it with me." I thought for a moment. "Maybe we could introduce a resolution underscoring our support for freedom of speech."

I could tell that Dora was listening intently, as she always did. "How far are you willing to go, Jake?" she asked in an unaccented tone.

I paused before responding. "If this turns out to be what you say it is, Dora, I'm in all the way."

After I put the phone down, I thought about the statement I was going to make and the one I just made to Dora. The first one seemed the easier of the two. I called Jamie in to have her arrange a brief meeting with my closest allies in the Senate. I definitely wanted to make a joint statement, and I was pretty sure the six or seven members whose names and faces were running through my mind would be willing to go along, if not spearhead a cry of outrage. After all, there were some things that were sacred in this country, and freedom of speech is one of them.

I wondered if I would really commit myself to Dora's plan even though I had been so clear on the phone about it. My statement to her was contingent but unequivocal. I had essentially committed myself to something I had vowed I would never do again. It was too outrageous to even contemplate deliberately, but I had to keep my mind focused on the fact that she was talking about killing. I am banking on her sordid explanation of events turning out to be hyped nonsense, no matter how compelling the immediate evidence. But the truth is in my guts I was torn. My esteemed surface life or a life of danger, intrigue, and possibly prison or death. It felt like lunacy to even contemplate it, but that is precisely what I was doing.

I also have to allow for the possibility that I was susceptible to getting caught up in a web of coincidence and paranoid thinking about things that might not be so serious at all. I reminded myself that my interest in Dora had more to do with her being a woman than her spearheading seditious activity to save the country. I did not really think I would surrender my objectivity so easily to my baser desires, but I had to allow for that possibility.

What ratcheted up by suspicion that Dora may be onto

something genuine was Maelstrom's arrest. Willy was irreverent and controversial, but he was a talk-show host, not unlike the kind the right had been using for years to trash the respected ethos of liberalism. These guys said the most outrageous things and, when criticized, wrapped themselves in the flag or religion or some other bogus way to avoid the issue at hand. They had succeeded in reducing the word "liberal" to a pejorative so much so that the other side started calling themselves "progressives" instead.

Maelstrom would not tolerate being dismissed so easily. He did not trash his opponents, although he teased them to the point of ridicule on occasion, especially when one would make a particularly foolish claim. What made him so compelling was that he stayed with the argument at hand. He did not allow himself or anyone else to get sidetracked by reducing an issue to, "Are you a good American or not?" His arrest suggested that the forces arrayed against him are not reasonable ones. Treason is a big word, and, as far as I know, no one had yet to cite a specific thing he allegedly did to betray his country. Something is terribly wrong here, and I am not sure what.

Chapter 11

Later in the day, I met with my colleagues and we drafted a statement. Contrary to the apparent mood of the country, everyone in our little group was pretty hopped up about this whole affair. It wasn't hard to get a consensus. We all agreed that the more people the better, so when we broke up we figured that among the seven of us we could at least double the number of senators who would sign on. I left the meeting feeling as if I had done something worthwhile.

After the meeting, I decided to ask Jamie and Sarah if they wanted to stop at a local watering hole for a drink after work. I thought I had been asking a lot of them lately and not giving them much information, and a little "in-house marketing" wouldn't hurt. I always thought it was important to keep in touch with staff people; they did, after all, run the operations that allowed me to function in august senatorial fashion.

So we went to The Hawk and Dove and ordered a round of drinks. There were quite a few other staffers in the place, and we all waived and acted jovial. It wasn't hard.

This little ritual helped me stabilize some. It was simple and concrete. We drank beer and talked about the office, the day to day stuff that makes up most of our lives, whether at work or at home.

It helped me feel grounded and a little more sane. For a couple hours, I didn't think of Dora, weird plots, or assassinations. I was just sitting with my friends, who happened to work with me.

It was Jamie who finally broached the touchy subject. "What about this Maelstrom thing, Jake?" She had a serious, unsmiling look on her face.

I shrugged, but then I met her look with equal seriousness. "Too early to tell, Jamie," I said. "It may just be some kind of fishing expedition. I haven't heard any specific charges brought against him."

Jamie continued unsure, "But treason? For God's sake, Jake, nobody is accused of treason. Timothy McVeigh and Terry Nichols weren't accused of treason."

I nodded, thinking that she was right. I believe the newscaster had been correct. Ezra Pound was the last person to be accused of treason, and his treatment at the hands of the authorities was as outrageous as anything he had done. I didn't really have an answer for Jamie, so I just shrugged again. "We'll see," I said weakly.

When I got home that evening, I was filled with cross currents of feeling that were hard to wrap my mind around. I thought about having another drink, but then thought I should eat first. I couldn't decide whether to eat out or in, but out of sheer inertia decided to pop a frozen entree into the microwave. As I waited for the annoying beep, I leaned against the counter watching the events of the day swirl by in my imagination.

I was picturing what it must have been like at Willy's house the morning of his arrest. *Did he see it coming? What about his family?* I don't know if Willy has children or not, but if he does I can only imagine how shocked and afraid they must have been. Kids are pretty accustomed these days to the sight of SWAT teams, but usually on TV, not in their front yards.

Layer two: *Do they really think they could pull this off? Rattle a huge and heterogeneous country like the US enough to turn it into a, a what? A theocratic oligarchy? Another Reich?* The sheer chutzpah of it made me lightheaded. *Hitler must be laughing in his grave.* The microwave beeped.

I ate the chicken florentine quickly because I didn't want anything to come between me and what was next. I wanted my gun.

So after a thirty second cleanup of the tiny mess I made in my early-twenty-first-century kitchen, I went to double check the lock on the front door. Then I pulled the old fashioned shades down on the windows giving onto the street. For good measure, I pulled the curtains closed. Then I took a breath and began the circuit. I started in the bedroom where the stock of the gun lay hidden at the far end of the top shelf of a good-size closet. I took it down, unwrapped it, felt it, and smelled it. I took it into the living room and placed it on the low coffee table.

Then I went into the kitchen pantry where the barrel was wrapped in rags and leaning against the back wall right next to the broom, mop, and bucket. I unwrapped it slowly, sighted down its length as if there were some possibility that the perfectly machined geometry could have been altered by leaning against the wall; then I walked it reverentially into the living room to lay it down next to its brother.

Next came the firing mechanism and the empty magazine from the guest room. It was taped to the backside of a drawer in a heavy chest. I removed every speck of tape and processed into the living room.

Finally, I reached into the storage space above the kitchen cabinets that held my traveling valises. The scope was beneath a false bottom in my leather carry-on. I dislodged it and placed it beside its siblings. The family was now together.

I sat down and took a deep breath, both to quell my rising excitement and to help focus the mind. Then slowly, methodically, and quietly I assembled it. When I was at the peak of my form and skill, I could assemble this magnificent piece of machinery in less than ten seconds. But I wasn't striving for speed now. This was liturgy, one to be done with decorum, with silence, with care, and with love.

With the gun assembled, I straightened my spine, raised the instrument to my shoulder, peered through the scope, and aimed at the farthest corner of the apartment. I slowly adjusted the scope until the visual field, which was only about twenty feet away, was crystal clear. Then I placed the gun on my lap with both hands wrapped around its heft.

I took a deep breath. Peace descended upon my body and clarity filled my mind. I knew at that moment that the promise I had made to myself—to never harm another soul—was contingent and not absolute. I knew that the rationalization for keeping the gun—I could have it if I didn't use it—was just a tactic to maintain the bond that I felt both with the gun and with the murderous vocation of my youth. These thoughts did not sadden me, but they were sobering. They were in the same category as many other recognitions that form part of adult life: that the woman you love is also most likely to be the one whom you can hate; that your dreams of an end point to worries and responsibilities is a myth; that you cannot contort yourself into being a person you are not. Clear, sober facts that don't require anything but mute resignation. Insights that deepen a person, that free him from the boundless prison of childhood.

I suppose this ritual of holding the gun and seeing myself for the killer I was is akin to the kind of thing many people experience in prayer: a reverential and awestruck feeling of not being alone, of fitting into your place in the cosmos. It's about strength; it's about love. If I could ever believe in a God, I would thank Him at this moment *for* this moment.

I do not know how long I sat there. I felt no need to pull the trigger—that day would come soon enough—I didn't even load it. For a long time, I didn't move. Just holding it in my lap and feeling it was sufficient for me today. I thought grimly that this might not always be enough, but that was an issue for another day. After an hour or two, I stood erect with the rifle at my side in standard military formation. I was whole. I was home.

Filled with clarity and purpose, I began to retrace my steps, disassembling the weapon and restoring the parts to their allotted dwelling spots. I felt myself breathing more freely. I was less frightened, in fact, I wasn't frightened at all. I knew where my power lay, and I knew how to find it. That night I slept deeply and dreamlessly.

Chapter 12

A couple days went by. Willy was released after a court threw out the preposterous charges against him, which boiled down to his making statements that some conservative interests did not like. They thought they had him because he had made a financial contribution to a charity that turned out to have links to Al-Qaeda, but it turned out that Willy did not have any day-to-day voice in the administration of the trust he had set up to contribute to the welfare of others on an ongoing basis. The charity in question was a front organization, but many people had fallen for the ruse, many of whom were in government and almost none of whom were treasonous.

I stayed up late to watch Willy's first show back, as did many Americans.

On the first show that Willy hosted after his return to TV, he laid out all the facts of what happened. He talked about the shock of waking up to gun-toting, black-suited troops at his door and surrounding his house. He described how frightened his wife and three children were, and how helpless he felt to reassure them because he was led away so quickly. He talked about the delays in getting his court-mandated phone call and the team of lawyers that kicked into action on his behalf. He also talked about the huge volume of supportive email and pledges of financial support to bolster his defense.

"As many of you may surmise," he said in an uncharacteristically sober opening monologue, "I am not an especially religious person." He paused, looked down for just a moment, and continued, "But these past few days I have felt a Spirit from across the land. I felt it in my family and friends; in those professionals—lawyers mostly—who worked tirelessly to help me; and most of all in the thousands of messages I received from people I will never meet who offered their support and encouragement." He looked directly at the camera. "I am deeply touched and grateful," he said.

Then his voice turned from serious to somber. "But now we have to look at this situation more deeply. We have to ask what is happening in our society that allows people to be confronted with such force in the face of concerns so trifling, so flimsy, and so innocuous that a few phone calls would have cleared it up. Why did a SWAT team show up at my home in the early hours of the morning when I would have gladly answered any concerns?" His eyes held the question in the air, and then he swung into his signature transition.

"To help address these questions, I have asked three people with some insight into these matters to join our discussion." The screen behind him lit up as the camera moved back for a larger view and revealed three large video screens. "Our first guest is Justice Priscilla Marberry, Appellate Judge for the District of Columbia. She has recently written a book questioning some of the uses of the Patriot Act. Welcome, Judge Marberry."

The prim and properly dressed middle aged woman on the huge screen nodded and said something about being happy to be here. There was polite applause from the audience.

"My second guest is Mr. Roger Bandera, Assistant Attorney General of the United States and a member of the America First Roundtable, a group of men dedicated to preserving American interests at home and abroad. Welcome, Mr. Bandera."

There was less than polite applause and a few catcalls. Obviously the studio audience was heavily weighted in Maelstrom's favor. The presence of a certified right-winger on the panel excited them; they smelled blood. I gaped at the TV because I was so shocked to see the name and now the face of the man that had knowingly or unknowingly led Dora down her recent path.

"And finally," Willy continued, "I want to welcome Dr. Isadore Hathaway, an associate at the Center for Law and Public Policy. Welcome, Dr. Hathaway."

The gaping hole in my face did not move. *Dr. Hathaway? The Center for Law and Public Policy?*

My Isadore? Paneling with nut-case Bandera? Just seeing her on TV in public made my knees weak and my face pale. *Is this safe?* I thought. She, of course, looked gorgeous.

Since the CLPP was a liberal think-tank, Dora got thunderous applause, as if she arrived on a rescue ship.

Despite my many questions and assorted emotional reactions, a couple things became immediately obvious to me. One was why I had not heard of Dora around DC. She was ensconced in the esoteric world of think tanks; organizations that are generally not known for carrying on their business in full public view. It also explained her extraordinary font of data and her keen analytic skills. I wondered absently what her doctorate was in. My eyes remained riveted to the TV.

Willy began with the Justice, probably out of a sense of decorum and respect for her office. He asked about her initial impressions, and she responded with liberal pabulum about protecting the rights of the individual and how that is more necessary than ever during a time of semi-declared war.

Then Willy turned his attention to Bandera. I missed the first few sentences because I was filled with jealously at the sight of this handsome man whom I knew dated Dora. *Asshole*, I thought. The idea of putting a bullet through his head struck me as momentarily reasonable.

But Bandera was surprisingly smooth and upbeat. He said that he was not directly involved in the matters regarding Willy's recent arrest but opined that there was a basis for the treatment accorded Willy over the last few days and that it was judged to be reasonable by the Justice Department, given his stature in the media and the heinous role of Al-Qaeda in sabotaging our system of government. Not just government but Western culture in general. He rambled on a bit about the centrality of individual rights and how these had to be balanced against the needs of the many. The entire time he spoke, he was smiling graciously and looking directly at the camera. It seemed rehearsed to me, but then again, I already hated the guy.

Then Willy turned to Dora. "Dr. Hathaway," he said looking at her with more familiarity than I would have expected. I thought I saw him wink and wondered how and how long they had known each other. "What is your response to what you have been hearing?" And then he moved his chair back slightly as if to get out of the line of fire.

Then Dora began shooting. "This outrageous and unconscionable act could only have been orchestrated by fanatics," she began. "Our preliminary analysis indicates that the Justice Department violated seventeen separate laws to arrest you in the fashion they chose. Despite what Mr. Bandera implies, there is no compelling national interest in assaulting you and your family as if you were an armed criminal."

Don't hold back, Dora, I thought sardonically. *Let these people know how you really feel.* The camera shifted back to Bandera for a moment. I could see the blood drain from his face, even though his face was still smiling. *Gotcha, you bastard*, I thought.

A free-for-all ensued, with the Justice trying to stay above it all but backing up every one of Dora's assertions.

"Isn't it true, Mr. Bandera," Dora asked, "that even the Patriot Act disallows military actions against civilians unless the threat is substantiated, immediate, and grave?"

Roger kept that smile going even as he fumbled around for an answer. "There are several statutes that pertain to this situation, which I am unfortunately not able to address publicly at this time," he stammered.

"Why not?" Justice Marberry broke in. "You consented to be on this show and said that you weren't involved."

Roger kept smiling. He looked absurd. He began to discuss vague legal precedents, and it was clear to anyone with an IQ in three digits that he didn't have a leg to stand on. He cited outrageous examples, such as Waco and Idaho. He even mentioned Jim Jones. He was obviously grasping at straws.

Dora, on the other hand, quoted law by chapter and verse. She cited specific legal precedents that forbade the federal government from assaulting its citizens except for the gravest of reasons. Priscilla also offered a plethora of data about the unconstitutional nature of the attack on Willy and his family.

Willy sat back with his arms folded and watched the battle unfold. After it was clear that the Justice Department had wildly overreached both its authority and its role and that Roger was not really contributing to the conversation, he rolled his chair closer to the screens.

"I think it is clear," he said in a steady voice which I was sure covered over the sheer glee he must have felt, "that the legal basis for this kind of activity is tenuous if it exists at all. This is what I have been hearing from the attorneys involved in my defense for some days now." He paused and looked at the three panelists. "And I have heard nothing here that even came close to changing my mind."

He ended the show with a little homily about the centrality of American rights. One of the things that I could never stand about liberals was their tendency to sermonize. He was right in what he said, but it sounded so patronizing. At the end, he thanked everyone. I thought he winked at Dora again.

Despite the cutesy liberal shop talk, I thought his show was outstanding.

But the thing I could not get out of my mind was his obvious relationship with Dora. *He had that comfort that only comes from previous contact, probably close contact and a lot of it. Willy looked to be in his midfifties; Dora was probably in her early thirties. Could they have dated at one time? Were they friends now?*

Nor could I get over Dora's public appearance and her involvement in a think tank. It never occurred to me to ask her directly what she did. I thought of her as Frank Hathaway's daughter. I assumed she lived off some kind of trust fund or that her involvement with the young women supported her. I felt colossally stupid.

I also wondered about Dora's frontal attack on Bandera and on the Justice Department. *Did she plan to go public with her fears? Was she no longer worried about what had happened to her friends? My contact with her had seemed for the most part clandestine, and what she asked me to do was surely not something she would want broadcast on national television. What was she really up to?*

I could ask her, I thought, *but not right now.* I needed to get my own ducks in a row first.

Chapter 13

Washington was beginning to heat up. Sometimes in June the weather can be downright pleasant, but toward the end of this particular June, the temperatures were climbing to August heights. I always stayed in DC through the Fourth of July because I am such a sucker for the patriotic outpouring. I love the fireworks, the crowds, and the flags. As far as I am concerned Washington DC is the center of the known world and Independence Day is its birthday. I think a lot of Americans probably feel that way.

I didn't try to contact Dora for the first few days after the television show. I had a lot of reasons. An old therapist once said that some reasons we know and some we don't. The ones I knew included the notion that I wasn't sure I wanted her to know that I had seen her, although you would have had to have been comatose not to have read about the Maelstrom show in the media. I mean all the media: the major newspapers wrote about it, the web was full of it, and it clogged more blogs that I could count. NPR did a segment interviewing Dora the next morning, and her momentum did not flag a bit. She was after these people, and she made no bones about her disgust with what happened. Still, she mentioned nothing about conspiracies, nothing about the group of twelve, nothing about takeovers and assassinations. She was all fiery outrage backed up by mounds of dry statistics and wrapped in a gorgeous package. The gorgeous part was hard to see on radio, but it was clear as day in my mind.

I also thought that maybe the affair with Maelstrom had set the bad guys back a bit. Now that he was free, it was as if someone had opened a window and let in fresh air. Regular Americans began to talk about it on talk shows and call-in shows around the country. In the main, the feeling was anger that the government was able to assault someone's home on such a flimsy pretext. What's next? was the general question. I was glad about the newfound interest in the case; the initially muted response was eerie.

It was Tuesday of the following week when Dora called me. I acted distant on the phone, but I was thrilled she called.

"How'd I do?" Dora began, assuming I had seen her.

"What makes you think I saw you, *Doctor* Hathaway?" I almost sneered.

Dora giggled. "I knew you'd watch," she said without a hint of guile in her voice.

I was doing OK until she giggled. It was the last thing I expected from this woman I was beginning to tag as the powerhouse she was. Charmed again.

"I thought you were great," I said candidly. "That was after I got over the fact that you were on at all. And that Bandera was on the same panel. That blew me away."

"Same panel, but not the same room. The technology for these shows is wonderful; you can be across town or across the world."

"And where were you?" I inquired.

"At the station." She paused. "Willy and I have been friends for some time."

There was a long pause. "I got that impression," I said. I stopped; I did not want to pry.

"Can you come over?" Dora asked in a voice that bordered on the cheerful. "I'd like to go over some recent developments with you."

I knew no was not an option; Dora knew no was not an option.

It made me wonder why she had even bothered to ask.

"Sure," I said. "When?"

"Now?" she asked.

"Give me an hour," I said, trying to maintain some semblance of authority in this relationship.

I put the phone down and wondered at my involvement with this woman. It had so many layers. I was charmed physically, intellectually, and in every other way I could imagine. And I was wary. Not just because of my general apprehension about intimate relationships—that was my default mode and I could see it coming—but because she had invited me to do something that civilized people just do not do; to kill people. It was more intimate than inviting me to her bed, more exposed than a tell-all memoir, and more dangerous than both. One thing was clear: Isadore Hathaway was no conspiracy-breathing nutcase unhinged from whatever moorings held her feet tenuously to the earth. She was deadly serious and capable.

I decided to walk over to her apartment just to see how long it took and because I figured it was a good way to kill the hour I gave myself. It also gave me some more time to think about this intriguing and dangerous woman. As I walked along Wisconsin toward K Street, I thought about the most compelling reason Dora held such powerful attraction for me. *She was the first person in— what? twenty-three or twenty-four years?—who knew what I had done. She was the first person who was not military or a medical professional who knew that I had killed people.* Even thinking these thoughts walking down K Street made me feel self-conscious, as if others could hear them, see me think them, or just know that I was thinking them.

But at the same time, I was exhilarated. When I told my story in the hospital—and it seemed that I told it, told it, and told it—there was in the back of my mind the constant awareness that I was talking in a protected environment; that my words were stripped of the normal power of words to be shouted or amplified and heard everywhere. They had limits. They could go no further than the walls and the filing cabinets of a sacred space. The staff could take them in but take them no further. Even if they talked among themselves, which I knew they did.

But Dora *knows*. She knows the way a normal person in a normal place knows. I could whisper to her. I could shout to her. I could even write to her—although these last two options would be unwise—but she knew me the way a "normal person" would know me. And she wants me around. Maybe just as an instrument that can serve her needs for now, but, nonetheless, I have some importance to her the way I am. Even because of how I am. This is unlike any experience I've ever had with a woman.

An hour was a generous slice of time for the ten-minute walk from my office to the Watergate Apartments. I came to the entrance of her building and kept walking, uncertain if I should arrive early or just wait the remaining fifty minutes. I thought of going to the coffee shop around the corner I had discovered my last time here, but then I thought better of it. I turned around and walked up to her building and pushed the button by her name.

"I'm early," I said when she buzzed me back.

"Great," she said as she pushed the enter buzzer.

Every step I took into that building felt like a step off a cliff. By the time I got to her apartment door, my head was swimming, my palms were sweating, and my breathing was labored even though the elevator demanded very little of me physically. I stood at her door a moment before I knocked, trying to catch a breath and right myself. It was to little avail.

Then the door opened of its own accord, and Dora stood there regarding me with a steady and expectant look. She did not move for a moment; neither of us spoke. Then she slowly extended her hand and took mine. She led me into the apartment and closed the door behind her and leaned against it. She put her arms around my waist and pulled me toward her. "Thank you for coming," she said without expecting a reply. Then she kissed me.

I kissed her back, hungrily, eagerly, and desperately. I took her arms and raised them above her head and held them so the work of our lips could continue unhampered. So that they could be the sole focus of what I knew was my intemperate love and desire for her. At that moment, nothing mattered but this woman in my arms, the woman who knew me, who wanted me, and who extended herself to me. My career, my past, my future, what I had done, what I had failed to do: these things no longer mattered. Only the luxurious present now counted, and it was here that I wanted to stay.

Chapter 14

Dora and I spent the rest of the day together, basking in each others' embrace, and making love time after time. We also talked, dozed, and munched on whatever we could find in her refrigerator. It wasn't unlike the wonders that much younger men experience with women when they get to know them intimately for the first time. But for me now this was the first time; the first time I was with someone who knew what I had done and what I was capable of doing. Who would join me in it and help me with it. Who would give it meaning and direction. Who would make it seem like the most reasonable thing in the world.

When evening came and the sky began to redden, Dora looked over at me and kissed me on the forehead. "This is not what I intended," she said softly.

Now she tells me, I thought. I didn't say anything.

Dora snuggled in more closely. "This is better than what I had intended," she said. I pulled her close.

I have always had difficulty savoring the moment. But being with Dora today was one of the few times in my life when I could let go and feel the texture and breadth of the moment, breathe the present air, not look forward or backward. The only other time I felt this way was when I was aiming a gun at someone.

But now the moment was breaking up. I held her body close, but my mind was already ranging down the probable future, a future where I once again begin to shoot people. I knew it could and would happen. I felt a twinge of regret for my public life, the life I pretended to have.

Dora, it seemed, was reading my mind. "Don't worry," she said. "We have time."

I looked at her with an arched eyebrow. "How much time?" I asked.

She took a breath and started explaining. "These recent incidents were trial balloons. They were testing the water. Unfortunately, they found good news and bad news. The good news was how sheepish the people were when Willy was first arrested. They might be up in arms now, but the first reaction was mostly silence."

Dora got up and went to the bathroom for a glass of water. She lay back down and took a long sip. "The other good news for them was that the 'industrial accident' went largely unreported and completely unsuspected."

"So what's the bad news?" I asked.

Dora looked at her half-empty glass. "The bad news for them was the later response to Willy's arrest, the way significant people from all across the country came to his aid. Not the general population, but enough outraged lawyers and civil libertarians to help him out. They think they underestimated that response." She looked down at her glass. "I don't think they will do that again."

"Will this set them back a bit?" I asked, trying to bring her back to me.

"Maybe, Jake," Dora replied. "How this played out was not completely unexpected. They may have contingency plans. Like any test, they use it to gather information, to hone their plan."

My mind began to wander. I wasn't ready to get back into the conspiracy mind-set. I wanted the closeness to this woman, the intimacy that was ebbing away.

"So what's your doctorate in?" I asked, apropos of nothing.

Dora looked at me and smiled. "Public policy," she replied. "Harvard Class of '96."

Harvard. Of course, I thought. *There was nothing about this woman that wasn't first class.*

"And how long have you been with the CLPP?"

"Almost ten years," she replied. "Right out of school."

Her disarming frankness only made me feel closer to her; plus, I appreciated any information I could get out of her.

"How about dinner?" I asked.

"OK," Dora said smiling.

And with that we both got dressed and prepared to go out for the evening. I was ready for fresh air, but I wasn't ready to let go of this day together. We decided to just go find a place and started walking. We found a tapas place a few blocks away, and found a high table in the bar. I ordered a bottle of good Spanish tempranillo.

As we munched on small portions of lamb, shrimp, scallops, and asparagus. Dora talked some more about her background. She was very much the serious, studious type. She idolized her father, but he was, like many politicians, not around home very much. So the idolizing she did was mostly from a distance. She described her mother as the anchor of her life. A little too subservient by contemporary standards, but a loyal, hardworking woman who played the hand that her youthful decisions had dealt her. Not a complainer; just a good wife raising her daughter pretty much on her own. It was clear that Dora loved her—perhaps with more genuine affection than her father, whom she idealized—and her voice shuddered momentarily when she talked about her death two years before that of her famous dad.

"She wanted me to trust myself," Dora explained. "But I think what I learned to trust was us together. We could do anything. When I would win some award, it wasn't real until I told my mom. When I got into Harvard, she smiled and hugged me. I just felt that the two of us could do it: play in the big leagues. When she died, I felt a loss of confidence that I had never felt before." She paused and played with her wine glass. "It was frightening."

But temporary, I thought.

"It took me a while to realize in retrospect that I was the one performing, doing the big league work. I was the one writing the papers, winning the arguments, getting hired by a national think tank. It just never occurred to me that I could do these things without my mother." She let out a long breath. "But after a while I found that I was still performing, still producing even though she was gone." A tear rolled down her lovely cheek.

Dora took a breath and straightened her spine against the high wooden chair. She looked across the small table and said, "I know quite a bit about your time with the military, Jake, but I don't know much about your home life." She looked at me sweetly from across the table.

The invitation hung in the air for a few moments. I had been listening intently to what Dora had been saying and I didn't want to change gears. Nor did I want to talk about my childhood. I may still have been irritated about her prying into my background. Whatever the reason, I ignored the invitation.

"I love hearing about your life, Dora," I said, making a lateral move, "Some other time about mine." I took a sip of wine.

After dinner we walked slowly back to her apartment. At the door, I put my arms around her and kissed her. "Good night," I said. "And thank you for today."

"My pleasure," Dora purred. I waited until she was safely in her building.

On my walk home, my mind was filled with images of the altogether incredible and, it seemed to me, improbable day. The pull of Dora and the pull of getting back into a part of my life that had long been buried were both powerful, almost inexorable. I could feel the stage being set between the forces of good and those of evil. Obviously, the gang of twelve were the bad guys, willing to subvert the government, harm and even kill innocent people, and conduct their nefarious schemes in secret. Dora, on the other hand, was a force of good. She was dogged, intelligent, well-grounded, and willing to confront the evil-doers in the light to the extent that this was reasonable.

The assassinations, however, were firmly in a gray area. Why so drastic a measure? Didn't this make the good fight suspect, as vile as that of the bad guys? Obviously in government, or at least in the military, killing was used in a lot of ways that seemed suspect but largely unknown to the public. That was the Alpha Unit, my outfit. We were under strict orders not to disclose anything to anybody, and we followed that dictum to a man. But Dora did not have government sanction. She was not, to my knowledge, affiliated with the military in any way.

The thought crossed my mind that Dora was cold-heartedly ensnaring me in this drama both to do her dirty work and maybe even to take a fall. It was not unheard of in the dark world of subterfuge for women to use their powers this way. Obviously, she had a nearly unerring read on how I function, on what I need and thrive on. This was a disturbing, even chilling thought; it contrasted sharply with the warmth and sincerity I felt with Dora throughout the day today. But I couldn't entirely dismiss it.

Chapter 15

The next morning I lay in bed and reached for the phone.

"Good morning," I said when Dora answered.

"Good morning to you," she said cheerfully.

"I had a dream that I spent the day with a gorgeous woman who catered to my every whim. What's the opposite of a nightmare?"

I could hear Dora smile through the phone. "Funny," she said. "I had a similar dream. There was this man. . ." And then she started giggling.

I don't know what it was about her giggling that charmed me so. It was such a middle-school girl thing to do.

"When will I see you again?" I asked.

"Soon, I hope," came the spontaneous reply. "But not today. I have to work on some articles for news magazines."

"OK," I said. "I have a job, too. But don't make me wait too long."

I hung up without detecting a hint of malice in Dora's voice. This may be a cockeyed way for love to happen, but it felt more like love than anything I'd ever felt before.

I got up and performed my morning ritual. It was still early. I didn't have to be on the Hill until ten, so I perused the paper, sipped coffee, and savored the way I felt about Dora.

Unaccustomed to feeling good for too long, I got dressed and hailed a taxi to go to work.

I was glad to be back in the office. The rhythm of the office is consoling in a way. The clatter of keyboards, the ringing of telephones, the bustle of workers going back and forth. The fact that all this activity took place in the deliberative body of the greatest country on earth added immeasurably to its appeal. I attended two votes, one for public works (yes, good for my state) and one for raising the threshold for poor families to receive Medicare benefits (no, bad for my state and my conscience).

After the votes, I saw Max in the hallway and suggested we do lunch. He was more than happy to get out of the building for a while. His administrative assistant was notorious throughout the Hill for being the meanest, most task-oriented camel-driver of the lot. Max stayed away from his office as much as possible. He valued Grace Mettelman's rigor and conscientiousness, but he couldn't stand her as a person. "Live Free or Die" must not apply to the office.

So we went to the nearest pub to grab a burger and a beer. Besides dodging Grace, Max's other pastime was working on health care. He too voted against the Medicare proposal this morning, and he was set to rail against the fact that the bill was even proposed. Max was a stout Puritan from the old school. While he did not disdain alcohol or dancing, he abhorred injustice, and throwing desperate families to the wolves of health care costs was one of his trademark banners. So he railed for the first ten minutes after we sat down.

"It's chilling, Max," I said, casually aiding and abetting his crusade. "What do these people think? That poor families can save enough money to cover hospital and surgical expenses? I tell you, Max, it makes you wonder whatever happened to *salus populi supremo lex esto*? The good of the people matters."

We railed on back and forth, two small voices singing from the same score. Then we fell into more prosaic news and gossip, the kind of talk that makes up about eighty percent of legislative conversation on the Hill.

"Did you see Willy Maelstrom's first show back?" I asked.

"Yeah," Max replied. "I thought Hathaway's daughter killed that asshole Bandera."

"She's bright all right," I said, suddenly aware that I was temporizing and not wanting to disclose my personal involvement with Dora. *My secret, I guess*, I thought. I felt protective, almost defensive.

We went on to other things. After the mention of Dora's name, I began to wonder if Max was on to any irregularities from the bad guys. Max was definitely not the suspicious type. He was gregarious and trusting.

"Max," I said, trying to sound more casual than I felt. "What did you make of Willy's arrest in the first place? I mean, didn't it seem a little over the top to you?" I paused to give him a chance to respond.

He did not respond right away. He looked into his glass, noticed that it was empty, and ordered another Heineken. Then he looked into his glass as if he were considering revealing something to me. It was full minute before he spoke.

"More than over the top, Jake," he said slowly, not looking at me directly. "I thought it was an outrage, even for this cynical town." His beer came and he poured it slowly down the side of his glass, carefully pouring the last couple ounces in the center to give it some foam. He looked at me head on. "I began asking around," he said. "I talked to Grim Shapiro over at Justice. You know Grim. He and I graduated law school together." Max's voice dropped to a whisper, "Grim would absolutely not talk to me on the phone. He changed the subject twice. When I brought it up again, he ended the conversation." Max's eyes went back to examining his beverage. "He called me later that same evening. He was nervous and agitated. He couldn't tell me details, but I got the distinct impression that the whole affair was orchestrated from very high up in the Justice Department; that the normal procedures were not followed. Grim said Justice was in lock-down; nobody is talking about anything to anybody. The staff has been told not to talk to the press, other branches of government, or anyone who does not have a court order." Max leaned back in his chair. I could tell there was more, so I didn't say anything.

He took a breath and started again, "I kept calling other people I knew. I called some of my contacts at the Marshal Service. I even called a couple guys at Langley. Same deal. No one is talking about it, and it seems everyone is watching everybody else. I don't remember anything like this." He returned his gaze to his glass. Then he turned his head sideways and looked at me askance. "It's like what you hear about the McCarthy era, Jake, except no one's talking about an agenda."

I sat and listened to Max talk. If I had any desire to share with him what I had learned from Dora, it was not on my conscious radar screen. I was more than accustomed to hiding the truth; it came as second nature to me. Or maybe first. I listened intently. I could tell his attention was piqued and that he wanted answers. The thought that this lunch was not a casual encounter flitted along the edge of my consciousness. Paranoia probably, but hard to know for sure.

Our conversation was interrupted by a sudden increase in the volume of the TV at the end of the bar. NBC had interrupted the baseball game for a special announcement. The screen flashed to a large head of a woman with a serious, almost grim expression. Even with the volume up, I had to strain to hear.

". . .and it appears that the illness is widespread," the large head said. "Hospitals in the Denver area are reportedly overloaded with the high number of sick and dying patients." The announcer's voice cracked audibly. She took a breath. "Preliminary estimates are hard to find, but the Eleven Mile Reservoir serves tens of thousands of Denver residents."

Silence slowly descended upon the lunch crowd. All eyes made their way to the forty-two inch flat panel screen.

"We also have new reports indicating that fish are dying by the thousands in the Eleven Mile Reservoir." The camera panned to a beautiful lake nestled in the mountains. The lens swept closer to the surface of the water, which was covered with dead fish lying on their sides. It was sickening.

"The governor of Colorado has declared a state of emergency, and the National Guard has been alerted," the voice continued. "FEMA has been called in and is flying emergency personnel to the Denver area to determine the exact nature and cause of the problem."

The screen cut to an interview with what appeared to be a public relations official with FEMA. He had a lot of ways of saying "We don't know anything yet." I figured he was a low-level employee, and he obviously didn't know anything. I looked across the table to Max, whose face was ashen.

"Oh, my God," Max finally said as a tear rolled down his cheek.

I was pissed. It was obvious to my mind that this was a deliberate act of sabotage. I had no doubt who was responsible. The rage swelled up inside of me, and I had to think hard to maintain control. I started breathing in a regulated but silent way, inhaling slowly through my nose and exhaling slowly through my mouth. This calms me and helps keep me steady when my anger is stirred up.

The woman on the screen returned. "To recap this hour's developing story: Thousands of residents of Denver, Colorado have become acutely ill due to an apparent poisoning of the water in the Eleven Mile Reservoir, one of the principal sources of drinking water for the Denver area. We have reports that there have been an unspecified number of deaths, and officials fear that the number will climb dramatically. All wildlife in the reservoir itself appears to have been killed as well. The Eleven Mile Reservoir is a large attraction for fishermen and outdoorsmen from all over the western part of the United States. . ."

I had to turn away and stop listening for a moment. These people are not backing off at all. I wondered if they had actually moved their timetable forward. I wanted to talk with Dora, but I knew I had to get back to Capitol Hill first.

"Let's go, Max," I said, throwing forty dollars on the table. "We need to get back."

Max did not protest. He was still gray, but the movement seemed to help. He got up wordlessly and followed me out of the small, dark tavern.

We walked at a good clip back to the Capitol, but neither of us spoke. I figured Max was thinking about how to respond, how to care for his constituents. I was thinking of what I could do to stop this murderous plot with violence in kind.

I left Max in the hall. My office was one direction; his the other. The vacant look on his face irritated me a little, but I also felt sorry for him. "Hang on, Max," I said. "We'll get to the bottom of this." I shook his hand and put my other hand on his shoulder. Then I turned and walked toward my office.

The place was a mess. The phones were ringing nonstop and people were either walking back and forth doing God-knows-what or sitting immobile by the radio and small television in the waiting room. Some people looked my way when I walked in, but for the most part, nothing changed.

Jamie was in my office arranging papers on my desk.

"Give me an update," I said.

Jamie took a breath. "Here's what we know: Evidently a large quantity of potassium ferrocyanide, a cyanide-based poison, was dumped into the Eleven Mile Reservoir just outside Denver. We think it happened after midnight and before dawn. There were several truckloads. We found tracks of heavy trucks on three sides of the reservoir." Jamie paused for a moment, as if to get her facts straight. "Despite the fact that this park is a hunters' and campers' mecca, no one seems to have heard these trucks enter or leave. At least no one has reported anything unusual."

Jamie took a breath and continued. "The first round of hospitalizations began around 8:00 a.m. This stuff is potent, and some victims were exposed just by brushing their teeth or showering. Others drank the contaminated water." Jamie paused again and bit her lower lip. "The death toll so far is about twelve thousand." She looked at me with sad eyes, struggling to maintain control.

I stared back. I could feel the skin on my face harden and my eyes focus. "Jesus Christ," I said, but I wasn't surprised. Poisoning a large reservoir like that will kill way more than twelve thousand people.

"The Senate is gathering in the chamber," Jamie continued, reacquiring her momentum. I always admired her strength, especially in a crisis. "The president has mobilized the Army; he may nationalize the Colorado National Guard."

At that point, Sarah arrived at the open doorway. "They found the trucks," she said. "It was just announced on CNN."

Thank God, I thought. *We need to catch these people before they vanish.*

I flipped on the television in my office. CSI teams surrounded the area where large building trucks were parked pell-mell in a small ravine. Cameras were kept at some distance. *Smart move*, I thought.

"I'd better get to the chamber," I said to Jamie. "Thanks for the update."

Legislators are dreadful in a crisis; a lot of panicked talk about irrelevant things. As always, there was a lot of cant about protecting our nation, even though the attack was essentially over. I knew nothing would come of this empty talk. I knew the damage had already been done. Till next time.

I huddled with my little cadre of like-minded senators, and we all agreed that we would support the president in whatever he chose to do by way of response. Then I took my leave. I knew most of my little group would want to be home with their families. The public doesn't often pay attention to the fact that senators and representatives are primarily people who care about their families more than anything, just like most people. But they are.

I wanted to see Dora. I stopped by my office, closed the door, and dialed her apartment. Then I dialed her cell phone. No answer. I left a message on the cell phone and told my staff that I would be out of the office for the rest of the day. I told them to contact me with updates throughout the shortening work day.

I headed home. I wanted to start making my own plans. I wanted to be more than a helpless bystander in this all-too-human drama. I wanted to start my new job as soon as possible.

Chapter 16

When I got home, I called Dora again. Still no answer. I was irritated, but I didn't think I really needed her for my next move. She had given me instructions the very first day I met her. I powered up my computer and went on-line to find the website with the twelve cameo heads. Then I thought better of doing this on my home machine. I grabbed my laptop and left the apartment.

There was a coffee-shop with an open-access wireless network that anybody could log onto. It had booths where I would be more or less screened from passers-by and where I could have a bit of privacy.

It took me thirty seconds to find the site that Dora had showed me with the cameos. The large cross loomed large on my small screen, and my stomach turned. Then I noticed the message right below the cross: "We pray for the victims of today's horrible attack on the good Christian people of Denver." It was enough for me to stop breathing momentarily. *When did this go up?* I thought. *I wish I knew more about computers so I could figure that out. Maybe I know someone who can. And they had the nerve to pray only for the "Christian people" in Denver. What about the Muslims, Native Americans, and Ba'hais?*

I refocused on the task at hand. I created a text file and copied the names of each head in it. I also included their job, which was listed on the site, and any other useful information, such as the address of their home or office, their church, any other affiliations.

I spent about a half an hour perusing the rest of the site. It was mostly sanctimonious scribbling about government, religion, spirituality, and values. There were also some screeds against the ills of our society. These latter were cloaked in surprisingly temperate language, but you could feel the animosity which lurked beneath the insipid text.

Whatever ambivalence I had about my role in this battle was vanishing. It was a battle, and either these fanatics would prevail and destroy our society or they would not. I was an elected member of this government, and I would do everything in my power to stop them. The future felt dark, as if Calvin had returned to Geneva with the intention of imposing his strict and doctrinaire ways onto the population. These people were trying to turn the clock back at least five hundred years.

My phone rang, and it startled me out of my ruminating. "Yes?" I said when I finally located the small unit in my pocket.

"Jake," the voice said. "This is Jamie. The FBI made two arrests about a half hour ago. Two men they think were linked to the trucks."

Great, I thought. *Maybe we can get a jump on this thing.*

"They're dead," Jamie continued. "They apparently had cyanide capsules in their mouths, and when the FBI moved in, they chomped down on them and released the poison."

"Jesus," I said, although I was conflicted about this. These were bad guys, and I was glad they were dead. Also, I was sure these were low-level operatives, and their deaths probably would not influence the investigation too much. The evidence that could be obtained would probably be gotten just as easily from their corpses as their breathing selves. I guess I wasn't so conflicted.

"Thanks, Jamie," I said. "Anything else?"

Jamie hesitated a moment. "There is something else, but it's unrelated."

I waited.

"Do you remember Guy Tessero, the chief district court judge from Milwaukee?"

"Of course I remember him, Jamie," I replied. "He was a big supporter of mine in getting appointed to the Senate."

"He died, Jake," Jamie said. "Apparent heart attack last evening. Mrs. Tessero called the office personally to tell you. When I told her you would not be back, she gave me permission to share this with you." Another pause. "I am so sorry."

I had to force myself to breathe. Nothing about this felt like a coincidence. It felt like murder. I took deep breaths from as far down my chest as I could to keep stable. After some minutes, I said to Jamie, "Thanks for telling me, Jamie. Do you have Ursula's number?"

She gave me the number, and I typed it into my open laptop. Then to Jamie, "Find out about the funeral arrangements, send flowers, and get me a plane ticket for the service."

After I clicked off from Jamie, I sat in my small booth and looked straight ahead. I knew I had to call Ursula, Guy's wife, but I wanted to make sure there was no trace of the rage and hatred I felt inside in my voice. I took a sip of coffee and tried to act as if I was OK. Then I picked up the phone and dialed the number.

Mercifully, I got her voice mail, with the voice of their youngest daughter saying the announcement. It was merciful because I didn't have to talk to Ursula right away—I could put that off perhaps until I got to Milwaukee—but it was also wrenching to hear the voice of a nine year old who had just lost her father. I left a short message extending my condolences and telling them I would be present for the funeral service.

I slowly closed the portable computer and turned to look out the picture window that gave onto the street. Summer in DC is a beautiful and sultry time of the year. The city glistened the way it always does in the sunshine, and I felt both the deep affection I had for this town and the revulsion that a small group of fanatics had the hubris to think they could control it, change it, and take it away. The more I thought, the more a sense of preternatural calm descended upon me. I was less anxious; I was clear. I knew the path I had to take, and I was prepared to take it all the way. I wondered absently if I would survive this drama, but whether I did or not did not seem to matter much. This was about matters more significant than my personal survival. All I knew is that I had to stay alive until I was done.

Chapter 17

I tried to call Dora again, but still with no success. I can only imagine she's up to her eyeballs in information, trying to build whatever case she could to stop these people from doing more damage. Then I went home and called Jamie about the funeral arrangements for Guy.

"Thursday," Jamie said. "At St. Anskar's Episcopal at 10:00 a.m."

"Thanks, Jamie. What about flights?"

"When do you want to leave, Jake?" Jamie asked. "There are many choices."

"Get me up there by late afternoon Wednesday, Jamie," I said. "I want to spend some time with Ursula and the children. Bring me back Sunday. I want to see some other people while I'm there."

"Got it."

I clicked off and leaned against my small kitchen counter. When you go from the sunshine world to the shadowy one, all the rules change; I had to review the new rules of my life with some focus so as not to get tripped up before I start.

From now on, I will have to keep my laptop with me at all times, along with a magnet powerful enough to erase the hard drive at a moment's notice. I will also have to transport the Remington sniper rifle to a secure location somewhere other than my apartment. I could not risk having someone find it in my apartment if and when the shooting started. I will also have to get a cash amount large enough to get me out of the country, along with the necessary papers, legitimate or illegitimate, and find a place to stash it securely. I'll develop an escape plan. These did not seem so much like the chores they were as they felt like planning a vacation or something; just things that had to be done.

I will also need some other equipment; parabolic microphones, night and day binoculars, and some kind of disguise, although I had never tried to disguise myself before. I chuckled at the clownish notion of dressing up to look like someone else.

An escape plan might be difficult for a United States senator. I thought about faking my death if it came to that, but I knew the FBI had resources that would most likely nullify my amateurish attempts to do that. I put this idea out of my head, especially because I thought the odds of my survival were considerably less than fifty-fifty. But that was an issue for another day.

Right now I had to decide what I could get done before I left for Milwaukee on Wednesday. That gave me a day to play with. Probably less, since I would have to go back to the Senate chambers tomorrow morning. I decided to focus on doing a few things.

I thought some things were best left to do in Wisconsin, especially since I was going anyway. It might actually be easier to do this in Michigan, which is much friendlier toward gun owners and purveyors of marginally licit military material. I would also be less likely to be recognized in that state than my own.

Getting the Remington to a safe but available location seemed like the most immediate thing to focus on. I considered a number of venues: a locker at Union Station, in the Metro, or at the airport. I did not think it would be a good idea to have it anywhere near a government building or an airport. I finally settled on putting it in several lockers at Union Station. There were always people there and it would be less liable to be vandalized than it would in the Metro. It would also be less suspicious than taking a gun to the airport.

I took a deep breath. I had done nothing with this gun except hold it for years. I was glad that I had gotten it so long ago, and by mail. It would be almost impossible to trace it to me. But still, it seemed like using a sacred object, a holy instrument that should only be used for worship, like pouring an evening cocktail into a communion cup. *Perhaps this is worship*, I thought darkly. *Killing mass murderers seems like a suitably holy task.*

I took the gun sections and wrapped them in cloth and put each of the pieces in small traveling cases. I would make three trips to Union Station; each time finding a separate locker in the massive building. I would walk with authority, as I assumed that, if anyone were watching, it would raise more suspicion for me to act timid and anxious.

The station itself was unusually quiet. The echoes of the marble floors are usually muffled by the sheer volume of humans and clothing, but today the marble allowed unchecked sound; each of my steps clattered across the huge rectangular space. The shops were largely empty, and there were police patrols throughout the station. I walked briskly across the main hall to the section where the lockers were. Even with the noise and the few people, no one seemed to be paying much attention.

I selected a locker with an easy number to remember. It was a multiple of twelve. There were enough lockers that were available for me to put all my equipment in lockers with multiples of twelve, making them easy to remember and easy to find.

After I finished loading the first locker and pulled it shut and turned the key and pulled it out, I turned and saw a guard with a German Shepherd about thirty feet away headed in my direction. I nodded to him respectfully but felt my stomach clutch. He nodded and kept walking toward me. I turned and walked slowly in his direction.

"Afternoon, officer," I said. "Lot of police presence here today."

"Yeah," he replied. "You wouldn't believe how many. They got everybody out and in the saddle."

"As well they should," I said. "It's turning into a dangerous place."

He looked at me straight on. "We'll get the bastards," he said. I nodded seriously. He kept walking. I also kept walking toward the door, away from him. I dared not look back.

It wasn't until I was outside that I could breathe again. I had made sure there were no fingerprints on that locker or on the valise. I had wiped the gun and the valise down both before I left the apartment. I only touched the key when I opened and closed and locked the metal door. The only prints were on the key, which was in my pocket. On the other hand, if that dog found anything, there were too few people in there for the guard to be confused. He would have easily been able to pick me out of photos. He may even have recognized my face.

I kept walking. I did not hear any sirens or alerts, but I had to re-think my plan for the remaining two cases. I wasn't even sure it would be wise for me to do anything with them today, especially if video cams were monitoring everything, as I a sure they were. It would have automatically looked suspicious.

It was clear to me that I would have to unpack the remaining pieces and leave them in their usual places at home. I would postpone planting the rest of the gun until I got back from Wisconsin.

On my way home, Jamie called to give me the flight details and to bring me up to date on what the Senate had done so far. She also told me the death toll in Denver had topped twenty thousand. This helped clear my mind and settle me down a bit; I was still anxious from my run-in with the guard and his dog. But my sense of purpose deepened.

Right after she hung up, my cell phone rang again. It was Dora.

Relief washed over me.

"Jake, where are you?" she asked.

"On my way home," I said. "Where are you?"

"In New York."

Damn, I thought. *That means I won't see her for a while.* "What's in New York?" I asked.

"I'll tell you when I see you," Dora replied. "I guess you're up on the news."

"Yeah," I said. "I'm up on it alright."

There was a slight pause on the phone. "I heard about Tessero," Dora said. "Jake, I am so sorry."

She sounded sincere, but my first thought was to wonder how she knew. It was probably news, but it was the kind of news that would be drowned out by the major catastrophe in Denver. I felt certain that the timing was not coincidental.

"Tell me what you think, Dora," I said without regard for protocol.

"I think you know what I think, Jake," was Dora's reply. And I did.

I let out a long stream of air. "OK," I said. "I'll be in Wisconsin until Sunday."

"I'll see you at the service, Jake," Dora said, to my complete surprise.

"You didn't..." I began.

"Yes, I did, Jake. Guy was an affiliate member of CLPP. He was an idea man."

I was beginning to resent the availability to information Dora had at her disposal, but it also felt reassuring to me that she knew a man I so respected.

"OK, then. I'll see you there." I clicked off.

This little contact with Dora renewed my spirit after the anxious moment in the station. I began to walk more quickly toward my apartment. An idea was forming at the back of my head. It started as a little notion but gained steam as I walked. It was about tactics. Sort of.

The idea was to shoot one of those web cameo heads soon so that the group knew that someone else knew what they were up to; to communicate to them that this will not be the sweet ride they might be thinking it is. The face of Roger Bandera was center stage in my forebrain.

Whoa, tiger, I thought. *You know that one is personal. So what?* I thought back. *With Guy's death, it all felt personal.* Funny how twenty thousand dead people on the other side of the country can shock and horrify you, but the death of a single person you know can take you over the edge.

There could be a message for me in Guy's death, if Dora was right and I was on one of their lists. It could be a warning. I hated this kind of thinking. Who ever knew the truth? My job was simply to put bullets in people, not analyze this or that message it might send. The message I wanted to send was clear as day to me.

Bandera might be first, but not until I get back. I don't have the time to devote to proper execution of a plan or even to devise a plan than would have a reasonable chance of success with minimal exposure of capture or death for me. I reminded myself grimly that there were multiple targets, and that I had to stay alive until I took all of them down.

Chapter 18

Besides heightened security at the airport, the trip to Wisconsin came off without a hitch. I had one carry-on bag and my laptop and no other metal on my person. I was accustomed to traveling light and was grateful for that. I hate airports.

I took a cab to the small apartment I maintain in my district. It wasn't fancy, but I don't spend much time there when I am in town, so I don't need much. When I am in my district, there is usually so much to do, I only come here to hole up and sleep for a few blessed hours. Of course, this may change, given current developments.

After a shower and change of clothes, I called for a taxi to take me to the funeral parlor where Guy's body was laid out. I walked in and people naturally deferred to me. Everyone knew who I was, and they knew that Guy and Ursula and I had a relationship. I spotted Ursula at the center of the room and at the head of a long line of sympathizers. She saw me and walked in my direction, quitting her post in front of the casket where her husband lay, a waxy version of himself.

Ursula and I hugged. I told her how sorry I was. She shook her head as if in disbelief. Then she leaned over and whispered in my ear. "I don't think this was natural, Jake," she said in the faintest whisper.

I pulled my head back and looked at her with a grim and shocked expression on my face. It wasn't faked. "We'll talk later," she said. "Thank you so much for coming." And with that, she walked back to the head of the line of mourners.

I stood in thought for a moment, and then I started looking around to see if there was anyone there I knew. Of course, there were. The group divided into three: people I actually liked and didn't mind seeing; people it was politic for me to touch base with; and the third, least savory group of people who were eyeing me and hoping to introduce themselves or be introduced. Those were the most excruciating ones.

I spotted Guy's two daughters over in the corner and walked in their direction. Evidently just in the nick of time, as two gentlemen in expensive suits had spotted me and were making their way toward where I was standing. I hugged the girls and reminded them who I was.

"I remember," said Theresa, the older girl. "You were at our house last Thanksgiving."

So I was. Guy and Ursula insisted on entertaining in voluptuous American fashion and put on a spread that was sumptuous even by Wisconsin standards. They made a policy of inviting people who didn't especially have any place else to go. Since I wasn't married and since my parents had passed away some years ago, I more than qualified. It was one of the few Turkey Day parties I actually enjoyed. I remember Theresa grilling me on what I did in Washington.

"So do all the senators sit in the Capitol building and talk about important stuff all day long?" she had asked.

I remember smiling. This was the kind of question that, coming from a stranger, would have been annoying. But I was happy to educate this bright and interested fifteen-year-old in how things actually worked in the nation's capital.

"No, Theresa," I explained patiently. "We do meet in chamber sometimes, but most of our work goes on in small offices in the

Senate Office Building across the street from the Capitol Building." Theresa listened intently. I don't know if she followed my explanation, but she did a great job of appearing to. I am fond of her.

Katherine, the younger girl, was more rambunctious. She had neither the patience nor the inclination to understand the machinery of government. She was, after all, only nine; and her priorities seemed to include running, jumping, and having as much fun as she could. But I suppose, because she was Guy and Ursula's daughter, none of this was done in an offensive way; she just loved being alive.

A genuine tinge of sorrow swept over me now as I was standing with Guy's two daughters, girls who would have to finish their upbringing without Guy's strong presence and clear determination. Without his support, and without his love. He loved the women in his life fiercely, his wife and his daughters. They were always his absolute top priority. Guy was political, but it never interfered with the execution of his duties and responsibilities as a parent. Not once. I respected him for that.

I respected Guy Tessero for all the usual reasons. He was an intelligent man of integrity who did not suffer fools gladly. He was a political supporter, but he had made it clear that he was available to me however I needed him to be. Confidant, mentor, mover, and a shaker. I was only beginning to explore the ways he could help me during the past two years. Now all that is gone. I hated whoever did this to him.

I also wondered what Ursula knew. Why would she suspect foul play? Guy was healthy enough, but he was a fifty-nine-year-old man who thought exercise was for children and who loved to sit around his outsize dining room table and eat and drink with as many friends and acquaintances as he could assemble. A heart attack would not be so unusual. In addition, if there was foul play, it should have been by someone who would remain undetected. Anything less than that would have been unforgivably amateurish.

In the middle of these thoughts, the two girls scampered away after spotting some of their friends arrive. I nodded and encouraged them to go. Grief is an adult preoccupation. They have plenty of time.

I spent some time working the room, moving from one first string contact to another, methodically avoiding dealing with people I didn't particularly want to see. There was a message in this; I didn't want anyone thinking that I was using this incident for political gain. I was here for Guy and his family. Period.

Later in the evening, I went up to Ursula and hugged her good-bye. I assured her that I was available to her if she should need anything. She nodded and thanked me.

Outside the funeral parlor, I took big gulps of the crisp Wisconsin night air. I loved the northern latitudes for never letting you forget you weren't in the south, that even hot summer days had relief in the evening and night hours. I hitched a ride back to my apartment with Todd Greenway, a lawyer I knew from my school days.

Todd asked if I wanted to drop by his place or get a drink somewhere. I looked at my watch. I was ordinarily not one to turn down such an invitation, but it was getting near ten, and I wanted to be fresh for morning, so I politely declined. He dropped me off at my place, and we said good-night.

I was glad I came. I can be such a loner, and it isn't often people I respect and care about invite me into their life. But Guy and Ursula did, and I feel attached to them. As I unlocked my apartment door, feelings of grief began to wash over me. With all that's happened over the past few days, the loss of Guy had not hit me. It did now. I sat down on the small love seat and tears flowed freely. This was out of the ordinary for me, but the stress of the past two days was part of it. I knew the number of dead in Denver would still be climbing. I knew there were others who were targeted for death by a maniacal group of religious fanatics. There was disbelief. I couldn't quite comprehend that they had been able to get this far. Especially after the fiasco with Maelstrom. What are they planning next?

Chapter 19

The next morning, I awoke early. Last night's sadness still hung around the edges of my mind, but I was looking forward to seeing Dora; the thought of seeing her dispelled some of the gloom. I wondered when she would be arriving. I kept an eye out for her last night, but she wasn't there. I would have known. My guess is that she'd be flying in this morning.

I did not have to wait long to find out. My phone rang just after 7:00 a.m., and her authoritative voice asked if I was up for breakfast.

"When did you get in?" I asked.

"Late last night," she replied. "And I skipped dinner, so I am ravenous."

I got to the restaurant a few minutes early to find Dora already seated. As I walked over to her table in the farthest corner booth of the place, I noticed that the look on her face seemed serious, sad, or strained; I wasn't sure which.

"Good morning," I said, leaning over to kiss her on the cheek.

She nodded but didn't say anything. I sat down. Neither of us spoke for a moment. Finally, I asked, "Dora, are you alright?"

She looked down for a moment and then shook her head, as if shaking the gloom away. "It's been a rough few days, Jake," she said slowly.

For the entire country, I thought. Then I realized that I had not heard any more news about Denver since I left DC yesterday. "Where is the death toll?" I asked, not exactly sure what Dora was referring to.

"It's still in the twenty thousand range," she said without skipping a beat, but I had the feeling that my reaction was off the mark, one of those I'm-a-blockhead kind of statements for which American men are so renowned.

On the other hand, I didn't want to pry. Dora had not told me she was going to New York. I had no idea what she has been up to. So after ordering coffee and pretending to look at the menu, I did not say anything. I looked at Dora expectantly.

Dora seemed to be trying to focus, or maybe she was deciding what to say next. To my surprise, for some minutes she did not say anything. This was odd behavior from my new friend and lover.

"Hungry?" I finally asked, risking another blockhead moment.

Dora took a breath. "I'm sorry, Jake," she said. "I have to admit I am a little shaken up by recent events." She paused for a moment. "Denver was worse than I thought and it happened sooner than I anticipated. Guy and I were close professionally. I considered him a mentor and always valued his input." She inhaled sharply, but her eyes teared up anyway. "I just can't believe he's gone."

I looked at Dora with a melting heart. The truth was that she was describing not only her own experience, but mine as well. I swallowed my urge to cry. I wanted to be there for Dora, who obviously had more heart than her analytic job and background suggested. I wanted to be strong for her.

I reached for her hand across the table and squeezed it gently. I nodded and waited.

The server came over and asked us if we were ready to order. Her voice automatically dropped as she approached the table. I guess she could sense that something was going on here that deserved respect. We nodded and ordered.

Dora began speaking. "Jake," she said. "Up until two days ago, I thought I had a handle on what was happening; I thought I could alter events somehow by gathering information, by getting you on board, and by working hard." She looked down and bit her lower lip in what would have been a charmingly seductive move had the circumstances been different.

"But this situation is bigger than me, than you, than the resources I have."

"Dora," I interjected. "Who else knows about this?"

She pursed her lips. "Before I contacted you, I tried to go to the FBI. I was cold-shouldered by some low-level hack who thought I was more suspicious than what I was describing. I think it was that guy who put periodic tails on me, the kind you saw the day after we met. Also, since some of the players were involved with the Justice Department, I did not want to specify anyone's identity. I didn't know who to trust."

She paused, and the server brought our orders in silence.

We both began to eat slowly, but our attention was riveted on what we were talking about. She put her fork down after a couple mouthfuls. "Then I tried other agencies: the CIA and the State Department. I tried to talk to some colleagues of my dad's. They are all insulated against cranks, which is what I must have sounded like to them. They were polite because of my father, I guess, but they all gave me the brush off. But I was so sure of what I was learning; that's when I decided to take matters into my own hands. That's when I decided to recruit you."

We resumed eating.

Dora finished her breakfast. She must have been hungry; I was still halfway through mine. She slid her plate aside and grabbed her coffee cup with both hands. "I can't stand this, Jake. I can't stand knowing things and not doing anything about them while thousands of people die and religious fanatics plot to take over the country." She was whispering, but the intensity of her voice was unmistakable. "I cannot sit by and let this happen to people I care about."

I glanced around to see if anyone was close. I couldn't see anyone, but Dora had positioned herself so that she had a full view of the room with no one behind her. I had to turn my head completely around for a view. Satisfied that no one was within ear shot, I leaned as far across the table as I could and whispered to Dora. "Ursula told me that she thinks Guy's death was deliberate," I said.

Dora's eyes widened. "What did she say exactly, Jake?" she asked.

"That his death was 'not natural'," I replied, looking straight into her lovely but steely eyes.

Dora pondered this for a moment. I could see the question on her mind was the same that was on mine when Ursula told me. How could the people who successfully engineered the catastrophe at Denver screw up so obviously with a single hit? It was incongruous.

Then the expression on Dora's face changed. It was if she had gained some encouragement that the bad guys were not some unstoppable juggernauts; they made mistakes. The mood at the table lightened perceptibly.

"We have work to do, Jake," she said.

"Yes, we do," I agreed.

I abandoned the rest of my breakfast when the server came. I asked for the check and it showed up within minutes. Dora and I stood up and walked to the cash register to pay. We did not need to speak. We knew what was next, even if neither of us wanted to say it aloud.

We went to the service as if we were married; such was the shared purpose we both felt as we faced the next phase of our lives. I don't know how Dora felt about attending the packed church service side-by-side, but I had a damn-the-torpedoes attitude and did not flinch a bit when cameras flashed in our direction. I was proud to be seen with Dora, a soul mate if I ever had one. A woman who was about to do things that she probably never imagined.

Chapter 20

The funeral service for Guy Tessero was sad. There were people in the world who did not like him, but none was present in the old church. Everyone was there because of their respect and love for their father, friend, husband, and co-worker. The priest gave a suitably simple but potent homily protesting the premature death of a valuable human being while staying within the defining myths of Christianity. This is terrible, but God has His ways. Whatever that means.

After attending both the service and the burial, Dora and I went to the large gathering at the Tessero household. I spotted Ursula in the middle of an overly reverential crowd and motioned to get her attention. She excused herself and walked in my direction. I introduced her to Dora.

"I know Dora," Ursula said. "How are you, honey?"

"Ursula," Dora said. "I am so sorry. This is such a loss for so many people."

The look on Ursula's face was both sad and distant, as if she was pondering something. "Please come with me," she said to both of us.

She led us into a small hallway behind the staircase. "Did you tell Dora what I told you yesterday?" Ursula asked me without preamble.

"Yes," I replied.

"Good," Ursula responded. "Because I do not want this to go unrecorded. I want people to know if he was murdered, as I suspect he was."

"But why…" Dora began.

"I don't know why," Ursula said. "But we were talking on the phone the afternoon he died. He said that he had a meeting right after work—about four in the afternoon—with two men from Washington who came in to talk with him about a project they were considering. Guy was vague, and, when I pressed him, he said that they were just as vague with him. But they said it was urgent, and that it was to be conducted in the strictest secrecy." A tiny smile curled the ends of Ursula's lips. "So, of course, he called to tell me about it." She paused as if gathering her thoughts. "Guy did not want to worry me, but his telling me was kind of a safeguard. There have been threats on his life in the past—as there have been with many judges—and this was our way of signaling that something might be amiss…" A tear fell from the eye of this sturdy woman. "He would not have called if he wasn't concerned."

"When Guy came home, he told me the meeting was one of the oddest experiences he had ever had with another government official. He said there were two men—a Geoffrey Adelburg and a Roger Bandera—who asked him about his religious beliefs."

At the sound of Bandera's name, both Dora and I froze and looked at each other briefly.

Ursula noticed. "You know these names?" she asked.

"Yes," Dora replied. "Both of them."

"So they are Justice Department officials?" she asked.

"Bandera is," replied Dora flatly. "Addelburg is with the State Department."

Ursula shook her head. Then she continued, "Guy told them his religious beliefs were none of their business, as stipulated by dozens of laws, the Constitution of the United States, and long judicial tradition. He said they listened, smiled, and apologized for taking his time."

Then Ursula sighed deeply. "He said he started feeling bad right after they left his office. He was feverish on his way home, and he died ten minutes after walking into the front door. He thought it was something they did, although he did not specify what that might have been. But he was pretty certain it was murder. He talked to me about this the whole last ten minutes of his life." She sighed again. "Except for the part where he told me he loved me and the kids and that he would always be in our hearts."

Dora and I waited as Ursula cried for a few moments. We both put a hand on her arm to steady her, to connect with her, and to let her know her pain was ours.

Then Dora spoke softly. "Was there an autopsy?" she asked.

"Yes, there most certainly was. Guy's doctor did not see the need of one, but I insisted. The results are due next week."

Dora thought for a moment, looking down at the hardwood floor. "Did you express your concerns to the doctor or to the medical examiner?" she asked Ursula.

Ursula looked at her. "I only said that I wanted to cover all the bases. That my husband was a judge, and if foul play was involved I wanted to know."

Dora nodded. "Good," she said. "That means they will take extra care with the results."

Ursula leaned over and hugged Dora. Then she did the same to me. "Thank you both for coming," she said. "It means a lot to me, and it would mean the world to Guy." She took a step out of the hallway, but then she stopped and touched me on the shoulder. "You could do a lot worse, Jake," she said, nodding to Dora. The she smiled at Dora and walked back into the living room.

I looked at Dora. "I agree," I said.

Dora smiled sadly. "Jake," she said, ignoring this last exchange, "I just cannot believe how fast this business is moving."

"Let's get out of here," I said.

On the way to Dora's rental car, we were both deep in thought.

We got in the late model sedan and drove in silence for a while.

"What do you know about Addelburg?" I asked the silence.

"Undersecretary of State for Latin American Affairs," Dora replied. "He's on the website."

"One of the twelve?" I asked.

"Yes, and a close contact of Bandera. We had dinner with him and his wife a couple times when I was seeing Roger."

It was Roger Bandera who was the almost palpable presence in the car.

"As good a place to start as any," I said.

Dora looked over at me, momentarily taking her eyes off the road. She did not say anything or change her expression; she just nodded.

"Let's go to Michigan," I said. "I have some shopping to do."

Chapter 21

The Great State of Michigan is indeed a great state. For every nutcase, militia member, and wannabe assassin. It has hundreds of stores selling guns and related paraphernalia. Toys for the guys who never got cops and robbers out of their system when they were seven. You can get anything in Michigan. And it's pretty legal.

The precise legality of it was not a major concern to me. Out in rural Michigan, I was just another guy with some bucks. I had brought a couple thousand dollars in cash with me for obvious reasons, and most of the proprietors of Michigan gun shops loved cash. It made their life easier and it shortened the time between closing and beer swizzling, which must be the major recreational pastime outside the major cities of the state. I love Michigan.

It took us thirty minutes from the border to find a suitable shop, one that had a billboard on the state highway announcing a warehouse full of the kind of goodies I was seeking. When we got to the large metal building, I figured there were at least two absolutely illegal firearms under the counter for every legal one we saw. And the legal ones were pretty potent: assault rifles, shotguns, automatic pistols, and rifles of every description. They also had related toys, the microphones, binoculars, and GPS trackers that made killing animals and people so much of an adventure.

I checked off the items on my mental list and found every single one of them at the store. I paid in cash and left; I don't think there was a complete sentence exchanged between me and the ragged looking character behind the counter.

"What now?" Dora asked, a little uncomfortable with how much delight I was taking in this part of the job.

"I think we should drive back to DC. We can talk about tactics on the way."

She looked at me askance but did not say anything.

"I'll have to go back to my hotel to get my things," she said.

"Why don't we stay over tonight and leave first thing in the morning?"

Dora agreed since the sky was already darkening. Truth was, we were both a little tired.

On the way back to Milwaukee, I kept thinking how easy this was for me. Forsaking my public life; taking a path that most people would regard as self-destructive lunacy. But it was me. It was me I found most engaging, most alive, almost intoxicating. I had some apprehension about the future but no real confusion or conflict.

I wasn't so sure about Dora. She was not being the hard-as-nails professional I first met and the one that millions of people saw on TV when she appeared on the Maelstrom show. She was quiet on the ride back, apparently lost in thought. I was thinking that this was the shortest honeymoon period I had ever had in a relationship. Then she spoke.

"I am sorry, Jake. Guy's loss was a big one for me. Not only that, but I was floored when the Denver thing came off without a hitch. I believe there are no suspects, and the bodies of the drivers yielded precious little by way of information. This all seems out of control."

As we drove across southern Wisconsin, I flipped on the radio. Fortunately, this rental had XM radio, and there were several all-news-all-the-time stations. CNN was recapping the events in

Denver, talking about how it was actually pretty easy to murder thousands of people, especially if you got the chemistry right. And evidently this round of terrorists knew their chemistry. The poison they used was a version of cyanide that maintained its potency even when diluted in thousands of gallons of water and even when it passed through filters normally used in purifying water in the US and elsewhere. A super-toxin, they were calling it.

I flipped to MSNBC. They had a panel discussion about the impact of the attack, and something one of the panelists said caught my attention.

"I think," the male voice said, "that we now have to ask the question: Can our government in its present form keep us safe? 9/11 and now this; the catastrophes are escalating dramatically in impact and lethality. More people are being killed. What have our leaders done to stop this? Is this the Achilles' heel of modern democracy?"

I glanced over at Dora and our eyes met for the briefest moment. I saw her tighten her grip on the steering wheel and set her jaw in a familiar iron pose. She was pissed.

"Geoffrey Addelburg," she said. "The very one." Her eyes turned acidic. "The guy with Bandera."

I listened intently. *Target number two*, I thought.

"Let's drive to DC tonight," Dora said. "I'll pick up my stuff at the hotel, and we can take turns driving. We'll get there by noon tomorrow."

"OK," I said. It didn't matter to me. But I could tell Dora was reconnecting with the fire she had in her belly about this whole affair.

Chapter 22

After stopping by Dora's hotel, we headed south toward Chicago and then southeast toward DC. We talked about targets. We never used that language, but it was clear what we were talking about.

"What do you need to start?" Dora asked as we drove through Chicago about midnight.

I thought for a moment. "What I really need is information, Dora. Habits, routines; stuff like that."

I was driving, and Dora was making notes on a piece of paper on her lap. She reached back for a black briefcase that was sitting on the rear seat and pulled it up front. She dialed what appeared to be a fancy locking mechanism and opened the case. She pulled out a small notebook.

"Mr. Bandera's schedule for the next three weeks," she said, opening it and pointing to the neat script in which the book was written. I glanced over at it as much as traffic and maintaining control of the car would allow. It was enough to see that we would know where Bandera was at every hour of every day for the next three weeks. My heart leapt. This is possible; it's going to happen. I tried to act calm.

"Impressive," I said to Dora.

Dora lay her head back against the headrest. "This is wretched business, Jake," she said. "I am afraid you are more comfortable with it than I am." She looked out the window for several minutes. "But I don't see any other way to stop these people."

As close as I was feeling toward Dora, I did not think I could explain to her what this whole experience was like for me. To say it aloud seemed to cheapen it. To say that I felt more whole at the prospect of killing people made me sound like a sociopath, and I don't think I really qualify for that diagnosis. I have a conscience. But I was trained to do things that someone in our society had to do, and my hope was to put my training in service to the good that I saw and against the evil that was encroaching on American life. It was about meaning, but it was excruciatingly personal. I don't think I can really explain it to anyone.

Instead, I decided to stick to business. "When do you think he is most vulnerable?" I asked.

Dora thought for a moment in silence. "Probably on the weekends. He often works at home alone for long periods of time and spends the evenings out on the town."

The thought of doing this on the weekend did not appeal to me. This was work-related; I thought it should remain strictly business—meaning Monday through Friday, more or less between nine and five.

Dora must have had a similar reaction. "The other possibility is when he is *en route* somewhere. His schedule indicates that he travels outside the office frequently during the week. Look here." She pointed to a few outside appointments. She bit her lower lip in thought. "But then we have to contend with the lockdown of the Capitol that is in force because of what happened in Denver."

"It's impossible to lock down a city completely," I said with more authority than I had about this matter. The fact was I didn't want to wait too long. Certainly not for the police presence to slacken. On the other hand, a sniper attack in the nation's capital might play right into the hands of the twelve. I thought on in silence.

Dora must have been having similar thoughts. "Is there a way to do this that doesn't look deliberate?" she asked.

"Maybe," I said, but I wasn't sure exactly how. "But it may be better to do it the old-fashioned way, if only to send an unmistakable message."

Dora did not balk at that; she just took it in and added it to her mental menu.

We talked on through the night as we drove through the blackness. As we approached Pittsburgh at about 3:00 a.m., it was clear that we needed a break. Even switching off driving chores was not keeping drowsiness at bay.

We stopped at a small motel just south of the city and checked in. We were less than four hours from DC, so we could still arrive early in the afternoon.

Once checked in, we both plopped onto the bed and breathed big sighs of relief.

"Good choice," I said, dragging myself up to disrobe so I could get more comfortable. I was a little uncomfortable undressing in front of Dora. We had only been together once.

"Um, are you going to sleep with your clothes on?" I asked.

Dora smiled. "Not on your life." Then she got up and retreated to the bathroom, picking up her travel case on the way.

She re-appeared ten minutes later smelling scrubbed and clean and sporting a small nightshirt. It looked sexy on her. In the meantime, I had removed my clothes and gotten into bed, by-passing my normal nocturnal grooming habits. I was beat.

"Yum," I said, leaning in her direction when she got into bed.

"Yum?" Dora said, looking at me as if she suddenly learned I was underage.

Before I could respond, I was asleep. I wanted to stay awake, to wrap her in my arms, to do what grown people who love each other do, but my fatigue got me. Fatigue with elements of apprehension, excitement, and spent adrenaline. The dreams were vivid: flying over the countryside, feeling exhilarated, potent.

It was 8:30 a.m. when I awoke. Dora was dressed and reading

the paper on the small chair. There were two cups of coffee on the little desk in the room.

"How long have you been up?" I asked.

"About twenty minutes," Dora replied. "Got you some coffee," she said, nodding her head in the direction of the small fake-wood desk.

"Thanks." I got out of bed, removed the lid from the steaming coffee, and took a sip, and headed for the shower. "I'll be presentable in ten minutes," I said.

Even with the shower going, I could hear that Dora had flipped on the TV and was scanning the news networks. No doubt looking for hints or clues.

As I was drying myself off, I yelled to Dora, "Any news?"

"No," she replied seriously. "Just yesterday's catastrophes."

We picked up our things and scanned the room quickly. Obviously we were both accustomed to traveling. We checked out on the TV and pulled the door shut tight.

Back on the road, things were calmer. I am not sure how Dora processes information; I know she is capable of assimilating mountains of it. I know she is capable of aggressive action. Over the past few days, I have seen a more tender, more emotional side to her. It was endearing. I who like to keep my distance have been moved to want greater closeness with this woman. New territory.

I guess I don't know what she does with her feelings when she's acting like a human computer. Of course, I really don't know what I do with mine when I am being a glad-handing politician. They just get pushed to the background, I guess. If I survive the next few weeks, I'll have to look into that.

At the moment, however, the realization that we were about to move from the discussion to the action phase became more and more palpable as we approached DC. A sobriety, a clarity descended on us. Neither of us spoke much. As the nation's capital came into view, I felt a silence I have never before felt. It was religious, almost, like the silence monks attain when they are all meditating in a room together. Or the natural silence that settles over the earth just before a thunderstorm or a tornado is about to hit. Eerie. Beautiful, but eerie.

Dora was driving on the last leg of our journey, and instead of turning west toward Georgetown or straight for her apartment at the Watergate, she turned east on New York Avenue toward Columbia Park Road. I looked over at her with a quizzical expression.

"A safe house," she said. "I was in New York to meet with some people who specialize in this sort of thing, and they set it up. Off the grid."

Just like the place in Ocean City, I thought. I still have questions about how far off the grid you could get in the capital city of a country that felt itself under siege. But I didn't argue the point. It would be better than returning to either of our apartments.

She drove to a small street in a part of the District with which I was unfamiliar. It was shabby but not seedy. Probably just poor. She pulled a small transmitter out of her purse and opened an automatic garage door. She pulled in without a word, closed the door, and killed the engine. Then she sighed.

"We'll be safe here for now," she said.

We got out of the car and Dora unlocked the door to the small house. It was clean inside; it looked as if someone actually lived there. I walked in first. It was about the size of a garden apartment, with a small galley kitchen, an eating area, and a living room space. It had one bedroom and a large closet.

The refrigerator was filled with food, as was a small pantry to the left of it. *This is too much like the movies*, I thought. What kind of company, agency, or person specializes in setting up safe houses? The only agency I knew that did that was the CIA. I felt certain they were not part of this project.

Dora glanced at the window, presumably to make sure the shade was drawn, which it was, and walked over to the corner of the dining area. She bent over and removed a small piece of base molding. It revealed a button, which she pushed twice. Soundlessly, the floor in the small hall we entered from the garage moved to reveal a hidden cache of supplies of a different sort. I walked over to it and looked down. It didn't take me long to spot a rifle, several handguns, and a few grenades. There was some other stuff, but it was too dark to see.

Then Dora was beside me with a flashlight. "I don't know if you can use this stuff," she said. "But here it is in case you can." She looked down at the hole, avoiding eye contact.

I took the flashlight and bent down for a closer look. The space was not large, about half the size of a coat closet, but it was packed with military grade hardware: plastique, detonators, wire, assorted types of guns and ammunition, and assorted bomb-making equipment. "Wow," I said.

"I just wanted to let you know this was here," Dora said. She led me back to the corner of the dining area and pressed the button again. Without a sound, the floor slid back into place. I walked back over to see if I could discern the outlines of the opening. I could not. Top flight construction work.

"OK," said Dora, "let's talk about the plan." She went to the car to retrieve the notebook that contained Bandera's schedule, and she sat down at the small table. I sat down next to her. She pulled out a sheet of paper and a pen, and she seemed poised to write something.

"You think the best time is when he is *en route*," Dora said. There was no sign of emotion in her voice; she was all analytic task-master.

The moment felt queer. When I was in the military, I was briefed on my mission, but I did not often participate in the actual planning. I did the implementation on the ground and at times had to improvise. I was familiar with tactics and planning, but mostly from an observer's perspective. Formulating a plan to kill someone seemed colder than actually doing it. I swallowed my reservations and forged ahead.

"Yeah," I said. "That way I can position myself from any one of a number of vantage points far enough away from the target."

We reviewed the times Bandera would be out of his office. We knew his destinations, but we did not know his routes. That probably wasn't a big problem, given traffic patterns and the ways DC streets are laid out. Unless he is deliberately trying to evade detection, his routes should be fairly predictable.

We selected three times when he would be vulnerable, one each for Monday, Tuesday, and Wednesday of the upcoming week. Dora produced a large map of DC, and I studied it to identify possible positions for me to station myself. Adrenaline was beginning to course through my body. I needed to calm myself down. I got up and walked into the kitchen and began opening cabinet doors until I found what I was looking for.

I returned to the table a minute later with an unopened bottle of Grey Goose and two glasses I found in an upper cabinet. "Whoever stocked this place knew what he was doing," I said to Dora.

She just shrugged. I wondered if she was being stalwart or if she was just warding off her own anxiety and ambivalence about this enterprise. I poured us both a glass of the transparent liquid. "Ice?" I asked.

She looked at the glass for a moment. "Please," she said, and I fetched some ice cubes from the dispenser on the front of the refrigerator.

"Here's to the future," I said, raising my glass and clinking it on hers. "The future," she replied in a small voice.

"Who did this place?" I asked.

Dora looked at me for a long moment. "I don't know that it's in your best interest to know," she said.

"Not in my best interest!" I exploded. Then my voice dropped to an acid whisper. "Dora, we are talking about my taking people's lives. My interests take on a certain importance because of that, don't you think?"

Dora looked away in that annoying way she has. As if she is

managing a defiant teenager. Then she turned her head to look at me squarely. "It is important for you not to know in the event that you get caught; you cannot reveal information you do not have." Her voice was monotonic: no emotion, absolutely even. Firm.

I glared back at her like a defiant teenager who just lost a point. I took a deep breath. "OK," I said acidly.

We went on to other things. We talked about how, how much, and how often we would communicate. We talked about how likely it was that the FBI had included me on their watch list because of my association with Dora. We talked in general terms of going down the list of the twelve cameo heads on the website. I got it that Dora thought we should not be in too close contact. I didn't like that.

At about 4:00 p.m., Dora drove me to my apartment. It was Saturday, and my staff wasn't expecting me back till Sunday evening. I was sad to leave Dora, but I needed some time alone, time to focus on how I would execute the first step of this plan. In the car, I kissed her gently on the cheek, and she touched my arm with her free hand.

"I'll be in touch, Jake," she said softly. I nodded and got out of the car.

Chapter 23

I was relieved to be alone in my apartment. I love Dora, but being around her for long periods of time drained me—it always did when I was around women one on one, even ones who were soul mates.

My apartment seemed empty when I walked in. It was not unusual for me to be away for days or even weeks at a time, especially in the summer when Congress was in recess. In another week, the office would be down to a skeleton crew, just enough people to track polling, deal with the constant flow of mail, and keep inertia away. But for the most part, after next week, I won't have any reason to be in DC. I will have good reason to be in Wisconsin, but I could really be anywhere. It was vacation time. I didn't have any junkets planned, although there were still a few possible trips where I could tag along. South Africa, I recall, and maybe Argentina.

I sat down on my sofa and considered the options. I had to retrieve the part of my gun from Union Station, but I didn't know if it was safe to do that yet. I wouldn't really have to use my own gun, but I wanted to. It would be very hard to trace. Plus, I knew how it felt; I knew its heft and balance. I didn't want to have to contend with a new piece of machinery right now.

I thought about Dora's idea that I dispatch Bandera in some

way that would not be so noticeable. I guess she meant poison or a bomb or something, but I wasn't very familiar with those methods. I am a sniper. I shoot people. I never considered doing it any other way.

So I thought about how this could be done. Despite my cavalier dismissal of Dora's concerns about the locked down capital, it would not be the easiest thing to pull off a clean shot in the middle of downtown DC and get away with it. But then again, I didn't really know. I hadn't actually sat down and devised a plan. That was what I wanted to do this afternoon. I got up and walked to the small desk in the corner of my living room. I pulled out a piece of paper and a pen. I put them on the coffee table and then went into my kitchen to make a pot of coffee. I needed to plan.

As I waited for the coffee, I looked around my apartment. It was a little warm, so I turned down the air conditioner to a more comfortable level. The thermostat was on the wall in a small hall outside my bedroom. The door to my bedroom was standing open, as it usually is, but something registered on the periphery of my mind. Something was amiss. I froze in place and scanned what I could see of the apartment from where I stood. I listened closely. My adrenaline was flowing; I could hear my own heartbeat.

Then I recognized it. The window in my bedroom was not closed. In fact, the door to the bedroom was not open all the way, as I thought it usually is. I listened even more intently. Could the bad guys have pegged me as someone who would stand in the way? If they knew about Dora, they could easily know about me. How careful was Dora? She was pretty flagrant when she evaded the FBI the day after we met. Somebody knows something about her. Or maybe, as she thinks, someone was just sending her a message; trying to scare her. The same could be true for me.

It was working. My blood kept pounding, and I slowly pushed the bedroom door all the way open. I was tense, ready to spring into action. I didn't hear anyone, but people can keep deathly still if they are trained properly. I had to know if someone had gotten the gun stock out of my bedroom closet.

I stared at the closet for a long moment. If someone was in there, I guess I had to defend myself. If they were armed, that might be a bad choice. But even the thought that an essential part of my sacred object might be gone or compromised in some way propelled me into action. I grabbed the cheap brass doorknob and pulled the door open as quickly as I could, hoping to startle anyone who might be in there. It was dark. And quiet.

Clothes were hung neatly on either side of the good-sized space, and there was no movement. I squatted to see if what I could see beneath the jackets, shirts, and hanging trousers. Finally, I pushed my arms against the hanging clothes. Nothing. Then I pulled back the organizer that held my shoes. My hands were sweating at the implications of a missing gun. Scenes of exposure, blackmail, and death threats filled my mind. I willed them away as I pulled the valise out of its hiding place.

As I felt the gun stock through the synthetic covering of the black carry-on, my heart rate began to decelerate. I took big gulps of air to regulate my breathing. I took the travel bag and set it on the bed and walked over to the window. The sash was about three inches above the sill, too small a space for someone to enter or exit. I thought back to determine if I had opened this window at anytime and perhaps forgot to close it. I didn't think so. After examining the glass to see if there were any unusual smudges or fingerprints, I closed the window completely and turned the sash lock on the top.

Then I remembered that this window only opens up six inches. I unlocked it and tried to open it all the way, and, sure enough, it jammed at about six inches. *Perhaps someone tried to get in*, I thought, and decided against breaking the window itself. But before I gave that more thought, I returned to the agenda of checking out the rest of the apartment. I closed the window and locked it. Then I turned and began as careful an inspection of my bedroom as I could. I looked under the bed; I checked the lamp for listening devices; I scanned the walls and ceilings carefully. Then I pulled the bed from against the wall and removed all the linens, examining each one in turn. Then I eyeballed the mattress and the springs underneath. When I was satisfied, I walked back out into the hall. I took the travel bag with me.

I checked the guest room with similar care. I took the firing mechanism and its own travel case from its hiding place and put it next to the other one in the hall. Then I checked every window in the apartment and every closet. I checked the kitchen and opened every cabinet door. I emptied each cabinet drawer. I looked into each cup and plate and glass and utensil. I tore apart the sofa and the chairs in the living room, looking for I wasn't sure what.

I knew this inspection was something I had to do, but I also knew it could not possibly reveal every possible way in which my apartment might have been tampered with. Snooping devices had gotten very small and very sophisticated in recent decades, and I didn't know enough about current technology to know if I could find them or not. What I did know was that the FBI or the CIA or some other government agency knew all there was to know about these things and had them at their disposal.

So I had to take extra precautions. I could not open the bags with the gun parts for fear of video surveillance. Nor could I speak about anything of substance aloud while in the apartment. I had to assume the phone was bugged. I wondered absently if cell phones could be bugged as well. I had to assume they could until I found out differently.

Suddenly the apartment that I had grown so fond of seemed like an alien and even hostile place. I didn't want to stay here, but this was my address in DC.

I had only taken a small carry-on to Wisconsin, and it was still sitting in the living room by the sofa. I decided to take what I needed for a longer stay, so I pulled down my large suitcase and started packing. To muffle noise, I turned on the stereo as loud as I could without disturbing the neighbors. It felt stupid to do that, but

I was not going to take any chances.

It only took me fifteen minutes to pack. I placed my gun cases in the larger suitcase and filled the remaining space with clothes. I hauled my belongings outside and hailed a taxi. I directed the driver to take me to the nearest car rental agency. It was close, within four blocks. Once there, I got in a short line to rent a Toyota Camry for two weeks.

The rental agency wasn't far from Union Station, and I decided to go ahead and collect my gun. I was filled with angry determination after abandoning my apartment. So I parked in the lot and strode into the Station with a pumped up sense of self-importance. Damn the torpedoes. I walked into the hall where the lockers were and went straight for number twelve. I pulled the small suitcase out of the locker, turned, and strode out of the station and back to my car. After pulling into traffic, I began to feel relief. I had all the parts to my weapon. Whatever else happened, I was whole again.

I drove across town to where the safe house was. On the way, I called Dora to tell her as vaguely as I could what had happened. She listened intently—only Dora can listen intently over a phone line—and communicated with equal vagueness that she thought the safe house was a good idea for now. She told me to make sure I wasn't being followed. It was business.

After I clicked off, I turned north and started checking my rearview mirror. No one. I turned back west and kept it up. After driving in a huge square, I was unable to identify anyone following me in any kind of vehicle. So I drove on to the safe house, my eyes never too far from the rear view mirror.

I pulled into the garage with the small transmitter Dora had given me. I didn't bring all my suitcases in, but I opened the trunk and took my overnight bag. Then I opened the large suitcase and took the smaller ones out with the gun parts in them.

After unlocking the door to the smaller apartment, I put my things down and looked around. It felt cramped but safe. I checked the windows and doors and made sure they were locked. Then I took my gun out and assembled it in under a minute. Anger soured the inside of my stomach, but no reservations clouded my mind. I pulled out the maps I had with me and began to plan.

Chapter 24

"It was a gas," Dora said the next afternoon when she arrived at the house.

"Gas?" I asked.

"Yes," she said. "Latest surveillance technology. It's a heavier-than-air gaseous substance that can coat an entire apartment or office for about a week." Her teeth were clenched. I could tell she didn't like this anymore than I did. "It coats the entire floor of all adjacent rooms up to about two inches."

"Your window was open for a reason. There has to be another source of air into a unit; otherwise the gas can become toxic. You would start having symptoms similar to those induced by carbon monoxide poisoning: headaches, nausea; that sort of thing." She sighed. "As a matter of fact, this substance is chemically related to carbon monoxide, but doesn't require a burning flame to be produced. It is remarkably stable and doesn't dissipate quickly the way most gases do. It can be transported and injected into a space in a few minute's time."

"What does it do?" I asked.

"It creates a type of echo chamber for sound, so that, with the proper equipment, everything you say or is said in a given space can be picked up within a half-mile radius."

I looked at Dora stonily. I was tagged. She knew it; I knew it. She was also probably tagged too. I felt slimed by some high-tech froth that didn't quite sound real.

We looked at each other in silence for a few moments.

I spoke first. "Tomorrow," I said.

She looked at me and sighed. "Tomorrow."

"How can I help you?" Dora asked.

I thought for a moment. And, as much as I did not want to say what I needed to say, I forced myself. "Leave town. Tonight, if possible. Go far away. And go as publicly as possible. Don't leave the country, but make sure whoever is watching knows you are not here."

Dora nodded. She was thinking. "I can't tonight," she said. "But I can leave in the morning, and I can make sure people know about it."

Then she picked up her cell phone and made arrangements to be in Boston by 9:00 a.m. I didn't know who she was talking to and didn't ask.

"Done," she said.

There was nothing else to say. She knew what would happen tomorrow; I knew it. After a minute, she got up, took my hand, and led me from the small couch to the small bedroom. And for two wordless hours we took possession of each other. We touched, hugged, kissed, clung, and acted as if our world was not going to come crashing down around us.

After Dora left, I knew it was time. I took the Remington apart and packed it neatly in a small lead-lined satchel that was only slightly larger than a typical briefcase. I reviewed the plan in my mind. The opening I would use in one building to aim and fire at a person walking out of another. The shot would be silenced, and it would be hard for anyone to hear it or to identify accurately where it came from, especially in the commotion that invariably followed an assassination. That was the easy part.

The hard part was getting set up in place. The place was the National Gallery of American Art.

Chapter 25

The next morning, I went into automatic mode. I dressed in the typical dark suit that members of the Senate wear routinely and took the case with my beloved Remington inside. I drove to the office and parked in the designated lot. I left the case in the trunk of my car. It was early for me—8:30—but my staff was accustomed to my erratic routines.

I greeted everyone as I did every day and walked into my office. Jamie followed.

She reviewed the schedule for the day. She also asked if I was going to join any of the groups of senators who were traveling during the summer break.

"I don't know yet, Jamie," I said truthfully. "Can you think of any specific reason I should select one of these?"

Jamie thought for a moment. I knew her background. She was from a small town in northern Wisconsin. Very Germanic. Very Lutheran and starchy. She shook her head. "No, Jake," she said. "I really can't."

After we finished the day's schedule and then the week's, I felt certain that I had sufficient blocks of time to do what I was about to do. "I have a luncheon meeting off-campus, and it may go till about three," I said, surprising even myself with the nonchalance of my voice.

Jamie nodded and walked out of my office.

I dug into the paperwork in front of me, which was comprised primarily of reading summaries and reports prepared by my staff of things they thought I should know about upcoming legislation. Since nothing was going to happen during this last week before the summer recess, I figured I was wasting my time. Except that what I was actually doing was not a waste at all. In my head, I was reviewing the plan I had devised to kill the first person I wanted to kill since that sultry day in Africa over two decades before.

The plan was simple; most good plans are. I drive to the Museum of American Art, set up my spot at the appointed time, discharge a single round, pack up, and leave. It was so simple I was a bit light-headed just picturing it in my head.

Of course, I knew the number of things that could go wrong was nearly infinite. That was the ubiquitous possibility in shooting people. But it was my fervent hope that this first assassination would come off without a hitch. Part pride; part wanting to prove to myself that I could do it; part showing off for Dora. Almost fifty years old and still wanting to show off for a girl. I shook my head.

The morning was going quickly enough. At about 10:45, I asked Jamie to call over to Max's office to see if he was free. Then I returned my attention to the paper-laden top of my desk.

A few minutes later, Jamie walked back into my office. She had an odd look on her face. "Max isn't in, Jake. His wife called him in sick this morning."

I almost didn't think anything of it. I nodded and said "OK." But then Jamie said that he had been taken to the hospital for possible carbon monoxide poisoning. That explained the odd look.

"It's July, Jake," she said. "Nobody gets carbon monoxide poisoning in July." She stared at me straight on.

I returned her stare. *No, they don't*, I thought, and the knowledge that Max had been hurt in this business enraged me.

"Get me the number of the hospital," I commanded in a stony voice. Jamie left to fetch it.

I took as deep a breath as I could, closed my eyes, and bent my head over my desk, close to the top. I felt I had been kicked in the stomach. This actually felt worse than realizing I had the gas in my apartment. I straightened and opened my eyes and looked out the window across from my desk. Beautiful summer day in DC, but none of the beauty touched me. My resolved hardened. I did not think that was possible, as I had been unaware of any hesitation since Guy's death.

Jamie came back into the office and gave me the number. I dialed it and nodded for her to leave. She hesitated a moment, and then she walked out the door. She had a frightened look on her face.

I held my breath as I waited to be connected to Max's room. A moment later, a woman's voice answered. "Hello?" It was Max's wife, Darlene.

"Darlene, Jake Telemark," I said. "I just heard about Max."

Darlene let out a long stream of air. "Oh, Jake, It's good to hear your voice. This morning was scary."

"How is Max?" I asked.

"I think he is out of danger, but he vomited half the night. His temperature rose and he said he had a colossal headache. It was a very tough night."

There was something in her voice I couldn't quite pinpoint. I wanted to ask why Max had gotten sick and she had not, but I thought better of it. It turned out I didn't have to.

"All the doctors and nurses asked me why Max got sick and I didn't know," she continued without prompting. "Jake, the truth was that Max slept on the floor in the library last night. We had an argument and he went downstairs." She was crying softly.

"It's OK, Darlene," I said because I couldn't think of anything better.

"We don't know why or how this happened." She hesitated. "I don't think the doctors believed me. They said I shouldn't return to the house until it was checked out thoroughly. Oh, Jake, I just don't know what to do." She continued the soft crying.

It was my turn to take a deep breath. I wasn't sure what to do either. I couldn't exactly invite them to stay with me; nor could I tell her what I knew about the gaseous substance that had crippled her husband.

"Darlene," I said. "I'll be over in about twenty minutes." I paused for a moment. "Just hold on. I think everything will be fine."

With that, we hung up. Darlene was a little bit reassured, but I wasn't. There was nothing about this that would be fine.

I looked up and saw Jamie standing near my door. She genuinely liked Max; most people did. She had the same worried expression on her face that she had ten minutes before.

"Jamie, I'm going to the hospital." I stood up. "I think Max will be alright."

Jamie gave a sigh of relief, and I internally reproached myself for reassuring everyone for no good reason.

The trip to the hospital took precisely twelve minutes. It was almost 11:00 a.m., and I figured I had plenty time to do this before my afternoon chore.

Being a senator does have its rewards, one of which is that most people defer to you automatically. Most senators are easily recognized throughout the District, and today was no exception. I parked in the lot and walked up to the information booth in the lobby of Georgetown University Hospital. An attractive blond woman asked if she could help me. I told her I wanted to see Senator Johansen.

"Yes, sir," she said promptly. And she gave me directions to a room on the third floor of the sprawling complex.

It was remarkably easy to navigate the halls and rooms of the giant facility. I found Max's room with no problem. Darlene was still sitting beside her husband, where I presume she was when we spoke fifteen minutes earlier on the phone.

I knocked gently on the door, and Darlene turned her head. Her face lit up and she got up and threw her arms around me.

"Oh, Jake," she said. "Thank you so much for coming."

I patted her gently back to her seat. I looked over at Max, who had an oxygen mask on his face. His eyes were half closed. "Is he alright?" I asked Darlene.

"The doctor said he was going to be fine," Darlene replied with no conviction in her voice. She still had a look about her that I couldn't quite pinpoint for a moment. Then I recognized it. Guilt. I knew that Darlene felt that she had almost killed her husband for some no doubt inconsequential argument the two of them had the night before. She probably wasn't thinking that her house had been invaded by fanatics who wanted information from Max.

I sat with Darlene for a few minutes and made small talk. Max was asleep, so she retold me the story in more detail, but nothing significant seemed to be added to it. Then a nurse popped her head in and excused herself before she walked over and checked Max' vital signs.

"Stable," she pronounced, smiling at Darlene; then she walked out of the room.

I turned to Darlene. "Is the doctor here?" I asked.

"I think so, Jake," she replied. "He was here just before I called you."

"I'll go check with him," I said, and I got up to leave the room.

I walked up to the nursing station and all eyes turned to me. "May I help you?" said the nurse obviously in charge.

"Yes, I'm looking for the physician attending Mr. Johansen,"

"That would be Dr. Conoria," replied the nurse. "I will get him for you."

Within two minutes, I was speaking with Dr. Edwin Conoria in a small consult room next to the nursing station.

"It looks as if Mr. Johansen will be fine," the doctor was saying, "although we won't know for sure for a couple days about residual cognitive effects."

"Residual cognitive effects?" I asked.

"Any brain damage that might linger. We know there's no gross damage, but what he inhaled was highly toxic, and there may be what we call residual effects: mild memory impairment, word-finding difficulties, stuff like that. Even if there are, they will probably diminish in a few months." He looked at me without a hint of guile in his face. "Mr. Johansen was lucky."

I nodded and didn't say anything for a few moments. Then I forged ahead. "Doctor," I said. "What could have caused this? Darlene—Mrs. Johansen—said you thought it was carbon monoxide. But it's July."

Edwin Conoria shrugged. "We are running tests on the substance now. We think it was probably carbon monoxide poisoning because of the way he presented when he showed up in the ER this morning. But it's not a perfect match. We can do some lab work to get a more precise read on what the substance was, but I am afraid that will take time."

I nodded. "But he'll be OK?"

The doctor nodded. "I think so," he said. "If something changes, would you like us to contact your office?"

I was surprised and pleased. "Yes, please." We shook hands and ended our conversation.

I was relieved. I walked back into the small hospital room and patted Darlene on the shoulder. I told her what the doctor had said. Then I went over and patted Max on the shoulder. I knew he was alive, but he looked to be close to death. I turned to Darlene. "I will be in touch," I said, and I left.

Driving away from the hospital, I had several thoughts. One was that what was in my apartment may not have been just about me, but rather about all the middle-of-the-road senators, including Max, upon whom the bad guys were spying. This may be something I could check out. That gave me some additional relief. I needed it because I couldn't stand to wait for another minute to get on with the day's task.

Chapter 26

The western wing of the National Museum for American Art is a sprawling building across the street and a block and a half away from the Justice Department. At about 1:15, Roger Bandera was scheduled to walk out the front door of the Justice Department Building toward a car waiting at the curb of Constitution Avenue. The car and driver were to take him across the Ellipse to a meeting at the State Department, where he was scheduled to have a luncheon meeting with, among others, Geoffrey Addelburg, the man with whom he traveled to Wisconsin to meet with Guy Tessero. The walk from the door to the car would take approximately ten to fifteen seconds.

At the southwest corner of the Museum, near the rear, is a lower level with windows that give directly to Constitution Avenue with a clear view of the sidewalk in front of the Justice Department. Even though it is on the lower level, the museum sits high. The window is positioned above grade, so that you can see the entrance of Justice above the heads of anyone strolling between the two buildings or in front of some of the other buildings that line the street. Because it is over a block away, it will be hard to pinpoint where the bullet came from. It's a perfect spot.

I parked on the street in front of the museum and pumped

quarters into the meter. Two hours. Then I took the lead-lined case from the trunk and strode confidently toward the main entrance of the museum.

Even in lock-down mode, Washington is a distinctly American phenomenon. That is, even when security is tightened, the city is still basically an open place. Excessive surveillance and restriction are just not American. So when I got to the metal detector and the guard just past the entrance to the museum, I put my case through the x-ray machine. I thought the lead lining would protect any detection of what was inside, but, as with all planning, I was acutely—and anxiously—aware that things could go wrong. They could have updated their equipment; they could have demanded that I open it; they could have prevented me from taking it into the museum itself.

Fortunately, the middle-aged, African-American female guard at the entrance recognized me. "Good morning, senator," she said with a big smile. I smiled back. "Good morning," I said. "Lot of business today?"

"Not much," she replied. "City's been quiet since Denver." She sighed as if the events in Colorado saddened her because of the negative impact they had on District tourism. She looked at me the whole time my case passed through the detection machine.

"It'll pick up," I said cheerfully, collecting my bag on the other side of the conveyer belt. "See you in a while."

I walked on through the enormous chamber that spanned the depth of the western museum wing. It was a beautiful place filled with beautiful things. There were some people milling about, looking at the paintings. But in general, it was very quiet.

I walked to the back of the room and found the stairs to the lower level. I made my way toward the southwestern corner and located the storage room I had picked out for my spot. I checked the time. Only 12:15. An hour to wait, to prepare. Plenty of time.

One of the many skills snipers learn is lock picking. It took a few seconds to open the door knob lock and enter the small room.

The space itself was almost empty. Some old wooden crates lined the walls, but it was clear that no one came here very often. I put my case down and pulled on a pair of plastic gloves. I didn't want any evidence, even though I did not think that anybody would identify this place as the source of the gunshot.

I began to turn the ancient crank that controlled the opening of the window. Judging from the dust, this window had probably not been opened for decades. It didn't budge. I stepped back to examine the window, the bottom of which stood at about chest height. Then I saw that there were screws holding the window in place. I knelt down to open my case, which had some tools in it. Fortunately, one of those tools was a screwdriver. I slowly turned each of the six screws that held the window closed. When I was finished, I turned the crank. The window opened easily. *Solid construction*, I thought.

I looked through the window at the bright DC day shining on the botanical gardens just to the west of the museum. I could smell the sweet scent of many different kinds of flowers combining their magic to create a new, wholly different smell. It was intoxicating. I breathed it in deeply. Then I knelt down to assemble my Remington.

Weapon assembled, I stepped back from the window so that no part of the gun protruded beyond the pane. I looked through the long scope to the entrance of the Justice Department Building and quickly adjusted the focus to a man in a dark suit walking jauntily along the boulevard. Then I turned the muzzle toward the doors through which Roger Bandera would be walking within the hour. Confident that I had done everything I could, I put my gun down, closed the window, and waited.

My mind was empty. I wasn't happy or sad, angry or pleased. I did not think of people I loved or my own death. I didn't think of anything. At some point during these minutes, I had fallen into the kind of trance that has probably been familiar to assassins down through the centuries. Numbness in the face of death. It seemed like the most reasonable thing in the world.

Time passed. I kept my eye on my watch. At 1:10, I reopened the window and lifted my Remington to the sill. The front entrance of the Justice Building is mostly glass, and through the scope I could make out who was walking toward the door. This gave me a few additional seconds to adjust my weapon, to follow my mark, and then to pull the trigger.

At precisely 1:12, Roger Bandera walked toward the door of the Justice Department and put his hand on the door itself. Well before 1:13, he lay dead on the sidewalk of Constitution Avenue. Having pulled the trigger, I put the Remington down, closed the window and screwed it back into place. I dissembled the weapon, and placed it neatly in the case. I removed the plastic gloves and threw them into the case as well. Then I closed and locked the case and left the small storage room where my past, present, and future met.

I walked back up the stairs and circled around the back of the large museum, casually holding onto my case and looking at the paintings on the walls. Then I smiled and waved to the guard, who had obviously not yet heard of any problem outside, and walked out the front door. I walked to my mid-size sedan and calmly opened the trunk. I put the case inside and drove off.

The car had been parked facing east, away from the pandemonium I could detect through my rear view mirror. I hesitated for a moment and then turned on the radio. The regular programming had been interrupted with reports from the nation's capital that someone had been assassinated. No one was sure who, but indications were that it was an official from the Justice Department. Then they announced the name: Roger Bandera. He had been shot right in front of the Justice Department Building in the middle of the day.

Why did that shock people so much? I wondered. *Better to shoot someone in the middle of the day, when you can see them clearly and where there is little chance of a rifle shot being recognized than in the middle of the night when the light is lousy and someone might see a muzzle flair. Only criminals kill at night.*

I drove on to the safe house and pulled into the small garage. I unloaded the case from the trunk and deposited in into the hidden storage space beneath the hall floor. Then I wiped the apartment down for prints, just in case, and left. I drove back to my office. I got caught in traffic and sat in my car as patiently as the thousand or so other drivers who were inconvenienced more or less on a daily basis by politics.

While I waited, my cell phone rang. It was Jamie.

"Jake, have you heard?" she asked.

"About Bandera? Yes, I just heard it on the news, Jamie."

She hesitated. "Are you alright?"

"Yes, Jamie, I'm fine." I said. "I think I'm caught in the traffic jam this thing caused. What's the reaction on the Hill?"

Jamie slipped into her Chief of Staff mode. "All the normal outrage and calls for investigation. He wasn't well known around here." She paused. "I couldn't stand him."

I wanted to smile. *Good taste, Jamie,* I thought. "I'm coming back as soon as I get through this mess. Hold the fort till then."

Then I called the guy I had arranged to see for lunch and told him that I wouldn't be able to make it because of the turmoil in the capital today. Maybe we could reschedule later. I explained to him that I was stalled in the traffic that clogged Constitution Avenue and the streets around Justice. He understood.

I clicked off and sat back and waited until the traffic crept along. I didn't mind. I had to remind myself not to smile too broadly or I might look suspicious. Otherwise, I felt that justice had truly been served this afternoon, and inwardly, I felt proud to be a part of it. Absently, I began to think about what I would do with my apartment. Nothing, I decided. If somebody thought I was a threat, staying away from my apartment just to avoid the gas might confirm in someone's mind that I was involved with the counterplot. I could easily return and go about my life with little chance of saying something that would incriminate me or jeopardize Dora's plan. In my mind, I would dare them to implicate me.

Chapter 27

When I got back to the office, the televisions were all on to CNN reporting the story that Roger Bandera had been shot and killed in broad daylight right in front of the Justice Department. There were short biographies of the man, pictures of him and of his grieving family. That included his parents and siblings, since Roger was not married. The news people were somber and respectful as they interviewed anyone with any kind of relationship with him.

Then the network turned its attention to the meaning of this and tried to speculate as to why an official of Justice would be killed at this time. Everyone tried to connect it to what had happened in Denver, but no one was having any luck making a credible connection. What they did have was a sense of impending doom, a feeling that things were going bad, a fear that more bad things might happen.

It wasn't until an interview with Richard Reed, Director of the Christian Covenant, that the connection was made.

"These events clearly demonstrate the failure of the secular government," Reverend Reed stated flatly. "They are reminiscent of the plagues visited on Egypt during the reign of the corrupt Pharaoh, who refused to allow the Israelites to depart. More desolation will be visited upon this country until we repent and turn back to our Christian roots."

So much for a pluralist society, I thought. Jamie was shaking her head. She looked at me with a look that wasn't exactly sad; it was a look of incredulity. I nodded for her to follow me into my office.

"How're you doing, Jamie?" I asked.

She sat down without being invited, a small but noticeable breach of protocol. "I don't agree with murder, Jake, but if it had to be someone, better a sanctimonious bureaucrat than Max Johansen or Guy Tessero."

I look at her squarely. *What did she know about these deaths? Was she just referencing recent people she knew or did she know something I didn't think she knew?*

"What do you mean, Jamie?" I asked gently.

She looked at me doubtfully. "I don't know about Judge Tessero, Jake, but I just can't believe that Max came down with carbon monoxide poisoning in the middle of summer. I think something is going on here that nobody is talking about."

I usually appreciated Jamie's candor. It was one of the reasons she's my chief. I sighed and paused a moment before I spoke.

"I asked Max's doctor about that, Jamie. He said they were running tests. We will know in a couple weeks if it was deliberate or not." I looked down at my desk for a moment, then back at Jamie. "He also said it wasn't a perfect match for carbon monoxide."

Jamie shook her shoulders as if to awaken herself from a bad dream. "I knew it," she said. There was bitterness in her tone.

"If something is going on, we'll know about it sooner or later, Jamie. Max has a lot of friends." I was making this up as I went along, but it sounded like something that had a chance to reassure my frazzled chief of staff and allow the day's work to proceed.

"I hope you're right, Jake," Jamie said as she stood up.

I spent the rest of the afternoon reviewing the same kinds of reports I had started on in the morning, but I kept the television on in my office. Nonstop coverage with little real news. Reed wasn't the only right-winger who purported to see the hand of God in recent events. Several reverends of his ilk brayed all afternoon about the failures of "the secular state".

Since when did the US government become so suspect? I wondered. *When did it go from being "our government" to "that government"? Did these people really want to return to the 'good ole' days', when people could be prosecuted for their beliefs or killed for disagreeing? Did we really want to reinsert religion into government, when the Founding Fathers worked so hard to draw such an unmistakable and useful line between them? Did we want to abandon the territory that science and rational discourse had held for the last several centuries? Did no one read history?*

One of the main reasons I kept the television on was not to produce materials for internal rants against fanatics. I hoped I would see Dora. After all, she did have some professional connection with Bandera in addition to dating him for a while. I did not know where she was, and she hadn't called me. I thought that was a good idea. But she did not appear on the screen, at least not on the channels I was watching.

At about 4:30, my private line rang. *Must be Dora*, I thought, and reached for the phone with anticipation. But when I picked up the receiver, there was no one. The line was silent. "Hello?" I said, and then repeated it. A sensation of fear rippled down my spine.

I still had the phone in my hand when Jamie came in and handed me a small sealed envelope. I put the phone down and looked at her quizzically. "A guy came up to the receptionist's desk and handed her a note saying he was deaf. Then another saying that this should be delivered to you personally." Jamie looked at me. "Do you want me to call security?"

I hesitated just a moment, just long enough to make the connection that Jefferson was deaf. "No, Jamie, but did you get a look at the guy?"

"Yes," she replied. "He was a large African-American man dressed in a business suit."

"It's OK, Jamie, thanks," I said. I'll take care of this."

As soon as Jamie walked out of my office, I slit open the dainty envelope. In small hand-printed letters, the note said "PLEASE COME WITH ME". I stood up and walked into the outer office. Jamie was leaning over Sarah's desk talking. "I'm leaving, Jamie, I'll see you tomorrow." Then to Sarah. "Good-night, Sarah." Then I walked out the main office door and took the elevator to the ground floor. When I got off the elevator, I spotted Jefferson instantly. He nodded his head in the direction of the front door, and I followed him to the BMW that was waiting at the curb.

After a wordless, hour-long drive through Maryland, we arrived at the cabin Dora had taken me to right after I met her. As Dora had done then, Jefferson pulled into the small, one-car garage and killed the engine. He motioned for me to proceed to the house. I looked at him quizzically and said, "What about you?"

It was apparent that Jefferson could read lips. He motioned that he was staying with the car, and insisted that I proceed to the cabin. I nodded, but I was uneasy. The area between the small garage and the cabin was about twenty yards. Anxiety flooded through my body, I felt like an easy target. I tried to suppress my fear and was successful only to the point of not throwing up. I kept walking until I got to the cabin door. I turned the knob and pushed the door open.

Dora was standing on the other side of the door. She looked at me with an expression I had not seen on her. She was doubtful, uncertain. I took a step into the cabin and looked around. She stepped back and allowed me to enter, but she did not touch me or hug me or give any inviting sign. There was no one else in the cabin. I stood there for a moment waiting for some cue from Dora, who finally gestured with her head for me to sit on the couch. I did, and she sat on the same couch on the other end.

"Dora," I said. "What's the matter?"

Dora cleared her throat. "I did as you instructed me, Jake. I was in Boston this morning. I just got back here a half an hour ago."

She paused. I had no idea where she was going.

Then her eyes filled with tears. "Three of my girls disappeared this afternoon," she said bitterly.

"Before I left, I told them to take cover, to have no further contact with the men they were seeing; to leave town if necessary. But three of them either did not get the message or did not believe me." She forced her lips together to stop herself from breaking down into sobs. "I can't contact them. I am worried sick."

I shifted my weight, not so much pulling up beside her as entering closer into her orbit. I put my hand on her shoulder. "How do you contact them?" I asked softly.

"I either call them directly on their cell phones or leave a coded text message." She looked over at me. "I sent the highest priority message for each of them to contact me. All of them did except for Melissa, Nora, and Jaclyn."

"Have you called them at home? Maybe they forgot their cell phones," I said stupidly.

Dora looked at me with appropriate disdain. "Of course I called them at home. And at work. No answer anywhere."

"Where can we look?" I asked.

Dora gave me a look of relief. She took my hand. "Thanks, Jake." Then she started talking about where they lived and worked. I took some notes in coded form on a piece of paper I had pulled from my pocket.

"Dora," I said. "I'll see what I can do."

Dora looked at me with drier eyes. She draped an arm around my waist and whispered in my ear, "Good work this afternoon," although I couldn't tell from her tone if she meant it. She thanked me again. I hugged her; and I left.

I walked slowly back to the car where Jefferson was still waiting, and I wrote the destination I wanted on a corner of the same piece of paper. He nodded, started the engine, and pulled the BMW out of the small garage. Within minutes, we were headed back to DC.

On the way back, I tried to think of how to proceed with

finding these girls. I didn't have a plan. Nor did I think it would be wise for me to use my staff or other resources to check on the whereabouts of these young women. I wondered why Dora had me hauled all the way past Ocean City to tell me this. I guessed she was wary of telephone communication. Since the drive back was going to take some time, I put this out of my mind, sank back into the soft leather seat, and tried to fall asleep. But even the undulating Maryland scenery was not enough to lull me into sleepiness given the events of the day. I was pumped. Adrenaline was not finished flowing through my body as the trance-like state from earlier in the day diminished. I felt a sense of satisfaction, but I also felt I had more planning and work to do. I wanted to get on with it as soon as possible.

The situation with the girls seemed to me to be a distraction. I determined to do what I could to locate them for Dora's sake, but I wanted to get back to my part in this affair as soon as I could.

In the gathering twilight, I felt the curve of my life, the valence that pointed out the path. I felt little by way of regret—none, really. Roger Bandera had been a part of a plot that killed thousands and might possibly kill many more. He and his band of fanatics wanted to stage a coup in which the voice of the majority would be subservient to the voice of a few. It was a medieval and ill-conceived notion, and every educated impulse in my body revolted against it; as did my more visceral impulses. It fell to me to play a small part in this drama of history, and I was reconciled to doing just that. In my mind, I flipped through the list of remaining targets.

Chapter 28

Jefferson dropped me off at my apartment, and it was dark by the time I arrived. I unlocked the door and flipped on the light, a little wary of what I might find. I had come to the conclusion that the gas they had installed when I was in Wisconsin wasn't just for me. They had evidently used it in Max's apartment and probably others as well.

As I went from room to room, I flipped on the light. When I got to my bedroom, I paused for a moment and then turned the light on. The window was still closed. I walked over to it and opened it. Then I went around the apartment and opened every window I could. I did not want to have the kind of toxic reaction Max had.

I suppose that if someone were listening, they could hear each window opening. And I suppose that the sound would tip them off that I knew what they were up to. At the moment, I didn't care. All I wanted was some fresh air. Fortunately, there was a breeze this evening, and it felt good.

I went to the kitchen to see what I could find to eat. As I did so, I flipped on the television. There was still a lot of coverage of the shooting earlier in the day. The FBI said they had no suspects and no leads. There was outrage, but it was muffled, except from like-minded types. Geoffrey Addelburg was interviewed because Bandera's secretary had told the press that was where Bandera was headed when he was killed. The interview with Addelburg must have been taped earlier in the day; I thought he looked rattled.

Good, I thought. *The message was received. You cannot just kill thousands of people without consequences. Without paying a price.*

I flipped off the television and sat down on the stool at the side of the kitchen counter that served as a bar. From my stool, I could see the front window of the apartment and the lit street lights outside. I recalled the feeling I had when I was in the Army as a sniper after I shot somebody. Or rather, I remember the lack of feeling I had. It wasn't numbness exactly, although it was related to it. It was a sense of rightness, of resignation, of being in the groove that was cut for me when I arrived on this planet. It seemed weird, even grandiose, except that it wasn't something to shout about. In fact, it was something to remain silent about, since it was only silence that allowed the feeling to persist, to seep down into my psyche and let me know that what I was doing. Although, to most minds, my path was morally repugnant, it was what I was here to do. Still sounds a little crazy.

After a while, I put my dishes in the sink and walked around the apartment again, closing most of the windows and turning out lights. I went into the bathroom, brushed my teeth, and looked at myself in the mirror. I saw neither reproach nor approbation. Just me. I turned out the bathroom lights and got into bed. I immediately fell into a deep and dreamless sleep.

Chapter 29

The next morning, I got up early and felt refreshed. I got dressed and drove to the office in a pretty good mood. Jamie came in with a cup of coffee and with the schedule for the day.

"How are you, Jamie?" I asked. One of the nice things about my chief of staff was that I liked her a lot, so the question wasn't mere formality.

Jamie looked at me with tired eyes. "I'm alright, Jake," she said. "But I can't help feeling that something big and bad is going down." She paused for a moment before continuing. "There've been a lot of meetings going on where you've not been invited." She looked at me. "Not just you, but none of the moderate Republicans."

I didn't say anything. We went over the floor schedule for the day. It seemed like the usual round of business. There was a vote scheduled for a bill I had been involved in, but that wasn't until later in the day.

"Jamie," I said. "In case you haven't noticed, there are several groups of my esteemed colleagues who do not invite me to their private meetings. The Senate is polarized, and the extremes only want the moderates involved at the last minute, and then only if absolutely necessary." Jamie shrugged, but did not otherwise respond.

"What?" I asked.

"That's true, Jake," she replied. "But it just feels different around here." She looked away. "Maybe it's just the Denver thing and Bandera's assassination. Everything feels unsettled."

I nodded, and we finished our business.

Since it was only a few days before the summer recess, I thought I would stroll over to the chamber and listen in. Much of Senate business is recognizing this or that person or institution or agency and it can feel self-congratulatory. But business does get done, and important matters are discussed routinely. I could read about what happens in chamber in the *Congressional Record*, but anyone can do that. To be there and be a part of the actual discussion: that's the honor of being a senator.

On the other hand, little business happens right before the summer break. Mostly people are preparing for their summer traveling or vacations. It's usually a pleasant time around Capitol Hill.

When I walked into the chamber, however, I got a whiff of what Jamie was talking about. Senator Hodges from Mississippi was giving an overheated speech about the present dangers to the Republic, including the Denver massacre and the assassination of a Justice Department official.

". . .and how can this be," the senator was bellowing, "that in our God-fearing nation, no one, no man, no woman, no child is safe from the diabolic forces currently roaming our country with impunity. Our sense of order is lost." He stopped for a moment and picked up a water glass to take a drink. Then he mopped his large brow and continued.

"My esteemed colleagues, we must look beyond a quick fix for this situation. We must repent. Repent! I say, and finish the work begun by our founding fathers to build a great Christian nation out of these United States."

I looked around. There were only about a dozen senators in the room, but the ones who were there were listening intently. *What kind of folderol was this?* I wondered.

Next up was Dick Gruber, the wacko from Maine who had wanted to arrest Willy Maelstrom.

Dick began speaking very slowly. This was odd, because usually he talks so fast that people can't understand him very well.

"I want everyone present to know that this is a momentous step, and that it has the full support of the Senate. . . "

What is such a momentous step? I wondered. Then I saw that each senator present had a shiny black packet at his desk; each one was treating it as if it were sacred.

Gruber continued, "So I ask that this proposal be granted by unanimous consent of the Senate, and that it become the basis for subsequent action among the states."

Hodges was making a move to second the call for unanimous consent, but I shot up first. "I call for a quorum," I yelled.

Everyone in the Senate chamber turned and looked at me. There were several minutes of silence.

"The rules allow me to call for a quorum if it looks as if there isn't one," I continued yelling. "I call for a quorum of the United States Senate."

Gruber glared at me with a hateful look on his face. "The senator from Wisconsin has called for a quorum, consistent with the rules of the Senate," he said. "Be it so ordered."

The clerk began to call out senators' names. I pulled out my cell phone and called Jamie. "Get the press in here, Jamie," I demanded. "Also, get our block of senators on the floor now." I clicked off.

There was silence in the chamber except for the clerk calling the names of each senator. Only occasionally would there be a response, since there were so few senators present. Within minutes, however, journalists began to arrive. A few minutes after that, some of my colleagues began to arrive.

I saw Hodges take his shiny black folder and put it under his desk. The other senators who were originally present looked as if they weren't sure what to do. After what seemed like an endless time, the roll call ended. "The Senate does not have a quorum," the clerk advised Gruber. Gruber looked around at the new people in the hall. "I order a recess for twenty minutes," he said, and stormed off the dais.

I signaled for members of my little cadre of senators to gather. We went up to the clerk and asked him to read the proceedings when this last debate started. We stood there and listened. And what we heard was dumfounding.

Hodges had introduced a call for a constitutional convention.

My cell phone rang. It was Jamie, who was out of breath. "Jake," she cried.

"What, Jamie?"

Silence on the phone. She was breathing heavily. "What?" I repeated.

She began to speak, her voice breaking up and cracking. "Jake," she said. "Thirty-eight state legislatures have introduced resolutions calling for a constitutional convention."

"What?" I cried. What I thought was a small but tightly-organized conspiracy had suddenly turned into a juggernaut.

I stood in the middle of the Senate chamber dumbfounded. This was obviously way bigger than even Dora had intimated. I looked around. Half of my small group were on their cell phones, no doubt having the same conversation I was having. We looked at each other, incredulous about what we were hearing.

Then I realized that Jamie was still on the line. She was obviously relating to me what she was watching on a news channel. "It looks like separatist and Christian groups from each of these states have organized to present these resolutions." She paused for a moment. "Some are right-wing and some are just plain nuts."

How did these groups pull off such a massive organizational effort under the radar? "What's happening right now, Jamie?" I asked.

"It looks like a few of the legislatures are getting ready to vote on the resolutions. The other ones are still talking." A pause on the line. "They're all red states, Jake. In fact, they are all the red states."

Jamie started spewing information. "Half the states have constitutional amendments banning gay marriage. A quarter of them require the teaching of Intelligent Design in science classes. Another two-thirds have outlawed stem-cell research. All of them allow concealed weapons." She was obviously relating what she was learning on whatever television stations she was watching.

She continued, "CNN has been polling all afternoon. That old guy who does their statistics is presenting their preliminary findings. Looks like at least some of the proposals are neck-and-neck."

I was ticking off the names of the twelve cameo heads in my mind, picturing the assassination of each. Killing them seemed like a pitifully small and ineffectual response. Maybe I could do it just for the satisfaction of killing those people who were trying to murder our country.

"We can stop this here, Jamie," I said. "Call every senator, tell them what is happening, and tell them to get in here."

At the periphery of my mind, I recognized that it was not like me to take the lead like this. I did not really care, but I am sure some of my colleagues will be surprised that the glad-handing, middle-of-the-road senator from Wisconsin is the one rallying the troops.

Jamie must have gone into overdrive. Within fifteen minutes, the chamber began to fill with senators. The din caused by the conversation was unlike anything I had heard in this hallowed room. Then a senator from California produced a direct TV feed into a small hand-held unit. As many people as could gathered around it; the rest of us hung back and listened to the shocking news. The conversational noise dropped; all that could be heard was the news commentary on the remarkable developments across the US in the red states.

I looked around. Gruber and Hodges were nowhere in sight. My mind was beginning to race. All of the extreme right-wing senators who were here when I arrived were missing from the chamber.

"Get out!" I shouted, almost without thinking about it. "Get out! Your lives are in danger!" The senators turned to me with questioning looks. Then we heard a loud explosion. "Get out!" I repeated.

Everyone began to run for the exits. I tried to determine where the explosion had come from. It was so loud I thought it came from inside the chamber, but I could not see any damage or even smoke. Then I saw it: pale grey smoke wafting into the chamber from the hall. Senators were covering their mouths and noses with handkerchiefs as they made their way through it. *It must not be poison*, I thought. I ran out into the marble hall in front of the Senate Chamber and found other senators and some clerks standing around something I couldn't see. I forced myself to the center of the small crowd and looked down. There, Dick Gruber lay dead, his right arm and half his leg blown off by what appeared to be a hand grenade. There was blood all over his torso, which had a large hole in it. The stench was overpowering. The smell of gunpowder, burnt flesh, and blood.

The sound of the explosion was so loud because of all the marble, I thought. Still, I was not so sure that the danger had passed. The capitol police and paramedics were running toward the crowd of senators. A stretcher was produced, but the police waved it off. Gruber was dead; this was a crime scene.

The police began cordoning off the area. They told the gathering crowd to step away. A perimeter had been set up at the entrances of the Capitol Building with officers in flack jackets and helmets and pistols drawn. They wanted the crowd to disperse, but they also did not want anyone to leave.

My cell phone rang. It was Jamie. "Jake, there was just a news report of an explosion on Capitol Hill. Are you alright?" she asked, the anxiety evident in her voice.

"Yeah, Jamie, I'm alright." In fact, I was feeling better because of the rapid response of the police and the medics. I wondered how this news could have made it to the TV screen so quickly.

I explained to Jamie what I saw and what I thought. I told her about how Gruber and his band had tried to sneak through a resolution calling for a constitutional convention with only a dozen senators present. Then I told her how those twelve men left as the others arrived and how everyone was listening to TV when an explosion went off. Gruber was found dead in the hall outside the chamber. It looked like an accident. My guess was that he had intended to throw the grenade into the chamber, but it must have gone off prematurely. *Score one for our side*, I thought.

Jamie listened without saying anything. When I got to the part about the capitol police and the medics and now the FBI, which was arriving as I spoke with her on the phone, she began to breathe again. *She is a committed government worker*, I thought; *I am lucky to have her.* "I'll probably be here a while, Jamie," I said. "But I'll come straight back to the office when I'm done."

The feds were questioning everyone who was in the building, so I figured it would take a couple hours before I could leave. I watched them work, carefully gathering clues and evidence. Nobody seemed to know what to think. They had not seen the kangaroo session I walked into barely an hour ago. I looked around until I saw the agent I thought was in charge of the investigation. I walked up to him.

"Agent Banks," I said, looking at the ID tag on his jacket. "I am Senator Telemark. I was here before all the commotion started. I might be a good person to start with."

Robert Banks looked at me with the unrevealing look of a seasoned agent. I must have passed whatever test he was giving me, because after a ten second look-over, he said, "Alright, let's start with what you know."

I told him in detail what happened from the time I walked into the Senate Chamber. I avoided trying to slant anything, but it was pretty clear that the small group that was here was up to something. Banks asked me a few questions, but mostly he took notes.

After I finished my explanation and answered the few questions he had, he asked me where I could be reached. I gave him my card; on the back I wrote my cell phone number. I also asked for his card, which he was reaching for just before I asked.

"If anything else comes up or you think of something else. . ." he said, handing me the small white card with black lettering.

"I will," I responded soberly.

I was cleared to leave, and I didn't waste any time getting back to my office. It was about 3:30, and Jamie, Sarah, and the rest of the staff were quietly going about their business with the televisions on. There was no idle chatter, and the silence was notable as soon as I walked into the antechamber.

I stopped at Sarah's desk to watch for a while with her and the rest of the staff. I figured they needed me around, not behind my private office door. From what I could gather, there were no states that had actually passed the resolution for a constitutional convention. Alabama and Wyoming had just begun voting. The rest were still talking or still getting ready for a vote. Some had adjourned because of what had happened here in Washington.

I was trying to make sense of what was happening. Obviously, the gang of twelve had decided that this was the moment to put their carefully crafted machinery into action. Maybe it was Denver; maybe it was Bandera's death; maybe they had planned to do it at this time all along. But it seemed to catch a wave of public discontent. Many more people than I ever would have expected were saying some version of "Why not?"

As I sat on the edge of Sarah's desk, I had a feeling that something wasn't quite right. I cocked my head at the television, thinking that maybe a change in the angle of approach would jog the incoming data into my conscious awareness. It worked. Not one person had mentioned religion or Christianity or God's will or anything like it. The language being used by the promoters seemed deliberately constructed to avoid it, much like the Intelligent Design folks never mentioned God, even though He was at the heart of their so-called theory. Clever. Worked pretty well for ID; I guess they thought it would work for taking over the country as well.

Wyoming seemed like a special case. Those few souls in the wilderness were just mistrustful of any government, even their own. They did not seem motivated by religion so much as by their insular orneriness. *Let them secede*, I thought.

It was obvious that the talk and the coverage were going to go on late into the night. The imagination of the country seems to have been captured, and pollsters estimated that fully a half of the country was tuned in. The unprecedented explosion in the halls of Congress had heightened the sense of urgency, of immediacy, and of fear.

I shook my head and walked into my office. I sat down in the capacious leather chair behind my desk and looked out the window. There was a term for the theory or the theology behind this, I thought, trying to remember what it was.

I turned to the computer on the corner of my desk and went online. I googled "radical theology" and got a lot of articles about the death of God. Then I googled "christian domination", and got a lot of sites about *Onward Christian Soldiers* and one about Pat Robertson with a reference to what I was looking for: Dominion theology, AKA Reconstruction Theology AKA Theonomy. All of these are names for the belief that Christians must strive for a Bible-based government to replace the one we have. A lot of mainline groups distance themselves from it in public, but an extreme group of Christians embrace it, and it has more sympathy from the faithful than many expect.

Shit, I thought. *These guys have been hiding in the tall grass for a long time, and it appears that now is their chosen time to do what they fanatically believe they are destined to do: dismantle the US government and replace it with a theocracy.*

I turned off my computer and walked out of my office. I needed to think. I needed some rest. I was going home.

Chapter 30

The District was eerily quiet as I drove the rented car to my apartment. I could almost sense the fear that was descending upon the city, maybe upon the whole country. There were other drivers on the road—it was only 5:30—but everything was orderly, almost mannerly. Much less speeding, much less honking; just a wariness as drivers eyed each other, trying to plumb their intentions.

I parked the car on the street near my apartment and walked up the steps to my front door.

Once inside, I weighed whether I should turn the TV on or not. On the one hand, I was sick to death of hearing about what had happened within the past ten hours, but on the other hand, I felt I needed to keep abreast of it. Morbid human fascination with calamity combined with professional interest.

I made some coffee and flipped on the television. CNN was following developments around the country and in Washington with a panel of familiar experts. Most of them scoffed—in a politically correct sort of way—at the notion that one disaster and a couple murders could compel the citizenry to abandon its government and turn to something unproven, unworkable, and unwanted by the majority of citizens. This cold-eyed realism gave me some solace, but I also thought this affair was far from over.

If these people could act so decisively and efficiently in carrying out their evil plans, who knew what atrocities we could be facing over the next days? I plopped down on the couch, put my feet up on the coffee table, and sipped my coffee. I turned the sound down because it was competing with my own interior dialogue. I wanted to think some of this through, although I wasn't sure the thinking would be helpful, as I had already embarked on a course that made me an active if not a major player.

If anything, I was itching to get on with my next job. I couldn't bear the thought that Geoffrey Addelburg was free and alive when Guy Tessero was dead. It was he along with Bandera, I was sure, who made the decision that Guy had to be "dealt with", in that polite turn of phrase favored by fanatics. Guy was dead, and the thought of his murder still brought hot tears of rage and sorrow to my eyes.

My private thoughts and feelings were interrupted by flashing from the TV screen. Wyoming had voted to secede! They had started by talking about a convention, a constitutional convention, not secession. But they had not interrupted their deliberations because of what was happening in far-away Washington DC, and in fact created an opportunity to take this a step further. For the first time since 1861, a state of the United States had elected to withdraw from the Union. Moments later, another flash: Alabama votes to secede. I stared dumbly at the television.

Commentators—no longer scoffing—were pointing out that these developments, while surprising, were catching a wave. The normally cool talking heads relating the news were visibly shaken. Their faces were pale despite their makeup, and the normally insouciant manner of even the most seasoned newscasters was absent; now it was clipped and terse speech. Everyone focused on the historic nature of these declarations, but no one had much else to say. They were blindsided, just as the country was.

Within a half-hour, it was clear that no one was exactly sure of the ramifications of these votes. Did the states have the right to secede? How many states were needed to force a convention? No one on the television seemed to know, but I had a feeling that a certain group knew exactly what the rules were.

I needed to sleep, so I turned the television off and went into the bedroom. The window was still open, and I thought it best to leave it that way, as a precaution. But sleep chose not to visit me then. I sat in the darkness looking out at the hot and humid Washington summer night. I didn't know about the particulars of how this would play out. I knew two things: one was that, as an elected senator, it was my job to preserve, protect, and defend the Constitution of the United States. The second was that I would do this both publicly by speaking out and privately by carrying out the agenda Dora had laid out for me in the spring when we first met. My insides turned cold. Nothing else mattered but these two things.

Chapter 31

I had apparently dozed off sometime after 2:00 a.m. It was now 6:00 a.m., and I opened my eyes to see dawn breaking over the buildings in my Georgetown neighborhood through the same window I had been brooding through last night. It was obvious that I was done sleeping, so I got up and took a shower, hoping that what I had witnessed yesterday had all been a perverse nightmare. I knew it wasn't, but it filled me with rage to even think about it.

As the coffee began to perk, I thought about Dora. I had to contact her. Maybe she had more insight or information about what was happening than I had. I pulled out my cell-phone and punched in her cell number. No answer. I tried her apartment with the same result. I was thinking of calling the think-tank where she worked, but then thought better of it because of the early hour. No one would be there.

I sat down at my small desk and opened my laptop. I listed the names of the remaining eleven men who were originally listed on the Christian website:

Geoffrey Addelburg
George Turner

Francis Kasselbaum
Ronald Edgars
John Truman Powers
Jason Reedy
Paul Venneman
Maximilian Grobe
Harold P. Stokes
P. Marshall Grandy
Jackson L. Lederman

I knew Addelburg would be next; I could feel the rage swell every time his name went through my head. I started to list what I knew about him and his habits. All the while, I was hoping that Dora had a dossier on him similar to what she had given me on Bandera. I judged that she probably did have one, and my untutored efforts to do the intelligence work seemed pointless.

I sat back in my chair and brought the coffee cup to my lips. Since I saw this as a mission, I tended to minimize the possibilities of identification or capture. I knew it could happen, but it seemed a distant and unlikely possibility. Recent events made an impression, however, and I wondered how deeply this network reached. I also thought that killing Addelburg right after Bandera might suggest a pattern to investigators. They might know about the trip to Wisconsin. They would know I was at the funeral. It seemed like a stretch, but people have been fingered for less. I needed to talk some of these things out with somebody. I needed to talk with Dora.

Where are you when I need you? I thought. *Always there*, I responded mentally. The fact was that, except for this particular moment, Dora had always been right where I needed her. I didn't think now would be any different. If she was as taken aback by recent events as I was, I can only imagine she was in overdrive, working whatever sources she had.

That reminded me of the three girls she couldn't contact. I

really didn't know how to go about finding them, especially if I wanted to do it quietly. Dora had given me the contact information she had on them and the protocols they used to maintain contact and evade detection. But the same thought kept going through my mind: I need to talk to Dora.

Where was she? I wondered. Since I didn't have anything to do before I went to work, I decided to go over to her apartment and see if she was there but not answering her phone. I got dressed, finished the rest of my coffee, put my laptop in its carrying case, and headed out the door.

On the way to the Watergate, my anxiety level began to rise. *Is it possible that they got to her? That they "dealt with" her as they had done with Tessero?* My heart began to race as I looked for a parking space near her building. I found one half a block away and got out and pumped money into the meter. I had to remind myself to slow down so as not to draw attention to myself. That was the last thing I needed.

Twenty feet from the door to Dora's building, I heard a car pull up and turned to see Jefferson leaning over to the passenger side window of the silver BMW. When he saw that I spotted him, he motioned for me to come. I got into the car, and we drove away.

I motioned, "What's up?" Jefferson understood but did not respond. Instead, he reached inside his jacket pocket and produced a note. I took it and examined it closely, as if it were a sacred thing.

Jake, if you are reading this, Jefferson must have found you. I am grateful. I have been extra careful these past few days because of the surveillance and because the plan is obviously moving into high gear. Jefferson will bring you to me and we can talk.

Dora

PS. Please destroy this piece of paper.

I breathed a long sigh of relief as I began to shred the small white linen stationary into little pieces. I took small lumps of shredded paper and threw them out the window at intervals. I guess my panic on the way to Dora's had been something that had been rumbling around in my unconscious more than I thought, and I was startled by how frightened I was that something had happened to her. I let myself relax a little.

I expected that Jefferson would drive to Dora's place in Maryland near Ocean City, but instead, he exited DC to the south, and soon we were driving through northern Virginia. *How many places could she have?* I thought. *Who knows?* I replied. I didn't think Jefferson would be forthcoming with information, so I sat back and prepared to enjoy the ride. It was only around 7:30, so I did not feel a compelling need to call Jamie. I thought I would see how the day played out first.

I pointed to the radio, which was not turned on, and Jefferson nodded. I flipped on the news channel, hoping to catch up on any overnight developments. I didn't have to wait long.

Several states had already decided to shift the focus from a constitutional convention to a vote for secession, apparently building on the momentum from last evening in Wyoming and Alabama. North Carolina, Mississippi, and Tennessee were slated to begin voting at 9:00 a.m. Alaska, Vermont, and Idaho were looking to begin voting after lunch. There was a news conference from the White House scheduled for 8:30.

It's about time, I thought. Gerald Aberland had not been president long, but long enough to know that it was his job to hold the Republic together. I had another forty-five minutes before he would address the nation. He must have timed the address in an effort to put a lid of these events, especially the upcoming votes.

I spent the next forty minutes wondering how these small groups could have been organized into such a coordinated undertaking with so little notice. The United States is an open society, so people can come and go as they please, but stitching together grass roots movements like this, which usually include more than a few hot-headed, stubborn, and independent-minded people who are not known for their ability to collaborate, seemed far-fetched and surreal. I hoped Dora had more insight into these events.

Chapter 32

Five minutes before the president was scheduled to speak, Jefferson pulled the BMW into a narrow road, which led to what appeared to be a landing strip with a single plane on it. A twin-engine Cessna 421C with its engine idling.

Jefferson pulled up right next to the passenger door and motioned for me to get out of the car and onto the plane. I looked at him doubtfully, and the faintest of smiles curled the corners of his mouth. He gave a second, more reassuring nod.

I thanked Jefferson and got out of the car. The temperature was already climbing into the eighties, and I could feel the perspiration on my clothes from the heat and from the anxiety. The door of the plane opened, and Dora was sitting in the cockpit with earphones on her head. She motioned for me to board.

I responded as I did to all of her commands, which is to say that I did exactly what she wanted me to do.

I am usually not a nervous flier, but small planes present their own obstacles. I tried to brush these aside. More than my anxiety, it was wonderful to see Dora again. If felt as if I had not seen her for months rather than the few days it actually was. I positioned myself in the seat next to hers and leaned over and gave her a peck on the cheek. She smiled slightly and motioned for me to put on my seat belt. As soon as I did, she revved the engine and started down the runway. I looked back to see Jefferson pull away and head back down the small road we had come up.

As we rose into the air, my qualms about flying in a small plane dissipated quickly. It was clear that Dora was in complete control of the small but comfortable aircraft, and I was more than just happy to see her. I felt at home with her.

After we reached a cruising altitude of about twenty thousand feet, Dora pulled the earphone away from her right ear so she could hear me. "Sorry I didn't call you, Jake," she said in a voice loud enough to compensate for the engine noise. "I've been busy."

I chuckled inwardly. *I am sure you have been busy*, I thought. "It looks like you only scratched the surface of this movement." There was a touch of hostility in my voice that I did not intend, but it was unmistakable.

Dora looked at me and nodded. "By a mile," she said, apparently unoffended by my remark. "That's why I've been so busy. And so careful." The plane banked slightly toward the left.

"Where to?" I asked.

"Georgia."

I looked out the window and thought for a moment. A red state. I had better call Jamie. I pulled out my cell phone and explained to Dora that I had to call the office. She did not object.

I told Jamie I would not be in the office today, but if she needed me or if something came up to call me on my cell. I thought she was a little disappointed, but it was hard to make out subtle cues with the engine noise. I clicked off.

I turned to Dora. "What's in Georgia?" I asked.

Dora turned to look at me. "Sanity, I hope. A meeting of friends."

I looked at the airspeed dial and saw that we were cruising at about 150 miles per hour. At that rate, I figured the trip would take us a couple hours, depending on where in Georgia we were going.

Dora engaged the autopilot and removed the headset. "Jake,"

she said. "This was more highly organized than I had every imagined." She looked at me intently. "Are you still on board?"

I looked at her squarely in the face. "I killed a man just two days ago, Dora. Yes, I am still on board." It pissed me off that she would question me after what I had done, but I knew she was probably just being thorough.

"Good," she said by way of reply. "I have been doing some digging. It looks like the twelve people on the website are in fact the core agents in this organizational effort. They apparently decided to join forces with a variety of fringe groups: SVR in Vermont, the Christian Exodus, Free State Wyoming, groups like that. They struck a deal, promising them less government in return for support. And for keeping quiet."

Dora paused for a moment to check her instruments. Then she continued, "The Bookkeepers is how the twelve identify themselves, the Book, of course, being the Bible. It's an innocuous name which downplays their religious fanaticism. Also, they kept religious language out of their negotiations. They only used it when they absolutely had to, playing to the fears of secularism on the part of the more crazy fringe groups." She paused and bit her lower lip. "They were more successful than anyone imagined."

My eyes were riveted on Dora, who had obviously been gathering information like a madwoman over the past few days. I admired her for her sheer capacity for work. I wanted to reach out to hug her, but I sat silently and listened.

"Jake, these people had this planned down to the day and time of their movements. What I thought were big clues from my girls' clients were nothing compared to the scope of this operation."

"Did you know the president was going to address the nation this morning?" I asked.

"Yes, but I don't think it will make any difference, unless he threatens force and intends to back up that threat. But having American soldiers invading individual states does not sit well with most of the population."

"They're banking on that, aren't they?"

"I'm afraid so," Dora replied. "They also chose this time of the year because so many legislators are on vacation. The legislative bodies barely have a quorum, but of course when they do it is filled by those people sympathetic to their cause."

We flew on in silence for a few minutes. Then Dora reached into a pocket and pulled out a flash drive. "Jake," she said. "This is all the information I have on the remaining Bookkeepers," she said. "It's quite detailed. But it is likely that they are all being especially careful since Bandera died. They may change the routines and schedules listed here. They may have heightened security." A stony look came over her. "I have to say that, when Roger died, I was a little freaked out. I knew it had to happen. I understood the logistical necessity, but…" She took a deep breath. "It's not something I am comfortable with. I still don't like it, but…" She tightened her grip on the steering control. "If these people live, more people will die. They may dismantle the most important intentional political experiment in human history. They must be stopped."

My heart went out to this beautiful young woman. I felt as if I were getting to know her more deeply every time I saw her. I took her hand and squeezed it.

Dora continued, "But I also think that the perverse advantage of what's been happening over the past few days is that a lot of people are scared and angry. Maybe more angry than scared. We're headed to Georgia to talk to some people who may be able to help steer the situation away from being so reactive." Dora reached back to the seat behind her and pulled up a piece of paper. "Here is a list of who we are seeing."

I took the paper and scanned the names. I had heard of a few of them, but mostly the names didn't mean much to me. "Who are these people, Dora?" I asked.

"Military brass, government officials, a few academics," she replied. "Some work in various branches of the government. Each of them has been cleared and accounted for with respect to their loyalties. Many of them have taken the same oath that you took. They are highly placed and intend to use their influence to counter the Bookkeepers."

I looked quizzically at Dora. "How, Dora? You already said that invading a member state of the US wouldn't fly."

"That's not the plan, Jake," Dora replied with an eerie sense of calm. "What we are going to do is expose the truth about how the Bookkeepers were behind Denver and the deaths of more than one federal judge. We are going to show the entire population of the United States what fanatics these people are. By the end of the week, they will be exposed for the frauds and evil people they are."

This did not seem like bad news to me, but I began to feel anxious about my role in what I was coming to think of as the counterinsurgency. I did not want seventy people to know that my role in the plan was to shoot people.

"You are here as a concerned member of the Senate," Dora said, sympathetic to my unspoken concerns. "That's all." She glanced in my direction. "It is my belief, however, that your other job is equally important. But for our purposes today, all you need to be is the senator you are."

I took a deep breath and relaxed a little. *OK, so this is how it will play out.*

We banked a little to the right and flew on in silence. Dora tried to raise a commercial radio station so that we could hear the president's message, but she had no luck. Silence fell in the noisy little cabin. Much earlier than I expected, Dora disengaged the autopilot and took active control of the aircraft. I could tell we were descending, but I did not see any place to land. I learned a long time ago, however, that pilots saw the world differently from non-piloting humans. They had instruments; they noticed cues; they were attuned to an infrastructure that most other humans ignored.

I was looking out the window and enjoying the beautiful

scenery of Georgia in full bloom when we suddenly began ascending again. I turned to Dora, whose face was pale.

"Dora!" I said. "What's the matter?"

Dora did not respond immediately. She had put her headphones back on, and she seemed totally absorbed in driving the lithe machine. We were banking sharply to the left as we rose. I watched the altimeter climb. I did not want to disturb her concentration. Seven or eight long minutes later, we were flying north at the same altitude we had used coming down. I had only taken my eyes off Dora briefly, just to judge where we were going.

Without consulting me, she banked left, and we were flying south again. We were climbing still higher. I saw the altimeter pass twenty-eight thousand feet and wondered what the ceiling was for this not very large aircraft. Dora pulled out a pair of binoculars and began scanning the ground below us. It did not take her long to focus in on what she wanted. She handed me the glasses.

"Look down there, Jake," she said. "At that hangar."

I took the glasses and pointed them in the direction she showed me. I saw a large building which I took to be the hangar with cars parked pell-mell around it. There was a long access road leading away from the building, and I could see what looked like moving gray-green trucks heading toward the building.

"What are they?" I asked, without removing the binoculars from my face.

"Georgia National Guard units is my guess," Dora replied with a flatness in her voice that hadn't been there before. "My guess is that they are going to surround the building."

My heart sank, as I am sure Dora's did when she first spotted the incoming vehicles.

"Are you sure...?" I started.

"Yes, I am sure," she replied coldly.

The plane was banking slightly. Dora was making a very wide arc over the ground below in the hope of not being detected. The altimeter neared thirty thousand feet, a height more accustomed to jetliners than to little twin-engine jobs like ours. I kept surveying the ground. The guard units were well-trained. When they got to the hangar, they split formation; every other vehicle went in the opposite direction so that within a few minutes the building was surrounded. Troops poured out of the personnel carriers with weapons drawn. My heart began to race. *This was the United States, for God's sake*, I thought. The last vehicle to enter the hangar area was a tank. An Abrams A-1 battle tank. I'd seen hundreds of them in the Army. After the other vehicles had surrounded the building, the tank sat with its gun turret facing the hangar straight on.

I pulled the glasses away from my eyes and looked at Dora. "Full court press," I said with no humor. "These guys are serious."

I put the binoculars back up to my face and resumed surveillance. It was mid-morning in the Georgia countryside, but we were almost five miles in the air, so it was impossible to hear anything. I leaned forward as if a few inches could extend the range of the already powerful optical instrument I was holding in my hands. Troops surrounded the building with weapons aimed directly at it. A smaller but still sizable contingent of people entered the building, also with weapons drawn. I felt my body tense.

There was no movement for a while. I waited but did not move. I automatically adjusted the lens to center on the building as Dora led the plane through a graceful ballet in the sky. I heard her speaking with what must have been a tower somewhere, but it was technical language that was indecipherable to my ears. I wanted to ask her what she was doing, but I couldn't take my eyes off the drama five miles below us.

Within a few minutes, the troops that had entered the building left. Then I saw the tank fire its main battle cannon directly into the building. It burst into flames. The troops surrounding the hangar kept their guns trained on it. What I was witnessing seemed unreal to me. I saw it, and I believed the testimony of my own eyes. My mind could not wrap itself around the possibility that state guard units could be firing on prominent citizens of the same country.

I forced myself to pull the binoculars away and glance at Dora. She was looking down through her window. She was pale and silent. She turned to look at me slowly. Then she reached back behind her seat and pulled out a camera with a telephoto lens. "Shoot as many pictures as you can, Jake," she said tonelessly.

I did as she asked. The long lens actually gave me a closer view, and I could see people running from the burning building, only to be shot by the soldiers on the ground. The scene sickened me, but I felt the emotional part of myself retreating. I was having the same kind of reaction I used to have when I took up my sniper positions. Cold, calculating, alert, emotionless. I kept snapping pictures with the high speed camera until smoke started to obscure my visual field.

"We can't stay here," Dora said, and the plane again banked in a long, slow arc toward what I thought was north. I didn't argue with her. Neither of us spoke. I snapped pictures until I couldn't see any sign of the activity below. Then we flew northward.

After about an hour, the plane began to descend. It kept going down until I thought for a moment that we were landing. This concerned me because I didn't see any possible landing strips. I looked over at Dora, who seemed to be barely breathing. She was engaged totally in the act of piloting the small craft.

After a moment, her eyes moved in my direction. "I am flying low to avoid radar detection," she said. Right after she said that, we were over water. "We are not returning to Washington right now," Dora said. "We'll go to my place in Maryland."

I didn't question her or argue with her or make any comment at all. It was clear that the Bookkeeper's plan was more sophisticated, more complex, and more comprehensive than either Dora or her highly-placed friends had recognized. It did not take a genius to understand that the seventy people who were killed this morning were at the heart of the movement to keep the US intact and to preserve the Union. I did not have the heart to ask who was left or what the other options were or what we could do from this point. I don't know if Dora knew. Smart and well-connected as she was, she was only one person. One person who underestimated the power, appeal, and resources of the rebels.

They were rebels. It wasn't enough to call them fanatics or extremists or even fringe groups. They were obviously a large network of people of superior organizational skill. They have been able to wangle their way into real power over real soldiers, not a small task in a country with such a strong patriotic base as the United States. I felt sick.

We swept back over land about an hour later. Dora seemed to know where she was going, and I still did not want to interrupt her concentration. We were still awfully close to the ground. I could clearly see the rooftops and the tops of trees. After about ten minutes, she banked the small plane and signaled a landing. Within ten minutes we were on the ground behind the cabin near Ocean City. She drove the plane into a small hangar that was mostly covered by old trees and vines. Then she killed the engine. She did not move for a few minutes. Then she removed the headset and looked at me with those sad, beautiful eyes. "I'm out of cards, Jake," she said simply.

I nodded slowly. I did not know exactly what to say to her, but I knew what I was going to do. I took her hand. It was moist. From fear, I guess, or maybe from the stress of flying so low over the ocean and over the Maryland countryside.

"We still have the job you gave me," I said. "It's something we can do regardless of whatever else happens."

Dora's eyes widened a little. It must have seemed like a small, futile option compared to gathering seventy important people in a single location in rural Georgia. But so far, it seemed to me that my job was at least able to be successful.

We tumbled out of the small plane onto the floor of the hangar. It had not seemed cramped in the plane until we got out, and be both stretched our limbs and breathed in the hot Maryland air. It was about 2:30 p.m. We walked toward the cabin in silence. Dora pulled the key from her pocket and unlocked the door. I waved her off, concerned that someone might be inside. She did not stop me or lecture me about how safe it was; she let me enter first and check out the space. She came in behind me.

Dora plopped down onto the couch and put her head in her hands. I have never seen her so dejected, so defeated. She sighed and lay down on the rustic piece of furniture, put her forearm against her forehead, and stared at the ceiling. I thought she might be running through options in her head, but then she shot up and stood straight up. She started yelling: "How did they know about this?" She turned her face in my direction with a look I barely recognized. "How did they know where we would meet? We vetted every single person in that building. We left no stone unturned." She turned away and walked over to the kitchen counter. She spread her palms on the counter on either side of her and leaned against them with her head down, as if in thought.

The she turned and looked at me again. "I am going over and over the vetting process and the people involved, and I can't find a single glitch. Not one person I mistrust or have misgivings about or worried about." Then she started to cry. Tears rolled down her face, and she hung her head as if in shame.

I walked over to her and touched her gently on the shoulders. I didn't say anything because there was nothing to say. I was not privy to the planning; I had complete confidence in her ability and judgment; and I did not question her loyalty either to her work or to her colleagues or to her country. And I loved her.

After a few moments, she turned toward me and put her head on my chest. She balled her fists, draped her arms around my torso, released her fists and dug her fingers hard into my back. She held tight. Her sobs became more intense. As her body heaved with the emotional storm, I held her close. I could see the pain she was in and felt sorrow for that; but more than sorrow I respected and loved this woman. I vowed to myself silently that I would never abandon her, never leave her. She might decide at some point she doesn't want me, but I would be available to her always. It was one of the few things that made sense in a world that was crumbling around us.

Chapter 33

Geoffrey Addelburg had a smug look on his face. My guess was that he was gloating from the coup in Georgia; it must have helped him recover from the shock of Bandera's death. He did not look like a man who had just lost a close friend and confidant. Nor did he look like someone who was about to die.

I had been tracking him since he left the State Department Building about ten minutes before. It wasn't hard to do; he was caught up in traffic on C Street. Not that it seemed to matter to him. For a while he was on his cell phone. Then he started reading something I could not see. He was in a comfortable, temperature-controlled cocoon.

I was on the top floor of the Indian Affairs Building across the street. Not many people realize that Wisconsin has a significant Native American population, and contact with Indian Affairs was something I did on a more or less routine basis, especially as my Native American constituents amassed more power and money through gambling and became more vocal. It was a cherished cause; in my heart I knew they had a lot to be vocal about.

The fact that I knew the head of the Bureau of Indian Affairs made my presence in the building considerably easier than it would have if I didn't know anyone. No one questioned me as I walked in for my appointment with George Wilson, the improbable head of the Bureau. Improbable because he was, for starters, a Democrat, and, beyond that, hailed from a state that hasn't seen a tribe of Indians since the days of the Revolution. But he was an affable man with a penchant for big cigars, and I liked him.

"So George," I said to him. "When are we getting the education money you promised my people?" I was teasing him; he and I both knew the money was being held up in Congress. I probably had more leverage than he had about when it would be released.

"As soon as those duffers stop trying to blow themselves up and get back to business," he responded playfully. He was yet another DC bureaucrat who did not mourn the death of Senator Gruber.

I just smiled. "You know it won't be back to business as usual until we get back in September, George. In the meantime, keep me posted of any extra funds you've got lying around. My people need it."

We didn't talk long. George liked many things, but the main thing he liked was keeping busy. Which meant that he didn't like shooting the breeze with elected officials on company time. Good bureaucrat, George was. Washington has a lot of them.

When we finished, I took my leave with a promise to see what I could jump start in Congress. George shrugged, knowing as he did that there wasn't a damn thing I could do until after Labor Day.

Walking up the steps toward the library, my body began to be possessed by the real and more urgent reason I was here. It was as if I were being taken over by a not-quite-alien spirit, a more serious, focused, and lethal version of myself. I did not dislike it.

I had planted the weapon two days before, on another pointless visit to some lower level officials in Indian Affairs who actually did have something to do with what was happening in my state. It was hardly difficult. What many people in the public world don't know is how easy it is in most ways to get away with small things that quickly add up to big things. Terrorists know this. Good snipers know it as well.

A small earpiece that was unnoticeable to anyone around me kept me abreast of Addelburg's movements. Dora was in the Interior Building across the street armed with high powered binoculars, what was known about his schedule, and a transmitter. My transmitter was buried beneath my clothes, and Dora could hear everything that I said or what went on around me. I had never worked so closely with someone else like this, and I had to admit I liked it, even though it tweaked my do-it-alone machismo.

I looked out the window and saw the State Department vehicle move slowly in the August heat. It wasn't moving much, but Addelburg didn't seem to mind. Washington was filled with summer tourists. I looked around the tops of the other buildings that lined C Street, but I didn't see anything. I checked with Dora in the clipped communications style we had practiced for this occasion.

"Clear?" I asked softly.

A few moments elapsed. "Clear," came the response.

The gun was assembled and ready to go. Addelburg was fortunately sitting on the right side of the car, so I had a clear shot. I knew the vehicle he was in had bullet proof glass; if he knew that, it would give him an unfortunate sense of security. Bulletproof glass was just an invitation for gun makers to make better bullets.

The bullet in question was a work of art. Double depleted-uranium coated pellets with dual explosive charges. The first would explode to penetrate the glass or the Kevlar or whatever else people hid behind; the second would decorate the target. Lovely. Through the scope, I aimed directly at the mark's head. He might be wearing a bullet proof vest, and I wasn't sure the bullet could work its magic against two barriers. It worked wonders against one.

After taking the shot, I pulled back below the window. As I did so, I heard three sharp sounds. I looked up and saw three holes in the window I had just used to view my target. Someone was shooting back. I was so shocked, at first I didn't hear Dora's voice. "Enemy fire."

"See it," I replied, quickly dissembling the weapon, putting it back into its place, and getting out of the top floor men's room as quickly as I could.

I slipped into the library, pulled a book off the shelf, and pretended to read. The enemy must have been using silenced weapons; the few other patrons in the library did not seem disturbed. They must not have heard anything. I didn't make any move to leave; that would only have made me look guilty.

As much as I could without suspicion, I looked around the light-filled room. There was another bullet hole in a window on the other side of the library, suggesting that the snipers couldn't pinpoint my exact location. "Calm," I said softly, so Dora could hear it.

"SWAT to IA," she replied.

"Losing stuff," I replied quietly. At a leisurely place, I took my book back to its spot and replaced it. I undid the radio equipment I had donned so carefully earlier in the day and stuffed the thin wires in between the pages of a random book. I took another book from another shelf back to the table. Within minutes three men in black SWAT helmets, flak jackets, and automatic weapons burst into the library. A young woman who looked up just as they entered let out a brief shriek. The half-dozen others just looked dumbfounded. I looked at the soldiers with a quizzical look on my face. A practiced quizzical look.

"Everybody stand up and move to this table," a tough-looking twenty-something barked to the dozen people in the room, rapping the table next to him with his knuckles.

"What is going on here?" a middle-aged man said with appropriate indignation.

The kid did not respond. Instead, he leveled his weapon at the white-haired man with a bow-tie. He motioned with his gun to the table near him. The man grunted but moved.

I moved too. I kept my eyes with the same practiced look of incredulity on the lead team member. I thought I detected a glance of recognition.

After we gathered at the six-foot long table, I turned to the leader and asked in a soft voice, "What is going on here?"

He looked around and did not say anything at first. Then he said in a low voice. "There's been a shooting, Senator. We are here for your safety."

"My God!" I replied. "Is Director Wilson OK?"

The young leader responded with his signature pause. Then he said, "Yes, I believe he is. The shooting was outside. But we believe it came from this building."

My eyes widened in surprise at what the young man had just said. But a measured sense of relief momentarily washed over my insides. *OK, they weren't really sure where it came from. They may or may not find the weapon. Even if they do, they could not possibly connect it to me.* I felt a faint sense of loss for a weapon I had revered for years. "What can I do to help?" I asked the young man who was clearly at a loss about what to do next.

The soldier lifted his weapon and leaned in my direction. "We were instructed to detain everyone in the building," he said. "I think the FBI will be here soon." He looked down for a moment, and then turned and looked me full in the face. "I'm sorry for any inconvenience, sir," he said.

"No problem," I said. "I was in the military myself. I know how these things go. Let me know if I can help." I sat back and looked at the other members of our ersatz group. "This may take a while," I said in a somber tone. "But it's important."

After about ten minutes, FBI agents began to arrive. They took pictures and treated the room like the crime scene it was. The third agent to arrive was Special Agent Robert Banks. As soon as he saw me, he walked in my direction.

"Senator Telemark," he said, extending his hand. He did not smile; nor did he say anything else.

"What happened, Banks?" I finally said, perhaps with more familiarity that the situation warranted.

He looked at me and emitted the slightest sigh I have ever

detected. "It seems there's been another shooting of a government official," he said. "An official from the State Department."

"Is he OK?" I asked.

Banks looked at me with a look that bespoke profound and conflicted feelings. "He's dead, sir," he said.

I closed my eyes in what I hoped looked like genuine shock. Actually, it was relief that my new bullet had found its mark. "Good God," I said.

Banks resumed his professional duties. "I need to ask you some questions," he said. Then he went through his routine. Where were you; how long have you been here; did you see anything unusual; why were you here, etc., etc. I was ready for all of them and answered with as much spontaneous earnestness as I could.

"Some senators go on junkets," I finished up. "I prefer to spend my time doing some homework."

Banks nodded and gestured that we were finished. "Call me if you think of anything else," he said, handing me a second card. The look on his face suggested that he knew this small action was perfunctory.

"I will," I said with the solemnity expected of a member of the Senate.

I walked slowly out of the library and down the stairs. I stopped by Director Wilson's office to make sure he was OK. He was surrounded by agents and SWAT team members. I raised my head to get his attention, and he saw me and shook his head sadly.

The scene outside was dramatic. Not a single car was moving, and there were police and federal agents everywhere. Pedestrians and motorists were standing around with car doors open. An ambulance had arrived and was removing Addelburg's body from the bullet proof limo that he had haughtily assumed would protect him. My sense of completion deepened. I decided to walk back to my apartment. I had to cross a couple cordons where police were questioning people, but they were mollified with an explanation and a wave of Banks' card.

On the way home, I pondered events as much as I could with the adrenaline still coursing through my body. I thought of killing as a small, isolated act, one that involved just me and my mark. There was always a higher purpose, but I seldom knew what it was; even if I did, it was always fuzzy to me. I was a good guy, so of course I was using my skills in service to a greater good, however that might be defined by the powers that be. But things were different now. Perhaps not different, but more personal, more immediate, more urgent. On this occasion, for one thing, I wasn't acting alone. Dora was also involved, and she was as willing an accomplice as I could ask for. But even more importantly, the goal did not seem distant; it seemed as pressing as eating after a long fast. Also, the scene on the street and the rapid response of what looked to be at least a paramilitary group injected a sense of grandeur into the simple act. This was something to which I had never been privy in my soldiering days. It was always me, my gun, and my target. Nothing else.

It wasn't exactly pride that I felt; it was more a sense that I had a role in the unfolding of important events, an importance that I never felt in the military because I never knew the details about why I was killing people. Feeling so involved underscored the clarity of my choice, but it also made me feel more responsible, more focused on the importance of my little role in the emergence of great events. It made me lightheaded and nauseated.

Chapter 34

The president's address to the nation the week before had not done much to help a complicated and still-unfolding situation in the country. He predictably served notice that individual states had no right to secede from the Union, an argument laid in stone by his distant predecessor, Abraham Lincoln, and that a constitutional convention was unnecessary because of the amendment process, which allows the citizenry to change the constitution any way they want. But he was apparently trying to be welcoming and inviting in his admonition that the errant states peacefully reconsider their decision to depart the Union. That may have been well-intended, but more than one pundit noted that it made him seem equivocal about where the line in the sand actually was. No mention was made of sending federal troops anywhere. The address did have some effect. The seceding states had not taken any additional action, and the push in other states seems to have become more subdued. It seemed that the whole country was holding its breath, waiting to see if the United States of America would weather this second assault on its integrity. News organizations were polling at a feverish pace, trying to discern the mind of the electorate. At the moment, that mind seemed confused.

Nor was there any report of the massacre in Georgia. Because it was August, many of the victims were not expected in their offices and were thought to still be away on vacation. There were scattered reports of missing people here and there reported by their families, but no general awareness of what had happened. This state of affairs weighed on Dora, who was doing her best to transform herself into a freedom fighter. Her former revulsion at the thought of killing people appeared to have vanished, and she was unflinching in the planning and execution of the latest plan with Addelburg. Nor did she flinch when the response was so forceful; she merely noted it and went looking for what kind of security arrangements had been increased.

The subtext of these developments was that our relationship was deepening by the day. We spent a lot of time together in various venues, planning, reconnoitering, and discussing options and targets. There was a lot of moving around for the purposes of evasion, but there was also a shared conviction that this was necessary because of the circumstances. We learned to read each other in increasingly minute detail. A nod, an eye movement, a simple shift in a single facial muscle was often enough to keep the conversation going. It was uncanny.

It was also new territory for me, the master of the short-term, never-too-close sexual relationship. Dora knew everything about me, and I was learning more and more about her. Not that she had the kinds of things to hide that I did, but I was fascinated to learn how she thought, how she processed information, how she related to me as a friend, cohort, and lover. She could shift among different temperaments rapidly, being alternately warm and engaging, cold and analytical, playful and mischievous. That part was fun.

What was not fun was watching the country move toward disarray and chaos. The United States has never been a stable country like the old nation-states of Europe, which were more homogeneous and more willing to formalize many aspects of their common lives. The US had always had a rough-and-tumble, make-it-or-break-it quality to it. But throughout all the early expansion, the foreign wars, the additions of news states, there had been an accepted framework, one that had endured for over two hundred years and was widely and deeply respected. Or so I had always thought.

The exception to that observation was, of course, the Civil War, which the current situation was resembling more and more. To most of those of my generation, the thought that the US might break up was just not on the radar screen. We knew about the Civil War—everyone studied it in school—but that was history in the irretrievable past. The idea that it could happen now in the midst of modernity was hard to grasp. It wasn't hard to grasp for the fanatical fringe groups that had cobbled a coalition for just that purpose, however. While they had different agendas, these disparate groups had one goal in common: to be done with what they referred to as Imperial America, and to replace it with separate political units that were smaller and presumably easier to govern and to control. The Bookkeepers saw themselves as the puppet masters in the unfolding of these events; they thought they could control the outcome and be left with the greater part of the former country to govern as they pleased.

Their inspiration in this work came from an obscure, presently deceased writer by the name of R.J. Rushdoony, a Presbyterian minister of Armenian descent who fancied himself a latter-day Calvin, writing a series of sermons he collected under the title *Institutes of Biblical Law,* after Calvin's own *Institutes* five hundred years earlier. Rushdoony preached Biblical Law for all society, and, even though he eschewed violence as a path toward that goal, allowed that it would happen naturally when most people freely embraced his form of Christianity. "Christian Reconstruction" is what they call it. One form of religion, one form of Christianity, and one form of religiously-inspired government for all. Chilling.

But apparently not so chilling for the Bookkeepers. So far, their plan seemed to be unfolding with a precision I would not have dreamed possible. Their network, their resources, and their timetable were all things even Dora in her detailed and thorough search for data had underestimated. As far as we could tell, the only fly in their ointment was the killing of two of their members. But beyond increased security, these did not seem to have much impact, did not seem to modify or impede the progress of their outrageous plot one iota. I tried not to think about this, and I especially tried not to talk to Dora about it. The impact or lack of it was seldom discussed because I didn't want to discourage Dora or reveal whatever doubts I may have about the whole enterprise. Doubt has no place in the snipering business; it saps motivation, introduces ambivalence, and makes a tough job even tougher. So if I had doubts, they were not available to me. Nor to Dora.

As for her, once the toll of the Georgia massacre became clear—which was immediately—something changed. Her commitment to our endeavor appeared to match mine in every respect. I could not detect any hint of her former qualms, not in her voice, her tone, or her facial expressions. She was completely on board. The thing we did talk about was where this was all headed. At first, Dora assumed that the plan was for the Bookkeepers to take over the US whole—simply to replace one form of government with another. But it was now clear that they had forged their alliances with promises of autonomy or independence for various states, maybe even regions. While perhaps not the original intention of their plan, the reality on the ground involved the break-up of the United States of America. Every time Dora and I talked about this, we were struck dumb both by the audacity and the lunacy of it.

The basic plan—to create an atmosphere of fear or even terror among the population—appeared to be working. There was an edginess people seemed to be feeling. Even if they were going about their business as if everything were normal; the fear was palpable just beneath the surface. People began to regard each others anxiously; they went out of their homes less; they huddled for safety.

About three days after Addelburg's shooting, we were huddling in Dora's Maryland cabin. It was unseasonably cool for August, and we had closed the windows and started a fire against the evening chill. We had been working all day on deciding who the next target was, and compiling everything we knew about him. We were locked in a discussion between two targets. Dora preferred George Treadman, the Chief of the CIA's Counterintelligence Division. She thought selecting him might put a dent in the shroud they had managed to maintain over their whole enterprise. I thought it should be Maximilian Grobe, the Chief of the Criminal Justice Information Services Division for the FBI, and for the same reason. We weren't exactly arguing, but we weren't coming to an agreement either. The fact was neither of us knew which one was the better target; we might as well have flipped a coin. Then suddenly, Dora stopped mid-sentence and stared into space for a few moments.

"There must be a time when they are together," she said. "Especially if they are working together surreptitiously to keep the curtains drawn over their whole operation." She turned to her laptop and started typing furiously.

For a moment, the elegance of Dora's solution hung in the air. *Nice going*, I thought, admiring her once again for her ability to integrate information and to see new paths when obstacles mount. Then I had my own think-tank moment.

"Why don't we see if all these guys ever meet together formally?" I said. I was a little embarrassed that this seemed like such an obvious thought. Dora cocked her head in my direction, away from the screen she had been looking at. She stared at me as if I had uttered something in a foreign language, squinting her eyes and then unsquinting them. Then she squinted them again. "Of course," she said. "I can't believe we didn't think of this before." Her statement wasn't harsh or judgmental—just matter-of-fact.

She got up from the small table where she was working and walked over to the coffee table in front of the couch, which was filled with paper, books, and other artifacts of scholarship. Her movements were accelerating, as if she were looking for something she had misplaced and was sure was in this pile somewhere. That was exactly what she was doing.

"Here it is," she said finally, picking up a flyer I didn't recognize.

After a moment of silence, I ventured the obvious. "Um, what is that?" I asked gently.

"It is the summer schedule of the United Temple Baptist Church of Northern Virginia," she said. She turned it toward me. There was a circle around a paragraph in the middle of the page. I walked over to where she was so I could read it.

"After the service, senior members of the Board will meet in closed session, along with their consultants and advisors, to chart future direction for the fellowship and prepare proposals for the next major conference."

I looked up at Dora. "You think some of our guys will be here?" I asked.

She cocked her head in my direction and smiled ever so slightly. "I think there's a chance they will all be there," she said.

"Give me a context here," I said plaintively if a bit too bookishly. It was better than asking Dora what she was talking about.

"I know that three members of the Bookkeepers belong to this church. I also know that they have met here in the past." She paused for a moment, lost in thought. "And who would suspect a church, especially one that has been around so long and has served the District as well as northern Virginia for well over a hundred years." There was bitterness in her voice as she came to the end.

I put my arms around her. "It's not easy keeping up with genius," I said softly. Her body was rigid and hard. Then she took a deep breath, and wrapped her arms around my body. "No, it's not," she said in a whisper. We stood there a moment, two people alone. I breathed in deeply and inhaled her scent. I would never want to be alone with anyone else.

The church meeting wasn't until the second week of September, which was only a month away; but it felt like ages as far as we were concerned. We had time to plan, time to scope out the setting, time to do everything we needed to do without rushing. Time poured into the gap that suddenly opened in our lives; time with all the pleasure that come with just being with someone you love. It did not matter what we would do this evening. We would in fact do what human beings always do when they are together. Talk, eat, relax, and love. What else was there?

Chapter 35

The next day, Jamie called. She was on vacation in Wisconsin, but she was monitoring calls through the office just to keep on top of things. My cell phone rang just before 10 a.m. "Jake," she began, "We got a couple calls that I thought would interest you. One was from Dr. Conoria, the doc who took care of Max when he was in the hospital." She gave me his number and then paused, as if waiting for a reaction from me.

"And the second one?" I finally asked.

"Ursula Tessero called," Jamie replied more formally. "She did not leave a message."

"Thanks, Jamie." I had the Tessero's number.

I clicked off the small unit and held it in my hand. *Truth-time*, I thought. I was unexpectedly anxious in both senses of the word: eager to speak with both of these people, and nervous about what I might hear. I looked across the small cabin at Dora, who was cleaning up breakfast dishes in the small kitchen. "I may have some information," I said to her back.

She turned her head and looked over her shoulder in my direction. "About what, Jake?" she asked.

"Ursula called the office this morning. Presumably the autopsy report is in." Then I reminded her about what happened with Max, something I had told her weeks ago, but it felt as if it had been months. "His doc said he would call the office when he had something."

Dora turned the water off, wiped her hands on a towel, and walked in my direction. "Could we call Ursula first?" she asked gently.

"Sure," I said, and I scrolled through my contact list to find her number.

Ursula answered on the second ring. "Hello?" she said.

"Hi, Ursula, Jake Telemark. My office said you called."

"Yes, Jake, I received the autopsy report yesterday afternoon. I thought you would be interested in it."

"I am," I replied when she paused.

I heard Ursula take in a long breath. She choked just a bit. *What a strong woman*, I thought. *This is probably not good news.*

"It was as we feared," she replied simply.

It was my turn to sigh. I glanced up at Dora and said to Ursula, "I am so sorry." It was a simple if partial truth. Rage welled up inside me, to be met by the satisfaction of taking out two of the people I was sure were responsible for the outrage of murdering a good and innocent man.

"Ursula, Dora is here with me. What can we do?"

There was a pause on the line. "I am not sure yet, Jake, but I can assure you I want to use this information wisely. I am open to ideas."

We talked about options in generalities. Neither of us said it, but we were both concerned about the possibility that this call might be monitored. I mentioned some names of people I thought were in a position to help her.

When I was finished talking with Ursula, Dora motioned for me to hand her the phone. I did, and she and Ursula spoke for a while. I wasn't listening. I was still nursing the rage I felt. Somehow two deaths of hated people for one loved one still seemed lopsided in the wrong direction. I was so lost in my tormented feelings, I didn't notice that Dora had ended her conversation. She walked toward me with tears in her eyes. She put her arms around me. "I don't know why I had hope that this would be otherwise," she said bitterly. She cried softly for a few moments. Then she pulled away, straightened herself, and said, "Are you going to call Conoria?"

"Of course," I said, although I felt it would be a replay of the same type of conversation. Not including the part about murder, of course.

In a minor health care miracle, I got straight through to Dr. Conoria. He told me that he had gotten the lab results of the toxicology screen on Max, and that the substance was unknown to the local lab. It appeared to be similar in chemical structure to carbon monoxide, just as he had said when Max was in the hospital, but it wasn't identical. He asked me if I wanted him to pursue it further. "No, Doctor, I don't think so," I replied. I thanked him for his time, his care for Max, and his thoroughness. Dora had been watching the conversation. We both shrugged. We knew what it was. There was a long time before either of us spoke. We were both deep in thought, possibly thinking about exactly the same thing. After about ten minutes, I looked at Dora and said, "These people could not have done this without massive financial and government support. I understand the government part, because they have so many highly placed officials, but what about the money part? Where are they getting all this money?"

Dora looked at me for a moment and then walked back over to her laptop. She turned the screen toward me and said, "I think they're getting a lot of it from that church."

Chapter 36

The United Temple Baptist Church of Northern Virginia lies just across the Potomac River from Washington, D.C. and just off the interstate. So it's easy to get to, which is one of the reasons it has become so popular with those members of Congress who are inclined to seek out church fellowship while in the capital. Northern Virginia is widely known to be at least fifty percent safer than most places in the District proper, and the congregation of United Temple was predominantly white. So it was comfortable for many staffers as well as for many of the bureaucrats who live across the Potomac.

The first time I drove around the church, I noticed its flawlessly manicured lawns and gardens. The neoclassical building itself was red brick and had freshly painted white trim. The columns in front looked as if no one ever brushed up against them. This was an American religious edifice at its best, ready to be photographed for a postcard or a wedding picture or some other festive event.

To the west of the church a large multipurpose building, designed to hold meetings, classes, or any other gatherings a large wealthy church might have. It too was flawlessly neat and tidy. On my second circuit, I noticed small surveillance cameras perched two on each corner of both buildings. I wondered what other security measures they might have taken, but nothing else was visible. An alarm system surely; perhaps also bulletproof glass. Because of the cameras, I dared not make a third pass. Two times around could be someone who is lost; three times is certainly someone who is casing the place. I drove off to a nearby diner to get a cup of coffee.

The diner was an upscale place, hardly anything like the authentically retro places it was designed to mimic. I ordered a cup of coffee at the counter and picked up a *USA Today*. It was the first time I had seen a newspaper in weeks. It was filled with stories about recent events, but with the editorially dumbed-down layout. It maintained its grade-school neutrality even on the editorial page, where it splayed two opposing viewpoints: should we or should we not remain one country. It offended me that they clung to their format even in the face of national crisis. The *Federalist Papers* this was not.

I closed my eyes and disengaged from the act of reading the paper. I needed to think about how to proceed. It was obvious that the United Temple Baptist Church was a fortress, one that I needed to penetrate. I opened my eyes but kept the paper in front of me as if I were reading it. My mind was far away. Alternative scenarios ran through my mind. Simply shooting people in or around this building was foolhardy. A larger tool was required: a bomb, perhaps, or a tank like the one they used in Georgia. Those seemed like far-fetched options, and I tried to clear my mind to focus.

After a while, it occurred to me that these plans were premature. I did not even know what was in those buildings; nor did I know where the closed-door meeting would be held. Despite Dora's enthusiasm for this plan, it seemed to me to be held together by some very whimsical assumptions. Such as (a) the Bookkeepers would meet in this location; (b) their meeting would be announced in a church bulletin; and (c) we could devise a way to locate and destroy the whole lot.

It was then that an idea visited my mind that seemed to hold the key to resolving both the assumptions and the obstacles weighing on me: I could join the church. I laughed out loud. It was a moment of gratitude that my parents had departed this earth, so outraged would they have been by the prospect that their only son would cynically join a church to kill some opposition politicians. I blushed a little. But sitting within a thousand yards of what could well be the home turf of this particular group was too much to resist. With a respectful internal nod to the people who raised me, I reached for my cell phone.

A very polite and sweet female voice recording answered and described a long list of menu options. There was this ministry and that ministry; this tribe and that tribe; this pastor or one of his assistants; worship schedules and special meetings for new members... That was selection number 7. I pushed it with no small measure of relief. I got another recorded voice that told me that newcomers were always welcome either to the church services themselves on Wednesday or Sunday or at the New Member Meeting held every Thursday evening at 7 p.m. It gave the location of the meeting and referred the caller on to a directions submenu for more information.

I thought the New Member Meeting might be a good place to start. I wondered absently if I knew anyone from the church. It seemed very conservative, so even if I did know anyone there, they would probably be from a wing of my party with which I did not fraternize. That worried me a little; my attendance might seem suspicious. I looked at my watch. I had a day and a half to worry about that. With my plan in place, I had no reason to remain in northern Virginia. I paid for my coffee, walked briskly out of the small shop, and headed for my car.

Out of the corner of my eye, I recognized a face that I knew. I didn't know it well, but I knew it enough to register it among a number of strangers in an alien place. It took me a moment to place it, and as I did so I saw that the body attached to it shifted course to intercept me on my way to my car. Recognition came when he was six feet away from me.

"Agent Banks," I said, looking him straight in the eye and extending my hand.

"Senator Telemark," Banks replied without hesitation, taking my hand and shaking it firmly.

We both stood there for a moment in the hot Virginian sun. I was waiting for him to say something, and I guess he was doing the same thing. When he did not speak, I finally said, "May I help you?" I figured he approached me, so the responsibility for the conversation was his.

"Perhaps," Banks said, but then he fell back into silence.

Now I don't work closely with the FBI, but between what contact I did have and the numerous TV shows about the agency, I knew they were seldom if ever at a loss for words. I looked at Banks with some concern. "Are you alright?" I asked.

He looked away, either because he was suddenly and uncharacteristically self-conscious or because he was looking around for people watching us. Finally, he asked, "May we talk privately, sir?"

"Certainly," I said. I was feeling some concern. I wasn't frightened; I was concerned one human being to another. Banks was clearly agitated about something; he looked as if he were either ill or doing something wrong.

"This is my car," I said, not wanting to walk back into the coffee shop I had just left. "Hop in." Banks seemed relieved and let himself in the passenger side front door as soon as I hit the remote lock. I got in the driver's seat, and we drove off. There is something intimate about driving aimlessly with someone, and my concern was not abating. So I breached protocol and asked, "Robert, are you alright?"

Banks seemed slightly relieved. "Senator," he said, not reciprocating the familiarity, "as an FBI agent, there are always dozens if not hundreds of laws that I can break when I speak with someone outside the Bureau." He paused for a moment. "I am not accustomed to breaking any of them."

I chuckled inside but dared not let it show. I am certain he was telling the truth.

He continued, "But this situation is different." He paused again and took several deep breaths. My heart went out to him. Whatever he was going to say must be terribly difficult for him. I glanced in his direction. He looked to be in his mid-fifties and had probably been with the Bureau since college. Most agents were. The Bureau was sacred to these people. I knew that and respected it. I kept silent.

"I am speaking to you because I have an idea that we may share similar concerns about what has been happening in our country." Another pause; more deep breaths. "You have gone out of your way to help me in the past. I looked into your background some. You are a good man and a hard-working senator." I glanced at him again. He was talking to the windshield and would occasionally look out the side window. I was beginning to feel anxious because I did not know what he knew; nor did I know where he stood with whatever it was that he did know. I did not think I could bear his generalities much longer.

"What is it, Agent Banks?" I asked as gently as I could.

"Would you please stop the car?" he asked. It wasn't a demand; just a request. I thought maybe he was going to vomit. I pulled over and stopped in front of some single family homes on an old city street. I kept the engine running because of the heat. I turned to look squarely at Banks, and he turned in my direction.

"Some months ago," he began. "I came across some evidence indicating that a highly-placed official with the Bureau may have been involved in the death of a young woman." He said this with authority. Evidently his qualms were beginning to subside.

"I decided to look into it further, but was stopped by my supervisor. When I objected, he threatened me with transfer or worse." His eyes flashed; he was clearly enraged by whatever it was that transpired in that conversation. "Even though every professional and moral bone in my body did not want to do so, I let it drop." His eyes narrowed. "But I did not forget it. I began—surreptitiously—to look into why the highest law enforcement agency in the country would not follow obvious leads which suggested that a government official was involved in a murder." How his eyes were flashing. "What I found astounded me."

I looked at Banks expectantly, fully engaged with what he was saying. "What did you learn?" I asked.

"Sir," he said solemnly. "I think a group of highly placed government officials is behind recent events and that they are trying either to take over or destroy the United States."

I did not bother to act shocked. "Walt Zimmerman was the guy involved with the dead girl," I said without emphasis.

Banks nodded. "A good friend of Roger Bandera," he said. "At first I thought the cover-up was just a friend thing. Even though that's outrageous enough and violates every oath I've ever taken, it at least made some sense." He took a breath and looked out the window.

"What changed?" I asked.

"A lot. For starters, another girl was killed a few months ago. Then three more a few weeks ago."

My stomach lurched. I thought of Dora. She would not take this well. She will feel responsible. Hell, I felt responsible and I didn't even know them. I closed my eyes in disgust.

"But those deaths are minor compared to what has happened since. The more I looked into Zimmerman and Bandera, I learned that they were involved with a group that was ostensibly religious in nature. I began picking up a pattern. They would meet, something would happen. They would meet again; something else would happen, all the way back to the first murder and to the unwarranted arrest of Willy Maelstrom." Banks had clearly been doing his homework. He did not try to disguise his bitterness. "Since I was waved off the initial investigation, I've had to do this all on my own. Not that I can't do that; I have resources. But I've had to do it very, very quietly."

Then he looked at me squarely. "My investigations brought me to that church. I'm betting you got there for the same reasons." He looked me straight in the eye.

Silence hung in the air between us. Banks looked down for a long moment before he spoke again. "I know you've been involved with Isadore Hathaway," he said without judgment. "I know she has been looking into the backgrounds of various government officials. I also know she had some kind of relationship with several of the women who died." He looked at me with sorrow in his eyes. "I believe she is in danger, sir."

"She had been on an in-house watch list of the Bureau's for some time, but mostly because she's such a liberal rabble-rouser. We did not get too close because of her pedigree, her job, and her reputation."

He continued, "A phone number we traced to her turned up on the cell phones of four of the girls who were killed. She has been under round-the-clock surveillance since last week. Nothing intrusive; but we have been keeping track of her whereabouts." He looked at me with a new seriousness. "Sometimes she has dropped out of sight. She may know we are on to her or she may just be an elusive woman, I don't know; but I do know that she has been spending a lot of time with you recently." He shrugged as if this were a mixed blessing.

"When I saw you scoping out the church, I figured you and Dr. Hathaway were looking into the same things I'd been looking into." He stopped, as if his part had ended.

I considered Banks carefully. I was fully aware that this could be some kind of trap, either sanctioned by the Bureau or by the Bookkeepers. I turned and looked out my window, deep in thought. My instincts told me to trust this man, although I would have liked some objective collaboration of that feeling. What he was saying was plausible and sounded sincere. Still, being wrong about this could get me into a great deal of hot water and it could hurt Dora. It was also true that, if what he was saying was true, I had to contact Dora as soon as possible. I turned back to Banks. "Why did you approach me today?" I asked.

Banks did not respond immediately. "One of the great things about the Bureau," he said, "is that we work as a team. We are trained that way. We each have extensive training and can act independently, but we prefer not to, and there aren't very many situations where going solo is called for. But I am up to my neck in information, and I am unable to talk with anyone about it. I believe the Bureau is compromised, so I can't talk to anyone there. I won't allow myself to talk with friends or even my wife about it; that kind of knowledge can get them into trouble, maybe even killed." Slight pause. "So when I saw you, I decided that you were one of the few people I know who might be able to handle this. Plus, you're a senator and have some influence." He almost chuckled. "A little more influence because a lot of your colleagues think you saved their lives and their jobs in the Senate last month."

He went on more earnestly. "I don't know who in the Bureau to trust. I was hoping you or Dr. Hathaway might be able to shed some light on this." He looked at me a little sheepishly. "Plus, I have some information that might help you," he said.

"What kind of information?" I asked with more irritation than the situation warranted. I was irritated that I had to make a decision about Banks with so little real information and no background.

Banks took a long breath. "The Bureau knows that there was a massacre in Georgia late last month," he said. "We also know that federal judges have been dying at an unprecedented rate, mostly by causes that seem harmless enough but, on further investigation, seem a lot like murder. We also know that none of this information is getting any press, and we are locked down. Nobody is allowed to talk."

Then Banks stepped out of his FBI persona. "I am a religious man, Senator. I practice my faith. I believe we are here to fight evil wherever we find it." He looked through the front window. "I am afraid I have found it. I will do anything to stop what is happening."

"You are giving me a lot of information, Agent Banks, and I will take it under advisement," I said. "You can be sure that the information you shared with me today is safe. I need some time to think about this."

Banks nodded. I believed at that moment that every word he said was sincere and reflected the behavior of a man torn between his loyalty to his agency and his loyalty to his country. But I needed some time. And I needed to speak with Dora as soon as possible.

"Where can I reach you?" I asked.

He gave me his cell phone number. "It's secure," he said simply.

I put the car into gear and headed back to the spot by the diner where I first encountered Banks. I pulled over next to the parking spot where my car was when we started. I turned in his direction and extended my hand. "Thank you," I said. "I will be in touch."

Banks nodded, got out of the car, and walked in the direction of the church.

Chapter 37

I watched Banks walk away for a few seconds and then pulled the car out into the street. I felt a sudden need to get away from this place; it felt like the Devil's lair. I also had to contact Dora as soon as possible, so I picked up my cell and speed-dialed her number.

She answered on the first ring.

"New development," I said tersely.

"Where?" came the equally terse reply.

"Same as Sunday," I said. I clicked off.

I was disgusted by these truncated conversations, but today I felt their usefulness. I sped up to get to the safe house as soon as I could. I figured Dora would be there by the time I got there, since she was likely already in DC. I hoped she would take evasive maneuvers. I worried about her as I had never worried about another person before. The thought of losing her...well, I couldn't even imagine it. Or rather, I could imagine it and it scared the hell out of me. I kept repeating her name inside my head. I felt protective; I wanted to shield her.

But when we were not actively engaged in planning or doing some task, Dora kept a measure of distance, even from me. I did not always know where she was. She planned it that way, and I agreed objectively that it was safer for me not to know. But I hated not knowing where she was at any given time.

Midway through these thoughts I realized I was speeding, so I slowed down so as not to draw attention to myself. I took a few deep breaths to slow my mind and body down. It would take me at least a half hour to get to the safe house, so I decided to think about what Banks said and to be extra careful about watching my own back. I was inclined to believe Banks. I could do a little checking, although that may be harder with the Bureau so locked down. But his big attraction was that he was inside that fortress and probably had access to information even Dora would have trouble acquiring.

I wondered what he actually knew about Georgia. It didn't sound like much. He did not mention any of the important people who were at that meeting. Nor did he mention Guy Tessero by name, suggesting that he may not have known of my connection to him. What I heard loud and clear, however, was that Dora was in danger. I needed to get to her.

The rest of the trip was spent going in circles, eluding real or imagined pursuers. By the time I got to the house, I was sweating profusely. I pulled in and was greatly relieved to see Dora's car already in the garage. I walked into the small house and threw my arms around her. Dora looked at me as if I were more than slightly off my rocker. We sat down on the shabby couch, and I proceeded to tell her about my encounter with Robert Banks. When I got to the part about the three girls, tears began to stream down her face. I found my own eyes welling up. I took her hand and held it. Neither of us spoke for a while.

Finally, I said, "He also said he thought you were in danger. Up till last week, they would do occasional surveillance, but now you're on 24/7 watch. He admitted that they lost you on more than one occasion."

"I suspected as much, Jake," Dora said with little emotion. "The FBI guys are not so subtle as they like to think. In any case, I have taken some countermeasures, even before this past week." She did not seem worried.

Dora took a deep breath. "Did Banks know that the Bookkeepers were meeting at that church?" she asked.

"I don't know," I said. "I did not ask him, but he was there looking for them. He was also aware of some previous meetings." I pushed ahead. "My plan was to attend a New Members meeting tomorrow evening. I thought I could scope out the facility." Then I went on to describe the security arrangements I noticed when I was there. Dora seemed to be listening, but I wasn't sure where her mind was. I was sure she wasn't finished with her grief about the deceased women she knew and cared for. Maybe she needed some time.

"Do you believe Banks?" she asked, surprising me.

"Yes," I said truthfully, "I do."

Dora looked at with an inscrutable face. I guess she was thinking. "We need to move on this, Jake, but I am not sure about Banks. Even if he's on the level and even if he's as upright as you think, he may be opposed to our methods."

No doubt about that, I thought. Still, I couldn't dismiss his potential usefulness to us. "Would you like to meet him?" I asked.

Dora thought for a moment. "I don't know, Jake," she said. "He might not want to take the risk if I am under surveillance."

I didn't know what to say to that. I knew that I needed to connect with Banks again, just to make sure he was on the level. On the other hand, I didn't know if I could tell that on my own. I wanted Dora to meet him.

"He's acting on his own, according to him," I said. "I don't think the surveillance will bother him."

Dora looked at me. "OK," she said.

I pulled out my cell phone and dialed the number Banks had given me. He picked it up on the second ring.

"Agent Banks," he said formally.

"Banks, this is Jake Telemark," I said. "Dr. Hathaway and I

would like to meet with you."

Banks did not say anything right away. I figured he was thinking either about whether this would be a good idea or the practicalities involved or both.

"When?" he asked.

"As soon as you can," I said, glancing at Dora.

"How about tomorrow?" he said. "There's a coffee house on Georgia Street in Silver Springs called *The Black Bean*. Could you meet me there at about 1:30?"

I repeated the time and place aloud and looked over at Dora. She nodded and shrugged at the same time.

"I will make sure it's clear," said Banks.

"We'll be there," I replied. I clicked off.

I turned to Dora, who was lost in thought. I could tell she was nervous, but I think that was only because I had gotten to know her so well. Her lower lip was trembling very slightly, and her jaw was clenched. She was trying to maintain control. I walked over to one of the stools by the breakfast bar and sat down. I motioned for Dora to sit on the other one.

"What do we do if he is on the level?" I asked her.

Dora looked at me and shook her head. "Last week I would have said he could help us assemble people to help the President maintain control over the country." She looked away. "But I tried that, and we ended up with the massacre in Georgia."

I did not have a ready reply for that, so I thought for a minute. Fortunately, before I had to say anything, my phone rang. It was Jamie.

"Jake, the President has called Congress back into special session to deal with the current crisis," she said. She was clearly agitated.

"When?" I asked.

"Everyone is to be back in chamber tomorrow at 11:00 a.m. The President is going to address a joint session of Congress at noon." She proceeded to describe how all congressmen were being called back, even the ones on overseas junkets. I looked at Dora as I listened. It was clear that there was no option. After I hung up from Jamie, I turned to Dora and said, "I have to go back to the Senate tomorrow. The President has called an emergency session of Congress."

Dora nodded. "What about Banks?" she asked.

I thought for a moment. "I don't know. Maybe we can arrange another time. I'll call him." But I did not reach for my phone. I wanted more time to think about it. I had a realization at the edge of my mind that Dora was not taking the kind of leadership in our relationship that she usually did. Georgia must have walloped her confidence. I wasn't sure I could be a very good stand-in for her. "Dora," I said, and looked her directly in the face. I stopped. She was crying. Not bawling; just allowing strands of tears to run down her face. She took my hand; I held it gently. I did not think she was up to major decisions right now.

"I'll call Banks in a little while and make other arrangements," I said softly.

She nodded but did not otherwise move.

Chapter 38

I drove to Capitol Hill the next day in silence. I had called Banks and explained the situation to him. I told him I would contact him again after I knew more about what the demands of the special session would be. Jamie had called this morning and said she would be back in the District this afternoon.

It wasn't a long drive, but I couldn't help thinking about Dora. She seemed so uncharacteristically lifeless and adrift. The rest of last evening was spent doing homey things: eating, cleaning up, and watching TV. Neither of us spoke much except for essential communications, and she went to bed at nine o'clock and fell into an apparently deep but restless sleep. This morning, she barely said two words to me. I was worried, but there wasn't a lot I could do right then. I had to get to the Hill.

I went directly to the Senate chamber, by-passing the normal routine of going to my office first. The place was loud and filled with people. Every senator was either there or on the way; some of them looked as if they had just stepped off an airplane. There were even two senators from Maine, since the governor of the state had appointed someone to replace the hapless Dick Gruber. A thick-necked, stocky guy with a football player's build sat in Gruber's chair, looking around the room somewhat anxiously, I thought.

The plan was to meet in the Senate Chamber and then proceed to the House Chamber, where the President would be addressing both Houses of Congress together. All of this, of course, is highly unusual: the only time the President ever steps foot in Congress is for the State of the Union speech in January.

I met up with Max and some other members of our little coterie of moderate republican senators. We chatted for a while. There was an odd ambience in the room; we were nervous, but we were also relieved that the President was showing some leadership. It turns out that Max was called back from his vacation with his family in Bar Harbor, where his wife's family has a little place.

I asked him how he was feeling.

"Great," he replied. "No residual effects that I can tell." Then more conspiratorially, "Whatever that stuff was knocked the crap out of me, Jake," he said. "I asked Dr. Conoria to follow up. So far the lab has not been able to identify the substance."

I did not respond. I wasn't sure if Conoria had told him about contacting my office. I thought it best left alone.

Max smiled. "The whole thing scared Darlene to death; she hasn't been this nice to me since our honeymoon." He smiled more broadly. "This should happen to me once a year." He chuckled and patted my back.

The gavel fell at that moment, and the Vice-President called for us to move to the House Chamber. Silence fell on the group of us, and we slowly filed out the Senate door toward what we privately called the lower house of Congress. In the House Chamber, silence also reigned. We quietly took our seats. No one appeared to have any advance notice of what the President would say. This was so unlike anything I had experienced during my time in Washington. No loud cavorting; no knowing glances: it was more like a high school assembly where the principal was going to announce the closing of the school or the death of a beloved teacher. Everybody seemed on edge.

There was a single television camera in the back of the room aimed at the podium. Nothing like the batteries of cameras and microphones that are usually present for even routine events. The Sergeant-at-Arms announced the arrival of the President, and Secret Service agents entered first, lining both sides of the aisle. Then President Gerald Aberland strode down the center aisle amid the silence of mostly gray-haired men and women. Polite applause started in the middle of the room, and most everyone picked it up. As the President made his way to the podium, Secret Service agents lined each side of the half-moon chamber. There must have been fifty of them. I have never seen so many seriously armed and determined men outside the military. Two took up positions in front of the podium on either side; two stood behind him on either side. They all turned to face the audience with their hands clasped in front of them.

"I want to thank everyone for coming," the President began. "As you know, there have been a number of tragic and troubling events in our country over the past few months. Primary among these has been the deaths of over twenty thousand of our fellow citizens in a deliberate terrorist attack near Denver, Colorado. This heinous act was an unprovoked assault upon the peace and tranquility of the whole country. My heart is with the victims and their families."

"In addition to that tragedy, which stands as the largest loss of civilian life this country has ever experienced, we have seen in recent days several states attempt to secede from the United States. Several weeks ago, I spoke to the country and stated that secession was not an option in our system of government and invited the offending states to reconsider their action. At the time, I made no threat of military action."

"What some of you may not know is that over the past three months, fifty-two federal judges have died under suspicious circumstances. Many of these people were friends of people in this room. Some were friends of mine. Autopsies have revealed that many of these men and women died in a way that was designed to mimic a physical ailment, but which was in fact triggered by chemical poisoning. In addition, we have had reports of surreptitious surveillance carried out against members of government and elected officials."

The President's voice was hardening as he continued.

"About a month ago, there was a peaceful meeting of highly placed officials, academics, and military people to discuss the wave of events that were sweeping the country. This meeting took place in rural Georgia, at an abandoned airfield which was rented for the occasion. Seventy prominent men and women were in attendance at this meeting." He paused briefly and looked at the assemblage. "All of them were murdered on the spot by soldiers dressed like American troops who had in their possession an Abrams A-1 battle tank."

The crowd shuddered, horrified by this news. The President paused and looked—glared—around the room. He continued, "A couple months ago, a prominent TV personality was arrested for a crime he did not commit on grounds that were so paltry as to be laughable. I believe this act was part and parcel of the same conspiracy that is behind these other atrocities."

Thank God he has linked these events together, I thought. I listened even more intently.

"I did not come here today to impose martial law or to threaten our civil liberties. I came here today to serve notice that terrorism in any guise will not be tolerated. I also serve notice to those states that are thinking of seceding: It is not permissible to extract yourself from the sacred union that our Founding Fathers established with much blood and grief over two hundred years ago and which was confirmed by the deaths of over half a million of our countrymen during the Civil War. You will nullify your secession resolutions or your legislatures and executive branches will be declared invalid, and new elections will be held within your states within the next thirty days."

"In the meantime, under the Emergency Powers Act, I am

assuming the rights accorded me under emergency conditions as these need to be implemented. These are sweeping mandates which will be used when needed to maintain public order and protect the territorial and political integrity of the United States of America."

"I have this to say to our friends and enemies abroad: The United States of America is committed to its existence and to its continued success. I assure you that we will abide by our treaties, continue our cooperation, and oppose any force that may try to take advantage of the current situation. So help me God."

And with that, the man whom everyone thought was so wishy-washy strode off the stage surrounded by a small army of bodyguards and walked out of the chamber. It wasn't until after he left the room that the applause began. Thunderous and sustained, it rocked the hallowed walls of Congress in a way that had not been witnessed since the end of hostilities in World War II. I was torn. On the one hand, I felt some hope for the first time in months. I was relieved that the President was on top of these developments. On the other hand, it seemed that Gerald Aberland had just declared himself a dictator, to the adulation of the very institution designated to prevent that from happening.

Chapter 39

A few days after the speech, Dora and I sat at a small table in the *Black Bean* coffee shop in Silver Spring, Maryland, waiting for Special Agent Robert Banks to arrive. Neither of us was saying much. Every once in a while I would stroke her hand or smile at her or make some other hopeful gesture or noise; but the truth was that I had not felt emotionally connected to her since my trip back from northern Virginia. I was worried about her, but she seemed impenetrable. She agreed to meet with Banks, and I had made the call and rescheduled our meeting. When I tried to talk with her about the President's speech, she just shook her head and did not offer an opinion.

In contrast to our silence, the media were going nuts. They hailed Aberland as a strong, decisive leader whose vow to preserve the Union was traced at every opportunity to the only other president with experience with rebellion, Abraham Lincoln. This seemed to me absurd, although I could feel some of the apprehension more than a few citizens felt in 1861 when Lincoln suppressed many civil rights and basically accorded himself absolute authority to deal with the impending breakup of the Union. It worked back then, but I had doubts about how well it would work now. I was also unsure of where Aberland stood in the grand scheme of things. Was he a Christian Reconstructionist? If so, the Bookkeepers' plan has been fulfilled. If not, the country was in for some hard times. I wished Dora would shake off her sullen despondency so we could talk about it. She was like an encyclopedia that could not or would not open.

At precisely 6:00 p.m., Agent Banks walked into the small but upscale coffee shop. He went straight to the counter and ordered a container of black coffee, paid for it, and ambled over to our table, taking a delicate sip of the hot liquid on his way. This kind of casualness did not fit with my image of him; but he was, after all, a cop, and maybe this was what cops did when they had a crack at good coffee.

Banks sat down without introduction. He looked at Dora for a moment and then said simply, "Agent Banks."

Dora nodded. "Isadore Hathaway," she finally said.

It was obvious that everyone was waiting and that neither Dora nor Banks was going to start. I finally said, "Agent Banks, when we met the other day in Virginia, you said some pretty serious things, including a conspiracy and threats to Miss Hathaway's life."

I let that hang in the air for a while.

Then I said, "I would like to hear more about these things."

Banks took a deep breath and then another sip of his coffee. He looked at both of us. It was apparent that he was in some sort of discomfort. My antennae were up and the big fear—that we were being set up—was not abating much. I could sense Dora on edge. Her breathing was shallow, and I thought I could detect an increase in her pulse rate. My anxiety was climbing.

Banks looked over and nodded to the man behind the counter, and I inhaled sharply. The other man walked to the front door and locked it, turning the OPEN/CLOSED sign around indicating that the shop was now closed. He drew shades down across the windows facing the street. Then the man disappeared through a door behind the counter where he had been working.

I pushed back from the table in a gesture that must have looked as belligerent as I felt it to be, because Banks looked me square in the eye and said, "Relax, he's a friend."

I rolled my head around in an effort to loosen some of the muscle tension that had been accumulating in the back of my neck. If this was a set-up, we were already gone. If not, I needed to be more self-possessed for the next step.

Banks took out a notebook from his inside jacket pocket and laid it on the table in front of me. He looked at me and then Dora. "This is what I believe is going on," he said.

For the next thirty minutes, Special Agent Robert Banks did not stop talking in the same monotonic voice that he used when he was questioning people. *This must be the voice he uses when he is briefing his superiors*, I thought. *Concise, fact-oriented, no extraneous material.* The tone and the dryness would, under ordinary circumstances, have been academic and even boring; but today the content made it riveting.

Essentially Banks had a bead on everything we knew about the Bookkeepers: their number, their names, their mission, and their positions. He also knew their connections not only to each other but to other groups. He had descriptions of some contacts they had had with radical fringe groups and listed about three dozen politicians who had been secret collaborators. He also had some information and a theory about what had happened in Georgia.

"That wasn't the Georgia National Guard," he said, as if he knew that was what I had thought. "They were members of a group called The New Georgia Republic, a secessionist group that basically consists of middle-aged white guys who dress up in uniforms and play soldier on weekends. They stole the tank."

Dora and I looked at each other. I could sense her mental wheels beginning to move. I held my breath; I did not want to hope too soon that the ice was breaking. But every bone in my agnostic body prayed that it would.

Banks continued, "This was their coup, their contribution to the mayhem the Bookkeepers started. Addelburg found out about the Georgia meeting because he had people going through the trash of anyone in the State Department who was in his twisted mind suspect. There was a New York phone number on a slip of paper that he had traced. Turns out it belonged to a professor at NYU who told his secretary where he was going that day. The professor had also given his secretary names of some of the other people who would be at the meeting." Banks paused. "I think he was bragging a little. But when Addelburg got a whiff of the political leanings of that little group, he started making calls."

Banks paused again and shook his head. "I think the plan was simply to surveil the meeting, but the NGR people had been excited that Denver came off so well that they decided to get into the act in a more dramatic way. In their mind it was like the battle of Bull Run, where the upstart rebels defeated the first attempts of the Union Army to stop the secession." Banks looked across the room; then he hung his head for a moment. "Evil bastards," he said almost under his breath.

Dora was breathing again. I had been looking at Banks while he was talking, but I glanced over at Dora and saw some color return to her face. She was not only breathing; I could tell she was thinking as well. It was not hard to see that she had felt that events in Georgia were her doing. Now she was hearing from somebody who seemed to know just how the meeting had been compromised. And it didn't involve her.

"John Wallaway," she blurted out. "A brilliant young economics professor from NYU. I didn't think he had enough experience, but three people disagreed with me and supported his coming. I thought he was too young and inexperienced."

Banks nodded but did not say anything.

Then the light in Dora's eyes began to dim again. I could tell that for a moment she felt exonerated, relieved of the guilt of the massacre. But the fact that this young and inexperienced professor had been killed needlessly was still an ache and a heartbreak. Dora stared at the table top for a full minute. Neither Banks nor I interrupted her.

After a while, she looked up. "He had a wife and a daughter," she said distantly. She shook her head. "What else?" she said, turning back to Banks.

"Addelburg was mad as hell that these overgrown cowboys had risked the entire plan by killing so many innocent people. It had not been a part of the Bookkeepers plan, which limited the mass killing to the one event in Denver. All the other killings were individual murders of people they were afraid would stand in their way. But before he could do anything about it, he was killed in broad daylight in the District."

"Agent Banks," I said. "How did you get this information?"

Banks looked at me without a trace of harshness. "As I told you the other day, Senator, I have resources." He paused for a moment. "I do not disclose them unless absolutely necessary."

I looked at Banks. If this was an act, he was a stellar performer. I took it from his tone that he did not welcome inquiries into his specific sources. My heart told me that this was OK; I would not want to compromise my resources if I were in his position. I could not help wondering, however, what he knew about how Addelburg was killed. At that moment, I did not want to ask, but I had to have some indication of what he knew or thought.

"Who killed Addelburg?" I finally said, hoping my color or tone of voice or anxiety did not change or show.

Banks exhaled sharply and looked at me square in the face. "I don't know. We think it was the same person or the same group that killed Bandera." He paused for a moment. "But we lost a lot of leads when the people in Georgia died. They were all opposed to the Bookkeepers, although none of them was known to be violent." He paused again. "So we just don't know at this time."

I noticed that he had switched to the first person plural; presumably he was sharing with us what the FBI investigation had dug up. He had crossed the line from his personal work to Agency work. An important line.

I nodded to Banks and then looked over at Dora, who was

showing signs of life again. She seemed to be struggling mightily with whatever demons were rumbling around in her head. She shifted in her chair, stretched, became immobile for a few moments, then became restless again.

"Are you OK?" I finally asked.

She did not say anything but nodded her head in large, deliberate movements. Finally, she said, "Yes, Jake, I think so."

Banks may have had more information, but Dora and I were a bit overwhelmed by what we had heard already to press him. There was silence around the small table. Banks sipped his coffee. Dora and I lost ourselves to our inner thoughts. Minutes went by.

It was Dora who spoke first. "What do you want from us, Agent Banks?" she asked, looking at him directly and sounding like herself more than she had in weeks.

Banks looked at her. "I need two things: I need evidence and I need more eyes and ears," he said. "Anything you might have about the events I just described would be helpful." He took another sip of his coffee. "What I laid out for you is what I believe actually happened, but I have to prove it. Any documentation you have would help in that task enormously."

Neither Dora nor I spoke.

"I also need some help with my investigation. As I mentioned to you the other day, Senator, I am doing this work on my own. My superiors would fry me if they knew what I was doing right now. I cannot do all the legwork by myself." He looked down into his nearly empty coffee cup. "So if you or people you know can help me, I have a list of observational targets I would like to gather information about. Most of them are going to be at a meeting at that church in a couple weeks."

I glanced at Dora before I spoke, but I wanted to be the one who responded first. "Agent, Banks, I believe you are a good agent and a good man; I appreciate your letting us in on what you have learned. But you are asking me to do things that I need to consider in the light of my role as an elected official; I need some time to think about it."

Banks nodded. "Fair enough," he said without rancor. "Keep in touch." He stood up, bowed slightly toward Dora and said, "Pleasure to meet you, Dr. Hathaway. I knew your father." Then he turned and slipped out a back entrance.

Chapter 40

Dora stared at the empty space that Banks had occupied a moment before. She was thinking. Then she turned to me and said, "Let's get out of here, Jake."

When we got into the car, which we had rented for the occasion, Dora motioned for me not to speak. We did not say anything all the way back to Washington DC, where we turned the car into the rental agency. Jefferson met us at the rental agency in the silver BMW. Dora gestured to Jefferson, and he began weaving in and out of traffic, turning often and keeping his eye out for anybody who might be following us.

As soon as the driving settled down, Dora started talking.

"He sounds genuine, Jake, but I don't know. There's something about him that seems almost too smooth, too comfortable dealing with someone the FBI has under round-the clock surveillance." She thought for a moment. "But then again, I am not sure I trust my instincts right now." She paused again; she was almost thinking aloud. "He said he knew my father, but that could mean that he met him on one or more occasions. Everybody knew my father."

I wasn't on the same page with Dora. I was thinking about two roads diverging in a yellow wood. *Do I get more deeply into this mess and help Banks? God knows what side he's really on. Or do I get out now while my actions are still undetected and go back to my senatorial life and do what I can from the halls of power, which will hopefully be restored when this crisis passes? Or do I try some combination of these?* I was all questions with few answers. I turned to Dora.

"Do you think we should help him?" I asked.

Dora looked at me thoughtfully. "I think the question is 'Can he help us?'" Dora replied. "He had an awful lot of information for one guy looking into a conspiracy involving at least hundreds of people."

"He cannot know about my role in killing Bandera and Addelburg," I said earnestly.

Something about that seemed to strike Dora as funny. She chuckled. "Your role? You mean tracking them, pulling the trigger, and killing them?"

I got the point. I had the starring if not the only role in taking out those two bad guys.

"I want to make sure that doesn't come to light," I said, chastened a little by the casual talk of murder.

Dora took my hand. "Of course not, Jake," she said solicitously. "I think we can manage that."

I wasn't so sure. I had a hunch Banks was a determined and forceful man. If what he was telling us was true, if he had uncovered all that information basically on his own, he was a force to be reckoned with.

We drove on for a while. It was getting late, and I was hungry. I suggested to Dora that we stop somewhere and get something to eat. She directed Jefferson to drive out of DC into northern Virginia. We both felt some assurance that we weren't being followed.

We found a place in McLean on Old Dominion Drive that was still open. Nice place: white tablecloths, flowers, candles on the table. It was a refreshing respite from the eat-on-the-run schedule we had been keeping. It almost felt like a date.

I could tell the meeting with Banks had been an important turning point for Dora, who was seeming more like herself. She wasn't out of the woods yet, but I felt hope that in time she would recover. I tried to be as solicitous as I could, meaning ordering huge amounts of food. Dora had not been eating much the past few weeks, and she was famished. We had two appetizers each, entrees, dessert, two bottles of wine and coffee. Dora apologized at one point, but I waved her off.

"No need," I said. "I'm just happy to have you back."

She looked at me sweetly and shrugged slightly. Before she could apologize again, I cut in. "I was worried about you, Dora; that's all," I said, taking her hand and squeezing it gently.

She smiled a muffled smile. Then she continued eating.

I love being with Dora; it does not really matter what we do together. Watching her eat with such gusto made me realize how relieved I was that she had turned a corner and how much I valued her and how much I appreciated who and what she was. Quirky, but lovable to the core.

Besides delighting in her coming back, I struggled with my own thoughts through bites of this or that delicacy. For the first time, I wondered if my killing those two men was the best thing to do. They were evil—there was no doubt about that—but I am not sure their deaths had much strategic value. It was hard to sort out my motivation, so I tried to stay away from those sticky issues. Gradually, my attention turned beyond myself, Dora, Banks, and the Bookkeepers and settled on the person whose behavior and motivations were a large question mark in my mind: Gerald Aberland.

I did not know much about President Aberland. He's a republican, so, of course, I voted for him. But he seemed like a non-entity. Not from the intellectual wing of the party—although that had shrunk in recent years—Aberland came up through the ranks. He was most recently governor of Tennessee and did an able job there by all accounts. He made all the right noises, pandering as our party has done in recent times to the right to garner their votes. He acted like "liberal" was a bad word, but he always seemed to me to have the heart of a moderate. I did not dislike him. I just didn't know him very well. And right at the moment I didn't fully trust him. The image of him addressing Congress held sway in the center of my mind as I watched Dora plow through more calories than I thought possible for a hundred and fifteen pound, size four-to-six female. She and I chatted through the courses, and it was great not to be talking about anything important. Through it all, however, I began to think of my gun, the one I had left in the Indian Affairs Building after shooting Addelburg. I was missing it. I wanted to go home, assemble it, take it in my hands, and feel its heft, its wood, its metal, its power. I had not been back to Indian Affairs to see if it had been found, and I knew rationally that it would be foolhardy for me to come anywhere close to that building, but the impulse was unmistakably there. It was irritating not to have access to the gun I had come to revere.

Finally, Dora and I finished dinner, and she sat back in her chair holding her coffee cup in two hands. "That was good," she said with a wide smile on her face.

I just smiled back. I was going to make a crack about her being a human combine, but I did not want to tarnish the moment. She was satisfied for the first time in weeks.

The check came and Dora grabbed it. "I would be too embarrassed for you to even see this," she said tauntingly. And she handed the server a credit card. Before she relinquished it, however, she had second thoughts and put it back in her wallet. In its place, she took out three hundred dollar bills and laid them on the black case with the check inside.

"Better safe than sorry," she said to me after the server departed.

"Always thinking," I said with no small measure of admiration. "Let's go."

We did not talk much on the way home. We held hands like middle-school children. I asked Dora to have Jefferson drop me off at my apartment. I was exhausted, and I just wanted to go to sleep.

Her face registered a little hurt. Maybe it was feigned. I am sure she was tired as well. "Do I get a rain check?" she asked.

"Absolutely," I replied. Then I kissed her. Not a peck, but a long, lingering kiss.

Before I could change my mind, Jefferson pulled up in front of my Georgetown apartment. I looked at Dora dolefully. "This man is entirely too efficient," I said. I kissed Dora again and opened the door. I was more than a little torn, but I decided my first instinct was probably the safest. I said good-night and watched as Dora and Jefferson drove off. I was glad he was with her; I felt she was safe.

Before I went inside my apartment, I sat on the front stoop for a few minutes. The late August heat was still beating down even at midnight, but there were people out, probably returning home from the theater or dinner or whatever else it was that humans did with their time. At the same time, it was quiet for Georgetown. So quiet I could hear voices coming from the bar a block away. *Probably filled with college kids returning from summer break*, I thought. For once, I did not envy them. They were going through a great time in their lives and probably have no idea how precious it will seem in retrospect. I am not sorry about the direction my life has taken, but I admit I had no idea when I was in college that the path would be so murky, so devoid of solid markers, the kind college kids live with every day of their academic lives.

Chapter 41

It did not take long to get a read on where Gerald Aberland was going with his newly declared powers. At the beginning of September, he announced the formation of a Presidential panel that was to serve as his advisory board during the crisis. This included some but not all members of his cabinet, the Joint Chiefs, some NSA people, and the head of the FBI, CIA, and FEMA. He also had assorted lower level officials. Some pundits scratched their heads at this. Why not use the cabinet he had and the access he had to those other agencies? What about Congress? What about the courts? But people were nervous, so they just waited and watched to see what he did next.

The President had some leeway in organizing himself and his staff during a crisis. But what stood out to me was one name on the list of people in this group: Maximilian Grobe, the Chief of Criminal Justice Information Services for the FBI. One of the Bookkeepers. I had no idea if Aberland knew that Grobe was one of the twelve or not. If he did not, it meant that one of the Bookkeepers had access to the highest level of power in a crisis; if he did, it meant he was in on it. Either possibility made me sick.

We were still two weeks away from the meeting at United Temple. Dora and I went back and forth about whether we should get involved with Robert Banks and whether or not we should attempt to use the meeting as an opportunity to destroy the Bookkeepers. We were having little agreement. It's not that we were on opposing sides in this conversation. Both of us kept changing sides, as we considered various reasons to bring Banks in or not; to attack the Bookkeepers at their meeting or not; to continue in our pursuit at all or not. We were lost.

Finally, Dora said, "Jake, it's just too risky to ask an FBI agent to assist us in eliminating ten people. So we have to either do it without Banks or not do it at all." She paused for a moment and thought. "I do not wish to spend the rest of my life in prison."

She was right, of course. As much as Banks' information would be helpful, he was a government agent. He was also, by his account, a highly principled man who would not, on the one hand, allow direct orders from his superiors prevent him from doing what he felt was right. On the other hand, it was hard to picture him participating in killing. He also knew about the church, so we would have a great deal of difficulty planning any kind of assault with his watchful eyes focused in that direction.

"OK," I said. "How would you feel about retiring to the south of France?"

Dora rolled her eyes, but not too much.

After a while, she said, "Maybe I was asking the wrong question, Jake. Maybe the question is whether or not we should help Banks. After all, he must have some powerful resources."

I saw the wisdom of this, but I was still nervous about it.

"What about your important and mysterious friends?" I asked Dora out of the blue one afternoon. "You know, the ones you fly off to see and never tell me about?"

Dora's face darkened. I immediately felt bad for putting her on a spot. I could anticipate her response.

"Georgia," she said simply. "We put all our energy into that meeting in Georgia, Jake. Most of my friends are dead." She looked away. "The others are afraid."

I was embarrassed beyond apologizing. "Let's call Banks," I said. "Maybe we can help each other."

Banks answered on the first ring. We arranged to meet later that day. After I clicked off, I looked at Dora. I cannot imagine how these past weeks have been for her. I don't know how or why she continues. Beyond the body blows, beyond the sophistication, I sensed a strong and committed human being. She would never stop.

Before we went to meet Banks, we gathered together some documents and photographs which we thought might be helpful in a criminal investigation. We went through each document, making sure there was no way to trace it to anything incriminating about either Dora or me. Then we drove to a metro station and deposited them into a locker. We wiped everything down, and removed the key, cleaning it of fingerprints and dropping it into a small zip-lock bag. We met Banks at a rest stop east of DC. We sat at an empty picnic table a distance from everyone else who was there.

"You said you needed evidence," Dora began. "In this locker are some documents and photographs which might help you."

Banks took the small bag, glanced at it, and put it inside his pocket. "Thank you," he said.

We all sat in silence for a few moments. It was clear that our fates were now intertwined.

"The meeting a week from Sunday," Banks said, breaking the silence. "There will be nine Bookkeepers there. Everyone except Grobe."

"What is your plan, Agent Banks?" I asked simply.

He did not hesitate. "We need someone on the inside. As near as I can tell, that building is a fortress. Not just cameras, but bullet-proof glass, armed guards, and metal detectors. They will be meeting in a windowless room in the interior of the building. Senator, this church is a meeting ground for high government officials. Since you are a member of the Senate, it would not seem unusual for you to want to get involved in their 'ministries.'" He peered at me intently. "What do you think?"

"I think I don't have time to join the church to get involved in the next ten days. Besides, Banks, anyone who knows me knows that I am not the church-going type."

Banks turned to Dora. "What do you think, Dr. Hathaway?"

Dora returned his stare but did not say anything right away. Then she said, "I don't think it is possible for us to set up any kind of system to get into that meeting on such short notice without tipping our hand. But what if we used the opportunity to arrest them?"

Banks looked at her blankly. He may have been thinking in the bowels of his brain, but there was not sign of life on the outside.

"I don't think we have enough to arrest them yet," he said. "Besides, as far as I know, they are not even under suspicion from Justice." He looked down at the trodden grass beneath the bench on which he was sitting.

A moment later, he raised his head. "It might be possible to detain them, however," he said. "If that stuff you gave me is useful."

Dora and I both looked at him. "How?" we said in unison.

"They will probably go through a tunnel from the church basement to enter and leave the building. That way, no one sees them enter through the main door. Even though they put this meeting in their church bulletin, no one really has any idea just how well-placed these people are or what the nature of the group is. They do not want to draw attention to themselves."

Banks pulled a folded up piece of paper from inside his jacket, which he still wore despite the heat. He unfolded it on the creaky wooden picnic table. "Here is a schematic of the church complex," he said. He pointed to the broken lines that ran from the church basement to the multipurpose building about fifty feet away. He also traced their arrival from the parking lot. "They will probably have heavy security," he said. "Especially after the shooting of two of their members."

Neither Dora nor I took our eyes off Banks. I don't know what she was thinking, but I knew what I was thinking. *Ambush. A narrow tunnel, presumably not known to many people. The targets close together.* My heart began to race.

"We can probably detain them either before they enter the tunnel or when they come out," he said. "But personally, I don't think it's a good idea to allow these people to spend too much time together, so I recommend we take them on the way in."

"How?" Dora asked. "With what resources?" She glanced at me but kept addressing Banks. "You said you were working under the radar. The Bureau doesn't know anything about this. How are you going to affect the detention of nine highly placed officials who are not wanted for any kind of crime?"

Banks did not reply right away.

"And who probably have very heavy security?" she added.

Still Banks did not reply. Instead, he brought both his arms together and wrapped each hand around the other wrist on top of the schematic on the splintered table. "We have some time to think about that," he said simply.

I leaned back on my bench, a little exasperated by this good man trying to do the right thing while going against the rules that he had lived by for over thirty years. He may have friends and resources, but I just didn't think he had the fortitude required to do the really hard thing. The thing that to my mind was once again obvious, necessary, and clear. This meeting was the opportunity; this was the time to put an end to this evil group. I had too many questions about where the President stood, where Banks stood, where the FBI or the CIA or the NSA stood to risk losing this opportunity if not to stop the mayhem, at least to deal it a major setback.

"Agent Banks," I said with as much authority as I could muster. "This is something we need to think about as carefully as possible. If you review the material in that locker and if is sufficient to get the Bureau going about this group, then we can use their considerable strengths and manpower to arrest all of them." I did not think for a moment that any of this was possible. I don't know how the Bookkeepers had hamstrung the highest law enforcement agency in the United States, but I know they did it and that they continued to do it.

Banks nodded slowly. "OK," he said. "I'll see what I can do."

With that we took our leave. Banks left first, and then Dora and I climbed into her sedan. We did not say anything at first. I was driving, and I kept glancing into the rear mirrors to make sure we weren't being followed. There was a fair amount of traffic, so it was hard to tell. After circling around for about a half hour, I drove on to DC. As we approached, the traffic slowed.

Dora and I looked at each other. I clicked on the radio, looking for a local news station. We caught the tail end of a story that was about an explosion. But we didn't hear what had been hit. It was obvious that traffic was slowed for miles. Without thinking too much, I crossed the median and got into the outbound lane. I did not want to be stuck in traffic, and I felt an urgent need for more details. I pulled into the first motel we came to and got a room. Dora was silent throughout this. She did not protest; she just let me take the lead.

When we got to the room, I went straight to the small TV and turned it on to CNN. Pictures of flaming material filled the screen, and the voiceover was describing the devastation.

The White House was on fire.

Chapter 42

Dora and I stared at the TV incredulously. According to the announcer, it was unknown at this time if the President and the First Lady were in the building at the time of the explosion. Judging from the extent of the damage, which was massive, it did not look as if anyone could have survived if they were in the main section of the building.

How could this happen? I wondered, doubtlessly along with most everyone else in the country. *The White House was impregnable: it had security systems on security systems. It also had fire suppression systems in place to quell any burning material. There were no indications that it had been a plane as was used on 9/11. It must have been sabotage. But how? Who? Why?* The newscaster was not helpful about these things; he kept restating unanswered questions.

There were partial screen cutaways to close up interviews with relatives of people who were thought to have been in the building. It was nighttime, so many of the day staff had already gone home. The cleaning staff was there and the regular kitchen staff. The White House was run like an antebellum Plantation House, with many servants and workers whose job was to make it look perfect always. Befitting the greatest nation on earth.

The network looked as if it were just filling in time as they provided pictures of the first serious damage done to the White House since 1812, when the British burned it to the ground. Finally, a piece of real news. The President was safe. At the first sign of trouble, the Secret Service had spirited him away to an unannounced location far from the place he called home. It was unclear if he was even in Washington. It was also unclear where Mrs. Aberland was.

Then the announcer began listing the names of some of the confirmed dead. It was sickeningly similar to that bright Tuesday morning in September of 2001. Lots of pictures; not much news; fatalities mounting.

Several officials were among the dead or missing: the heads of the FBI and CIA; members of the National Security Agency; several members of the new Presidential panel. Some escaped, among them Maximilian Grobe.

There was some news. "It now appears that this blaze was intentionally set," the newscaster was saying, as if relieved to have something to talk about. "Early indications are that a chemical substance was fed into the building and then ignited with a high intensity instrument. Whatever that substance was was found on the bodies of several of the victims."

This was not an accident. I looked at Dora. The look of horror on her face was similar to what I saw in Georgia. I reached out and put my arm around her. "Come on," I said. "Let's get something to eat." I pulled her away from the TV and switched it off. "I think we know who did this," I said.

She did not resist at first. She limply allowed me to redirect her attention away from the television. I thought I was going to lose her again to the apathy I had seen in her the previous few weeks. But then she pulled her arm away. "Those sons of bitches!" she yelled. She put both her hands on the back of a worn wooden chair and hung her head between her arms. Her arms were taut, and I could see her knuckles whiten as they squeezed the back of the old chair. She was breathing heavily, taking in long slow breaths in through her nose and exhaling slowly through her mouth. She was trying to maintain control. She slowly turned her head toward me. "We've got to kill these people, Jake," she said acidly. "Soon. At that meeting."

I nodded because I preferred Dora angry and alive rather than passive and depleted. And because I couldn't think of a single reason not to kill them all. Except for the matter of Robert Banks and the FBI, but I did not think at that moment that this would stop us. "OK," I said.

It was clear that Dora wasn't going anywhere. "Let's use their preferred method," she said with a tone so devoid of emotion that she could have been teaching a biology class. "Let's use poison. We can plant it in the tunnel in the Church. It is probably their most vulnerable spot. Let's see if we can't show these people once and for all that they cannot get away with destroying this country."

Chapter 43

It turns out that Dora did have a few remaining contacts, one of whom was a weapons specialist, the guy who had a hand in collecting the tools buried in the floor of the safe house in DC. Dora contacted him to discuss possibilities. I was unclear how much he knew, and she did not allow me to meet with him or even talk to him. She took care of all that by herself.

What this man proposed was using a vicious neurotoxin called batrachotoxin, a substance found in a certain species of South American frogs and favored by the indigenous peoples of Columbia to tip their hunting darts. Extremely lethal even at low dosages, all that is required is that it break the skin. To that end, he provided us with five canisters which were filled with tiny metal shards that looked like glazing points. The canisters were filled with propellant gases which, once triggered, would provide enough force to easily pierce through normal clothing, especially the type likely to be worn in mid-September. In other words, we had the twenty-first century equivalent of poison darts. Dora's contact has connected the triggers to a timer and to a remote triggering device, such that all we had to do was set it up to detonate at a selected time or trigger it manually.

Simple in theory, I thought. Of course, there were a few details, such as finding a way into the church basement, locating the tunnel, and setting these things up undetected. It was entirely possible that security might sweep the tunnel before the Bookkeepers walked through it. One thing was clear: I had to get into that basement. I guess I was going to join the church after all.

With only a few days to go before the next New Members Meeting, I called the church and inquired again about membership. I pushed menu buttons until I spoke with a real person. I wanted everyone there to know who I was. There were two reasons for this: one, I wanted some consideration because I was a senator; secondly, I did not want in any way to act as if I were undercover. I wanted everything to be done in the light of day. Fewer questions, even given that more than one person will shake his or her head about the liberal senator from Wisconsin joining a conservative Baptist Church.

The woman I spoke with, Irene, was sweet as could be. It was clear that she was from somewhere further south than the Virginia/Maryland border. Or maybe she was just old Virginia. Mellifluous voice, unctuous, she never stopped addressing me as "Senator Telemark". She asked if I would prefer to attend the Wednesday service before the Thursday meeting, and I told her that I would be honored to attend both. She was pleased. I am also sure she spoke with her superior as soon as she got off the phone. These places thrive on the powerful, and it would be a feather in her cap to announce to her boss that she had snagged a senator to join their august assemblage.

After I hung up, I turned to Dora, who had been listening the whole time. "I'm not sure I can pull this off, Dora," I said. Religious people make me nervous; I could hear the skepticism in my own voice.

Dora smiled and kissed me on the cheek. "Who knows, Jake, maybe this will end up with your turning to religion after all."

Doubtful, I thought. We began to talk plans. By necessity, I would have to play this by ear. It is possible that they will give new members a tour of the facility. They may even give me a private tour, given my status.

The Wednesday Worship Service was the easy part. It was spottily attended, but there were more people there than I would have thought for a Wednesday morning. I recognized staffers from the Hill and some other folks. Even a lobbyist or two. I was surprised that I had some familiarity with the hymns they sang, and I joined in with as much gusto as my talentless voice would allow. Blessedly, the service was followed by donuts and coffee in the church basement. I followed the elderly ushers as they directed me down a flight of steps near the rear of the church that I had not noticed when I entered. It seemed to be the only access point to the lower level.

I had never seen a church basement. I had always imagined them to be medieval places, with stone walls and slotted chains. I guess this is one of the reasons I am not so religious. This one looked nothing like that. The walls were perfectly plastered and painted in light colors. The lighting was bright, provided by recessed fluorescent tubes throughout the ceiling. There were several doors which led off a main central room. None of these was marked, so I assumed they were for storage.

Irene, the church secretary, was the first to introduce herself. She looked just like her voice: large, warm-hearted. She extended her hand in a way that suggested I lean forward to kiss it, but I shook it instead.

"Senator Telemark," she exclaimed. "Welcome to our little church. Let me introduce you to the pastor." She put her arm on my back and gently led me to a tall man who was standing by the coffee and donut table.

"Pastor Williams," she purred. "Allow me to introduce our newest member, Senator Jacob Telemark." She bowed slightly, and the pastor extended his hand in a limp handshake. It felt creepy.

"Welcome, Senator," the white-haired man in his mid-sixties said, "to our little church."

I wondered why they kept referring to it as "our little church", when it was obviously both large and well-endowed. *Southern understatement*, I guessed.

"Thank you, Reverend," I said politely. And then, because I have never in my life known how to speak with members of the clergy, I pushed onward. "Nice complex you have here."

The Reverend, who was at least as uncomfortable as I was in this ridiculous small-talk situation, took this bait with great relief. He launched into the history and construction of the Union Temple Baptist Church, noting that it was started shortly after the Civil War and built by former slaves from the surrounding plantations. He seemed to think that this was a good thing, but I wondered if and how much those hardworking people were ever paid. I wondered aloud if the old complex had nineteenth century curiosities, such as secret doorways and tunnels.

"Yes, yes it does," the Reverend averred with increasing enthusiasm. "In fact, there is a tunnel which connects all the church buildings, including the parsonage, the multipurpose building, and the church." As he said this, his head tilted to what I gauged to be the northeast corner of the room, where a door exactly the same as all the others stood silently closed and where the schematic said the entrance to the tunnel was. This was blessing enough for one day.

We chatted on for a bit, and I met some other worshipers who had heard the word "Senator" and decided that I was worth a second look. A queue was beginning to form, so I glanced at my watch, apologized because I was late for an important appointment, and left.

Once outside, I inhaled deeply and let out a huge stream of air. *Why do people do this?* I wondered. *Boring songs, bad coffee, and ho-hum donuts.* But I felt sure than I had obtained the basic information I needed. I had scoped out the stage for the next act in this drama.

Chapter 44

The New Members Meeting the next night was held in the multipurpose building near the church, in a corner room with windows. Irene was there, but the pastor was not. There were about eight of us "new members" sitting around a table asking questions and talking about what we were looking for in a church. It was a very American scene. There were two former Catholics, assorted Protestants, one other former Episcopalian, and a couple of people who wore their agnosticism on their sleeves. All were looking for a church that was convenient, friendly, social, and not too demanding. The agnostics arrogantly talked over any conversation involving God or Jesus or beliefs. They seemed to want either a place to drop their kids off or a place to sneer at true believers. I found them repulsive. My own agnosticism is a very private thing.

"Do we get a tour of the facility?" I asked cheerfully after I tired of listening to people rationalizing their senseless behavior.

"Why, of course," Irene exclaimed. This seemed to be her default mode of speech. She exclaimed everything.

And tour we did. We walked the entire multipurpose building, one classroom-like room after another. We walked all around it on two floors. But all the rooms we toured were on the outside. I could feel my mind beginning to glaze over.

"What's in here?" I asked, nodding to a door on the interior side of the hall.

Irene did not skip a beat. "Why, that's our board meeting room. We keep it locked because there are important files and records in there." She did not sound the least bit defensive or even guarded. We moved on. As we were descending the stairs, I asked as nonchalantly as I could, "Do we get to take the tunnel to the church?"

Irene smiled broadly. She had been present for the conversation with Pastor Williams. "Why, of course," she exclaimed liltingly. "I had intended it as a surprise for you, Senator."

The thought crossed my mind that she was flirting with me, and I glanced at her left hand. It was ringless. I blushed ever so slightly. "Why, thank you," I exclaimed.

The tunnel was clean, dry, and well lit. The walls were either plaster or drywall. No shelves; no places to plant anything. Same fluorescent lighting recessed in the ceiling, just like the church basement, where the fifty foot tunnel led. We emerged into the church basement through the same door that Pastor Williams had indicated when I spoke with him. Then we continued the tour through the church and sanctuary and ended up in the parsonage, where Pastor Williams and his wife had coffee and pastries. *The path to religion must be through the stomach*, I thought darkly. The pastries were delicious.

I drove home thinking about how difficult it would be to plant the canisters in the clean, uncluttered, and sterile environment that was the United Temple Baptist Church of Northern Virginia. It not only felt unlikely; it felt impossible. I planned to share these thoughts with Dora when I got back to the safe house, but she was in the shower, so I got a cup of coffee and flipped on the television. The White House fire was still the story on all networks all the time. The death toll was in the twenty-to-thirty range: miraculous for the intensity of the blaze. President Aberland had come on earlier in the evening to assure everyone of the continuity of government and of his commitment to rebuild the White House. He also expressed gratitude and grief for the brave members of the Secret Service who saved his life, some of whom gave their own in the process. He did not say anything about his wife, who was nowhere to be seen.

Some more facts had come to light about the fire itself. It appears to have been a hydrogen fire. Somehow that common gas had been pumped into the White House, which was very well insulated. Hydrogen usually dissipates quickly because it is lighter than air, but the volume in the White House was great. PVC containers had been found melted around the building. That explained how they got past the metal detectors. The first was ignited on the first floor and quickly spread to the second, despite the fire suppression systems activating quickly. Many of the fatalities died because of asphyxiation due to the intensity of the fire using up all the oxygen in the building so rapidly.

The effect on the psyche of the nation was unmistakable. Denver had been terrible, but the White House was the symbol of American power and supremacy. More than the Capitol or the Supreme Court, even more than the Statue of Liberty, the White House stood for stability, power, and American principles throughout the world.

Then the reporter turned his attention to something that started as a small thing but began to grow. Evidently people from each state were converging on Washington DC. There was to be a day-long gathering in front of the burned out executive mansion and a candle light vigil in the evening. At first, the media thought that perhaps ten or twelve selected people would come from each state. But the roads and airways and train tracks leading to Washington were jammed. Thousands of people were arriving; maybe hundreds of thousands. It appeared that the population of the nation had reached some kind of critical mass, and the citizenry was crying out for order, for restoration, and for their government.

If the Bookkeepers had planned this, maybe they deserve to run the country; that thought flew through my mind. But I did not think that they had planned this or even anticipated it. This demonstration seemed to come from another place, a place of devotion and strength, not fear or subservience. Thousands of people wanted to send a message. And they were coming in person to do it.

I had not heard the shower stop or Dora get out until she was standing next to me wrapped in one large towel and drying her hair with another. "What's up?" she said, and it startled me a bit. I looked up and pointed to the television screen.

Dora stood rapt. A helicopter was aloft with a camera aimed at the huge crowds assembling in front of the White House and spilling onto all the adjacent side streets. She sat down next to me and watched. A commercial interrupted the action, and we both turned and looked at each other. Dora had a tear in her eye, and so did I. I shrugged. She wiped her eye.

"How did it go at the church?" she asked after a while.

I looked at her. "Tough," I said. "All neat and tidy; no place to hide anything."

It was Dora's turn to shrug. She nodded toward the television and said simply, "We'll find a way, Jake."

Chapter 45

We did not hear from Banks on Saturday. Nor did we find a way to use the containers Dora's contact had provided us. I began to think we needed another way to eliminate the Bookkeepers, elegant and satisfying as poisoning these men would be. We looked through the weapons cache beneath the floor in the safe house, which was becoming our house. There were plenty of alternatives. Guns, knives, hand grenades, and self-propelled grenade launchers.

As we considered these materials, a thought kept flitting around the edge of my mind. *How did they get hydrogen into PVC containers?* I wondered. Because it is so flammable and so light, it always comes in heavy metal cylinders with double control flow mechanisms. I asked Dora to check with her guy. She left the building to do this, I guess so I would not somehow intuit the guy's cell phone number when she dialed it. She was not gone long and was putting away her cell phone as she walked back in the house through the garage entrance.

"Not hard," Dora said. "There's a company out in the Midwest that specializes in these things. They've been providing it that way for over a year. They can pack a lot more hydrogen in a single vehicle that way, since the gas is so light anyway. When the containers are also light, they can pile them high. In fact, my contact believes that whoever did the White House probably got their supplies from this company."

"What's the name of the company?" I asked.

"Westover," Dora replied.

I opened the laptop and searched the company name. Yup, there is was right on the home page: bragging about their new light conveyance systems for hydrogen and other gases. I had never thought about flammable gases before, so I actually found the website interesting. They carried carbon monoxide and related flammable gases, but they also carried helium and a variety of other nonflammable gases, including xenon and krypton, which I thought up until that moment was a substance from the planet of the same name used on earth to debilitate Superman.

I searched the site for the Board of Directors on a hunch. I was rewarded with two names with which I was very familiar. Geoffrey Addelburg and Maximilian Grobe. I motioned for Dora to come look and angled the computer toward her. Her mouth dropped open, but no sound came out. Finally, she said, "We've got to get this information to Banks." Almost without thinking, I picked up my cell phone to do just that. For the first time since I've been calling him, however, Banks did not pick up.

"Jake," Dora said. "This seems too, um, amateurish for these guys. That they would actually use a company in which they have an interest to destroy a national monument and kill many people. Too easy to trace." Dora fell into her pensive mode. I did not dispute what Dora was saying. It was unforgivably foolish, if that is what they indeed had done. On the other hand, we did not know for certain that they had procured their gas from this company. I did not think much more about it, except to note mentally that, even if they used a different company, they knew a lot about gases and probably a lot about chemistry.

Midway through these thoughts, my cell phone rang. It was Banks returning my call. I told him what Dora and I had found. Banks was quiet for a moment. Then he said, "Westover is part of a larger conglomeration that provides a lot of chemical products to industry around the world." I was dismayed for a moment that he already had that information, and I thought it was odd that he had not said anything about it before. Then he added, "I just learned about this yesterday, Senator." There was something about Banks' tone that I found disconcerting. I wasn't alarmed; it just didn't sound like his normal, flat-affect way of speaking. Then he said something that really surprised me. "Things are coming together, Senator." I did not respond right away. "The information you and Miss Hathaway gave me was useful," he said.

Finally I said, "What's next, Agent Banks?"

"I am not sure," he replied. "I have to take the information I've gathered to my superiors."

"Is that safe?" I asked. There was a pause on the other end of the line.

"It needs to be done very carefully," Banks replied.

I do not know if Banks was afraid, but the slightly strained way he said these words was evidence of something: fear, caution, apprehension. Neither of us spoke for a few moments. Then Banks said, "Senator, listen very carefully. At the rest stop where we last met, there is a utility room with shelves holding mostly cleaning supplies. Underneath the shelves eighteen inches from both corners is a false tile. Press on the rear left corner of it and it will come free, beneath it is a hole lined with stainless steel. In that hole is everything I've got from my investigation. If you do not hear from me by Wednesday at noon, get those materials and use them in any way you can." He paused. I could almost hear him perspiring over the phone. "Do you understand?" he asked.

"Yes," I said quietly.

"Good." And he clicked off.

I turned to Dora. "Banks is going to his superiors," I said. "He's scared." Then I told her about the cache at the rest stop in Maryland. Dora thought for a moment. "Are you going to church tomorrow?" She said with a touch of irony in her voice.

"You bet," I replied with none.

Chapter 46

Pastor Williams stood at the front of church greeting his congregation as they entered. He was good; he not only remembered my name, but he knew everybody by name and asked specific questions about the well-being of family members who were not in attendance. There were many more people attending this Sunday service than had been at the Wednesday one. I saw Treadman and Kasselbaum arrive, even though the board meeting was not until next week. I guess they came every week if they could. I did not recognize any of the other Bookkeepers.

When Kasselbaum saw me, he nodded. "Senator," he said with just enough officiousness to let me know he thought my being here was insincere. Or at least, that was my read on it.

I also wondered if my presence here was really a surprise. Board members might be alerted to new members routinely, especially if they were members of Congress. I did not know; all I knew was that it was too late for me to try to cover over my presence or to equivocate. I bowed slightly to the Executive Assistant Director for Law Enforcement Services of the FBI and kept walking toward a pew in the middle of the church but near the side aisle. I wondered if this was one of the people Banks would turn to. *Probably not*, I thought; *we had given him the names of the people we suspected of being Bookkeepers.*

Banks' job was more complicated. This was one of the men he had to keep information from. I did not know if the field agent had any confidantes in the Bureau, but I prayed he did. People he could trust and who could be trusted not to go to one of the several Bookkeepers highly placed within the Bureau itself. In other words, somebody who would be willing to risk his or her career to do the right thing.

As the service began, everyone rose and started singing. The congregation seemed genuinely warm and involved in the service. Several people shook my hand by way of welcoming me to their community. I have to admit I did not dislike the experience. But I had to focus on ways we could intercept the Bookkeepers. My eyes flitted around the church, but no idea presented itself. I allowed myself to pray for guidance—a vestige of my childhood perhaps—and it felt comfortable and familiar. Then I noticed a middle-aged man leave his pew and walk with difficulty toward the back of the church. As I followed him with my eyes without turning my head, my attention was drawn to small surveillance cameras located on a loggia on either side of the nave. I also thought I perceived movement, possibly guards. Banks had mentioned guards, but these were the first indications that I had of them.

What had seemed a moment before to be a typical church service filled with welcoming Christian souls now began to reveal itself as the tightly controlled hub it was. The actors were good: Irene, Pastor Williams—they could not have found more convincing players. I wondered absently if they were in on what really went on here, or if their unknowing complicity simply guaranteed that they played their roles with more vitality. It did not really matter to me. Anger was rising inside me, and I took the opportunity to leave my pew in the middle of the church to head to the back where I thought the bathrooms were and where I assumed the middle-aged, white haired man had gone. I slipped into the side aisle and headed to the back of the church, so my departure did not create a lot of commotion.

I found the bathroom and listened intently. I pushed gently on the door. It was locked. I guess the gentleman was still inside. I leaned against the stone wall and waited patiently, relieved to be away from what now seemed to me to be a charade in the middle of this lovely old church. I wondered how many of those present really knew what this place was about and what an abomination it was. That's what galled me. These bastards used the cover of religion deliberately to shield their nefarious actions from scrutiny. Even for an unreligious man such as myself, it was an outrage.

I heard the toilet flush softly and then the sound of running water. Within a minute, the old man opened the door and ambled out, heading back to his pew. I entered the small washroom. It had a single smoked-glass window that sat high, too high for anyone to observe even if the window were clear. I leaned over the toilet bowl and rolled my head around to relieve some of the tension and to inspect the ceiling of the small room without seeming to. I saw it immediately, a tiny device perched on top the mirror. It could not have been a video feed; it had no lens. My bet was that it was a microphone. I quickly looked again around the whole little room, but I did not see any other devices. I suppose these people had a basic sense of decency not to spy visually on people relieving themselves. On the other hand, I could not imagine who would use this small space to plot against them out loud. It didn't matter; I know paranoia was not a rational force.

For the sake of the microphone, I made noises as if I were vomiting. I truly did want some fresh air, but I also wanted to quit this desecrated place and then look around some more. I left the washroom and walked outside into the fresh air. I took several deep breaths and leaned for a moment against one of the huge colonial columns that lined the front of the church building. I did not notice the man approach until he was almost at my elbow. "May I help you, sir?" he asked with solicitousness mixed with authority. I looked at him; he had a wire leading from his ear into the collar of his blue blazer. Another guard.

"No, no thank you. I just got a little lightheaded in there," I said with some truthfulness. "I just needed some air." The guard did not retreat. He stood in a parade rest stance and did not say anything. I took deep gulps of air. Finally, I look at him and said, "Is something wrong?"

"No, sir," he replied. "I was just waiting to see if I could be of service."

I looked at him askance for a moment. "Thank you, but I think I'll be alright," I said.

The young man tilted his head very slightly, as if listening to instructions through the ear piece. "Very well, sir," he said. Then he turned and walked away.

I stood there for a few more minutes. I was certain that I was being watched, but I did not want to look around too dramatically so as not to give any indication that I was suspicious. After a while, I went back to my place inside. Pastor Williams was just beginning his sermon. I slunk down the side aisle and re-took my place. Sermons are a peculiar type of speech that I never warmed up to. Alternatively stern and patronizing, often rambling and nearly incoherent, there have probably only been one or two during my entire upbringing that I thought were worth the time or energy. Pastor Williams' was no exception to this general rule. He seemed a pleasant enough man, and his tone was largely conciliatory, but I wondered at several points if he was beginning to demonstrate symptoms of dementia. He wandered; he went off on tangents; he lost his place. But he was mercifully brief.

The rest of the service was uneventful. I did not partake of communion. I thought it would be unseemly, and not a bone in my body wanted to strengthen my connection to this place in any way. After the service was over, everyone headed out the main door, where Pastor Williams was greeting people again. I uttered the obligatory compliment for his sermon, and he responded with an equally obligatory invitation to join them for still more coffee and donuts in the basement of the church. I had been hoping for that; I wanted another look at that tunnel.

There were a lot of people in the church basement. It seemed like an especially friendly group, and most of the people who were upstairs seemed to be cramming into this small place. I did not see Treadman or Kasselbaum; I guess they were beyond simple church socials. But I did see a couple of the new members who were at the meeting on Thursday, and we waved and nodded as if we had known each other for a long time and had been thrown into a new sea of people without direction.

After a while, I began to think that some of the participants had come to see the senator from Wisconsin who was a now joining their community. There was for all practical purposes a line forming in front of me. Irene appeared at my shoulder and asked if I wanted more coffee and, before I could respond, took the paper cup from my hand and re-filled it. She also brought me an especially messy jelly donut.

The cardinal rule of social gatherings such as this is never say anything critical or unpleasant. So I smiled as Irene handed me the oversized and overly sweet donut. At least it meant that I couldn't shake anyone else's hand. I resumed chatting with people who came up to me. It felt like a funeral. After about fifteen minutes, I turned to Irene and asked if there was a washroom anywhere near here. She pointed to the corner of the room, the same door that led to the tunnel. Feeling lucky, I headed in that direction. My hands were sticky, and I opened the door carefully. Following the directions Irene gave me, I found a small windowless washroom right on the other side of the door. I had not noticed it before.

Inside the small washroom, I looked around while I ran the water and washed the sticky goo from my hands. No microphone; no video camera that I could detect. I quickly dried my hands, left the washroom, and walked into the tunnel. I did not see any surveillance cameras, but I knew that did not mean there weren't any. I took out a small digital camera from my pocket and snapped pictures of the walls and the ceiling. I hoped there was enough light to capture the images. I did not want to spend too long in the tunnel. After snapping the photos, I slipped back into the large reception room that was the church basement, and resumed greeting people and responding to people who were greeting me.

"All better, Senator?" Irene asked, coming up to me from behind. She had placed a hand on the back of my jacket. Gingerly, as if not to be intrusive, but it felt as if she were looking for something. A wire, perhaps.

"Yes, thank you," I replied with a smile. "Those jelly donuts are good but sticky."

Irene just smiled in that overbearing way some southern women have of letting you know who was in charge.

"Irene," I said to her with equal unctuousness, "thank you so much for your hospitality. I think I am going to like it here." She extended her hand, and I shook it gently.

After locating Pastor Williams, I said my good-byes, thanking him for his hospitality and his service. Pastors love to be recognized as important. Within a few minutes, I was outside the building and headed for my car. Out of the corner of my eye, I saw a young man who may have been the one who stopped me earlier. If not, he was dressed identically. He was moving in my direction. About ten feet from my car, he caught up with me. "How are you feeling, sir?" he said with more solicitousness than authority.

"Fine, thank you," I replied without stopping. "See you next week."

I got into my car and drove off. I don't know if there was anything else he wanted to tell me. Maybe his boss had told him to be nicer. I don't know; I just wanted to get away from this poisoned place.

Chapter 47

Back at the safe house, I uploaded the pictures onto my laptop and opened them in Photoshop. They were dark but visible: I could make out clearly the images of the tunnel. I had taken pictures of the walls and the ceiling so as to double check for any kind of opening or air duct. I was encouraged by the fact that there were no visible surveillance devices either in the small washroom or in the tunnel itself. I used the Photoshop utility to sharpen and brighten the images from my camera. They turned out to be very serviceable. I could see additional openings on either side of the fluorescent light fixtures: I guessed that these were vents to the outside.

I pulled out the schematic that Banks had given me and looked for air vents. Yes, they were set about ten feet apart along the entire length of the tunnel. But it wasn't apparent from the schematic or the photographs how they vented to the outside. *It had to be somewhere*, I thought. I guess I was going to attend another church service on Wednesday.

Dora had left me a note that she had gone to Harold's to get some groceries for dinner. Harold's Fine Foods was a small market where we shopped occasionally. It wasn't far from the safe house. I made some coffee and paced around the small house thinking about the next step. *Would we be able to pull this off?* I wondered. I had my doubts about the canisters. They were exotic and no doubt lethal, but it was not immediately apparent to me how we could position them for maximum effect. In addition to that, there were still quite a few unknowns: how many guards were there? Where were they stationed? What about other countermeasures? It all seemed very risky.

There was also the question of Agent Robert Banks. He seemed sincere, but I was still mistrustful that he was simply one guy collecting the quality of information he said he was able to get a hold of. It still seemed possible to me that he could be setting us up. Even if he weren't, he could easily get tripped up by sharing his intelligence with the Bureau. We know who the Bookkeepers are, but we don't know how many people they have in other positions of responsibility who are part of their extended network. In the middle of these interminable thoughts, my cell phone rang. Once. That was the danger signal that Dora and I had arranged. It meant that she was in trouble, that she was caught, or that she and/or I and/or the safe house had been compromised somehow. If the phone rang again within sixty seconds it would mean that all was clear. If not, I had to move fast.

I held my breath and watched the second hand on my watch sweep around the dial for a complete single revolution. During the last five seconds, I let my air out, realizing that there would be no all clear. I had to get out of the house. I ran into the kitchen and grabbed a dish towel, which I moistened and wiped down everything I might have touched or that Dora might have touched. I grabbed my laptop and my travel case which contained my clothes and threw them into the car. I collected some weapons and the poison dart canisters and threw them into the trunk. Then I pulled out of the driveway with my heart pounding. Once on the street, I headed for downtown DC, but I dared not exceed the speed limit.

There were only a few other cars on the road. It was Sunday

afternoon, after all, and the safe house was in a part of town that wasn't known for leisurely Sunday drives. I made a large arc around the neighborhood and drove past the house for a second look. Still dark; no movement. I didn't see anything that looked suspicious. The safe house might still be safe, but I would never take the chance to go back and look. Not without contacting Dora.

But contacting Dora was for the moment impossible. We had worked out a protocol: if the signal was sounded, I would wait to hear from her. If I did not hear from her within twenty-four hours, I was to contact Brian McClintock, her supervisor at the think tank where she worked. I did not know this for sure, but I thought that McClintock had some additional significance in Dora's life. He may have been in on what she was doing, or he may have been her connection to the larger network she had used. At the moment, twenty-four hours seemed like a very, very long time.

I was instinctively driving toward my apartment in Georgetown, but as I passed the Capitol, I wondered if this was a wise move. If Dora had been compromised, whoever had her might be looking for me as well. I had too many emotions going on to think clearly. I was worried about Dora, worried about myself, and worried about exposure. I was angry that I had no idea what Dora's plans had been. She had always been careful, but...

I pulled over into a spot by the Tidal Basin that was open. I took in long deep breaths in an effort to calm myself. It did not look as if anyone was following me, but honestly I was having so much trouble concentrating I could have missed someone. I must have sat there for twenty minutes. No one came. My phone didn't ring. I was barely breathing. I got out of my car and walked toward the water. It was still very hot in the District, and the heat seemed to target me, beating down with its relentless energy. I tried again to breathe deeply. I walked quickly in an effort to combat the paralysis that seemed to be enveloping my body and my mind.

It all came down to Dora. I could not, would not go on without her. If something happened to her, our project and maybe even our country were doomed. All I could see was fear and blackness. I slowed down to a stroll and looked out over the water in the Tidal Basin. I used to love this spot, the way I loved Washington DC, Georgetown, and the United States. It was as advanced as civilization got, and it was my home. I never felt anything but lucky to be born here and to be a part of the governance of the place I loved more than anywhere on earth. But now bitterness crept into my mind, and it was associated with this place. Not with the Basin, but with Washington DC itself. The place I revered was being desecrated, vitiated by forces that were so powerful they could remove the woman I loved from my life.

I could not let this happen. I could not let them have Dora. I did not know at that moment what I would have to do, but I vowed to do anything it took to locate her, to find her, to bring her home safely. Home was wherever I was. This is not the ordinary way I thought of love; it went way beyond sex and romance. It had to do with truth and with meaning. I would find her and help her. Or I would kill those who hurt her.

Chapter 48

I got back into my car and headed back toward the neighborhood where the safe house was. I was headed to the grocery store she had mentioned, the one we used most often to provision the small house during those times when we spent a lot of time there. It was a small place; more like a greengrocer than a supermarket. Like a lot of small stores in poorer neighborhoods, the prices were terrible, but the supply was decent.

After circling twice around the block, I parked on the street about a hundred feet from the entrance. I surveyed the street as best I could. It was Sunday, so there were few people out. I slowly got out of my car and walked into the small but densely packed food shop. Harold's son Max ran the place. He was in his seventies; I assumed Harold had died many years ago. Father and son looked just like each other, as you could see in the pictures that popped up here and there on the few open spaces of wall that were not covered by merchandise.

"Hey, Max," I said, acting as if he knew me. "Have you seen this woman?" I placed a picture of Dora on the counter.

Max looked at the picture without registering any emotion. "Sure," he said. "That's Dora."

Relief ran through my body, but just for a moment. "Have you seen her today?" I asked.

Max look at me and thought for a moment. "No," he said, shaking his head. "I haven't seen her in a few weeks."

The relief evaporated as I tried to think of the last time Dora had gone to this market. I was uncertain. It could have been a couple weeks, but I couldn't be sure. We did not always use this place; we varied it the way we vary many things to minimize the chance of being caught in a routine. These ideas were swimming through my head like so many mute fish; they clouded the obvious reality: whatever happened to Dora happened before she got here.

"Max," I said. "Are you sure?"

Max thought again in that irritatingly slow way. Then he grabbed a dog-eared notebook. "Yep," he said, engrossed in the worn pages. "She hasn't been here since the second of September."

"You make a note every time somebody comes in?" I asked without thinking.

Max smiled. "Yep," he said with more than a little pride in his voice. "Every time."

Something did not seem right about this situation, but I could not put my finger on what it was. I wasn't thinking too clearly. Max did not seem to be covering up anything. He probably kept a running log to pass the time or to see who his customers were or for some reason perhaps he did not really comprehend. I looked at my watch. It was just after 3 p.m., and I was making small progress. I thanked Max and left.

I stood on the hot concrete of the sidewalk for a few minutes pondering what to do next. Then I walked up and down both sides of the street to see if I could determine if any struggle had taken place. I did not want to focus on this too directly, but I was looking for blood. After two trips up and down the block, I did not see any blood or any sign of a struggle. I got back into my car, started the engine, turned on the air conditioner, and just sat there. I had no idea what to do next.

I must have been in something like a trance. I do not remember time passing or thinking anything in particular. I did not even hear the knock on my window right away. I head a muffled sound that sounded far away that my radar picked up at the edges of my awareness. But it kept coming, and I was finally swept back into the world it was coming from. It was Banks. He was pounding on my window, and he did not look happy. I guess he was frustrated. I touched the button, and my window slowly went down. "Banks," I said.

"Are you OK?" Banks asked with a worried look on his face.

I looked at him. "No, I am not. Dora's gone."

"I know," Banks said; and at this my attention snapped completely to what we call the real world. "Let me in."

I did not know what he meant at first. But as he started to walk around to the other side, I realized he wanted me to unlock the doors to my car. I did; Banks got in the other side. "Let's get out of here," he said.

I shook my head to finish off any residual tranquility and swung into action. Bank acted as if he knew something. I had to find out what it was. And for the moment, I had to trust him.

"Where to?" I asked.

"Go downtown," he said. "Take Maryland Avenue."

He sounded like he had a goal in mind. "Why downtown?" I asked.

"Because that's where we might find out where Miss Hathaway is," Banks replied.

I looked over at him, but he was looking out the windows. He was looking around; I presume to see if we were being followed.

"What happened, Banks?" I demanded.

"Some federal agents picked her up," he replied. "They got her this afternoon. On the way to the market."

"How?" I demanded. Dora was always very, very careful.

Banks shrugged. "Max has been on our payroll for years," he said. "And before him, Harold, his father, was on it."

I looked at him in disbelief. "Spying on poor people?" I asked.

Banks was still looking around. "Part of a network," he said simply.

We drove down Maryland Avenue past Stanton Park. "Take Constitution," Banks said, and I obediently turned west on Constitution Avenue. After we passed the Capitol, he said, "Stay on Constitution."

We were obviously heading for the Justice Department, but you did not just walk into that building and demand to see a detainee.

"Why do they want Dora, Banks?" I asked. "On what grounds can they detain her?"

I heard Banks sigh. "She was picked up by some agents who are in cahoots with Kasselbaum and his group. I was monitoring the comnet system, and I happened to hear that they had gotten her."

"What's comnet?" I asked.

"It's our communications network. It's how we agents keep updated on who's wanted, who's been nabbed, and who's on the most dangerous list. It's a network that uses a combination of voice and data sources. It's very efficient."

But then he continued, "I don't think her name was supposed to go out on the network, but one of their guys must have slipped up and it got sent out."

I pondered this for a while. I could not think of a single reason why Banks would let me know these things if he were on the other side. This is not how a set-up operates. But the fact that he knew where Dora was or at least who had her filled me with appreciation that he had shown up.

"What do we do now?" I asked.

"First," Banks said. "We have to find out where they took her. It probably is not the Justice Department; but that's a good place to start."

Why? I wondered; but I did not say anything. Banks obviously had a better handle on this situation than I did, and I did not want to stand in his way. There was an ache in the pit of my stomach, though; I wanted to ask Banks something I was afraid to ask him.

"Agent Banks," I said, speaking slowly and forcing my voice not to quiver. "Is there a chance they will hurt Dora? Or kill her?"

Banks did not reply right away. "Senator, these are evil men. They are capable of anything." He paused. "But that said, I do not think they are likely to hurt her before they find out what she knows and who her contacts are."

I took another breath. "What about torture?"

Banks shrugged. "I don't know, Senator," he said. But he said it with soulfulness in his voice. At this moment, my hesitation about Robert Banks vanished. He was an honest man intent on doing the right thing. And he had a soul. I decided to believe him. We drove past Justice to an entrance to an underground garage. Banks handed me a pass for the machine that controlled the entrance gate to the garage. It swung open, and we drove in. I handed the pass back to Banks. He directed me to parking spot with his name on it. I stopped the car; killed the engine; and turned to Banks. "OK," I said. "Now what?"

"You stay here. I'll be back in fifteen minutes. If I am not, drive out through the same entrance you came in on. The gate will open automatically. Do not return to the safe house; it's been compromised. Go either to your apartment or to a hotel. I would suggest a hotel."

He paused and looked at me with some apprehension in his eyes. "I will find you," he said.

Banks got out of the car and vanished through a steel door. I sat in the driver's seat, where it seemed I had been for ages, and rolled down the windows. It was comfortably cool in the underground garage, so I turned off the engine. It was also quiet. Sunday. I kept my eye on the clock on the dashboard of the car or on my watch. Minutes went by slowly. I was thinking that Banks did not give himself much time. I also wondered if he had had time to work more with the information we had given him the week before.

Eight minutes went by. I was thinking of what hotel I should go to. Banks did not say why a hotel; nor did he say I was under surveillance or suspicion. But if someone was watching Dora, they no doubt knew something about me; they were also watching me with her. That would have been ultimately unavoidable. I hate to lose, and right now it seemed as if the bad guys were winning. That was my last thought before the steel door re-opened and Banks returned. He got in the car without a word. Then he looked at me and said, "Let's go."

"What did you find out, Banks?" I demanded. Even as I did this, I started the car and was pulling it out of the parking place.

"In a moment, Senator," Banks said, motioning with his head to the video monitors on each corner of the lot.

We pulled back onto Constitution Avenue, and Banks motioned for me to continue west. As soon as we cleared the garage, he began speaking.

"They took Dora to a house near the Naval Observatory. Turn right here," he said, pointing to Virginia Avenue. "It is a FBI safe house on Hall Place."

I turned and looked at Banks. Hall Place is near Georgetown and is filled with students. Seemed like an unlikely place to take a hostage. We drove on in silence for a while. I had questions, but I was beginning to trust Banks, so nothing seemed pressing except finding Dora and getting her away from whoever was holding her. After a few minutes of silence, Banks pulled out his cell phone and punched some numbers. When he was connected, he barked some numbers into the phone. He paused for a moment. "Go Hall," he said and clicked off.

I look at him with a question on my face. "Back-up," he said.

"Back-up?" I replied. "Who? How do you know who to trust?"

"Most agents are very good men, Senator. Not just good men, but exceptional human beings. Even the bad ones. They got into this because they were too idealistic." He paused for a moment. "Too damned young," he said with more than a touch of bitterness in his voice.

As we approached the area within a couple blocks of Hall Place,

Banks motioned for me to slow down. About a block away, he motioned for me to pull the car over and park. He opened his jacket and pulled out two pistols.

"I understand you were in the military, Senator," he said without emphasis. "You might need this."

I took the ten millimeter Glock, checked the magazine, and pulled back the firing mechanism. It was too comfortable. I had no doubt that I would use it if I needed to. I stuck it in my waistband. Banks handed me two extra clips, ten rounds each. We got out of the car and walked slowly toward number 15. There were a few students around, but not too many. I listened intently, but I couldn't hear anything that sounded like Dora or federal agents.

Two doors away from fifteen, Banks nudged me toward a darkened doorway. "I'm going to call one of these guys on his cell. I am going to give him a code which he will recognize and tell him to bring the detainee out the back of the building. I don't think he will be able to verify the orders; Kasselbaum is not available, even on comnet." He looked me straight in the eye. "The front is covered. I will take charge of Dr. Hathaway in the rear of the building. You stay in the gangway. Do not display your weapon or fire it unless you see me pull mine out first. Do you understand?"

"Yes," I said. "What happens if they don't hand her over peacefully?"

"Chances are if they come out with her they will have taken the bait," Banks replied. "When we get her, I will walk her back through the gangway to the front of the building. Got it?"

"Got it," I replied.

He made the call.

As we turned into the gangway, I saw four guys pull up in a Lincoln Town car, identical to the one that chased Dora and me a few months ago. Seems like years ago. Two got out and headed toward the building. They moved quickly but did not appear hurried. They were calm, well-trained. The other two pulled a little further down the street and stopped. I could see the driver redirect the side mirror for a better view of the entrance and the second floor windows.

Halfway down the gangway, Banks motioned for me to stop. He went on to the back of the ancient brick structure. From my spot in the narrow space, I heard a screen door bang against the door jamb. Then I could hear conversation, but I could not make out what was being said. I strained to listen. I couldn't tell if Dora was there, but I presumed that what Banks said was true and that they had brought her out. Then I hear storm door bang against the jamb again. I assumed whoever had brought Dora out had gone back inside. But I couldn't be sure, and my heart was beating so rapidly I could hear the blood running through the veins in my head. I tried to slow my breathing as silently as I could. Little sounds echoed in this brick enclosure, and I did not want to make any audible movements. I was frozen.

Within ten seconds of the second door slam, Banks and Dora appeared in the gangway, walking swiftly in my direction. Dora looked dazed, but she was being guided by Banks, who had a firm grip on her upper arm. Banks motioned for me to move toward the front of the building. By the time I got to the front sidewalk, Banks and Dora were right behind me. The driver had pulled the Lincoln around to the front of number 15 and one of the men was holding a rear door open.

"Give me your car keys," Banks demanded. I did, and he tossed them to the man holding the door, nodding with his head in the direction of where we had parked my car. Then he shoved us gently but authoritatively into the back seat of the town car. He got in the front seat. As soon as the door closed, the driver took off, leaving two men on the sidewalk in front of the building and one who had gone around back. I looked around. They had their hands in their jackets and were approaching the door of number 15.

I inhaled deeply and put my arm around Dora. She looked frightened and confused. I imagined that she did not know what was happening here. "It's OK," I said softly. "These men just rescued you."

Dora looked at me not comprehending. She opened her mouth, but nothing came out. She looked at Banks. She looked at the men sitting in front of the car. Banks was listening to the conversation. He looked at Dora and nodded his head. "That's true, Dr. Hathaway," he said. "On behalf of the Federal Bureau of Investigation, I apologize for what happened to you today. Those men—the men who took you—were under the influence of the Bookkeepers."

Dora looked at him but did not speak right away. She squeezed my hand. She looked at me softly. I nodded.

"Thank you," she said to Banks. Then tears rolled down her face. No one spoke.

Finally, Banks said, "We have some additional information that we think is useful. The main piece is that Frank Havrakos, Assistant Director of the Secret Service, is going to be inducted into the prime Bookkeeper fraternity at their meeting next Sunday."

I could hear the bells going off in Dora's head. "That's how they pulled off the attack on the White House!" she exclaimed.

Banks nodded. "We think so," he said. "Although, we do not know the particulars. We are working against the odds here," he said cryptically.

Dora looked at him quizzically.

"I mean," he went on, "that there are only a small group of us in the Bureau that we know about who are onto what is happening." He looked away for a moment; then back to Dora. "We are going to have to detain those guys who held you; if we do not, they will alert everyone that we are operating out of protocol." There was acid in his tone.

It had cost him a lot to rescue Dora, I thought. Dora must have had a similar thought. "Thank you again, Agent Banks," she said. "What can I do for you?"

Banks thought for a moment, although it seemed he was just

organizing his thoughts. He did not seem at all equivocal about what he was going to say. After a moment that only felt like a long time, he said, "We have to take these people out at the church."

No one spoke. I noticed the driver squeeze his fingers more tightly against the large steering wheel.

Banks continued, "We don't have a lot of men. We need you two in order to pull this off in a way that is effective. And maybe even deniable."

Dora and I looked at each other. Neither of us responded.

Chapter 49

We drove along in silence. Because I could not bear it any longer, I finally said, "What do you mean, 'take out'?"

Banks turned his head in the direction of the back seat of the car, but he did not make eye contact with either of us. He thought for a moment, then he looked me straight in the eye and said, "Eliminate; destroy; kill them."

Oh, I thought. More silence in the car, my stomach was beginning to roil. I felt the familiar but always private pull of two paths: one leading to a kind of exposure I had never experienced before; the other a safer path of continued dissimulation, acting like a public servant but harboring my own private and sometimes murderous agenda. The only thing I knew for sure is that I did not want to make a decision at that moment. I did not look at Dora, but I could feel her body temperature rise sitting next to me.

"And how do you propose we do that, Agent Banks?" I said, forcing my voice to remain even.

"We can supply with intelligence, some means, and logistical support. What we cannot supply you with is people. Maybe me and one other guy, but that would be it."

"How many are in your group, Agent Banks?" I asked.

"Six," he replied. "The five of us you saw here today, and one other guy. He was busy diverting Kasselbaum."

Precious little support, I thought. I could feel my body moving toward depersonalization; my feelings were receding into the background. A sense of unreality was making the edges of my consciousness fuzzy. My intellectual awareness was available, but I was losing a sense of myself as a person. I wondered absently if this was what it was like to be on an airplane you knew was going to crash. *Probably*, I concluded.

I was also conflicted: I had begun to trust Banks, but I could not fathom how or why a longstanding agent of the FBI could talk so easily about murdering people. No matter how noble, murdering people is still illegal. He knows the dangers of trying to implement this plan using other FBI agents, much less a United States senator and a prominent think-tank analyst. The risks of exposure were very high. Maybe he was trying to get me to do work he could not in his own conscience get away with, but it still felt suspect. I was sloughing off my previous assent to trust and backing into a more familiar mode of suspicion.

There must have been a few moments when I was totally detached from the reality inside the car because I saw Banks' lips moving before I heard the words coming out of his mouth. I struggled to focus on what he was saying, but it took me a moment to actually hear the words he was speaking right in front of me.

"...we know the dangers, here," he was saying. "We know you've been working to expose these people. We do not see an alternative. If you want to prevent the country from breaking up into smaller parts and fall into the hands of fanatics, we must act decisively. We are too small a group to pull it off. But we have reason to believe the two of you would sign on."

Dora spoke up, "What are you referring to Agent Banks?" she asked without hesitation.

Banks grimaced. It was easy to tell that he did not want to disclose more than he absolutely had to. But Dora must have been very important to him; important enough for him to attempt an answer to her question.

"The Bureau has had you in our sights for some time," he began. "It has gotten more intense lately, but we have been collecting intel on you for some years now." He paused and looked across to the driver's side window. "It was suspected at high levels that you were a part of a vigorous countermeasure. At first, this was framed as your being a suspected part of a terrorist ring. Later it became clear that you were part of the resistance to the Bookkeepers' plan."

Banks paused again, looking for the right words. "I told you earlier that the skirmish in Georgia was due to some overly zealous weekend warriors, and that was true. But it was also true that the end result was widely regarded in the upper echelons of the Bureau as a win for our side, even if at the time we had no idea of how unscrupulous the rest of their plans were. Or how connected they were to the other disasters that had taken place." He stopped.

At the mention of Georgia, Dora tensed. Those wounds were still fresh. Her jaw stiffened, but she did not speak.

Banks continued, "So after the affair in Georgia, scrutiny of you became a high priority. There was some mention that you might have been involved somehow in the two assassinations of the Bookkeepers who were killed in DC. No proof, but a strong suspicion. They were so worried, they apparently decided to detain you in anticipation of the meeting on Sunday."

"There's more," Banks said. "We believe that the attack on the White House was designed to decapitate the government, to remove the normally powerful American president who could stop the implementation of the rest of the Bookkeepers' plan. President Aberland's speech signaled strong leadership and led directly to the attack. We believe that they now think their moment has come to take advantage of the disarray that followed the attack."

Banks turned to face us both, taking in both of us with his gaze. "I'll level with you. We diverted Kasselbaum, and we need to detain the two agents who took you the other day. We do not have a long time to plan. Kasselbaum is going to know by tomorrow at the latest that his men were ambushed—he will likely think they were killed. He is also going to be thinking of a leak in the Bureau, as only people from our agency would know just how to divert someone off the comnet system. He has a lot of people convinced that his agenda is the most patriotic one. If he is able to utilize the resources of the FBI to consolidate his scheme, the Bookkeepers have a good chance of pulling off the dismantling of the United States. We move now or it's over."

Dora and I looked at each other and then looked down. I finally broke the silence, mostly in an effort to stay grounded in this surrealistic present. "Where are we headed now, Banks?" I asked.

"We've arranged a safe house for you in Lexington," he replied. "Far enough away, it will probably be outside their net." His tone was matter-of-fact.

"Probably" did not sound too reassuring. But I had no vision of an alternative, so I did not say anything right away. Dora had started looking out the window at the warm Virginian landscape. A couple hours passed; no one had said a word. I leaned back into the oversized seat and tried to focus. Failing that, I shut down my mind and let myself doze a while. When I awoke, Dora's head was lying on my lap. She was sound asleep.

It felt that we had been driving for quite a while, and I began to look for mile signs to Lexington. I put my hand gently on Dora's head, not wanting to wake her. Before I saw a sign, we were pulling off the highway.

The black Lincoln turned off the highway and right at the first cross street. It did not look as if we were in a city; it looked more like a rural area. We kept driving. The silence in the closed up car was beginning to cloy. Everyone except Dora was awake, but no one was speaking. The gauntlet had been thrown. I was trying to digest the options, and I guessed that Banks and the other G-Man were wondering about what path I would take. Silence felt like the safest thing, but it was not the most comfortable one. I wondered absently if they would kill me if I refused, but I had no real way to assess that. The fact that they had gone way out of their way to spring Dora from her captivity seemed like the bottom line. These guys mean business.

The other reality that seemed most compelling to me was that the odds of my surviving this whole affair seemed dimmer and dimmer. Maybe I could go back to my seemingly tranquil life as a senator, but I had already been targeted as an obstacle to the Bookkeepers. Maybe I could help kill some of them, but the guard I saw and the security I observed at the church looked formidable. We had some means, but arranging them into a coherent, effective, and safe plan seemed powerfully unlikely.

On an intellectual level, death seemed OK to me. It was never something I would volunteer for, but my life did not, on its own, seem to have much consequence. I made small contributions; I helped people. But it was obvious to me that my most intense and most important role on this planet was to kill people. It was engaging in that dark enterprise that blessed me with meaning and purpose, even if it chipped away at my sense of myself as a good and moral person. But I could not allow myself to be a party to harming Dora. She was the first woman whom I ever loved beyond sexual interest, and I would not put her in harm's way. Could not, would not, will not.

At that point in my musings, Dora stirred. She sat upright and stretched, looking around as if surprised that we were all still there. She had a small smile on her face when she first roused herself from sleep, but as she began remembering where she was a more sobering attitude showed itself on her face. Not a frown exactly, but a serious look. She looked over at me; I squeezed her hand. She squeezed mine back.

"Are we close?" Dora asked the three silent men arrayed before her.

"Close," replied Banks, apparently not wanting to get caught up in a conversation.

The driver, who had not said a single word since we got into the vehicle hours ago, pointed to an opening in the brush beside the rural road on our right. "There," he said.

Banks nodded. The driver turned off the rural road onto a graveled drive almost completely obscured by trees. About halfway up the road, he stopped the car. Banks looked at the driver, who nodded. We slowly drove closer to the farmhouse. It looked deserted. Both agents got out of the car with their guns drawn. I reached for mine with one hand and took Dora's hand with the other. The driver entered the house from the front; Banks from the rear. After a long minute, they both appeared at the front door and waved for us to enter. Dora and I glanced at each other and then got out of the car and walked toward the front door.

The inside of the farmhouse looked a little less abandoned than the exterior. The space was one large room with a small kitchen in one corner. The paint on the walls was old and the room was swept out, but it did not seem very clean. There were some simple pieces of furniture: a rickety table with cheap wooden chairs; a TV stand with an old black-and-white unit on top, complete with a rabbit-ear antenna; a worn couch and side chair; and a small coffee table. Four cots.

Banks walked around to where the kitchen was and opened an ancient refrigerator door. It was filled with food items hastily assembled. Eggs, milk, cold cuts, bread. We were all hungry, and it appeared to be the only option at the moment.

"Anybody hungry?" Banks asked. Then he began pulling out the food items, placing them on a small counter. "Come help yourself."

The taciturn driver finally turned to Dora and me. "Name's Russ," he said simply. He shook my hand.

We gathered at the small kitchen counter as if at an altar. Nobody said much, but it felt a lot like a last meal.

Chapter 50

"Pastor Williams," I said as warmly as I could at the beginning of the Wednesday service. "Good to see you again." I shook his hand.

"Likewise," Pastor Williams said, responding in kind. In fact, it seemed as if he were much happier to see me than I him. He has that kind of self-consciousness common among the clergy. More comfortable with God and the Divine Mysteries than with human beings. I shook his hand.

I do not know how I learned superficial social behavior so well. For the most part, I've always been a loner, but I keep a persona in my back pocket for occasions like this. Times when I have to be social or pleasant or at least bearable. But it never feels like me; it never ever feels anything but strained and rehearsed on the inside. I learned a long time ago, however, that no one can see inside my body, and the social graces people do see fall well within the range of the expected. I am glad about that.

What I am not so glad about is the anxiety inside of me. I was at the church for one reason, to plant the canisters we had gotten from Dora's nameless accomplice. This was today's part of the plan that Russ, Banks, Dora, and I hammered out over the course of the last three evenings at the safe house in Lexington.

"Impossible!" I said on Monday evening. "Too much security in place; I am too visible a presence; I have no idea what is inside those ducts."

"Maybe not impossible," Bank replied with a calmness that was beginning to drive me crazy. Did this guy never get worked up? "There are magnetic adaptors that will cling to metal ductwork. If that fails, there are Velcro tabs that can be quickly cemented in place."

"What about the guards?" I demanded.

Again, no hesitation. "We believe that there are fewer guards during the week," Banks said, specifying neither the "we" nor the "during the week".

I looked over at Dora, who shrugged her shoulders. "Jake," she said. "You are the only one with a legitimate entrée into the church. There is no one else."

I felt volunteered. So I spent a lot of time with those canisters, learning exactly how they worked, how to set the timers, how to aim them for maximum effect. In the back of my mind, I couldn't shake the notion that this was a Keystone Kops plan. People should be killed with a proper weapon: a gun or maybe a bomb. But aerosol-propelled poison frog piss? It just did not seem right.

"Technically, it is not frog piss," Dora explained when I shared my objections. "It's actually a toxin specifically generated for defense." She smiled a tiny, tiny smile. "If that makes you feel any better," she said.

It did not. But I knew I was outgunned on this issue, so I agreed to go to church on Wednesday and attempt to install the canisters in the ducts and hope that no one discovered them before Sunday after services, when the Bookkeepers would parade through the tunnel on the way to their meeting in the multi-purpose building. This was all fine in theory, but there remained a number of obstacles on the ground. For one thing, there aren't too many people at the Wednesday service, so there was no large-crowd cover. The attendees present were mostly pious and elderly women who relished any opportunity to attend church services but who do not move very swiftly.

Secondly, I had to find a way to get downstairs carrying the five shaving-cream sized canisters with timers and remote switching devices attached. This turned out to be more doable than I thought; they were taped around each of my legs and hidden inside my suit coat. They felt bulky, but I was convinced they were not visible from the outside. I would be okay so long as no one kicked me.

Finally, I had to get down to the church basement unnoticed, and this struck me as the most improbable part of the plan. There were numerous sub-problems with this. I had to stay as invisible as I could to whatever guards or cameras might be watching. I had to be able to disappear from the sight of those who did notice me. We took several precautions. Jefferson dropped me off at the church, so I did not have a car for anyone to watch. I was to signal Dora from my cell phone when I was ready to be picked up. We had decided it would be best if I left during the service.

It was good to see Jefferson. Dora had protected him from knowledge of the safe house, where we had been spending so much time, so it had been awhile since I'd seen him. He dropped me off with characteristic efficiency. He even nodded approvingly, apparently happy to be back in business.

I began to fidget during the sermon. Evidently Pastor Williams saved his best work for the weekend, because this particular talk was so convoluted and recondite that I could not even find a topic sentence, much less imagine what one might be. My eyelids started to droop. I shook my head back and forth to stay awake, and as soon as he finished the sermon and the congregation rose I slipped into the side aisle. I was sitting near the rear of the church, so it was a short walk to the back. I headed first for the restroom that I knew was wired for sound.

Once inside, I splashed water on my face to help me focus. I watched the small microphone as I dried my face, wondering if anyone was listening. It did not matter much. I was not headed back to the service, no matter who was listening.

I had a vague outline of a cover story if someone discovered me in the church basement, but I had to admit it did not hold much water, even in my mind. Something about forgetting my schedule or the bulletin or some other useless artifact that absolutely no one would go out of his way to retrieve. I was feeling reckless. The real motivation for doing this was that Dora would not have to do it. I felt I was protecting her, even though I knew there were no other candidates for the job.

I walked out of the small washroom and found the stairs to the basement. I looked around for guards but did not see any. I also scanned for cameras, but I couldn't see any of those either. I took a deep breath and descended the dimly lit staircase.

At the bottom of the stairs, there was a small windowless space that led to double doors which opened into the large gathering room. I put my ear to the door to see if I could hear anything. I made a point of not putting my hands on any thing unless I absolutely had to; even then I would use a handkerchief to prevent fingerprints. I did not want to use the latex gloves I had brought with me, not this early in the process when someone might come up to me. The small cloth would have to do. At first, I did not hear anything, so I placed my hand on the brass door knob and slowly began to open the door.

Then I froze. It was a faint sound, barely audible on the expansive carpet that covered the gathering room in the church basement. I listened more intensely. There it was again. I heard the unmistakable sound of humans breathing. They were trying to muffle the noise, but I could still hear it. Through the small slit in the door, I scanned what I could see of the room. There were no lights on, but there was some light streaming in through the high windows on either side of the large meeting room. I detected movement to the left. I squatted down. Then I saw it: Irene and the guard who had stopped me on Sunday, engaged in a common and primal human activity, albeit one usually conducted in a private bedroom after dark. Irene was on her back with her head tilted back facing the ceiling in the direction away from me; the guard was facing her.

I had to stifle a laugh. I closed the door very slowly, so as not to draw attention to it, but I did not think there was much of a risk of that couple hearing anything short of a gunshot. I look around the small hall where I was standing. There was a door underneath the stairs that I had not noticed before. I opened it. It was a small closet that housed an air handler for the HVAC system. With more than a little relief, I entered the small space. The periodic noise of the air handler would mask any slight noise I might make. In addition, it seemed unlikely that anyone would be entering this mechanical space.

The air handler had obviously been retrofitted into the old building, which was constructed decades before anyone thought of air conditioning. I pulled out a small penlight and looked around the dark area. A trunk line from the unit went directly into the meeting room where the love nesters were doing their love nesting. The ceiling throughout the basement was a dropped acoustic ceiling, the type seen in basements throughout the US. Cheap, sound dampening, and easy to install. In this little room, I could remove some of those two-feet-by-four-feet tiles and hoist myself up to see clear across the meeting room to the tunnel area. The trunk line cooled both parts of the basement.

The ceiling must have been lowered many years ago. Instead of the wires that are usually used to support the frame for acoustic tiles, there was a wooden frame built across the entire expanse of the original ceiling. It was dusty and looked as if it had never been disturbed, but it also looked sturdy in a way modern construction often doesn't. It looked if it could support a man. Maybe even a large man.

I listened more intently to see if I could hear Irene and her consort. I learned to my delight that the duct from the meeting room made a serviceable telegraph, broadcasting their sounds with more clarity than one would expect considering the distance covered. I was acutely aware that this property worked in both directions, so I kept myself perfectly still. I was so excited about the prospect of using this space for an entry to the tunnel; I had to deliberately keep myself from making any noise.

In keeping with the natural cadence of human sexual behavior, the dalliance on the church basement floor soon came to its climactic end. I imagined a scene I could not actually see: two faces expressing satisfaction, perhaps a quick kiss, the fumbling of re-dressing quickly. Perhaps even a whispered "I love you" in either one direction or two. My guess is that, if it came, it emanated from the mouth of Irene, who, while attractive, had a good twenty years on her paramour. My guess is that his motivations had more to do with overcoming boredom, notching his belt, and indulging what must have seemed like another harmless conquest.

In another few minutes, I heard the door to the meeting room open. In an ageless tradition, one of them no doubt quit the meeting room alone. My guess: guard. Within five minutes, I heard it open again: Irene. I chuckled to myself.

Without hesitating, I hoisted myself onto the wooden frame to test its strength. Like many things built in the thirties and forties, it was built not just to accomplish a goal—in this case lowering the ceiling—but it was built to withstand time and abuse. The space was about three feet high, so there was plenty room to crawl amid the beams. I moved as quickly as stealth allowed, not wanting to make much noise. I headed for the tunnel.

As I went, I put my penlight in my mouth both to light my way and to search for traps, obstacles, cameras, or any other thing that could turn this piece of good fortune into a disaster by exposing me. So far, it looked like what it was: a sturdy piece of construction that easily held my considerable heft.

Every few feet, I stopped to listen. There was a chance that what I thought happened by way of the love birds' departures was not what actually happened. But no sound came to my ears, no matter how intently I listened. I got to the tunnel and was able to examine the air ducts that joined the air conditioning outlets over the tunnel. They were seamless, and as such unusable for dispersing the aerosol toxin. But a one-eighth inch space separated the air ducts from the trunk line of the air conditioning system, and this was more than enough of an opening to set the deadly aerosol containers.

I situated myself so that I could dislodge each of the containers from its hiding place beneath my clothes. I placed the penlight on the frame facing me and fished the latex gloves out of my inside pocket and put them on. Then I set each of the canisters in a line on the wooden frame and turned my body so that I was lying on my abdomen facing them. I took each canister and set the timer. I also activated a manual remote in the event of timer failure or in case the time frame changed.

I took each canister and aimed it downward at an angle, securing each one with Velcro straps and duct tape. I did not trust the magnets to hold for the four days between now and Sunday. It was not hard to figure how to cover the entire space. A crisscross pattern from canisters placed at different angles on different ducts would blanket at least twenty feet of the tunnel with the tiny poison darts. That should make quite an impact.

I picked up the penlight and examined my work. I backed up to look at it from a different angle. I allowed myself the thought that this foolhardy plan might work after all. Then I heard sounds below me. The doors of the meeting room were opening and people were entering the meeting room. I smelled the aroma of coffee and heard the clatter of cups and dishes. Someone was preparing for the after-service gathering, setting up the coffee and donuts.

No one was speaking, so I began to think that maybe only one person was doing this. After a few minutes, I heard the door close. I listened for maybe a minute, thinking this might be my only chance to get out of this outrageous and unexplainable situation.

Satisfied that no one was in the room, I crawled on all fours across the wide expanse of the meeting room ceiling. When I got to the air handler room, I swung myself down to the floor. I was breathing heavily and was aware of how dirty I must be. I had worn a gray herringbone suit because it does not show dirt so easily, but I had just traversed a space that had no doubt lain undisturbed for decades, collecting layer after layer of dust. I had no mirror to check my appearance. I dusted myself off as much as I could. My hands were black. I did not think I was presentable.

Then I remembered the bathroom near the entrance of the tunnel, the one with no listening devices. I did not think I had much of a choice. If I showed up at the post-service gathering like this, it would instantly be known that I was up to something. I cracked open the door of the small closet and listened. No noise. I took a quick breath, and sprinted across the windowless space to the gathering room door and threw them open. Empty! I sprinted across the room and made it to the tunnel door, which I opened.

Once in the bathroom, I was shocked to see the face in the mirror. Black soot covered a good part of my face in addition to my hands. My hair was disheveled and there were black marks on my jacket and pants. As best as I could, I cleaned up these marks using the industrial-smelling soap in the dispenser.

In the midst of these ministrations, I heard voices of women and a few men. I could hear Pastor Williams' voice clearly above the rest. Then I heard Irene's voice near the Pastor. I did not move; I stood in the bathroom trying to concoct a story as to why I was here. I also tried to think if I left anything anywhere. I couldn't think of anything. I wondered where the guard was. Just filling in the blanks with information I had no way of knowing. I just stood in a near trance-like state.

After about twenty minutes, the number of voices began to decrease. I heard the doors to the meeting room close one last time and then silence. I waited another few minutes before I turned around and opened the door to the small washroom. I walked out into the meeting room. The lights were still on. Church people are fanatical about wasting electricity, so I knew someone would be along to turn them off. Halfway across the meeting room, Irene entered the double doors.

"Senator Telemark!" she exclaimed.

"Irene," I said, nodding to her.

She looked at me askance. "Are you alright, Senator?" she asked.

"I think I'm OK now," I responded truthfully. Then the dissimulation: "I must have eaten something for breakfast that disagreed with me."

Irene stood in front of me for a moment regarding my appearance, which must have struck her as odd. Then in a curious blend of solicitude and flirtation, she said, "Why, we must get you some medical attention."

I looked at her for a moment, as if disoriented. "I think I'll be OK, Irene," I said. "I just need to call my driver."

"Yes, of course," she said, circling her arm around mine and leading me out of the room. "Let me help you."

She escorted me out of the church basement, up the stairs, and into the sunshine of the bright Wednesday morning. I took deep gulps of air, savoring the freedom I felt being released from that stuffy and evil place.

I thanked Irene one more time and pulled out my cell phone to call Dora. After leaving her hand on my arm for an inappropriately long time, Irene finally turned, smiled lasciviously, and re-entered the church building. I turned and walked down the white marble steps. Jefferson was just pulling up.

Chapter 51

It was too bad Jefferson could not hear: I had a lot to talk about, ranging from good fortune to misfortune to nearly incredible stories of the salacious Irene, who seemed to scout out potential sex partners as she breathed. But I sat in silence, mulling over events and wondering if this plan could possibly work.

The outlines of it were straightforward enough. I attend the Sunday Service and the after-service gathering. The timers on the canisters are set for 12:30, the time we figured the Bookkeepers would be walking through the tunnel. But if that changed, I was to signal Dora, who would press the trigger for the canisters to do their lethal spraying. Simple. *Way too simple*, I thought. *There are at least a thousand things that could go wrong.*

Banks alluded to contingency plans, but he was vague about these. He had left the house in Lexington on Tuesday with Russ, and neither Dora nor I had heard from him since. My trust level was equivocal about Banks. He had obviously gone way out of his way to help us, especially Dora, but he always seemed to be holding something back. Some secret or some thoughts or something that made him seem mysterious. Maybe it was just his temperament. I trusted him, but between his arcane behavior and my typical mistrust of people, this did not come naturally.

I met up with Dora at a small restaurant outside Arlington. It felt good to be in a public place, but I was apprehensive. Jefferson dropped me off with a nod and drove off. I do not know where he went.

Dora asked how things had gone. I told her every detail, especially savoring the part about Irene and the guard. She had a dark look on her face as she listened, as if she disapproved. She did not appear to see any humor in a situation I thought was the only entertaining segment of the entire scenario.

"Dora," I said. "What's the matter? Why are you being so stern about this?"

"It just seems so sick to me, Jake," she said after a minute. "And pathetic." She looked down into her coffee cup. "These are the people who want to take this country back to some idealized nineteen-fifties era where people are civil and pleasant on the outside but allow their passions to run amok in secret. It makes me sick."

I looked at Dora for a moment. It was easy to understand her reaction as she explained it, but we did not know for sure if Irene or Pastor Williams or even the guard was in on what was really happening within the confines of the church property. I shared these thoughts with Dora.

"No, we don't, Jake," she replied. "But this kind of attitude allows a lot of things to go unquestioned." She shook her head. "I don't mean to be so schoolmarmish about this; it's just that, while she's catting around for sex, the country is being destroyed right under her stupid nose." Then Dora laughed. Not laughed really, but chuckled. "I guess it really pisses me off that she's so stupid," she said smiling.

We talked about other things. One thing we did not talk about was the upcoming Sunday, when we would be called upon to murder ten or twelve of our fellow human beings for the greater good. We sat in silence for a while, looking out onto the bright Virginian sunshine. After a few minutes, I looked over at Dora and put my hand on hers. "You OK?" I asked.

She looked back at me with no movement: no nod or gesture; no apparent emotion. Just a blank look. Then she sighed. "I don't know, Jake," she replied. "I guess so." Then she looked away. "The fact is I don't feel much of anything. I think this situation is just so... pathetic, unnecessary. It just all seems so... so uncalled for." A tear rolled down her cheek. I squeezed her hand.

I had a sense of how she felt. It had to do with being involved in killing people. Killing people is different from hurting someone either deliberately or not. Humans are almost endlessly resilient and can recover from almost anything. Except death. That's why putting an end to someone's life, even accidentally, takes you into a different world, one that most people thankfully do not have to experience. Doing it at all changes your life, but doing it consciously and deliberately changes you more deeply. I was feeling a little guilty at not explaining this to Dora before she got involved in this side of things.

But just now I did not say anything. I squeezed her hand and nodded and acted as if this were just another passing feeling she was having, even though I knew better. The secret truth of my reaction was that I was glad she was in it with me. It was hard on her, but being close to someone with whom you shared this intimate an experience went a long way toward relieving the desolation I always felt around other people. I had one person close who really knew what it was like to end the life of another. It was a secret and immoral pleasure. But a pleasure nonetheless.

Dora's cell phone rang. She looked at it a moment before she picked it up. She looked at the tiny screen. "Banks," she said simply.

I was relieved. He had been out of touch for a couple days, and it took a toll on both Dora and I. Dora listened quietly to whatever Banks was saying and then clicked off without a word.

"He wants to meet us. Now. Here."

"He knows where we are?" I asked incredulously.

Dora shrugged. I did not say anything, but I could feel my breath becoming shallow. I looked around as casually as I could. I was on alert. Dora had not said anything threatening, but the situation felt dangerous. This wasn't right. How was Banks tracking us? What was so urgent? It did not add up.

I did not have to wait long to find out what Banks wanted. Within ten minutes, he drove up.

"Dr. Hathaway, Senator," he said without introduction. He sat down at our small table.

No one spoke for a moment. Dora looked down at the table. My antennae were up, wondering what was really going down here.

Then Banks spoke. "The Bureau is onto us. They found the guys we were detaining. They arrested our guys." He took a sharp breath and glanced out the window. "They are not following protocol in their interrogations," he said with resounding bitterness in his voice.

All of us knew exactly what he was saying. They were torturing the men Banks had brought into his counter conspiracy. This was obviously very painful for Banks. The Bureau was his home, a part of his belief system. He must be feeling enormously betrayed. But our agenda had a specific focus. What did Banks' cohorts know? What could they reveal?

Banks did not seem inattentive to our concerns; it was just hard for him to talk, he was so angry. He was doing physical things to get himself back under control: taking deep breaths, tensing and relaxing the muscles in his body. Finally, he was able to speak.

"None of the others know what you two are up to. Russ knows, of course, but he is with me." He looked away again; the struggle was still not over. "We're going to ground." He gritted his teeth. "This means we won't be much help to you. I need to share with you now exactly what we know."

He proceeded to do that. He described who in the Bureau was in charge of rooting out those who were labeled as traitors. He gave us some information about weapons caches. He also gave us some names of people who might be able to help with additional information. All in all, it wasn't much.

"How did you know how to find us today?" I asked.

Banks looked at me with the age-old demeanor of a twelve year old who had raided the cookie jar. "GPS tracker in Dr. Hathaway's shoe," he replied. Then, as if to reassure us, said, "That's all."

Without thinking, Dora kicked her shoes off and shoved them under the bench she was sitting on.

"If we learn any new information, we will contact you," Banks said. Then he pulled out a cell phone from his inside pocket. "If you think of something that we might know that would help you, call me. Use this phone; it's a no-contract, prepaid phone with two thousand minutes on it. Very hard to track. My number is preprogrammed: press and hold the number two. If we need more than two thousand minutes, the battle is probably over." Then he thought about what he had said. "If you need more time, get another phone just like this. Pay cash."

Banks shook his head and looked at Dora, then at me. "Gotta go," he said. He stood up, nodded to the two of us, and walked out of the restaurant. Dora and I watched him walk through the door to the car waiting for him. Russ was behind the wheel.

"We've got to get out of here," Dora said, standing up and pulling her cell phone out of her purse at the same time. I threw some money on the table, and we stood up and walked out of the restaurant. Dora in her bare feet. Jefferson appeared within minutes to collect us. Dora made a hand signal to him I did not recognize. "Evasive action," she explained without my asking. *Jefferson must be well-trained*, I thought.

Jefferson was one of the best drivers I had ever seen. He went into the evasive mode with great finesse, at all times maintaining the speed limit, but making a lot of turns and keeping his eye on the rear view mirrors every few seconds. I did not know where he was heading, and at that moment did not care. Dora and I were both seated in the back seat of the BMW. She turned to me and said, "We have three-and-a-half days until Sunday. I think I can get us a place to hide out, but we need to plan for all contingencies."

From the way she said it, I thought she meant the contingencies that included our deaths or our utter failure.

Chapter 52

The announcer on the radio said that the President would address the nation on Thursday evening. Dora and I were ensconced in a small apartment she said belonged to a friend of hers who was out of town. I hated that she was so cryptic about these matters, especially because we were pretty much thrown together with each other as the major support.

Nonetheless, we were both eager to hear what the President had to say. There had been little information forthcoming since the fire at the White House. The major news networks had contented themselves with reviewing and re-reviewing the history of the building and the plans for its refurbishment. The President took up residence at Blair House, the official guest residence for the President, where he continued to conduct the business of the nation, receiving official guests and doing whatever else Presidents do. By all accounts, Aberland liked the connection with Harry Truman that his residence there implied. Truman was the only other president ever to live there; he did so when the White House was being remodeled during his administration.

Congress had postponed its regular post-Labor Day session. Its members were doing the same watching and waiting that much of the country was doing. Everyone was mum about the President's agenda. His speech to Congress last month had been distributed to the media, which had in turn played and replayed it many times. It seemed to give solace to the restless and frightened populace. At the same time, however, precious little additional information was forthcoming from the President. The country was moving forward, albeit tentatively and slowly.

Most of the seceding states had nullified their secessionist proclamations. Most pundits attributed this to Aberland's threat of throwing the officials out of office and to the return of a greater majority of cooler heads, who had been on vacation or otherwise engaged when the resolutions were passed. Wyoming was a holdout, but it still had a few weeks before the deadline the White House had given the states.

There were few arrests of terrorists or insurgents or anyone of note during these past few weeks. At least few that had been reported. The President had accorded to himself sweeping powers under the Emergency Powers Act, but it was unclear how or if he was using these. The media, long known for chasing down every piece of information it could legally compile, did not have much to chase, and they were taking the same watching and waiting attitude of everyone else. There was some criticism of the administration, but it was muffled. The threat and fear of public disorder loomed large in the American mind, a fear not felt since the Depression or perhaps since the Civil War. Also, the fear of reprisal, either from the administration or from whoever was engineering the recent mayhem, weighed heavily on the public consciousness.

So like tens of millions of our fellow countrymen, Dora and I sat on a small loveseat facing the television and waited for the leader of the free world to clue everyone in on the state of the United States.

The announcers did not have much to say in anticipation of the speech. Aberland had not requested time from the networks; he had demanded it. Nor had he released a copy of his remarks in advance. You could sense resentment smoldering beneath the powdered and tailored heads of network announcers and analysts; they had long enjoyed increasingly deferential attitudes from public officials. They did not like being treated like the reporters they were. *Screw them*, I thought; *it's about time.*

They did not even know where the President was going to be speaking from. In a highly unusual move, the administration had informed them that it would provide all of the networks with a single live feed from an undisclosed location from which the President would speak. This added to the air of mystery, fear, and resentment.

A camera zoomed in on an image of Gerald Aberland seated at a nondescript wooden desk in a leather chair with the Presidential Seal of the United States behind him. He was dressed in a simple blue suit with a maroon tie. It was impossible to determine where he was.

"My fellow Americans," he began. "It has now been several weeks since the destruction of the White House, one of the most outrageous acts in our history, even our recent history, which has been tainted by multiple outrageous acts."

"My purpose in visiting with you this evening is to share with you where the situation in our nation stands. Our goals are to maintain the Union and to protect our citizens from further aggression. With respect to our first goal, all of the states that passed resolutions of secession have nullified them, as I directed them to do last month. The most recent is Wyoming, which voted for nullification earlier this afternoon. I welcome our fellow citizens back to the United States without reprisal or prejudice. The Union has been preserved."

"With respect to our second goal, the situation is more complicated. At this time, we do not know for certain who is behind these attacks, but we have a general outline of their intentions. We believe there has been an alliance among various disaffected fringe groups who managed to band together and direct their common hatred against what they regard as the American

Empire. Haughty and self-righteous, these people believe that their private fantasies and desires trump the gradual and imperfect development of American culture. They believe their lofty goals—of religion, of independence, of autonomy—justify any means, as witnessed by the heinous acts we have seen in recent months."

"During these past few weeks, we have intensified our efforts to determine the leadership of this unholy alliance, and we have stepped up our investigations into possible future plans they may have to continue their efforts to intimidate our citizens." He stopped and looked directly into the camera. "We believe they remain committed to chaos as a way to power, much like the Nazis in Germany in the 1930's." Aberland frowned deeply. "It pains me to report, however, that, at every step of the way in the midst of these investigations, we have been obstructed by highly placed officials in every major department of the federal government." He paused again to glare at the camera. His face had a wild aspect; it was unclear if he was angry or if he was losing his mind.

Aberland did not sidestep his reaction. "It disgusts me to think that a few discontented, disloyal, and deranged individuals could choose to assist in the murder of their fellow citizens and the destruction of our national symbols. But such is sadly the case. Fortunately, I have been in public service for many years, and along the way I have developed a network of very solid relationships with other government officials, some of them highly placed, some not. I believe all of these men and women are dedicated, selfless public servants, as are the majority of workers throughout the large bureaucracy of the United States. I assembled many of these trusted individuals myself to assist in the conduct of our ongoing investigations. Several of these heroic Americans died the night of the fire at the White House." Aberland did not even try to disguise his bitterness, his contempt, or his grief.

He collected himself. "But fortunately, most survived; not all members of that panel were in attendance that evening at the White House, and they were mercifully spared."

"Since that fateful evening, we have had to meet in a more circumspect way. There are traitors among us. We devised a plan to remain dispersed in an effort to avoid being targeted further by discontented elements within the government itself. We have not published the names of everyone on this special commission. We are in more or less constant communication by high-tech voice transmission technology that allows us to confer privately and safely. Using these methods, we have been able to continue our work and our investigations. By being especially careful and selective in our communications, we have determined that it is highly likely that some of the people involved in recent events were strategically placed members of the bureaucracy. One man was originally on the Presidential Panel itself. Some of the people we have identified have been detained."

"Fortunately, the memory of the American bureaucracy is long, and its respect for American traditions resilient. Most civil servants have remained loyal to the government and have been invaluable in helping to identify the obstructionists who have interfered with the process of justice even as they proclaim this to be their solemn and sacred duty." Aberland's eyes blazed. "I speak with you tonight to declare to you that we will not rest until all of these people have been brought to justice. Their plans have succeeded in instilling fear among the American people, and in compelling its lawful government into secret operation. I assure you this is temporary." He sat back a bit in his chair. "I do not say this simply to be reassuring. I say this with full knowledge that the major part of the United States government machinery remains loyal to the United States and to what it stands for. This includes all branches of the military, which has been tireless in its efforts to cooperate with our investigative work."

"At the same time, I want to be realistic. We are not out of the woods. These people remain committed to the destruction and dismantling of our way of life. We believe they are planning further terrorist acts designed to cow the American people into

325

submission. We believe they remain committed to their goal of establishing a different kind of America." He shook his head as if even he couldn't believe it. "Whatever their motivations, we will continue to seek them out and bring them to justice, holding them accountable for the atrocities they have visited upon this great nation. Be assured that the work continues. I will speak to you periodically to give updates on the situation. Thank you and good night."

And with that, Gerald Aberland signed off, leaving the Great Seal of the President of the United States to command the entire screen.

The networks took up their commentary in a type of daze, as if they had just been visited by a ghost. They repeated the main themes of what the President had said, but they soon settled on the overall impression left by this carefully crafted and controlled exercise; that impression was one of a secretive and careful Chief Executive who basically said that the threats to the country were greater than any of his listeners expected, despite the nullification actions among the states. Unfortunately, it appears that Gerald Aberland's effort to reassure the nation had the opposite effect.

Dora and I sat in silence for a while. The impact of this small, dedicated group of fanatics was stunning. They knew the specific points of pressure. They succeeded in cowing a powerful government into hiding. We were speechless. I don't know precisely what was going on in Dora's mind, but mine was wondering just how many people were bound to the Bookkeepers by conviction, contract, or chance. *Just what kind of impact would killing the remaining Bookkeepers have, even if we succeeded in doing that? Would other leaders just rise up in their place? Had a desire for order overridden the American zeal for freedom? Was fear alone to be the basis of our Union?*

I was also thinking about what Aberland said, or at least implied: that there remained at his disposal a coterie of loyalists; that he had control of the military; that he was making progress in ferreting out the evil-doers. But I also wondered if he was referring to Maximilian Grobe as the traitor in his midst. *Was he still in his close circle of advisors? Did he know he was one of the plotters? Was he keeping him close deliberately? Or would he be victimized by a close associate?* Many questions; few answers.

My thoughts were interrupted by Dora, who was on a different track. "You can bet the Bookkeepers are pleased with this speech," she said. "Aberland just confirmed to them that they had succeeded in putting the government on the defensive." She was talking to me because I was there, but she was actually thinking out loud. "I think they will try something even bigger, a *coup de grace*. They obviously don't think the military is a significant obstacle; they got this far without it." She sat back on the love seat and stared into the ceiling. "I am trying to think: What would I do if I were a fanatic intent on destroying the current government and had managed to put it on the defense and wanted to do away with it altogether?"

"I would destroy Washington, DC!" she blurted out after a moment. "The White House is already in ruins, but other powerful symbols of the American democracy are in abundance. And almost all of them are in Washington. I would destroy them and give Aberland's successors no place to return to." She looked at me with a sense of resignation on her face. "I think that's what they are going to do."

"How?" I asked, not completely on board with the concept of destroying the entire capital of the United States.

"Pick your poison," Dora replied with a touch of sarcasm in her voice. "Nuclear weapon, chemical bomb, fertilizer bombs strategically placed. There are a lot of ways to finish off a wounded animal. Or maybe they could just render it unlivable for decades with chemical sprays or some other exotic method. They have shown some competence in this regard." She shook her head.

As we talked, our attention had been drawn away from the television, which was still on and which was still dominated by the

President's speech. We both happened to look at the small screen again and noticed that they were interviewing Richard Reed, head of the Christian Covenant.

"...and this speech makes it clear once again," he was saying, "that the government can no longer protect us. We must now turn to God and put our faith in Him to save us."

Samuel Johnson was close: Patriotism is only the second last refuge of scoundrels, I thought. *Religion must be the ultimate one.*

Chapter 53

Small acts are funny things. Sometimes they make a big difference; sometimes only a tiny one. Neither Dora nor I had any idea of what the impact of our small act would be, assuming that we could pull it off. We spent the rest of that Thursday of the President's speech and the next two days focusing on one thing: The elimination of the Bookkeepers. We hoped that it would have a big effect, but we did not know if it would have any impact at all.

We spent our time just being together: talking, cooking, eating, and making love. We seemed to move with the kind of solidarity that one sees in older couples who have been together for many years, who know each others' limits and play to each others' strengths, who behave more as one organism than two. It was comfortable, but there was a feeling of resignation to it. We were resigned both to what we were to do on Sunday and to the fact that it might be futile, whether we succeeded or not. We did not say this out loud, but we were also resigned to the fact that we might not survive it. The Bookkeepers were in our minds riding a wave of triumph. They were well-insulated and well-protected. There were many of them and two of us. The odds just were not in our favor.

It was raining on Sunday morning. The service was at ten o'clock, and Dora and I decided to go out to breakfast. There was, we figured, some small chance that we would be spotted or accosted or detained, but neither of us felt that it was likely, and, truth be told, I don't think either of us cared. We were committed to doing what we had been planning to do, but if something interfered with it, so be it. Neither of us thought nor felt that the fate of the nation rested upon our shoulders. We were just contributing one small act. For whatever effect it had.

Jefferson had dropped us off at a small restaurant in northern Virginia. He parked the car and handed Dora the keys. Then he bowed slightly and walked away.

"Where's he going?" I asked as we entered the restaurant.

"I don't want him involved in the actual act," Dora replied matter-of-factly.

We got a table and sat down. It was only 7:30, so there were plenty of choices. The waitress came, and we ordered coffee and juice.

"So who is Jefferson, anyway?" I asked Dora with uncharacteristic bluntness.

"What do you mean?" she replied.

I looked at her, wondering if she was just avoiding the question. "Well, he's part bodyguard, part chauffeur. Sometimes you seem to treat him like your personal valet; at other times you go out of your way to protect him. Like now. What gives?"

Dora sighed and took a sip of coffee. "Jefferson's family and my family were close. When Jefferson was a teenager—something of a wild teenager—he and his parents were involved in a terrible automobile accident. His parents were killed. Jefferson was pretty banged up and spent a long time in recovery. That's when he lost his hearing. When he got out of rehab, he came to live with us; my father insisted. And my dad, who did not have a son and who pretty much left child-rearing responsibilities to my mother, took up caring for Jefferson with a devotion neither my mother nor I had ever seen. It was touching. I resented it some at the time, but even I thought it was a good thing. And a natural thing, given how close his family had been to ours."

She took another sip of coffee and continued, "Jefferson was angry for a long time. He would wail at night. We never knew if he was awake or dreaming, but the anguish he felt was something that broke our hearts. My father gave him a lot of outlets for his rage: he got him a martial arts instructor; he tried music lessons; he spent hours on end with him. He would even take him to work. Jefferson and I also spent a lot of time together. He's a little older than I am, but he liked having me around. We developed a way of communicating. Not American Sign Language or anything like that, but our own private system. Hand signals mostly, but facial expressions as well. Jefferson is terrific at reading lips." The tone of Dora's voice was softening as she talked about Jefferson in this tender way.

"Of course, other kids made fun of him and of us. Even though he was deaf, he knew it and hated it. On more than one occasion, I had to pull him off some mouthy kid who made a wrong move. He couldn't hear what was being said, but he had a finely honed sense of what was going on around him." She looked down at the table. "I love Jefferson," she said simply. "I don't want to expose him to harm."

This was a much more satisfying answer from Dora than I was expecting, and I luxuriated for a few moments in the bond it created between us.

We talked about other things. Almost everything, in fact, except what we were going to do around noon.

We ordered breakfast, and, when it came, ate mostly in silence. I felt unhurried, close, almost contented. It seemed as if life as we knew it would end sometime around 1:00 this afternoon, highlighting the sanctity of this moment, of this morning ritual. It might end completely or partially or in some way neither of us could recognize. But the ending itself felt certain.

We finished breakfast and still had over an hour before we had to be at the church. I suggested we drive around for a while and review the plan one final time. Dora went along with that; I guess she did not have an alternative.

She tossed me the keys to the BMW, and I unlocked it and opened the passenger side door for her. As she passed in front of me, she paused to kiss me, a serious kiss on a Sunday morning. Then she got in and I walked around to the other side of the car. I got in, started up the engine, and drove off.

We talked about the plan. It was simple. My job was to monitor the Bookkeepers' position, especially their movement through the tunnel from beneath the church to the multi-purpose building where they would be meeting. We had three signals. If they headed through the tunnel when we predicted they would—about 12:30— I was to do nothing. If they were in the tunnel before that time frame, I was to push a preprogrammed button on my cell phone. Then Dora could trigger the canisters manually. If it looked as if they would not be in the tunnel until after a five-minute time frame around 12:30-12:35, I would signal with a different button; in that case, Dora could disable the canisters from their automatic dispersal. If that happened, I would signal her yet again with a different preprogrammed button when they were in the tunnel. In that scenario, she would also manually trigger the devices.

This required three different cell phones, but that was easy. Dora had one, and we acquired two other prepaid ones with a minimum amount of minutes. She said she was going to line them up on the passenger's seat to keep them straight. I had no doubt she would.

We drove around the soggy neighborhoods around the church. It was a typical quiet Sunday morning in northern Virginia. No doubt similar to Sunday mornings around the entire country. After reviewing the plan, there wasn't much to do but switch drivers so that Dora could drop me off. We did that on a quiet side street, and Dora got in behind the wheel. After adjusting the seat, she looked at me full face and said, "Here goes," and drove off.

She dropped me off right in front of the church so that I did not have to walk far. I had not thought to bring an umbrella, but the rain was letting up, and it was easy to dodge the raindrops in a sprint up the marble steps to beneath the protection of the portico. People were gathering on the steps; many of them had the presence of mind to bring appropriate rain gear. I spotted Pastor Williams just inside the vestibule of the church. I also spotted three men in blue blazers who looked exactly like the amorous guard I had encountered on my last two trips here. Each had an earpiece, and each was surveying the crowd. *If there are three right here, there must be many more posted around,* I thought. I was glad that our plan did not include anything more threatening in my possession than a cell phone, something which was probably in the pocket or purse of every person present.

I shook Pastor Williams' hand as I passed in front of him. He welcomed me warmly. He seemed a bit anxious. It was hard to tell if he knew something was up or if he was uncomfortable with the increased security or if he was just being his shy and somewhat disorganized self. The impression had been forming in my mind ever since I met this man that he was not privy or even significant to the events which transpired right under his nose. They probably selected this place or him because he was so kind and so committed to doing what pastors did, that is, attending to the spiritual needs of his congregation. I pitied his *naïveté*.

I entered the nave of the church and found a place in the middle on the right side. I liked having easy access to the side aisle, a habit I acquired as a boy who was forced to attend church services on a regular basis. Going in and out of the main aisle drew a lot of attention but almost no one paid any attention to people moving up and down the side aisles. Easy escape.

The service began with a rousing chorus of *A Mighty Fortress is Our God*, that powerful hymn by Martin Luther that became the battle hymn of every persecuted Christian since the reformation. To my mind it underscored just how self-righteous and arrogant these people were; but I also recognized that to their mind they were probably doing something great and noble. Misguided surely, but I could feel their commitment to their chosen path. There was a power in the church that I had not sensed before. I wondered how many people in the congregation were aware of or involved in what was happening and what was going to happen. I felt sharply the sense of being in an enemy camp.

As the service wore on, the tension did not soften. Even Pastor Williams' sermon extolling the role of religion in public life and its especial importance at this critical juncture in our nation's history seemed like encouragement to move forward with whatever diabolical plans the Bookkeepers had devised. Maybe I was wrong about Williams; maybe he knew exactly what was going on and was supporting it. Or maybe someone else had written his sermon. The longer he talked, the more I was struck by how different it was from the previous samples of his work that I had encountered.

These people plan well. When Williams was finished, the congregation applauded. I clapped my hands in the hope of fitting in. During the applause people stood up, and, as we did so, I glanced up at the balconies that lined either side of the nave. I spotted at least three guards on each side. *This place is under heavy security and is not concerned about who knows it*, I thought. I shuddered a bit, not so much in fear as in awe at the time, talent, and treasure invested in this project.

Throughout the rest of the service, the intensity did not abate. At communion, some people made spontaneous proclamations, common in evangelical circles but not so common in upscale neighborhood churches like this one. The final recessional hymn was *How Great Thou Art*, and there did not appear to be anything but full-throttled voices in the hall. The effect was thunderous and dramatic. When the hymn ended, the congregation began filing out. Everyone was headed downstairs; no one left. This may have been partly due to the rain, which had resumed with some force, but it felt more like a reflection of the common commitment of these people to the ideals expressed in the upstairs liturgy. They were soldiers ready to fight and die for their cause. And to kill and maim as well.

The service had lasted for an hour and forty-five minutes, which meant that the time frame for the social was probably only going to be another forty-five minutes. I was relieved at that. I knew I was not visibly anxious; I was in a dissociated state, going through the motions of greeting people as an actor might, smiling and nodding and showing concern but all the while keeping my eye on my real agenda of bringing an end to the lives of the Bookkeepers. This part felt familiar if it felt like anything. But dissociation does not feel like anything; it specifically feels like nothing at all.

Fortunately, I did not have to worry about having people to talk to. I saw several people I had met before and many people seemed to recognize me. There was a group of people who were more than a little interested in making contact with me, and I was happy to watch the time go by doing this mindless kind of conversation. I did not attend to the presence of the Bookkeepers, but I saw some of them engaged in strained but casual conversation. A couple of them seemed anxious; a couple others seemed disinterested. Some had smiles on their faces. Pumped up, I guess.

As these social things so, there was a rhythm to the affair. The noise in the room got progressively louder and built toward a crescendo; then noise began to level off and begin to drop as people left or finished their conversation. The peak hit about 12:20.

I began glancing at the wall clock every few seconds. Time had slowed dramatically. I had to force myself to breathe. At 12:24 I pushed the button on my cell phone without bringing it out of my pocket, signaling Dora to disarm the canisters. It did not look as if anyone would be in the tunnel until after the chosen time frame.

12:30 passed; then 12:40. There were probably half as many people in the room as there were at the beginning. There were still people around me, so it was natural enough for me to stay. At about 12:45, Irene came up to me from the side, slipped her arm around mine, and asked how I was holding up. I nodded as dispassionately as I could. She moved into a spot directly in front of me, cutting off the contact with the others who had gathered around. She was flirting feverishly; I wondered if she had been drinking. Gradually, the small group of people who had been standing around began to drift away. *Probably in disgust*, I thought.

At about 12:54, I saw a couple of the Bookkeepers nod to each other and move toward the tunnel. Fortunately, Irene was standing directly between me and the tunnel door, so it was easy to glance over her bobbing head to track their progress. They moved as one animal. As if on cue, each of the Bookkeepers headed for the door. Within ninety seconds, the door closed quietly but firmly.

I took Irene's right hand with my left and squeezed it in what I hoped was a seductive way. Her hand was clammy with desire. With my other hand, I reached inside my trouser pocket and pushed and held the number three. I smiled at Irene, took my hand out of my pocket and placed both her hands in mine.

"You have been a delightful hostess, Irene," I said. As I did this, I looked around. There were probably thirty people still in the room. Two of them were guards. "But unfortunately, I must be going."

There was no noise from the tunnel, no screams, no report of any kind. I waved to some of the people who had been waiting around me and walked out of the basement meeting room and went up the stairs. It was still raining, but Dora was waiting at the bottom of the church steps. I waved to her casually to get her attention, as if this were necessary, and got in the car. We drove off.

Chapter 54

The headline in the Monday morning paper said it all: *Religious Leaders Slain in Terrorist Act*. It detailed how ten members of the Bookkeepers, a group of committed religious leaders, and two guards had been killed on their way to a meeting after a church service in northern Virginia. No one knew what the motivation was, but it was being billed as yet another assault on our safety, on our freedom.

The President was to address the nation at 11:00 a.m. Eastern time.

Neither Dora nor I knew if we had succeeded in our plan until late Sunday afternoon. Then we learned that it was Irene who had found the bodies of nine Bookkeepers, one prospective new member, and two guards. She, of course, fell into a state of hysteria when she opened the door to the tunnel—*no doubt looking for her next conquest*, I thought—and her screams and cries brought others who in turn brought the police, who arrived within minutes.

That was all the public was told. What they were not told was that, in the course of the investigation, detailed plans for a nuclear explosion over Washington DC were found, as well as extensive documentation about past and future terrorist acts against the people of the United States. That was to be the topic of the press conference the President was holding Monday morning.

We knew this because Robert Banks called us late Sunday to tell us what had happened. After he described the events in his typical monotone and detailed what was found, he said, "There is someone here who would like to speak with you."

"Who?" I said, a little apprehensive.

"President Aberland," Banks replied.

I did not register the name for a moment. Then it hit me, and my eyes widened and my palms began to sweat. I looked across at Dora, who was staring at me expectantly, not having a clue what was happening.

"Senator Telemark," Gerald Aberland said. "I extend to you the thanks of a grateful nation. Unfortunately, because of how these things work, this will be the extent of my ability to thank you. But be assured that we recognize that your government's investment in you was not wasted."

"Thank you, Mr. President," was all I could think of to say.

I clicked the phone off. I could not speak for a few minutes. Dora came over and put her hand on my arm. I began to cry, then to shake, then to fall into her arms. I lay there for a few moments after the storm subsided. I still could not speak.

After a while, of course, I did speak. I told Dora what Banks had said and what Gerald Aberland had said.

We watched the news conference on Monday morning. On the podium with the President were his Vice-President, his Chief of Staff, and Special Agent Robert Banks.

Dora and I smiled at each other. And held each other close.

About the Author

Paul Martin Midden is a practicing psychologist and author. His first novel, *Absolution*, was published in 2007 to positive reviews. His work is character-driven and reflects years of experience in clinical practice. He lives in St. Louis, Missouri, with his wife and children. Visit him on the web at *paulmidden.com*.

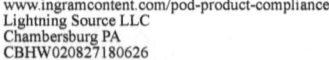